한국 희곡 명작선 04

전설의 달밤

한국 희곡 명작선 04

전설의 달밤

홍원기

평민사

홍원기

전설의 달밤

화진   호숫가 카페 〈고인물〉의 여주인.
규명   머구리. 60대.
명각   대학교수 40대.
각수   소방사 30대.
수호   20대.

'화진'의 카페 〈고인물〉.
뒤쪽으로 호수가 보이는 큰 통창이 있다.
창문 안쪽이나 너머는 전설을 재현하는 또 다른 무대가 된다.
한편에 스탠드형 가라오케 모니터(노래하는 사람만 보는)가 있다.
간판은 카페이지만 밤에는 술과 안주를 파는 '노래주점' 같은 곳
이다.
상수에 주방으로 통하는 바텐더 칸막이. 하수에 출입문과 화장실
이 설정된다.

[밝힘]

'화진포'에 얽힌 '장자못' 또는 '고청' 전설을 꺼리로 삼은 연극이
다. 전설 속 인물은 〈이화진-富者〉〈고청-며느리〉〈스님〉이다.

'머구리'는 바다 속으로 잠수해서 물고기를 잡아 올리는 '잠수어
부'이다. 배를 타고 가까운 바다로 나가 작업한다. 잠수복(헬멧)
과 배로 연결한 생명줄(숨 쉬는 라인)에 의지해 숨을 쉰다. 근대
이후에 주로 동해안에서 생겨난 직업으로 제주의 해녀와는 다르
게 남자가 한다.

#1 늦은 밤

수호의 카메라 플래시 터지면서… 번개천둥!
가라오케 반주에 맞춰 규명 노래한다.
화진 명각 각수, 춤추며 분위기 맞춘다.

수호   네…! 억수 같은 빗줄기 원수 같은 천둥번개 요란한 오
       늘 이 밤도, 이렇게 세월 죽이고 첫사랑도 지우면서, 흘
       러간 유행가로 내일을 안다리 걸면서, 높은 음은 악으
       로 낮은 음은 뽀대로 뭉개면서, 저기 저렇게 사라지는
       노래의 진실을 찾아 달려가고 있습니다. (사이) 네 그럼
       여기서 잠깐, 오늘도 이렇게 한결 같은 마음과 화끈한
       씀씀으로 이 호숫가 카페 〈고인물〉을 찾아주신 단골님
       들을 소개해 올리겠습니다.

사내들, 수호에게 팁 찔러준다.

화진   아이 뭐야 끝내자는데. (바텐 안으로 간다)
수호   아참! 순서가… 카페 〈고인물〉의 CEO마담이신 이화
       진님!

화진   (바텐 안) 오늘은 이만! 커피 내릴 테니 커피로…

각수   좋지요, 향기롭게 정신 번쩍 나는 우리 화진씨 커피! 꽉 채워주셔요!

수호   네, 밤도 늦을 만큼 늦었고 날씨도 엉망진창이니, 오늘은 이만 우리 마담께서 제공하시는 커피로 해장들 하시고 돌아가시랍니다.

규명   커피는 무슨… 치우라우! 야 근데 지금 어데 누구한테 떠드는 기야?

수호   저기 새들이요… 호수에.

각수   비 오는데 뭔 새?

수호   비가 오나 눈이 오나 새는 새, 다만 날개 잠시 접었을 뿐.

명각   새들도 세상을 버렸어. 텃새는 날아가고 철새는 아니오고.

각수   철새가 왜 안 와, 때 되면 다 오는데.

명각   나참… 상징이요 시적 상징…

수호   네! 이번 여름에도 어김없이 우리 카페를 찾아주신 여름철새 조명각 교수님!

각수   뭐가 교수야, 시간강사지

수호   네 그동안의 탁월한 연구활동과 강의실력으로 어느 대학의 교수님이 되셨다네요

화진   어머 그래요? 축하해요!

규명	야 글면 당장 한턱 쏘라우!
명각	좋습니다. 쏘는 거라면 내가 자신 있습니다. 여기 술 줘요! (기관총 쏘는 흉내 내다 줄에 걸려 넘어진다)
각수	(가라오케 주변의 배선을 살핀다) 이거 배선이 영 엉망이네. 화진씨, 여기 소화기 갖다놔야겠어. 이 건물 화재보험은 들어놨어요?
규명	기걸 왜 나한테 물어.
수호	내, 우리 도시의 불침번. 불이면 불, 목숨이면 목숨, 촌각을 다투는 위급상황은 다 맡겨다오! 119소방사 문각수님!
각수	야 나 목숨은 책임 못 져. (지포라이터로 담뱃불) 불, 불이라면 내 전문이지.
규명	마빡에 피도 안 마른 아새끼가 어데서 맞담배질이냐.
각수	저 낼모레면 마흔이거든요.
규명	기래 아직 총각 딱지도 못 뗐니?
각수	그 딱지 봤어요? 딱지가 뭐야.
규명	봤다. 날밤 까고 찜질방에서.
각수	어허 이 어르신… 마나님 작별하시더니… 변태 되셨네.
수호	네. 이 고장의 토박이 유지이시며 또 젊어서는 저 동해바다 밑바닥을 이 잡듯이 훑으셨던 머구리 박규명님!
규명	야 머구리가 뭐야? 잠수어부! 햐 오늘 같은 날 들어갔으면 해삼 멍게 성게 개불 섭조개 싹 훑어오는 긴데. 낮

에는 날씨가 여간 좋았잖니. 야 여기 술 더 개져오라!

화진　(커피 내온다) 자 이걸로 입가심 하시고… 드셔보세요!
　　　하와이 코나예요. 아주 가볍고 상큼해요.

규명　뭐 코나? 코 나온다 치우라! 우리 술 깰 때까지 술 마시
　　　면서 그냥 놀자!

명각/각수　(합창하듯) 오예! 커피도 술도 마담과 함께. 취하고 깨는
　　　것도 우리 화진씨와 함께!

규명　스톱! 술 깨는 덴 노래가 최고야. 하던 대로 돌아가면
　　　서. (마이크 잡는다)

화진　(마이크 뺏으며) 아이잉 나 졸려 (사이) 제발 나 좀 혼자 있
　　　게 해줘요. 뭐야? 날이면 날마다 문 열자마자… 벌써
　　　몇 시간째야?

규명　혼자 있으면… 매상은 누가 올려주고?

화진　아이씨… 그러네.

각수　(옷매무새 고쳐 잡고) 저기… 생각해 봤어요?

화진　뭘?

각수　나하고… 그러니깐… (속삭) 전세금 인상 때문에 카페
　　　접는다는.

화진　그래요, 고민 중이에요.

각수　그러니깐… 그럴 거면… 나하고… 뭐랄까… 그게…

화진　뭐가?

각수　(갑자기 심각해진다) 노래로 할게. (노래번호 찍는다) 나 그

대에게 모두 드리리. (반주 나온다)

명각 (잽싸게 마이크 잡고 나선다) 이건 내 노래요.

각수 이거 왜 이래요?

명각 내가 찍었다구요.

각수 뭘?

명각 노래번호

각수 그래 박사님은 번호만 계속 찍으슈. 화진씬 내가 찍었으니.

명각 내가 찍었다니깐요.

규명 야. (화진 보며) 야가 또뽑기판이냐 찍고 찍게. 치우라.

명각 소방사가 불이나 끄지, 찍긴 누굴 찍어.

각수 그래 불이다 불. 내 가슴 속에 불! 이건 아무나 못 꺼. 안 그래, 화~진?

화진 내 이름 거꾸로 해봐요!

모두 진화!

각수 안 돼! 타오를 껴, 밤새도록.

규명 마이크 이리 내고, 날래들 꺼지라우! 오늘은 나의 단독 철야콘써트! 저 바다 속 헤집던 머구리 폐활량으로! 화 화 화진을 위하여! 화! 사월과 오월의 화!

'화' 반주가 나온다. 규명 노래한다. 명각 각수도 따라 부른다. 마이크 쟁탈전 치열하다.

수호   그날 밤, 세 남자의 노래다툼은 저렇게 치열했습니다. 자기들은 열심 절심 신명도 낳겠지만 듣는 사람은 참… 노래라는 게… 하는 너, 듣는 나의 주고받는 느낌이 교감해야 되는데 저토록 혼자서만 악 악 대는 건, 노래가 아니라 소음공해 음향적 폭력이지요. 그래서 저는 시간도 잘 가고, 하는 이도, 듣는 이도 조용해질 수밖에 없는 꺼리 하나를 제안했습니다. 그건 바로 저 호수에 얽힌 이야기!

모두   (사이) 뭐, 화진포 전설?

수호   예! 비 오는 이 밤하고도 잘 어울릴 것 같고… 제가 이번에 포토스토리를 하나 만드는데 (사이) 사진이야기책이요. 내 사진에다 어떤 이야기를 넣는 거죠. 그래서 이 화진포를 찍고 있는데, 여기 얽힌 전설이.

규명   기래서 맨날 카메라 잡고 폼 잡았구만. 다 찍었니? (사이) 기럼 책 내면 되지, 뭔 전설이야기야 고리타분하게.

화진   너 또 그 전설타령이니? 빨리 끝내라.

수호   그게요. 그 전설이라는 게, 말하는 사람마다 다르더라구요. 뭐가 확실한 전설인지 좀 헷갈려서요.

명각   전설은 전하는 사람마다 달라야 전설이야. 하나같이 똑같으면 그건 정설이고 역사지. 여기 전설은 전국적으로 퍼져있는 장자못전설이야. 옛날엔 이 호수 아래가 이화진이라는 자가 살던 마을이었대… 어? 그 이화진하고 우리 화진씨가 이름이 같네.

화진 어머 그래요?

명각 이거 뭐야, 우연을 빙자한 필연인가?

각수 인연으로 배배 꼬는 운명?

규명 그 어려운 말로 복잡 떨지 말라! 간단해 이야기는… 그 이화진이 처음부터 부자는 아니었거든.

화진 그건 나도 그런데… 그럼 나도 나중에 부자 되겠네.

각수 진짜 그렇게 된 사람 눈앞에 계시잖아. 이번에 수십 억.

(순간 규명 손으로 각수의 입 막는다)

규명 치우라우.

화진 뭐요?

각수 모르던 땅문서가 나왔는데 근데 그 땅이 글쎄…

규명 그 쫑알 방정떨지 말고 들어보라. 그러니깐 (오랜 사이) 얘기가 어떻게 되지?

각수 아 그거야.

규명 시끌! 국어공부 빡쎄게 한 박사가 이야기하라우.

각수 그 얘기라면 여기 토박이인 내가 더 잘 알죠.

명각 내 전공이 야담과 전설이요. (사이) 해봐요! 틀리면 내가 바로 잡아줄게

각수 나참… 번데기 앞에서 주름 잡으란 말이오? 하시오!

명각 나참… 토박이 앞에서 토산품 팔란 말이오? 하시오!

규명 에이 내가 할게 (사이) 얘기가 어떻게 되지?

모두   에이! 술이나 마셔.

수호   내가 할게요. 대신에 이야기가 틀리면 곧바로 말해주세요! 그 어느 한 옛날에, 이 화진포가 호수가 아니고 그냥 움푹 파인 농경지일 때. 이화진이란 사내가 살았어요. 그는 아주 가난했어요. 남의 집 머슴살이도 하면서 열심히 돈을 모으고 그 돈으로 논과 밭을 사고… 그래서 어느덧 이화진은 인근 고을에서 제일가는 장자 즉 부자가 되었지요. 심지어 지가 머슴살이를 하던 땅주인을 머슴으로 부리기도 했습니다.

화진   에이 설마, 그 주인이었던 놈은 배알도 없대니?

셋   쉬!

수호   그러던 어느 날, 오늘같이 비가 주룩주룩 오는 날. 화진이가 머슴들을 데리고 소 우리를 고치고 있는데.

화진   아참 나도 주방 설거지해야 돼.

셋   나중에!

수호   저 금강산 자락 건봉사에서 온 중, 스님 하나가 동냥을 나왔습니다. "나무아미타불 관세음보살! 시주 시주!"

규명   시주? 야 내가 너 줄 건 이것밖에 없다. 가져가라! 하고 소똥을 그 중한테 줬어.

수호   "예 감사무지로소이다. 아미타불!" 중은 아무 말 없이 그대로 돌아서서 대문을 나갔어요. 그때 안마당에서 절구를 찧고 있던 며느리 '고청'이가 그 광경을 목격했습니다.

화진   고청? 성이 고씨인가? 심청이하고 성만 틀리네.

명각   청! 청이란 이름은 다 팔자가 쎄. 심청 고청… 청, 뭔가 청승맞잖아.

모두   쉬이.

수호   그 고청은 이래서는 안 되겠다고 생각! 그대로 절구방 아 내던지고 신주단지처럼 애지중지하는 쌀독을 통째 로 들고 중한테 달려갔습니다.

화진   어떻게? (바텐으로 달려가 와인병을 들고 나온다) 이렇게?

셋   감사아미타불!

수호   "시아버님이 스님께 큰 죄를 지었습니다. 부디 저를 보 셔서 저희 아버님을 용서해주세요! 그리고 이거!" 해봐 요 그대로!

화진   (그대로 한다)

셋   어허 뭘 이런 것까지.

수호   그대의 갸륵한 마음… 그대만은 내가 살리겠소. 지금부 터 무조건 내 뒤를 따르시오! 그리고 그 어떤 소리가 나 더라도 절대 뒤를 돌아보지 마시오!

화진   왜?

셋   하라면 해! 그게 전설이야!

수호   그리하여 며느리 고청이는, 중의 뒤를 땀 뻘뻘, 가슴 두 근, 다리 휘청 따라가는데

셋	꽈과광!

진짜로 천둥번개 친다. 화진이 비명 지르며 얼어붙는다.

수호	뭐해요? 돌아봐!
화진	왜?
수호	왜? 왜? 왜? 절대 뒤를 돌아보지 말라는 그 중의 말이 더 궁금하기도 했던 고청이 마침내, 고개를 돌려 뒤를 보고야 말았다. (사이) 돌아봐요!
화진	돌아보지 말라며.
수호	그 며느리가 돌아봤다니깐.
화진	난 그 여자가 아니야.
각수	아 진짜… 전설! 재현드라마도 못 봤나?
명각	중요한 건 돌아보지 말라 했는데 돌아봤다는 겁니다.
화진	왜 돌아보지 말라는 거지?
각수	그래야 돌아보지…
명각	그 이유가 궁금해서…
각수	돌아볼 거야 말 거야? 한참 신나가던 판에 뭐야 이거.
규명	야 집어치고 술이나 마시자!
명각	에이 그만하고 우리 가지요!
셋	(나가는 척 하다가 각자 숨는다)
수호	자 자 그럼, 뒤를 돌아볼 수밖에 없었던 그 궁금증의

시간을 드리겠습니다. (천천히) 하나 둘 셋 넷 다섯 여
섯 일곱.

화진 (돌아본다) 응 뭐야 다 어디 갔어? (사이) 갔니, 그새? 에
이 시원하다. 찐득이들. 야 문 닫고 간판 불 꺼. (순간 비
명)

셋 (소리 없이 나타나며, 수호가 하는 이야기를 몸짓으로 표현한
다)

수호 마침내 고개 돌려 뒤돌아보니, 아 이를 어쩌랴, 차마 못
볼 지경! 거대하게 밀려드는 저 거센 해일! 거역할 수
없이 잠겨드는 운명의 터전! 지금까지 살던 집과 온 동
네가 온통 물바다! 그리하여 우리의 착한 며느리 고청
이는 그대로 멈춰 선 바위가 되었다는 화진포 전설!

화진 재수 없어! 왜 우리나라 전설은 여자만 시련을 당해?

명각 (뜨악한 분위기 바꾸려고) 음… 그런데, 고청이는 바위가
된 게 아니라, 그런 상황 자기 운명이 너무 억울 원통해
서 스스로 목을 매서 죽었어요, 저기 저 고청고개에서.
그 혼은 고청서낭이 돼서 고을사람들한테 제삿밥 얻어
잡숫고. 지금도 그래.

수호 그래요?

명각 그 며느리가 바위가 된 건 내륙지방 전설이고, 이런 해
안가에서는 자결을 해. 그래 나중에 서낭신이 되고, 어
부들이 섬기는 풍어의 여신이 되기도 했지.

화진　죽긴 왜 죽어, 뭘 잘못했다고? 내가 그 여자라면…

각수/수호　(아부 떨며) 어떻게 하실 건가요?

화진　… 몰라. 하여튼 말도 안 되고, 화나고, 재수 없는 전설이야. 왜 여자만 귀신이 돼?

수호　귀신이 아니라 여신, 서낭당의 여신이잖아요.

각수　우리의 여신을 위하여 건배! 음~ 이 커피의 향기 죽인다!

수호　자 전설 속의 여신, 고청을 위하여! 막잔 건배 하시고 그만들 그만. (빈 잔이다)

명각　술이 없는데, 좋았어. 이 와인! (스님 흉내) 이건 아까 시주하신 거니 계산에서 빼시지요! 이거 좀 따 봐요!

화진　안 돼. 이 와인은 누구 오면 마시려고, 내가 아끼고 아끼는 거야

셋　(문득) 누구?

화진, 섬뜩하게 다가와 와인병 낚아채서 바텐으로 간다.
규명, 화진에게 뭔가 말하려다가… 창가 쪽으로 가서 호수를 바라본다.
화진, 말이 없다. 와인 끌어안고 터지려는 울음 참는다.

명각　역시 청이란 이름은 청승맞은 건가…

화진　난 그 청이가 아니거든요. 그만들 가세요! (수호에게) 야

너도 꺼져.

규명   어이 박사! 그거 알아, 그 시아버지 이화진이가 아끼고
아끼던 금절구가 아직도 저 호수 밑에 있다는 거.

셋   금 금절구요?

규명   그래, 지금도 보름달이 뜨면 호수 밑에서 누런빛이 솟
아올라, 달빛에 반사되는 금절구 때문에… 진짜야. 내
눈으로 봤어.

뜨악한 정적.

명각   … 많이 드셨군요, 술?

각수   금절구? 뭔 개떡을 치는 금절구. 상황파악도 못하고 뭔
주책 뺑바가지.

규명   뭐야 이 자식이 (각수 멱살을 잡는다) 한 번 붙어볼래?

각수   아 벌써 이렇게 붙어 있잖아요.

명각   자 자 이거 놓으시고… 이제 그만 갑시다! 화진씨, 내
내일 또…

규명   (명각의 멱살도 잡고) 내기하자고, 그 금절구가 있으면 니
네들 뭐 내놓을래?

각수   그 빛이 안보이면?

규명   내 재산 다 내놓겠다. 니들은?

각수   시키는 대로 하지요, 일평생.

명각   평생 스승으로 모시겠습니다.

규명   좋아. 각서 써! (수호에게) 종이하고 볼펜 가져와!

화진   재미있겠다. 내일모레가 보름날이야.

규명   화진이는 어디다 걸래?

갑자기 불이 나간다. 화진이가 꺼버려서

각수   (어둠 속에서) 뭐야 이거? 합선인가? 건물주가 누구야?
          소방검사 제대로 받은 거야, 뭐야? (사이) 아야! 누구야?

#2 보름날 밤

수호의 카메라플래시 터지며 밝아진다. 수호의 카메라에 대포 같은 망원렌즈가 달려있다.

창 밖에 대고 연신 셔터 눌러대는 수호. 창밖 날씨 잔뜩 흐려 있다.

규명 명각 각수 들어온다.

규명 뭐 휘엉청 밝은 보름달을 보게 된다고… 내 이제부터 기상청 일기예보 믿으면 개아들놈이다.

각수 잘 됐죠 뭐. 먹구름 덕분에 전 재산 안 날리고.

규명 (째린다)

명각 자 자 내기는 없던 걸로 하시고, 오늘도 그냥 한 잔 하지요. 여기 맥주 줘요!

규명 아니 이렇게 흐린 날 맥주 마시면, 이 가슴 속에 씁쓸한 거품만 껴. 쏘주가 좋지 쾌청하게 맑은 쏘주… 어이 박사, 쏘주… 피 토할 때까지 마셔봤어?

명각 (아니라고 몸서리친다)

규명 그렇게 마시고 토하고 나면, 온 세상이 소주처럼 투명해져. 다 보인다고. 이 눈앞에 있는 나무 바위 산 호수

바다… 그 속안에 뭐가 들어있는지. 사람들 가슴 속도 보여, 무슨 생각을 하는지. 돈도 마찬가지야. 평생을 토해내도 다 다 못쓰고 죽을 만큼 돈이 있으면, 다 보여… 저 인간들이 나한테 뭘 원하는지. (수호를 그윽이 째려본다) 너 지금 술 마시고 싶지?

수호   어떻게 아셨어요? 예!

규명   야 기럼, 카메라 들고 개폼 떨지 말고, 냉큼 술 개져오라!

수호   예!

규명   (각수를 그윽이 째려본다)

각수   아 뭘 봐요?

규명   지금 화장실 가고 싶지?

각수   … 예! (화장실 간다)

규명   저 작자하고 너무 어울리지 마!

명각   예? 왜요?

규명   그 금절구 분명히 있어. (명각을 심각히 째려본다) 안 믿지?

명각   예!

규명   거봐! … 지금 노래하고 싶지?

명각이가 가라오케 번호 누른다. '이등병 편지'를 노래한다. 수호가 소주와 안주를 내온다. 같이 잔 부딪치고 마신다. 규명, 자리를 뜬다.

수호   구름 잔뜩 낀 하늘 때문에, 저 호수 밑바닥의 금절구가
       뿜어낸다는 광채를 두고 건 내기는 유야무야 되었습니
       다. 이대로 두면, 그 금절구가 있다 없다 날밤을 새며,
       죄 없는 소주병들만 일렬종대로 늘어놓게 생겼습니다.
       (사이) 저… 그런데요. 그 이야기 속에 고청의 남편, 즉
       이화진의 아들은 왜 등장 안하는 거죠? 이상하잖아요.
       그렇게 큰 부잣집에 시아비하고 며느리만 사는 게.

화진   (통창 앞에서 밖을 바라보며) 음… 그거야 (사이) 어디 갔겠
       지, 그 아들.

수호   어디요?

화진   (막연히) 저기.

수호   저기… 어디요?

화진   …

명각   그 아들 이야기는 전설 속에 없어. 그래도 아들이 있긴
       있었겠지. 내 생각에는… 이건 내 생각인데, 한 번 들어
       볼래요? 그 아들이 어디 갔는지.

       수호가 조명 스위치를 만져서 실내조명을 어둡게 한다.
       통창 밖에서 호수의 빛이 들어오면서… 화진이의 모습이 실
       루엣으로 보인다. 전설 속의 '고청'의 모습을 닮은 듯하다.

명각   며느리 고청이는 매일 매일 절구질을 해야 했어요. 그
       땐 곡식을 절구로 빠서 먹었으니. 벼는 쌀로, 겉보리는
       알보리로… 근데 시아버지 화진이가 가만히 보니 그 절
       구질이 그냥 절구질이 아닌 거라. 아가야! 웬 절구질을
       사납게 해대냐? 그러다 절구 깨지겠다. 그만해라! 그런
       다고 군역에 간 네 서방… 못 돌아온다. 난리 끝난 지
       벌써 몇 년이냐… 필시 어찌 된 게야. 죽었겠지… 아니
       요. 살아있어요. 저는 서방님을 믿어요. 이렇게 이렇
       게… 미친 듯이 절구질… 아니다 아가야! 그놈하고 너
       의 인연은 끝난 게여. 미련 버리고 재가해라! 너를 보살
       펴줄 괜찮은 사내가 어디 있을 거다. 새 출발해라! 그럼
       내 재산 반을 네 몫으로 나눠주마. 그래도 고청이는, 아
       니요 돌아와요! 꼭 살아서, 살아서 돌아와요! 저는 그렇
       게 믿고 기다리고 믿고 기다리고 믿고 기다리고…

       규명이가 끼어든다.

규명   그런 절구질로 쪼개졌어, 나무절구 돌절구 쇠절구가
       (전설 속 화진으로) 아이구 괜찮니? 어허 이놈의 절구. 내
       이번에는 순금으로 절구를 만들어주마. 그래서 저 호수
       밑에 금절구가…
각수   파토 파토! 거기서 왜 금절구가 나와요?

24

명각 그래요. 중요한 건 며느리 고청이의 갈등이란 말입니다. 그 갈등스런 마음을 절구질로 드러낸 거구요.

규명 시끄러! 박사 이야기 틀렸어. 금쪽같은 자기 아들을 오매불망 기다리는 며느리한테 재가를 하라니. 또 그 많은 재산을 재가하는 며느리한테 갈라준다고? 누구 좋으라고?

화진 맞아. 그 아들은 분명 살아있는데.

수호 그걸 어떻게 알죠?

화진 그거야… 여자의 본능이지. 여자는 알아. 멀리 떨어져 있어도 자기가 사랑하는 남자가 어디서 뭘 하는지.

수호 그럼 지금 어디서 뭘 하는데요?

화진 응? 누구?

수호 그 남자요… 사랑한다는?

화진 몰라!

수호 아신다면서?

규명 누가 누구를?

명각 아… 이 와인… 같이 마실 남자.

화진 그거 손대지 마!

수호 정말 누굴 기다리는 거예요?

모두 (화진을 응시한다)

화진 (창가로 간다) 올해는, 고니도 안 날아오고… 오늘밤은 달님얼굴도 영영 못 볼 것 같네. (오랜 사이)

수호 그러니까 누군데요?

화진 과는 다른데 같은 학번인 남자.

수호 네?

화진 삼수를 해서 내가 오빠라 불렀지.

각수 아 네.

화진 우리는 아무도 모르게 사귀었어요. 남들이 알게 되면, 우리사이에 어떤 흠집이라도 날 것은 두려움 때문에… 자기가 정말 아끼는 구슬은 다른 아이들한테 절대로 보여주지 않는 아이들처럼… 그런 사랑을 했어요, 우리는…

수호/각수 … 그래서요?

화진 행방불명 됐어.

각수 행불… 어디서?

화진 군대에서.

규명 왜? 뭣 때문에!?

화진 모르겠어요. 어느 날밤 갑자기 그냥 사라졌대요.

각수 갑자기 사라지다니… 귀신인가?

화진 오빠 고향이 이 근방이래요.

수호 그래요? 같이 왔었나요, 여기.

화진 군대 가기 전에 딱 한 번… 그때 오빠가… 호수가 다른 말로 뭔지 아니? 고인물. 고인돌은 죽은 사람들이 하늘로 가는 문이고, 고인물은 산 사람들을 다시 만나게 하는 거울이야. 수만리 날아갔던 철새들도 다시 날아와, 서로의 날개를 비춰보는 시간의 거울. 너와 나의 마음이 여기에 고여 있으면, 내가 어디를 가더라도 꼭 다시 돌아와, 너와 나의 얼굴을 이 호수에 비춰볼 수 있을 거야… 그땐 남들 다가는 군대 가면서, 너무 감상 떤다고 생각했죠. 근데 오빠가 사라지고 나니깐, 아~ 언젠가는 이 호수가로 돌아올 작정을 하고 어딘가로 갔구나… 그런 생각이… 그래서 이렇게…

각수   기다린다, 무턱대고? 이런 젠장 열녀춘향이 울고 가네. 그 증발도령은 언제 암행어사가 돼서 돌아온대나?

명각   디엠지에서 행불됐으면, 사망했거나 월북일 텐데… 뭘 믿고?

규명   디엠지? 거기인 줄 어떻게 알아?

명각   (당황) 그러니깐… 후방서는 그런 일이 거의 없잖아요 (사이) 내 생각에는… 그렇게 사라졌다면, 군대를 안 갔어도, 어디론가 떠났을 남자 같은데. 그런 남자를 언제까지 기다리고 있을 거죠?

규명   돌아올 때까지.

각수   미쳤다, 요즘 세상에.

규명   사람을 사랑을 약속을 믿고 기다리는데, 요즘세상 저즘세상이 어디 있어? 돌아올 거야, 걔가 말한 대로… 철새처럼.

각수 철새면, 때 되면 또 날아가지.

규명 걱정 마! 돌아오면, 내 그놈을 붙박이 텃새로 만들어 놓을 테니.

수호 어떻게요? 그 사람 잘 아세요?

규명 (당황) 아 아니… 내 주특기가 머구리잖니. 그 애 돌아오면, 저 호수로 들어가서, 금절구 꺼내설랑, 턱 갖다 앵겨주는 기야. 아니 세상에 제 품안에 금절구 끌어안고 있는데, 어느 남자가 다른 데로 날개를 펴? 안 그래?

화진 글쎄요. 난 절구통이 아니라 S라인이거든요 (사이) 이제는 기다릴 만큼 기다린 것 같고, 나이 먹는 것도 겁나고, 올려 달라는 전세금도 감당 안 되고… 그만 정리할 때가 된 거 같아요. (사이) 저 와인 확 따버릴까?

각수 그거 좋지. 내가 산다.

명각 아니. 저건 내가 산다고 했어요!

규명 저건 따면 안 돼! 내가 산다. 얼마면 돼?

화진 대체 왜들 이래요?

수호 그럼 경매로 할까요? 네, 좋습니다. 자 지금부터 경매 들어갑니다.

규명 필요 없어. 백지수표 줄게! (품에서 종이를 꺼낸다) 원하는 액수 적어.

각수 돈벼락 맞은 머구리 아니랄까봐서 진짜.

규명 진짜 뭐? (사이, 화진에게) 난 내 돈 내 마음대로 쓸 테니,

넌 니가 원하는 대로 금액 적어! 와인 어디 있어?

명각/각수 안 돼. 그건 내 거야.

규명이가 움켜쥔 와인병을 뺏으려는 명각과 각수. 서로 뺏고 움켜쥐고 다투다가,
병이 튕겨져 공중으로 솟아오른다. 화진이가 몸을 날려 병을 끌어안듯이 움켜쥔다.

화진 (비명) 왜들 그래 정말! 뭐야, 그래 사봐! 얼마, 내가 얼마짜리라고 생각하는데? (와인따개 병에 꽂으며) 이건 내가 따고 내가 마실 거야. (울음 터트리며) 아이씨… 이거 왜 이렇게 안 따져?

규명 (달려가 와인병 붙잡고) 것 봐! 이것도 열리기 싫다잖니, 자네 맘처럼… 미안 미안. 내가 사과할게. 나 돈 같고 유세 떤 거 아니야. 자네를 지켜주고 싶어서 그런 거지.

화진 (울면서 규명을 끌어안다가 문득) 아저씨가 뭔데 왜 나를 지켜줘요?

규명 (당황) 그러니깐… 나는 저 호수 밑에 있는 금절구를 믿거든.

화진 … 난 S라인이라고 했거든요. 이 손 치우세요!

각수 아 진짜, 티켓다방인가, 어딜 더듬거려.

규명 이게 더듬은 거야? 야가 안쓰러워서 살짝 쓰다주어 준

거지.

명각 (버럭) 그러면서 왜 또 더듬어요? 정말 화딱지 나서 못
봐주겠네. (나간다)

규명 아니 왜 그래? 내 맘은 그거 아니고… 결백하다구. (따
라 나간다)

수호가 카메라 들고 따라 나간다.

각수가 주위를 둘러보더니 잽싸게 가방에서 소화기를 꺼낸다.

각수 저… 이거!

화진 뭐죠? 소화기 주방에 있는데.

각수 이건 나를 위한 거요. 잘 보관해 둬요! 언제 이 가슴이
확 타오를지 모르니깐. 그때 사용해주세요!

화진 왜, 가슴에 신나 뿌려요, 향수 대신?

각수 그게 아니고 (사이) 내 손 좀 잡아주세요! 아니 내가 잡
아 줄게요.

화진 진짜 왜 이래 (소화기 들고) 뿌린다. 확!

각수 맘대로 해! 이 몸은 그대 향한 사랑의 화염방사기니깐.
(화진이 안전고리 빼려하자 소화기 끌어안으며) 화진씨… 맞
죠? 그때 그 폭우 속 계곡에서 떠내려가면서 나한테 살
려달라고 손 내밀던 그 처절하게 가엽고 애타도록 아름
다운 아가씨?

화진   아니라니깐, 내가 몇 번이나 말했잖아.

각수   예 아니어도 좋아요. 그때부터 내 인생은…아 그때 내
가, 이 손을 구 센티 아니 삼 센티만 더 내밀었어도, 그
녀를 살릴 수 있었는데. 그때 나를 바라보던 그녀의 눈
이 화진씨라니깐. (사이) 아니라고 그럴 거죠? 그래도
좋아요. 화진씨 처음 본 순간, 내 빛나는 소방복에 걸고
맹세했으니깐. 이 여인이다! 내 인생의 모든 걸 받쳐 구
해줘야 할 영혼이… 당장 여기서 떠나요, 나하고. 진부
령에 근사한 카페 자리도 알아놨어. 아니 우리 결혼하
면 이런 거 안 해도 돼요.

화진   (약간 심난하게) 정말?

각수   그럼요! 진구! 걔 절대 안 돌아와.

화진   진구? 그 이름을 어떻게 알아? 응?

수호, 어느 사이 들어와 지켜보다가, 몰래 사진 찍는다. 카메
라 슈터소리에 자기가 깜짝.

수호   (들어오는 척) 뭐해요? 보름달 나왔는데.

창밖으로, 흩어지는 구름 사이로 밝은 보름달.

각수   (창가로 가며) 얼씨구 그러네… 봐 안보이잖아, 금절구

31

광채.

수호　(하품하며) 오키나와 바다 밑에는 바위 깎아 만든 인공구
조물이 있고. 대서양 어디엔가 가라앉은 아틀란티스대
륙이 있겠죠… 그 금절구 저 물밑에 있을 수도 있어요.

각수　소 방귀 꾸면서 지구 온난화 유발하는 소리 하고 있네.
야 무슨 금절구야? 있다면 소똥이나 잔뜩 있겠지. 그
구두쇠영감이 중한테 퍼줬다는.

수호　맞다, 소똥! 아까부터 궁금했는데, 이화진은 왜 하필 스
님한테 소똥을 줬을까요? 시주하기 싫으면 그냥 돌려
보내도 됐을 텐데?

화진　(각수에게) 이봐요? 어떻게 아냐구, 그 이름?

각수　(외면, 딴청 떨며) 어떻게 아냐면… 왜 소똥을 줬냐하면…
이유는 간단해. 이건 내 생각인데. (잠시) 그 구두쇠 영
감탱이한테 그 중이 찾아왔어 (중 흉내) 어허~ 사방팔방
수소문 해봐도, 아드님 같은 사내를 봤다는 집도 절도
사람들도 없더이다. (이화진 흉내) 살아있어, 내 아들은.
갠 절대로 무책임하게 죽어서도 죽을 수도 없는 몸이
요. 금쪽같은 아내를 놔두고… 또 지가 물려받을 아비
의 재산을 놔두고 (중 흉내) 열 길 물속은 알아도 한 치
사람 속은 모르고… 인명은 재천이오. 아드님은 필시
죽었거나 살아있어도 귀향의 뜻이 없는 겁니다. 허니
이제 그 부자지정의 집착 버리시지요! (이화진 흉내) 못

간다 이놈! 내 아들 찾아준다고, 네가 **뺏어간** 쌀가마가 얼마인데, 이제 와서 발뺌을 해? (중 흉내) 허허 그것으로 흉년기근에 허덕이는 중생들을 구제했지요. 진정코 그 아들을 살리고 싶으면…

어느 사이, 규명과 명각 들어와서 각수의 이야기 듣다가.

규명   (이화진이 돼서) 예? 예! 어찌하면 우리 아들을 다시 만날 수 있겠소?

각수   (흠칫 놀라나 곧바로) 아 예… 저 곳간에 있는 전 재산을 보시하시오!

규명   전 재산? (사이) 내가 소똥거름 져 날라서 농사져 모은 내 재산이다. 그러니 이 소똥이나 가져가라! 이 똥만도 못한 땡중놈아!

각수   이런 젠장할 보살! 머지않아 큰 환란이 닥칠 것이니, 한시바삐 저 곳간 다 비우시고 이 집을 떠나시오!

규명   무슨 환란? 다 내놓고 떠나고 싶어도, 저 금절구 때문에 못 간다. 썩 꺼져라, 이놈아!

각수   파토 파토! 아 또 금절구가 왜 나와? 얘기를 도와주려면 잘 도와주던가.

규명   이치가 기렇잖아. 나한테 제일 소중한 건 화진이 아니 고청이고, 화진이 아니 고청이가 제일로 아끼는 게 금절구니깐.

각수   오호 그토록 소중한 고청 아니 화진씨라 전세금 올려 받겠다?

규명   (순간) 쉿! 입 닥치라!

화진   전세금? 아저씨가 왜 전세금을… 뭐죠?

각수   인사드려요, 이 건물 주인장이십니다.

모두   예?

각수   그… 맨날 전세금 올려달라는 주인이 바로! (사이) 이래 봬도 내가 검사요, 소방검사! 내 구역에서 내 말 한마디 면 집 개증축 절대 못해. 건물주가 누구인지도 다 알아. 이 건물의 소유주가 여기 박규명씨란 걸 얼마 전에 알 았네요. 놀랄 일이죠?

화진   그게 정말예요. 나 놀리는 것 아니죠?

규명   (잽싸게) 전세금 올려달라고 한 주인을 저 호수 물 싹 마 를 때까지 패줘야 한다고 말한 게 나지. 그래 난 맞아도 싸. (사이) 화진이가 이 카페를 얼마큼 소중히 여기는 지… 알고 싶어서… 안 그렇다면 벌써 전세금 핑계대고 문 닫고 떠났겠지. 그런데 아니었어. 이 카페는 화진이 인생에서 제일로 중요한 것이야. 걱정 마! 전세금 인상 취소야. 그리고 이 카페도 금으로 발라줄게, 내가. 이 인테리어도 다시 해!

화진   기가 막혀서… 아저씨가 뭔데, 내 인생을 전세금처럼

	들먹거려요?
규명	아니 그냥 나는.
각수	진구 아버지니깐.
규명	닥쳐!
화진	뭐 뭐라고요, 아저씨가?
명각	아 아… (사이) 저기 달도 저렇게 떴네.

규명   … 그래 나다 나. 네가 기다리는 그놈아가 내 아들이다.
         하나뿐인 내 아들.

화진   아하하 알았어요. 그래서 처음부터 가게자리 알아봐주
         고, 텃세 막아주고, 매일 찾아와 매상 올려주신 게 다…
         진구오빠 아버님이라구요? 그런데 왜? 나보고 감동받
         으라고? 그럴 거면 더 더 있다가, 내가 그 이름 애타게
         부르면서, 저 물속으로 투신자살하는 순간에 말씀하시
         지, 그럼 감동 따따블일 걸. 아 감동 감동스러워 미치고
         팔딱 뛰겠다.

규명   아니 아니야 그렇게 오해하면 못써! 난… 난, 처음에 네
         가 진구가 어디 있는지 안다고 생각했어. 그놈아가 탈영
         을 하고 숨어있으면서, 나 몰래 너를 이리로 보냈다고.

화진   그래요. 그랬어야 했어요. 그런데… (뭔가를 말하려다가)

규명   알아. 인제는 다 알아, 그 무정한 놈을 기다리는 우리
         화진이 마음.

화진   (눈물 맺힌다)

규명 기래… 우리 이렇게 손잡고, 기다리자! 돌아올 거야, 그
놈아 돌아오면 깜짝 놀랄 걸, 애비가 엄청난 떼부자가
됐다는 걸 알면. (밖에 대고 외친다) 진구야, 빨리 돌아와!
난 이제 바다 밑이나 훑는 머구리 아니다. 내 재산 다
네 거 된다! 하하하.

명각 끝끝내 돌아오지 않으면… 어떻게 하실 거죠? (화진을
본다)

규명 와! 와! 그놈은 당연히 돌아올 거고 꼭 꼭 돌아와야 해,
우리 아바이가 돌아와야 되는 것처럼. (사이) 우리 아바
이 함경도서 혈혈단신 내려오셨어. 인물 훤하고 성깔
툭 부러지는 요샛말로 인기짱이었댔지. 기런 남자 가만
두면 바닷가여자 아니지. 그래 내가 태어났고. 삼팔따
라지 사위가 못 마땅하지만, 끼니 때울 보리쌀이나 심
어먹으라고 비탈밭 한 귀퉁이를, 내 외조부가 떼어주셨
지. 그때부터 한 십여 년을 우리 아바이 정말 쇠골 빠지
게 일했어. 농사판 산판 노가다판 닥치는 대로 뛰어들
어 돈 모으고 그 돈으로 땅을 사두셨던 거야, 아무도 모
르게. 그걸 나중에 벽장서 땅문서를 발견하고서 알게
됐지. (사이) 내가 철나고, 그냥저냥 먹고 살만 하니깐,
배를 타셨어. 그거 위험하다 웬 팔자에 없는 뱃일이냐
고 오마니는 대고대고 말리셨지만… 그 배를 타고 나가
면 쪼끔이라도 더 더 가까이서 고향냄새를 맡을 수 있

다고… 그렇게 삼사 년 배를 타셨댔는가? 그러다가…
야 나 눈물 마려우면 꼭 술 고프드라. 술 좀 줘!

화진   (술을 따라준다) 오빠도 술 마시면 꼭 할아버지이야기를
했어요.

규명   기래? 다 나한테 들은 거지. 기깐 놈이 뭘 알갔어. (품에
서 사진 두 장을 꺼내며) 그놈이 제 할아바이를 **빼다** 박았
어. 봐!

화진   (사진 보며) 예… 이 사진 저 주시면…

규명   기래. (준다)

화진   (사이) 할아버님이 납북인지 사고인지 모른다면서요?

규명   그때 풍랑은 좀 심했지만 다른 배들은 다 돌아왔거든…
납북일 거야. (사이) 돌아오실 거야, 우리 아바이. 그래
서 지금까지, 그 땅 안 팔고 있었어. 이 땅은 아바이 것
이니, 돌아오실 때까지, 누가 뭐래도, 그 어느 놈이 간
빼주고 꼬리를 쳐도 절대 팔 수 없다. 그렇게 눈 딱 감
고 버팅기고 있었지.

각수   그랬더니 그 땅이 억 억 수십억!

모두   (탄성 지르며 박수)

각수   나 같으면 이 건물, 등기 째로 이전해주겠다, 화진씨한
테.

규명   (버럭) 안 돼! 그건 내 재산 아니야. 내 아바이 꺼 고대로
내 아들한테 물려줘야 돼. 진구 돌아올 때까지, 한 푼도

허투루 남 못 줘.

각수   화진씨가 남인가요? 타관객지에 와서 청춘세월 다 받치며 진구만 기다렸는데 (버럭) 요즘 세상에.

화진   (분위기 뜨악함 무마하려고) 각수씨가 뭔데, 왜 그래? 그럼 내가 이 날 이때까지 아버님 아니 아저씨 재산 노리면서 여기서 산 게 되잖아. 아 진짜 말하다보니 열 받네… 이거 왜 이래? 내가 누구를 기다린 것도 여기서 이렇게 사는 것도 또 여기를 떠나고 말고도 내가 선택하고 내가 결정해. 나가! 다 나가! 오늘 영업 끝났어. (수호에게) 야, 너도 사진 그만 찍고 꺼져! 너 알바 쫑이야.

수호가 욱! 문 박차고 나간다.
잠시, 어안벙벙 침묵 흐른다. 명각, 벌떡 일어난다.

명각   오늘, 카페 완전 쫑내! 영업폐쇄! 화진씨! (사이) (아무 번호 막 누른다. 노래반주 나온다. 노래 안 하고 마이크에 대고 말한다) 나 나 나 오늘 화진씨한테 한마디 하겠습니다. 미안합니다, 화진씨! (무릎 꿇으며) 내가 다 책임지겠습니다.

화진   예!?

명각   (감격에 겨워) 화진씨, 이 손 잡아주세요!

각수   (무릎 꿇으며) 안 돼! 이 손 내 손을 잡아야 돼, 화진!

규명   내… 진심으로 사과한다. 조금만 더 가다리자! 여기서
        나하고… 우리 진구… 이제 와서 포기할 수는 없잖니.
        (손 내민다)

        화진, 손을 비비며 고민하다가 바텐 박스 안으로 가 와인병을
        품에 안는다.
        수호가 문 벌컥 열고 뛰어든다.

수호   절구 금절구다! 맞아요, 아저씨 말이 맞아. 봐요, 저기
        호수 한가운데!

        열린 문과 통창 밖으로, 호수 한 가운데서 솟아오르는 금빛
        광채가 보인다.
        모두 창가로 간다. 놀람과 두려움의 환호성 내지른다.

화진   아 뭐야 저거? 그럼 그 전설이 진실인가?

규명   거 봐라! 내 말이 맞지! 금절구 진짜로 있다. 내 말은 틀
        림없다. (환호하며 나간다)

명각   아~ 뭐야 저 광채는? 그날 밤… 그 빛도 저거였나? (뛰
        쳐나간다)

각수   왜 그래요! 저 금절구 내 꺼야. (따라 나간다)

화진, 따라나서려다 돌아선다.

화진   꺼내! 꺼내서 보여줄 수 있으면…

암전.

#3 얼마 후

휘영청 밝은 보름달
규명, 느긋 초조하게 술을 마신다.

수호 세상엔 믿을 수 없는 사실과 믿어야만 하는 환상이 있습니다. 저 호수 한가운데서 솟아오른 금절구의 광채가 바로 그런 것이었습니다. 도저히 믿을 수 없는데 사실이었고, 분명코 이 눈으로 봤으니 믿어야만 하는 환상이었습니다. 어쨌든, 두 사나이는 그 광채를 향해 뛰어들었고 헤엄쳐 나갔습니다. 그러나!

뛰어 들어오는 명각 각수. 흠뻑 젖은 팬티바람의 몸이 애처롭다. 빈손이다.

각수 에이… 죽고 싶어서 환장했어? 헤엄도 못 치면서, 그렇게 무턱대고 뛰어들면 어떡해요? 몇 분만 늦었어도 당신 지금 물귀신 됐어요.
명각 오늘 같은 밤이면… 죽어도 좋소.
각수 죽을 거면 혼자 죽지. 왜 나를 붙들고 늘어져요?

명각   오늘 같은 밤에 혼자 죽는 건… 저 달에 대한 예의가 아
         니요.

         두 사내, 턱 부딪치며 오들오들 떨며 달을 본다.
         화진이가 우아한 춤동작으로 수건을 던져준다.
         죄송 억울한 자세로 수건을 받아든 둘, 옷을 찾아들고 화장실
         로 간다.

수호   (규명의 시선을 받으며) 뭘 그렇게 보세요! 앗 또… 내가
         무슨 생각하는지 아세요?
규명   너 지금, 내가 왜 저 호수에 안 들어갔는지 궁금하지?
수호   (놀람) 예!
규명   왕년에 동해안 제일의 머구리라면 잠수에는 도가 텄을
         텐데.
수호   예 예!
규명   출출하니 술 한 잔에 안주발 땡기고 싶지.
수호   아 역시. ('최고'라고 엄지 치켜보이며 술잔 받는다)
규명   마셔! (사이) 너 지금 네가 소주를 마셨다고 생각하지.
         아니야. 소주가 네 몸 안으로 뛰어든 기야. 그 소주는
         곧 바로 네 몸의 일부가 돼야 돼. 그렇지 않으면 넌, 그
         소주를 토해낼 수밖에 없어. 잠수도 마찬가지. 내가 물
         에 뛰어드는 순간, 내가 물과 하나가 돼야 돼. 그렇지

않으면 물이 나를 토해내. 죽는 거지. 이해가 안 되니? 물에서 죽은 몸뗑이는 반드시 떠오르잖아. 그건 물이 그 몸을 토해낸 거야. 저놈들, 그렇게 안 된 게 다행이지. (사이) 뭘 그렇게 빤히 봐?

수호   아직 말씀 안하셨거든요, 왜 물에 안 들어 가셨는지.

규명   (쓸쓸) 술이나 마셔!

화진   잠수병, 아주 치명적인. 깊은 물에 들어가면 뇌신경이 꼬이고 마비돼서 곧바로 시체로 떠오르신대, 우리 진구 아버님. (사이) 나도 한 잔 주세여!

규명   야이 많이 했어. 그만 하라. (사이) 너도 봤지? 봤으니 믿는 거지?

화진   술이나 주세요!

규명   아이구 그래 그래. (술 따른다)

각수 명각 옷 차려 입고 나온다.

각수   저놈의 달님은, 여전히 뻔뻔스레 떠있네. 저 때문에 멀쩡한 사나이들 죽다 살아난 걸, 몽땅 목격했으면서

명각   달은 여자거든. 매일같이 살짝쿵 모양 바꿔가면서, 남자 약 올리는.

각수   맞아. 어떨 땐 완전히 사라질 때도 있잖아.

명각   그래서 그믐날엔 귀신들이 활개를 쳐. 달처녀가 없으니

깐, 심심적적 외로우니. 우리 그런 귀신 되지 말자!

각수　　근데 왜 반말이냐? 우리 서로 존대하는 사이였잖아요?

명각　　야 너와 나는, 저 전설의 고인물을 함께 들어갔다 나온 사이야. (노래한다) 너와 내가 아니면 누가 지키랴 / 전설의 호수에서 헤매는 여인.

각수　　좋다. 말 놓은 기념으로 한 잔 꺾자… 요!

명각/각수　너와 내가 아니면 누가 꺼낼까/ 전설의 카페에서 외로운 여인.

규명　　거기, 물귀신 되려다가 퇴짜 맞고 돌아온 소방귀신 박사귀신, 이리 와!

각수　　누구 보고 오라 가라? 화진씨 이리와 우리랑 한 잔 해줘!

규명　　주접 그만 떨고, 여기 계약서대로 시키는 대로 해! (금절구 두고 사인한 계약서 꺼낸다)

각수　　어디 봅시다! (다가와 읽는다) 호수 밑에 금절구 있음이 확인되면 갑의 승리로 인정하고 을과 병은 갑이 시키는 대로… (사이) 있어요, 금절구? 없잖아, 빛만 잠깐 보였고.

규명　　빛이 보이면 그 밑에 절구 있는 거지.

각수　　그 절구, 누가 봤냐고?

규명　　봤잖아, 그 금빛.

각수　　빛이 절구요?

규명　　금절구가 있으니 금빛이 나온 거지.

각수   글쎄 그 금절구 누가 봤냐고요?

명각   아직까진 우리가 이기고 있는 겁니다.

규명   나… 이런… 배운 놈까지 더 말도 안 되는 억지를.

각수   억지는 지금 누가 부리는데. (사이) 꺼내오든지 사진이 라도 찍어오든지, 물증이 있어야 이기고 지는 거 아니 요. (수호 보고) 그거 수중촬영 되냐?

수호   (절대 안 된다고 몸서리친다)

규명   오냐 좋다. 들어간다. 내가 들어가서…

화진, 규명이 들고 있는 계약서 낚아채 갈기갈기 찢어 공중으 로 날려버린다.

화진   뭘 봐! 당장 꺼지든지 술이나 마셔들!

명각 각수, 자기들끼리 따로 떨어져 소주를 나눈다.

수호   야릇하고 어색한 침묵이 오랫동안 흘렀습니다. 우리 몸 안으로 소주가 뛰어드는 소리만 홀짝홀짝… 언제나 내 품에서 커다란 외눈을 껌벅이며 이 전설의 호숫가를 찍 어대던 이 카메라도 꾸벅꾸벅 졸기 시작하던 바로 이 때. 드디어 난, 아스라한 이 달빛의 끝자락을 붙잡고 마 지막 퀴즈를 던졌습니다. (사이) 그렇다면 우리의 고청이는 도대체 왜 무슨 생각으로, 그때 그 고갯마루에서 뒤를 돌아봤을까요?

각수 그때… 뭔 소리가 났겠지.

수호 폭풍우, 쓰나미 밀려드는 소리, 사람들의 아우성 뭐 그런 소리겠죠. 하지만 스님이, 그 어떤 소리가 나더라도 절대 절대로 돌아보지 말라했지요. 그런데 도대체 왜 왜? 왜? 고청은 뒤를 돌아봐야만 했나요? (화진에게 와인병 주며) 그 답을 맞히는 분한테 드리세요!

화진 왜? 니가 뭔데? (사이) 좋아. 나도 갈등스런 이 밤 빨리 끝내고 내 갈길 정하고 싶어, 더 기다릴지 말지. (각수 명각 규명을 둘러본다)

셋 음…! (고개 끄덕이며 각오를 단단히 한다)

수호 자 그럼 누구부터? 아 잠깐. (화진을 이끌어 통창 앞에 세운다) 이렇게 서 있다가, 그 생각을 맞히는 사람을 향해 돌아보세요!

창문 밖을 향한 화진, 작은 허밍으로 그 어떤 노래를 부른다.
셋, 서로 먼저 이야기 하라고 미루다가.

명각 (벌떡 일어나, 스님 목소리로) 절대 절대로 뒤를 돌아봐선 안 되오! 즉 금기! 인간이 하고 싶어도 하지 말아야 할 그것. 하지만 금기는 인간의 욕망을 오히려 부축이지.

고청은 금기를 어기고 뒤를 돌아봄으로써 인간적인 승리를 얻은 거야. (사이) 돌아보세요! 지금까지 그대를 옥죄고 있던 시간의 사슬, 그 금기에서 벗어나세요!

수호 (화진의 반응 살피다가) 네 아닙니다. 다음!

각수 여자 마음은 그렇게 추상적인 게 아니지. 아주 구체적이고 매우 자잘하고 너무 실생활적이야. 불난 집에 가보면 알아. 온 집안에 불길이 번지고 있는데, 베란다에 빨래부터 챙겨서 나와. 난 그런 게 여자만의 매력, 능력, 마력이라고 생각해요. 고청이가 뒤를 돌아본 건… 마당에 두고 온 금절구 때문에…가 아니라 마침 그때 벼락이 금절구를 때리면서 빛이 버번쩍… 놀라서 돌아볼 수밖에… 돌아봐줘요, 제발!

수호 아 아닙니다. 다음!

규명 다 아니고… 고청이가 막 고갯마루를 넘어가는 순간, 어떤 소리가 들렸어. 고청아! 여보, 나 돌아왔어! 난리 통에 군에 갔던 신랑이 그때 돌아온 거야.

화진, 서서히 고개 돌려 규명을 바라본다.

규명 고청아!… 화진아!

화진 … 네. 돌아올 거예요.

규명 됐어 됐어 이제 그만. 자 기분이다. 우리 밤새도록 평생

토록 노래하고 놀자!

수호　네 그럼 어떻게 할까요? 이 와인? 딸까요?

화진/규명　(동시에) 안 돼!

규명　이건 진구가 돌아오면 마실 거지? 잘 보관해둬! 하하하.

명각　아니! 아드님은 돌아올 수 없습니다.

규명　그게 무슨 소리야!

명각　(작정한 듯 소주잔 비우며) 내가 진구의 마지막을 지켜봤으니까요.

규명　뭐 자네가?!

명각　네, 죄송합니다. 제가 박진구 일병의 소대장이었습니다.

규명　아닌데? 사고 조사할 때 부대를 몇 번 갔었어, 내가.

명각　진구가 사라진 다음 날, 저는 전역신고를 해야 했습니다. 물론 사고조사 때문에 며칠 연기가 됐었죠. (사이) 진구는 특별 관심사병이었습니다. 가끔가다 환상과 현실을 구분 못했어요. 영화 공동경비구역을 흉내 내며, 저쪽 애들하고 축구를 하겠다고 달밤에 공을 갔고 튀기도 했습니다. 제대 말년에 더 큰 사고라도 칠까봐, 일부러 내 당번병을 시키면서 가까이 했어요. 진구는 전공이 법학이었지만 나를 깜작 놀래키는 문학적 재능이 있었어요. 그래서 우리는 같은 동아리 선후배처럼 어울리며 문학과 사랑과 인생을 이야기했지요.

규명 기런데?… 대체 그놈이 어떻게 된 거냐구?

명각 그날… 부대교대를 앞두고 마지막 매복을 나갔는데…
오늘처럼 보름달이 훤하게 뜬 밤이었죠. 내 전역을 축
하한다며 수통을 건네주더군요.

수호 술을, 최전방 GOP매복에서?

명각 커피였어, 애인이 보내준 원두커피로 뽑은… 그 커피,
너무 쓰면서도 아주 달콤하더군요. 첫사랑의 키스처
럼… 사진도 보여줬어요. 둘이 같이 호수를 등지고 찍
은… 달빛에 비춰진 사진 속의 여인이 살아있는 듯 아
름다웠어… 바로 그때 하늘 높이 날아가는 철새들이 보
였어. 아! 저 새들 보름달 등에 지고 바이칼호수 간다.
같이 가자! 가다가 가다가 쉬어가자! 함경도 어디쯤 할
아버지 고향에서. 잠꼬대처럼 중얼대더니 그대로 벌떡
일어나서 휘청휘청 저쪽으로… 거기 서! 철커덕! 월북
으로 판단한 우리 소대원들이 자물쇠 풀고 총 겨눴어.
쏘지 마! 돌아와! 쏘지 마! 돌아와! (사이) 그 자식은 돌
아오지도 돌아보지도 않고 그대로 달빛어둠 속으로 사
라졌어.

규명 월북했다고? 제 할아바이 찾으러? 그런데 왜 탈영 실종
이라고 했어?

명각 남북정상회담, 월드컵! 그땐 그런 사건이 발생하면 안
됐고, 사건이 났어도 그냥 덮어버려야 할 때였어요. 지

휘계통에서도 개인적인 사건이길 원했고. 나도 당장 전역신고를 해야 했으니깐. (괴로워한다)

수호 월북! 정확한 정황인가요?

각수 (어처구니없음) 월북? 말이 되나. 그땐 수많은 탈북자들이 압록강 두만강을 목숨 걸고 넘을 땐데 어느 미친놈이 월북을 해.

규명 그래… 그래도 월북했다면, 살아 있는 거잖니. 돌아올 수 있어. 세상이 바뀌고 있으니.

명각 아니 아니요! 그리고 얼마 후… 저쪽 어둠 속에서 터지는 지뢰 폭발음. 연달아 쏟아지는 기관총소리. (사이) 시신은 아마 저쪽에서 처리했을 겁니다. 의거월북자를 오인 사격했으니, 저쪽에서도 사건을 덮어버렸겠지.

화진 아니야 아니야! (명각의 가슴을 때리며 울부짖다가 무너진다) 그런데 왜 왜? 인제 와서 나한테.

명각 제대하고 난, 이 악물고 그 사건을 잊었고… 잊자! 잊자! 잊어버리자! 그건 한국남자라면 누구나 가는 군대에서 얼마든지 일어날 수 있는 일이다. 절대로 뒤돌아보며 살지 말자! 앞만 보고 살자! 살자!… 그랬어야 했는데… 그 녀석이 남기고 간 이 사진 만큼은 버릴 수가 없었소.

명각, 사진을 화진에게 준다. 화진, 받지 않는다.

규명이 사진을 뺏어 바라본다.

규명   갔다구, 너 혼자? 네 옆에 요렇게 어여쁜 인연을 놔두
고… 이놈아.

각수   진구… 지가 하고픈 대로 놔뒀으면, 지금 비행사가 돼
서 저 하늘을 날고 있을 텐데. 우리 고등학교 선후배들
사이에서 진구는, 희망이고 자랑이었어. (울컥) 야 너는
꼭 네 희망대로 공사나 항공대 가서 비행기 탈 거다. 그
비행기 나도 태워줘라! 네 덕에 우리도 이 지겨운 바닷
가 벗어나 저 넓은 세상 좀 가보자! 그런데 내 아들만은
서울대 법대를 가야한다는 그 대책 없는 고집으로… 서
울에 있는 대학을 겨우 삼수 만에 들어가더니… 육군땅
개로 박박 기게 하더니…

규명   기래 나, 그 고집 하나로 내 아들 키웠다. 잠수병으로
뼛골이 뭉그러지면서. 그 어느 놈의 도움도 응원도 없
이. 에이 빙신 같은 놈. 지 앞가림이나 잘하지… 누가
지 할애비 찾아오랬나? 국가와 민족도 해결 못하는 그
일을 왜 제가 하겠다고.

규명, 술을 따라 마시려다 술병으로 이마로 치고, 깨진 술병
으로 자해하려한다.
울부짖는 규명을, 수호와 각수가 붙들고 늘어져 겨우 말린다.

화진   네, 그 누구의 잘못도 책임도 아니에요. 스무 살이 넘은 사내자식이 그 누구를 핑계 대며 제 인생을 해까닥질 할 수는 없는 거죠. 그 남자는 자기가 가고픈 데를 간 거고, 나도 내가 오고픈 길을 왔을 뿐. 그래요. 지금까지 난 내가 한때 오빠라고 부르며 의지했던 한 남자의 그림자만 쫓으며 살아온 거예요. 여자라는 이유, 여자라는 핑계를 대면서… 헌병… 군수사대가 몇 번 찾아왔었어요. 탈영의 원인 거의 다 여자문제다. 혹시 아는 거 없느냐? 없다 모른다고 했죠. 우리들의 약속을 저버리고 한 마디 말도 없이 사라져버린 오빠가 도저히 이해가 안 되고 믿고 미워서… 하지만 곧바로 그렇게 된 게, 내 책임일 수도 있다는 생각이 들었어요. 우리나라 남자는 언제까지 그 개뿔 같은 군대를 가야만 하냐고, 안 가면 안 되게냐고, 내가 떼를 쓴 적이 있었어요. 그 말이 가시가 돼서 그랬다면 내 책임이다. 책임진다, 기다려야한다, 난 그 남자를. 계절이 되면 돌아오는 고니를 기다리는 저 호수의 마음처럼… 하지만 이 고인 물에는 덧없이 흘러흘러 술에 절은 내 젊음만 고여 있을 뿐. (사이) 됐어요. 이제 돌아들 가세요! 나도 이 가슴에 고여 있던, 썩은 진물 다 뱉어버리고, 내 시간의 원점으로 돌아갈 테니, 더 이상 여기 남겨둘 미련도 추억도 보물도 없으니… 결코 뒤 돌아보는 일은 없을 거예요.

화진, 바텐을 통해 내실로 향한다.

규명   화진아! (사이) 여기서 더 살면서 기다리면 안 되겠니?
        진구는 돌아올 거야. 돌아올 수 있어.

화진   … 죽었어요.

규명   아니야. (명각의 멱살을 움켜쥐고 몸부림) 너, 분명히 말해!
        니가 봤어? 진구 죽는 거 봤냐구? 말해! 우리 아들 살아
        있다구 말해! 살아서 저 북쪽으로 갔다구. 그러니 얼마
        든지 다시 살아 돌아올 수 있다구. 내가 억만금을 들여
        서라도 빼내올 거야. 요즘 중국 연변엔 그런 브로커들
        많다잖아.

명각   (고개 젓는다)

각수   놓으세요, 이거! 죽었다잖아요. (순간, 주먹으로 명각의 어
        구창을 날린다) 너 이 새끼, 그대로 있어, 당장 헌병대에
        고발해서 죗값 치르게 할 테니. (핸드폰 꺼내든다)

수호   (차갑게) 동작 그만! 내가 여기 있습니다.

화진   가! 다 필요 없어. 나한텐 다 끝난 일이야. 다 꺼져 버려!

규명   안 된다. 진구가 돌아올 수 없는 길을 갔더라도… 화진
        아, 여기서 그냥 이대로 같이 살자!

화진이 고개 젓는다. 그리고 말없이 내실로 들어간다.
내실로 들어간 화진을 향하여 규명 소리 지른다.

규명   내 재산 다 네 것이 될 수 있어. 넌 여기를 떠나면 안 돼!

명각   (웃는다)

각수   야 이런 상황에… 왜 웃어? 안 아프냐?

명각   웃기잖아. 저 전설의 호수가… 전설은 소설이 아니야.

각수   뭔 말이야?

명각   저기 저 물 속에 있다는 금절구… 그건 전설이지. 근데
       진구 그 자식은 소설을 썼어. 제 마음, 제 욕망대로…
       나도 그렇고.

수호   그건 또 뭔 뜻이죠?

명각   넌 사진을 왜 찍니? 무엇에 대한 증명이고 무엇을 기억
       하려고?

수호   내가 보고 기억하고 남기고 싶은 그거요. 보세요! (카메
       라 파인더 조작하며 본다)

각수   뭐야, 이건?

수호   어라? 아까 분명히 찍었는데, 그 금절구 광채… 그냥
       어두운 물결만 찍혔네.

각수   … 다 꽝이고 뻥이야. 우리가 술기운에 달빛에 취했던
       거야.

명각   그래… 가자! 다 꺼지라잖아.

각수   그래… 가라면 가야지. 그나저나 우리 화진씨는 어디로
       가려나?

규명   아~~ 이런 개아가리 같은 놈들! 전부 꼼짝 말고 있어!

내가 꺼내온다. 저 호수 밑에 금절구. 그거 꺼내 오면 다들 내 말 대로, 내가 시키는 대로 한다, 그랬지. 너 화진이도! 그대로 있어! (웃옷 벗어젖히며 뛰쳐나간다)

각수　어… 저 양반… 잠수하면 그대로 (사이) 안 돼, 말려!

각수가 규명을 쫓아 나간다.
명각, 천천히 자기 가방을 찾아들고 나가려 한다.

수호　조명각 중위! (사이) 아니 교수님이시죠. 저… 그 전설에 대해 마지막으로 하나만 더 묻겠습니다.

명각　묻지 마! (사이) 전설은 전설로 있어야 살아있는 전설인 거야.

수호　그럼 이제부터 박진구 일병의 실종 건도 전설이 돼야겠네요. 저 달빛 아래 그 어디에선가 영원히 살아있으려면 (사이) 그렇게 돼야겠죠?

명각　… ?

명각이 천천히 걸어 나간다. 수호, 명각을 잡아 세우고 품속에서 신분증을 꺼내 보여준다. 움칫 놀라는 명각. 수호 핸드폰을 꺼내 전화를 건다.

수호　충성! 헌병 한수호 전화 드렸습니다. 하하하 예! 저도

압니다. 곧바로 귀대해서 전역신고 하겠습니다. 여기
상황이요? 다 해결 됐습니다. 박진구는 말입니다 탈영
도 사고사도 아닌 것 같습니다. 네 지금까지 적확한 첩
보 획득 못했습니다. 월북이요? 에이 요즘에 어떤 또라
이가 월북을 합니까? 예! 아무튼 탈영도 월북도 아닙니
다. 원인불명의 행불 아니면 증발이라고 하죠, 뭐. 더
이상 박진구를 추적할 필요도 가치도 없다고 판단됩니
다. 저의 제대와 함께 이 사건도 종결하시죠! 하하하 전
행운이었습니다. 군무이탈 체포조하면서 전공인 사진
도 병행하구요. 옛! 귀대해서 제대 턱 화끈하게 쏘겠습
니다. 충성! (사이) 이제 일병 박진구의 증발은 전설이
됐습니다. 자 가세요! 가거든 다시는 뒤돌아보지 말고
사세요! 전설은 전설로 남겨두고…!

천천히 문을 나서려던 명각, 멈칫 그대로 선다.
호수로 날아드는 고니들의 울음소리.

명각   그 전설에 대한 마지막 질문은 뭐지?
수호   (씨익 웃으며) 그 아들은 과연 저 새들처럼 돌아올까요?
        (사이) 어 이 분들 진짜 어디로 갔지? (나간다)

홀로 남은 명각. 잠시 내실 쪽을 응시하다가… 바닥에 버려진

사진을 집어 들고 망설이다가 두 쪽으로 찢는다. 사진의 한 쪽은 버리고 한 쪽에 입 맞춘다.

달밤을 스치는 고니의 처연한 울음소리.

명각, 통창으로 달려가 마치 소총을 들고 있는 양 정조준 하더니 쏘는 시늉을 한다.

환청처럼 자동소총소리 울려 퍼진다.

명각 다다다당! 다다다당! 탕! 야이 이놈아! 내가 널 얼마나 믿고 아꼈는데… 야이 돌아이 새끼야! 가버려! 너 같은 새끼한테 이런 여자는, 너무 아깝고 책임도 못 져. 내가 책임진다. 그래 너는 가고 나는 여기 있다. 하하하 내가 쐈다. 내가 내가 죽였다. 죽어 죽어 죽어라!

명각, 미친 듯이 웃다가 울다가 웃는다.

가방을 든 화진이 나타난다.

명각 들었니? 내 말? 내 마음? (사이) 내가 그랬어. 아니 내가 그럴 수밖에 없었어. 그날 밤은 달빛도… 사진 속의 너의 얼굴도 너무 밝고 아름다웠어.

화진 (와인병 내민다) 따줘!

수호 (밖에서 목소리, 멀리) 어디… 지금 어디 계세요?

각수 (밖에서 목소리) 야야~ 안 되겠어. 빨리 119 불러!

수호   (서로 가까워지며) 형님이 119잖아.

각수   아저씨! 어디 계세요!

각수/수호   어어 저거 뭐야?

뻥! 명각이 와인병 딴다.

통창 너머, 저 호수 한가운데에서 누런 금빛 광채가 솟아오른다.

명각, 멈칫 통창으로 달려가 밖을 내다본다.

화진   그거 알아요? 그 남자와 내가 했던 약속. 그때 우리는 탈출을 계획했어요. 이 지긋지긋한 땅덩이 벗어나 저 넓은 세상 어디든… 그 남자는 영화를 나는 커피를 공부하러… 제대하면 곧바로 오기로 했는데…

화진, 와인을 바닥에 쏟아 붓는다.

고니들 울음소리, 해일처럼 밀려든다.

#4 몇 년 후

카페 인테리어와 소도구가 바뀌었다.

바텐더 박스 안에서 청바지에 허름한 셔츠 걸친 각수가 커피를 내리고 있다.

말끔한 정장차림의 수호가 통창을 내다보고 있다.

수호   그날 밤 이후, 그 두 남녀는 이곳에서 사라졌고… 저도 이곳을 떠났습니다. 제대하면서 사진을 그만 뒀습니다. 더 이상 카메라라는 기계의 눈으로 이 세상을 바라볼 수도 기억할 수도 없었습니다. 그래서 계획했던 그 사진집도 이 세상에 나타날 수가 없었습니다. (사이) 오늘도 그날처럼 달밤이네. 그때 이렇게 찍었는데… (빈손카메라로 촬영하던 기억을 더듬는다)

각수   (커피 내오며) 아깝다, 전공 못 살려서. 사진 안하면 뭐해?

수호   형님은요?

각수   물에 빠진 사람을 둘이나 못 살린 게 119 할 수 없잖아. 그 대신에 향기 좋게 정신 번쩍 들게 하는 커피로 행복을 주자. 마셔봐! 내가 볶은 하와이안 코나.

수호   이 카페?

각수 너 제대하고 곧바로 소방복 벗고 커피 볶아댔다. 꺼져
가는 가는 내 젊음 들볶듯이… 그게 벌써 몇 년이냐. 카
페는 작년 여름에 개업했고 (사이) 너 지금, 이 카페 누
구한테 인수했냐고 묻고 싶지?

수호 아 예.

각수 그 어르신이 유언장에 다 정리 해놨더라. 아들 진구가
돌아올 때까지 모든 재산은 지자체가 관리한다. 단 이
카페 건물은 세입자 화진의 소유로 한다. 근데 그때 이
후 사라진 화진씨가 안 나타나는 거야. 그래서 시에서
이 건물임대수익을 탈북민 자녀들 장학금으로 하기로
(사이) 너 지금, 화진씨는 어디 갔고 왜 안 나타나는지
묻고 싶지?

수호 아니요. 여기 오다가 만났어요?

각수 뭐… 어디서?

수호 여기 오다가… 진부령휴게소에 잠깐 들렀는데 기념품
코너에 낯익은 와인이 있더라구. 그래 한 병 사들고 막
출발하려는데, 길 건너에서 손을 흔드는 여자가 있더라
구. 윈도우 내리면서 봤더니 마담, 아니 화진 누님인 거
야. 급정거하고 내리려고 했더니, 손짓으로 일행이 있
다며 막 그냥 가라는 거야, 이쪽 바다 쪽을 가리키며.

각수 무슨 소리야? (사이) 죽었어… 여기 떠나고 얼마 후에…
달리는 버스에 뛰어들었대.

수호 아닌데… 내가 분명히 봤는데… 여기서 만나자고 했는
데. (가방에서 와인병 꺼낸다)

고니들의 울음소리 천공을 가르며 솟구친다.
통창 밖으로 어슴푸레한 그림자들이 나타난다.

막.

한국 희곡 명작선 04

전설의 달밤

초판 1쇄 인쇄일   2019년 1월 16일
초판 1쇄 발행일   2019년 1월 25일

지 은 이   홍원기
만 든 이   이정옥
만 든 곳   평민사
           서울시 은평구 수색로 340 [202호]
           전화: (02) 375-8571(代)
           팩스: (02) 375-8573
           http://blog.naver.com/pyung1976
           이메일 pyung1976@naver.com
등록번호   제251-2015-000102호
 정 가   6,000원

  ※ 이 책은 사단법인 한국극작가협회가 한국문화예술위
     2019년 제2회 극작엑스포 지원금을 받아 출간하였습니다.

Federal Efforts to Develop
New Evaluation Methods

Nick L. Smith, *Editor*

NEW DIRECTIONS FOR PROGRAM EVALUATION
A Publication of the Evaluation Research Society
SCARVIA B. ANDERSON, *Editor-in-Chief*

Number 12, December 1981

Paperback sourcebooks in
The Jossey-Bass Higher Education and
Social and Behavioral Sciences Series

Jossey-Bass Inc., Publishers
San Francisco • Washington • London

Federal Efforts to Develop New Evaluation Methods
Number 12, December 1981
     Nick L. Smith, *Editor*

New Directions for Program Evaluation Series
A Publication of the Evaluation Research Society
Scarvia B. Anderson, *Editor-in-Chief*

New Directions for Program Evaluation (publication number
USPS 449-050) is published quarterly by Jossey-Bass Inc.,
Publishers, and is sponsored by the Evaluation Research Society.
Second-class postage rates paid at San Francisco, California,
and at additional mailing offices.

Correspondence:
Subscriptions, single-issue orders, change of address notices,
undelivered copies, and other correspondence should be sent to
New Directions Subscriptions, Jossey-Bass Inc., Publishers,
433 California Street, San Francisco, California 94104.

Editorial correspondence should be sent to the Editor-in-Chief,
Scarvia B. Anderson, Educational Testing Service, 250 Piedmont
Avenue, Suite 2020, Atlanta, Georgia 30308.

Library of Congress Catalogue Card Number LC 80-80074

International Standard Serial Number ISSN 0164-7989

International Standard Book Number ISBN 87589-859-9

Cover art by Willi Baum

Manufactured in the United States of America

Ordering Information

The paperback sourcebooks listed below are published quarterly and can be ordered either by subscription or as single copies.

Subscriptions cost $30.00 per year for institutions, agencies, and libraries. Individuals can subscribe at the special rate of $18.00 per year *if payment is by personal check.* (Note that the full rate of $30.00 applies if payment is by institutional check, even if the subscription is designated for an individual.) Standing orders are accepted.

Single copies are available at $6.95 when payment accompanies order, and *all single-copy orders under $25.00 must include payment.* (California, Washington, D.C., New Jersey, and New York residents please include appropriate sales tax.) For billed orders, cost per copy is $6.95 plus postage and handling. (Prices subject to change without notice.)

To ensure correct and prompt delivery, all orders must give either the *name of an individual* or an *official purchase order number.* Please submit your order as follows:

Subscriptions: specify series and subscription year.
Single Copies: specify sourcebook code and issue number (such as, PE8).

Mail orders for United States and Possessions, Latin America, Canada, Japan, Australia, and New Zealand to:
Jossey-Bass Inc., Publishers
433 California Street
San Francisco, California 94104

Mail orders for all other parts of the world to:
Jossey-Bass Limited
28 Banner Street
London EC1Y 8QE

New Directions for Program Evaluation Series
Scarvia B. Anderson, *Editor-in-Chief*

ERRATUM

D. Baugher (Ed.). *New Directions for Program Evaluation: Measuring Effectiveness,* no. 11.

p. x, 105 editor identification should read:

Dan Baugher is an associate professor of management in the
Lubin Schools of Business Administration, Pace University,
New York City.

Contents

Editor's Notes

Evaluation is a rapidly expanding enterprise that has made remarkable progress in the last fifteen years. The practice of evaluation can be seen at all levels of federal, state, and local government, and it is now a common activity of many private and public agencies and corporations. While debate about the cost, utility, and effectiveness of evaluation continues, there is little evidence at present to suggest that the national interest in improvement and control of programs and policies through evaluation is lessening.

It is generally acknowledged that the primary impetus for the use of evaluation has come from the federal government. Through the creation of evaluation requirements in such areas as health, justice, education, housing, and welfare, the federal government has fostered a social movement, created a general climate of accountability, and channeled resources into the development of evaluation methods, training of practitioners, and widespread implementation of evaluation activities. It is doubtful that the increasing professionalization of evaluation (as evidenced by the emergence of professional societies, technical journals, standards of practice, and so on) would have occurred without this federal interest in, and support of, evaluation.

In addition to creating the mandate and resources for evaluation, the federal government has also been influential in the improvement of evaluation methods and the creation of new approaches. As it became clear that many existing procedures lacked applicability or utility, efforts were mounted to revise current methods and to look for new alternatives.

The purpose of this sourcebook is to bring readers up to date on some recent advances in evaluation methods that have been sponsored by five federal agencies: the Office of Service Delivery Assessment of the Department of Health and Human Services, the National Institute of Justice, the U.S. General Accounting Office, the National Institutes of Mental Health, and the National Institute of Education. The efforts reported in this sourcebook certainly do not represent all the work being conducted in this field by these agencies or by others. The chapters that follow do, however, describe some of the most innovative work being done and provide a sampling of possible new directions for program evaluation methods.

Michael Hendricks begins this sourcebook by describing the

work of the Service Delivery Assessment (SDA) unit of the Department of Health and Human Services. Required to provide evaluative data on national policy issues to the Secretary within three to five months, SDA staff have developed a field inquiry approach that relies less on the controlled studies of traditional social science and more on the open-ended, flexible field inquiries of sociologists, anthropologists, and investigative journalists. The procedures reported here for conducting national-level studies that result in policy and evaluation reports routinely sought and used at the highest agency levels offer genuine alternatives for improving evaluation at state and local levels as well.

In the next chapter, George Silberman summarizes the variety of research conducted by the National Institute of Justice to improve criminal justice evaluation methods. He reviews a large number of stimulating projects designed to clarify the nature of important variables in criminal justice evaluation, to generate procedures for estimating certain data when such data cannot be collected, and to improve the analysis of criminal justice data once they are available. The methods discussed draw on existing procedures in such areas as sociology, psychology, mathematics, and zoology, and they provide new techniques for conducting evaluations in health, education, and other areas as well as in criminal justice.

Next, Bruce W. Thompson discusses a system developed by the U.S. General Accounting Office for evaluating the quality and dependability of large computerized modeling procedures used by policy analysts and decision makers in the federal government to estimate the effects of program and policy changes. Evaluation of these complex systems requires the combined skills of statisticians, computer scientists, policy analysts, and substantive specialists. The evaluation procedures that have resulted from these efforts are finding use by model developers and model users both inside the federal government and elsewhere.

In Chapter Four, Charles Windle and Eugenie Walsh Flaherty examine some values commonly held in mental health service work, such as humanitarian service, rationalism, individualism, mental health, and community involvement. They then review some newly emerging evaluation methods, especially those sponsored by the National Institutes of Mental Health, and assess their level of compatibility with the dominant mental health values. Their analysis not only provides a useful review of new mental health evaluation techniques but illustrates the use of philosophical and value criteria in judging new methods. Theirs is an insightful departure from the standard, solely technical review of new methods.

The final chapter includes a summary of the work of one multi-year project funded by the National Institute of Education. In this chapter, I review not only the need for new methods in educational evaluation but also a rationale for the programmatic development of new methods. Of special interest is the summary of new techniques and conceptual distinctions that have been adapted from such fields as philosophy, journalism, architecture, geography, and art for use in educational evaluation — techniques and distinctions that are equally applicable in such areas as health, housing, welfare, and justice.

These chapters provide a stimulating array of new methodological alternatives for evaluation in a variety of practical areas. The methods range from highly technical stochastic modeling procedures to field-oriented interview procedures and philosophic analysis procedures. Each reader should find something in this volume to stimulate his or her interest in new directions in program evaluation methods.

Nick L. Smith
Editor

Nick L. Smith, director of the Research on Evaluation Program at the Northwest Regional Educational Laboratory in Portland, Oregon, served as president of the Evaluation Network in 1980. He is editor of two new books on evaluation methods, Metaphors for Evaluation: Sources of New Methods *and* New Techniques for Evaluation.

*An innovative new evaluation unit in the U.S. Department of
Health and Human Services is regularly briefing the Secretary
on the services delivered to clients at the local level.*

Service Delivery Assessment: Qualitative Evaluations at the Cabinet Level

Michael Hendricks

For the past three years, an unusual group of federal employees has
been walking the field with migrant farmworkers, observing tenants'
meetings in public housing projects, riding along with meals-on-wheels
volunteers and crisis intervention teams, and following legal proceedings in both courtrooms and judges' chambers. These unlikely bureaucrats, members of the Office of Service Delivery Assessment (SDA) in
the U.S. Department of Health and Human Services (HHS, formerly
the Department of Health, Education, and Welfare, HEW), have
made countless visits to nursing homes, Social Security offices, community mental health centers, hospitals, Indian reservations, boarding
homes, senior centers, kidney dialysis units, daycare centers, rural
health clinics, and other sites at which HHS-funded services are provided for clients.

The author wishes to thank Sue Clain, Dennis Coughlin, Richard David, Milton Fick, Ted Koontz, Mike Mangano, Alan Meyer, Jack Molnar, Bill Moran, Sylvia
Rivers, Nick Smith, Jan Tebbutt, and Charles Windle for their helpful comments on
an earlier version of this chapter.

N. Smith (Ed.). *New Directions for Program Evaluation: Federal Efforts to Develop New Evaluation Methods*, no. 12.
San Francisco: Jossey-Bass, December 1981

These site visits and the accompanying discussions with clients, front-line service providers, local administrators, program officials at the local, state, and federal levels, and many others knowledgeable about service delivery are not part of any audit, investigation, research study, compliance review, monitoring exercise, or traditional program evaluation. Instead, they represent an innovative approach to program evaluation—an approach that relies less on the social science model and more on the open-ended, flexible observations and discussions familiar to sociologists, anthropologists, and investigative journalists. After four years of operation, this approach, unique in the federal bureaucracy, provides regular reports and briefings to the Secretary and other top HHS officials.

Service Delivery Assessment was established in January 1977, when Joseph A. Califano, Jr., was appointed Secretary of HEW. Califano had been Lyndon Johnson's domestic advisor and was therefore quite familiar with the decision-making processes used by cabinet members. Califano felt that the Secretary of a department as large as HEW had information needs that could not be satisfied by the traditional systems. He, like Peter Drucker, saw that the chief executive of a major organization could easily become isolated and insulated from the front-line activities of the organization. "When top management has to depend totally on abstractions, such as formal reports, figures, and quantitative data, rather than be able to see, know, and understand the business, its reality, its people, its environment, its customers, its technology, then a business has become too complex to be manageable. A business is manageable only if top management is capable of testing against concrete reality the measurements and information it receives— that is, its abstract figures, data, and reports" (Drucker, 1973, p. 681).

Califano resolved not to be insulated from conditions and activities at the local level, so with then Inspector General Thomas D. Morris, he sketched requirements for the SDA function. First, this new system was intended not to replace the traditional information systems but to supplement them with information from the "client's end of the pipeline." Second, only in-house federal employees were to conduct SDAs; outside contractors were not to be used. Further, only a small staff (currently three professionals) were to manage the SDA function from Washington; the bulk of SDA employees (currently fifty professionals) were to be located in the ten regional offices around the country. Third, SDA was to study a wide variety of topics relating to health care, social services, income maintenance, and (in those days) education. Fourth, SDAs were to be completed very quickly, typically within three to five months after the assignment.

Finally, and perhaps most important, SDA was required to focus on the delivery of HHS-funded services, not on such other aspects as management objectives or long-range effects. The latter concerns were judged the proper domain of evaluability assessment, traditional evaluation, or research studies. "I mandated the development of Service Delivery Assessment (SDA) because I believe that our offices need continuing, rapid access to information about how HEW programs function from many perspectives at the local level" (Califano, 1978). Thus, SDAs are mainly focused on the input, process, and output of service programs.

In emphasizing service delivery, SDA embodies a concern of many evaluators: "the critical feature of human services is that they are highly operator-dependent and difficult to standardize. Hence, it is always problematic whether a treatment is being delivered as designed, whether the mode of delivery is adding some unintended treatment to the basic one, and finally whether a treatment can be delivered in a reasonable way at all by the typical human services organization" (Rossi, 1978, p. 596; Freeman, 1980). Rossi (1978) identifies eight different ways in which service delivery systems can fail: no services are delivered, agencies "cream" the most treatable clients and do not serve the most needy, the method of service delivery dilutes or negates the services, services vary in uncontrolled ways from site to site or even within sites, only a "ritual" compliance with delivery procedures occurs, services are too sophisticated for clients, clients are too heterogeneous for a single service, and clients reject services completely or in part. The purpose of SDA was to assess these and other possible weaknesses in service delivery programs.

Assignment by the Secretary

One noteworth aspect of the SDA process is the personal involvement of the Secretary of HHS. Through all four years of its operation, every SDA project has been personally selected and assigned by the current Secretary. This top-level assignment of projects contrasts with other evaluation activities in HHS, and it can occur in two different ways.

First, the Inspector General, who manages the SDA process for the Secretary and who possesses functional management authority over all SDA staff, prepares an annual workplan for the Secretary's review and approval. After soliciting proposed topics from all Assistant Secretaries, Commissioners, and Principal Regional Officials, the Inspector General forwards approximately twenty topics to the Secretary for consideration. Rather than automatically approving these suggestions, the Secretary typically selects between ten and twelve from this list and adds an additional five to seven topics not originally suggested by the Inspector General. These fifteen to nineteen projects then comprise the annual SDA workplan for the fiscal year.

However, the SDA process is designed to respond to the Secretary's changing or emerging needs, and high-priority studies can be initiated at any time via a second, informal assignment process. For example, the Secretary has requested the Inspector General to conduct quick studies of the arrival of Indochinese refugees and the first implementation of the low-income energy assistance program. In both instances, SDA teams were at local sites when problems first began to appear, and they were able to suggest specific remedies for the program to consider. Such "emergency" studies can be completed within ninety days of assignment.

The Secretary's reason for assigning an SDA varies. Some programs are suspected of having operational problems that may be correctable with close examination. Others may be experiencing or planning major changes that will affect operations at the local level. Expiring or proposed legislation can prompt an SDA assignment, and some programs have high visibility in the department, Congress, or among citizens. Some programs warrant special attention because of their size or complexity, and still others simply attract the personal interest of a Secretary.

For whatever reasons, the SDA workload has expanded during each year of its operation. In the first year (1978), seven SDAs were assigned and completed. Following this successful trial year, the number of assignments jumped to fifteen. In 1980, Secretary Harris assigned seventeen topics to SDA: civil rights enforcement, toll-free telephone lines to Medicare Part B beneficiaries, restricted patient admittance to nursing homes, low-income energy assistance, community health centers, availability of physician services to Medicaid beneficiaries, end-stage renal disease, health systems agencies, Title XX services, National Health Service Corps, HHS services to public housing residents, Medicare physician assignment, child abuse, Indochinese refugees, daycare linkages with health care and social services, nutrition services for the elderly, and developmental disabilities.

Preassessment

Once the Secretary has determined the SDA workplan, the Inspector General assigns each project to a "lead" regional office. SDA is a highly decentralized function, with a staff of three professionals in Washington, D.C., to manage SDA on a day-to-day basis. The remainder of SDA staff—approximately fifty professionals—are distributed among the department's ten regional offices. (Regional offices are located in Boston, New York, Philadelphia, Atlanta, Chicago, Dallas, Kansas City, Denver, San Francisco, and Seattle.) While this decentralization parallels the SDA philosophy of remaining close to actual service delivery, it probably results more from the availability of these regional staff, who were planning and evaluation specialists under a former administration.

The first task for the lead region, and for the three to four "support" regions assigned to assist it in all phases of the project, is to conduct a preassessment aimed at understanding the reality of local conditions and reaching an understanding of the important issues to pursue during the study. The former goal is important, since "knowledge of how the actual activities are being carried out is needed to determine what can be measured, what those measurements would be, how much they would cost, where they would be obtained, and how reliable and valid they would be in describing a program's activities, processes, outcomes, impacts, and effectiveness" (U.S. General Accounting Office, 1977, p. 4). SDA considers this a critical aspect of the project's development, and it probably devotes more resources to determining possible respondents, possible contact settings, and required methods than most evaluations do. Several site visits are conducted immediately after assignment to allow SDA staff members to get their feet wet, and these site visits are explicitly patterned after the open-ended approach favored in Scriven's (1972) goal-free evaluation (see also Harrington and Sanders, 1979). Visits are also made to program officials at both the state and federal levels to obtain their perspectives on services and activities. Finally, a brief literature review of major studies is conducted.

The second goal of preassessment, reaching a consensus on the issues to pursue, is even more important. The Secretary's mandate for the study can either be very specific about the issues to be explored or it can be quite vague and general. In the second case, the lead region is responsible for defining the issues and scope of the study. The initial site visits, discussions with state and federal officials, literature review, and previous experience help its staff in this process. However, since SDA serves the Secretary and top department officials, much effort is spent contacting those closest to the Secretary for their views on the particular topic being assessed. Such persons include special assistants, policy coordinators in the Executive Secretariat, the Deputy Undersecretary, the Undersecretary, or even the Secretary. "In order to have data used in the way we prefer, then we need to assure that the evaluation is oriented toward specific questions which are of interest to the manager and which are program-related" (Cox, 1977, p. 505; Rossi and McLaughlin, 1979; U.S. General Accounting Office, 1976).

In addition to their use in clarifying the issues to examine, pre-assessment discussions with top department officials also help in determining the types of information needed by the Secretary. Does the Secretary need a representative snapshot of reality that describes local conditions, clients, and operations as a context for understanding how services are actually delivered? Does the Secretary need an early warning of potential or emerging problems that could develop into major headaches unless corrected? Does the Secretary need an objective view of issues about which there are differing opinions within the department? Or does the Secretary need an analysis of best operating practices, which can then be transferred to other delivery sites? SDAs have provided these and other types of findings to fill specific needs of the Secretary.

Designing the SDA

After finishing preassessment, the lead region has sufficient understanding of both the operations at the local level and the issues at the national level to design the full-scale SDA. At this point, SDA departs radically from the traditional social science model of evaluation. For a variety of reasons, an SDA project includes no control groups, no single treatment that can be identified and isolated, no pre-tests, no control over client condition, and little quantitative measurement. Instead, SDA has borrowed methods from a variety of disciplines, including investigative journalism (Guba, 1978), "particularly responsive evaluation" (Stake, 1975), sociology, anthropology, and policy analysis, which allow a subjective, open-ended examination of processes and outcomes in a complex, dynamic situation.

The primary technique for gathering SDA information is one-to-one personal discussion with a wide variety of respondents at the local level. The variety of perspectives, a key feature of SDA, is essential to gaining a full picture of service delivery. Assessment of clients' perspectives of service delivery is surprisingly rare among federal evaluation efforts; in fact, some claim that SDA may be the only federal mechanism for providing regular client input into the top decision-making process of a department.

However, since SDA staff have learned that clients often respond favorably to services regardless of their actual quality (a fact also noted by Scheirer, 1978), information is also sought from others close to the delivery process. "Focusing on the different perspectives among different groups seems to be our best technique for exposing cultural bias. Clients describe a service agency differently from agency workers or administrators, . . . and their views are important for the total assessment of a program" (Cochran, 1978). One excellent example of the diversity of perspectives that SDA seeks is contained in a study on domestic violence, which sent teams to hospitals, shelters for battered women, private homes, police stations, jails, judges' chambers, community centers, city service agencies, schools, township government offices, and on routine cruises with crisis intervention teams.

A second technique for gathering SDA data is to observe local conditions and activities. In the study of migrant farmworkers, for example, much was learned by observing the living conditions and interactions between migrants and health and social service officials. SDA teams sometimes attend already scheduled meetings. Observation of local school board meetings taught SDA staff much about the allocations being made for education for handicapped children. Sometimes, staff also examine documents that are available at sites. In an assessment of Social Security services to the public, examination of letters from SSA officers verified the complexity of terms and processes that had been mentioned by clients. Still another technique for gathering information lies in retrieving data collected at the local level that, for one reason or another, are not forwarded regularly to state and federal program managers. Often, these local data can indicate the accuracy or inaccuracy of data upon which decisions are being made at higher levels.

In addition to specifying the types of respondents and the methods to be used in gathering information, the SDA design outlines such things as the sites to be visited. Unlike many evaluations, SDA does not require random-sampling procedures to select sites. Instead, each SDA samples only those sites that fulfill its particular needs. For example, an SDA that aims to describe the average service delivery site would deliberately exclude sites known to be very poorly managed, very well managed, very new, very turbulent, or atypical in other ways. The typical SDA only visits between fifteen and thirty local sites, so an SDA looking for the average site cannot afford to visit sites that deviate much from the norm. However, an SDA focused on best practices or on service problems might wish to exclude average sites and look instead at sites suspected of being deviant.

Staff

As mentioned earlier, SDA employs no outside contractors; all stages of the SDA process are conducted by employees of the Department of Health and Human Services. Fortunately, these SDA staff are highly talented and dedicated professionals, for the SDA task is a difficult one. Staff need public policy skills in order to refine the issues of importance to the Secretary in a constantly changing national environment; they need political and social skills in order to gain access to local projects without the oversight of federal, state, or local program officials; and they need technical skills in order to design ways of guiding open-ended discussions without losing flexibility, record pertinent information from lengthy conversations, and analyze findings.

Of course, SDA shares the need for highly skilled staff with all evaluation efforts. However, qualitative evaluations like the SDA process are highly dependent on the information gathered from complex interactions with respondents and situations, and they require a greater level of staff input than evaluation efforts do. Qualitative evaluations produce no findings that are not filtered through the eyes and ears of evaluators before they are recorded. "Human observers are the best instruments we have for many evaluation issues" (Stake, 1975, p. 16; Brickell, 1976). Unfortunately, not all instruments, human or otherwise, are created equal.

An SDA attempts to maximize staff abilities through two methods. First, all staff assigned to an SDA complete a training session prior to site visits. This session which may be held in a central location with all project staff who usually number between ten and fifteen, or separately in each regional office, usually lasts between two and three days and covers such diverse topics as the purpose of the SDA, background on relevant programs, issues being assessed, design of the SDA, settings and respondents likely to be encountered, and analysis and reporting plans, and it provides practice with instruments necessary for recording observations or discussions. Given the variety of this information and the short time for training, it is inevitable that SDA staff must sometimes rely on past knowledge and expertise while on site.

However, not all members of SDA teams share the same knowledge and expertise. Since there are only fifty SDA staff in the ten regional offices, SDA teams are often augmented with temporary staff from various federal programs and staff offices. Sometimes, these staff have never participated in an SDA, or they have never visted a local site to determine the state of service delivery. Training is even more vital for these non-SDA staff, although there are acknowledged limits to the ability to train qualitative evaluators (Scriven, 1975).

Thus, the second way in which SDA maximizes staff abilities is careful selection. Increasingly, SDA relies on full-time SDA staff for most, if not all, of its activities. While early SDAs involved between sixteen and twenty-four team members, recent studies have used fewer team members, almost all of whom have been full-time SDA staff. In recent studies, some lead regions have conducted SDAs with between three to five SDA staff from their own immediate offices. This approach ensures that staff are highly knowledgeable and highly experienced, but suffers from the disadvantage of excessive travel demands and the danger of too narrow a perspective on the issues of interest. However, SDA staff generally agree that, whenever feasible, it is probably a wise decision to rely more on SDA team members than on others.

Conducting Site Visits

As noted earlier, perhaps the single most distinctive feature of SDA is the emphasis on site visits to actual service delivery locations. Unlike evaluations that rely on existing data, mailed questionnaires, or site visits by other (typically contracted) analysts, SDA sends its own staff to gather information that will later be reported to the Secretary. As former Undersecretary Hale Champion remarked while discussing Service Delivery Assessment, "You've got to go out and look at how actual individual people are affected" (Demkovich, 1979, p. 1000).

A typical SDA involves visits to between fifteen and thirty sites across the nation, with a team of two or three staff spending three or four days at each site. Given the average of five discussions per day per team member, each site visit can yield between thirty and sixty discussions. As a result of logistics and other duties, the number of discussions yielded by a typical site visit is closer to the lower number. Given an average of twenty sites, most SDAs produce approximately 600 discussions with a variety of respondents.

This variety of respondents embodies the first of two objectives for an SDA site visit: comprehensiveness of perspectives. Team members deliberately seek out all viewpoints on the program and services being assessed, so that no single perspective dominates the findings. This requirement to uncover differing viewpoints almost automatically precludes the use of randomized selection procedures, another way in which SDA differs from traditional evaluations. While some respondents can be identified in advance and by random selection procedures, others can be discovered only on site or by referral from another respondent. Since the referral is to a specific individual, it is difficult to see how random selection procedures could be applied. Instead, such techniques as haphazard, quota, and judgment sampling are employed (Demaline and Quinn, 1979).

For example, an SDA team assessing health maintenance organizations (HMOs) can identify all HMOs receiving federal funds and use stratified random sampling to choose the HMOs that team members will visit. However, since each HMO employs only one executive director, sampling of these persons is not possible. It is true that staff of each HMO can be selected randomly, either by simple random or by cluster sampling, but leaders of a rival health group probably cannot. Also, it is difficult to apply random procedures in selecting among the few officials responsible for monitoring a particular HMO. Thus, while SDAs can use a combination of random and nonrandom selection procedures, most respondents are selected by nonrandom methods.

The second objective for an SDA site visit is flexibility in pursuing information. While the preassessment process has provided the lead region with a set of issues that appear to be relevant for service delivery, the SDA process explicitly recognizes the possibility that issues of equal or greater importance may surface from site visit discussions and observations. "Responsive evaluation procedures allow the evaluator to respond to emerging issues as well as to preconceived issues" (Stake, 1975, p. 15). It is in this area of flexibility that the parallel between an SDA team member and an investigative journalist is most pronounced. Once on site, all SDA team members, especially the more skilled SDA staff, become very investigative and pursue unexpected information vigorously.

A second, recent attempt at maintaining responsiveness to emerging issues alternates site visits with analysis in each regional office. After the first week of visits, team members often can suggest interesting leads for all regional staffs to pursue. By holding a national conference call before teams make the second set of visits, the lead region can elicit the unexpected issues and investigate them systematically in subsequent discussions and observations. Both strategies allow SDA to obtain the type of serendipitous information that does not appear regularly in normal department information systems.

Analysis

The intensive, comprehensive, and flexible efforts during site visits typically yield between 400 and 600 discussions that involve a wide variety of respondents and cover a wide variety of issues. Such rich data are beneficial in highlighting emerging issues, effective local practices, national consistencies and regional variations, and the viewpoints of respondents most knowledgeable about local reality. Perhaps of even greater benefit is their propensity to illustrate the critical intervening variables that make or break service delivery but often escape notice in less intensive evaluations (Hendricks, 1980).

However, such a wealth of information is a mixed blessing, for it is sometimes extremely difficult to analyze properly. Unlike more traditional evaluations that use fairly standard analysis procedures, qualitative analysis of information has no established guidelines. Most disciplines that employ qualitative analysis recognize the process as one of consensus building by iterative steps of gathering information, checking for patterns and trends, and seeking new information to verify or refute preliminary hunches (see Guba, 1978, for a discussion of such procedures used by journalists as "circling," "shuffling," and "filling.")

The SDA process uses three separate techniques in its attempts to reach a consensus. The logic is that three different techniques, each with its own strengths and weaknesses, can illustrate consistencies and deviations better than one technique used alone. Such "triangulation" is intended to shape and refine the perspectives and knowledge of the lead region staff who must declare and present the SDA findings.

First, each region involved in site visits completes a site or regional report, using a format developed by the lead region. Generally, these reports follow the outline of the issues to be addressed, but they also contain room for unexpected information or comments from team members. Second, each discussion is typically recorded using some type of discussion guide prepared by the lead region to ensure that important issues are discussed and that relevant information is captured. These guides are photocopied and forwarded to the lead region for further analysis. Depending on the SDA and the preferences of the lead region, this analysis can range from a thorough reading of all guides to a computer analysis of coded responses. The quantified findings are then used in conjunction with the regional and site reports — as a supplement, not as a substitute.

The third, and perhaps most important, analysis technique is a two-to-three day debriefing session involving all lead region staff and the leaders of teams from other regions. At this session, the lead region discusses each issue and solicits views from every team leader. Consensus or differences are noted, findings are ranked in order of importance, the report is outlined, and some tentative suggestions for change may be drafted. SDA studies differ from many evaluations in that the debriefing sessions are generally afforded more weight in establishing the studies' findings than written reports from the field or quantified results from individual discussions.

The findings that result from an SDA are of three kinds: description of local conditions and activities, comparison of services against one or several standards, and interpretation of the findings from the lead region's perspective. The description of local conditions and activities is important, since the SDA process has been intended to serve as the eyes and ears of the Secretary since the outset. In fact, one of the motives for establishing SDA in the first place was to supplement the Secretary's ability to visit delivery sites. It has been a continuing value of SDA to increase the understanding of local reality among top-level department officials.

However, the simple description of service delivery is not sufficient, since information must be placed in context to be meaningful. Accordingly, SDA makes appropriate comparisons between the services being assessed and selected standards. These standards can include the hypothetical performance of ideal services, the original aims of legislation or regulations, other services to similar clients, past service delivery, or service delivery under ideal conditions. As is true with most other aspects of SDA, the appropriate standard for comparison depends on the unique topic and objective of the individual SDA.

After describing the services and comparing them to appropriate standards, the SDA team adds its own interpretation to the findings. While the Secreatary and other top officials may disagree with these interpretations, it is important, for both the immediate and long-term viability of SDA, that this information be provided. Interpretations can identify strengths and weaknesses of service delivery, barriers to better performance, best operating practices, relationships between findings (particularly notions about causes and consequences), and issues that bear further analysis. While it is difficult to document how such interpretations are reached in general, SDA teams have found it helpful to shift back and forth between individual findings and a larger perspective while analyzing the study findings.

Reporting Findings

Once the analysis has been completed, the findings are presented to the Secretary in two forms. The first reporting mechanism is a short written report, typically between fifteen and twenty pages in length, with perhaps three to six pages of appendixes. Drafts of this report are reviewed by a variety of persons within the department, including SDA staff, officials from the program being assessed, policy coordinators in the Office of the Secretary, planners and evaluators, and others knowledgeable about the issues of interest. Following the revisions prompted by reviewers' comments, the report is forwarded to the Secretary. Since reports are kept short and understandable (Staats, 1980), the Secretary reads almost every one.

The second reporting mechanism is an oral briefing, usually involving a twenty-minute presentation and forty minutes of questions and answers. This briefing, which generally involves between eight and ten well-prepared charts and handouts, is first presented to key staff from the program and the Office of the Secretary. This trial run provides an opportunity to identify missing information that must be obtained, prepare for likely questions, and polish the presentation style of lead region staff.

The final briefing is for the Secretary, although key staff from both the program and the Office of the Secretary also attend, depending on the topic being presented. Due to the history of Secretary-level support for SDA, these briefings typically attract the highest echelons of the department. For example, a recent briefing on restricted patient admittance to nursing homes included the Secretary; Undersecretary; both Deputy Undersecretaries; the Assistant Secretaries for Planning and Evaluation, Legislation, and Management and Budget; the General Counsel; the Director of the Office for Civil Rights; the administrators of the Social Security Administration, Public Health Service, Health Care Financing Administration, and Office for Human Development Services; and the heads of the programs being assessed. Since top-level managers often do their most important communicating orally (Cox, 1977), these briefings for the Secretary allow SDA to present its findings in the most effective and personal manner possible.

Impact

It is a well-known fact among evaluators that public policy decisions are made incrementally and that no single set of findings can hope to influence major decisions by itself. "Research impacts in ripples, not waves" (Patton, 1978; Cox, 1977). The experience of Service Delivery Assessment is no different, and thus it is difficult to cite specific examples of immediate use of SDA findings to alter programs. Instead, SDA is used like all other evaluation data: It provides one set of information that is combined with many other sets of information to create an overall framework for viewing a program or services.

Even so, there are several ways in which SDA findings have

affected HHS programs. First, some changes have occurred as a result of SDA reports and briefings. Often, the Secretary ends an SDA briefing with assignments to various agency administrators and program heads. Usually, these assignments involve preparing an action plan for providing further analyses, but sometimes they serve to change programmatic directions. For example, following the SDA briefing on Indochinese refugees, the Secretary adopted the primary recommendation and doubled the current allocation for English language training. On another occasion, the Secretary halted a planned national strategy and ordered demonstration projects suggested by the SDA team.

A second way in which SDA has had impact is better informing the Secretary and other top department officials about service delivery at the local level. In speeches and memoranda, by personally assigning the SDA workplan, by reading reports, and by continuing to schedule SDA briefings, the Secretary has affirmed the value of SDA in fulfilling this informative role. While this top-level support is important for any evaluation system, it is especially critical for a system like SDA, which must gain and maintain the attention of high-level officials for the study to be completed.

Third, key staff within the Office of the Secretary use SDAs in better fulfilling their own roles. Policy coordinators in the Executive Secretariat, who are responsible for preparing and reviewing briefing materials for the Secretary, routinely use SDA reports to supplement materials sent to the Secretary. For example, staff from planning and evaluation units consulted an SDA on the first year of the low-income energy assistance program when drafting regulations for the second year of operation, and staff from the Office for Civil Rights have taken an increasing interest in SDA findings that illustrate inequities in service availability at the local level.

Fourth, program officials themselves use SDA reports the better to manage their own operations. In one instance, a new program within the department used a recent SDA on that program, along with two other documents, as an overview and introduction to the program for incoming staff. Illustrating the adage that "imitation is the sincerest form of flattery," the Office of Human Development Services initiated a process known as Delivery Level Assessments to provide the same type of client-level information obtained from SDAs. Unfortunately, budget restrictions have severely curtailed the efforts of this new unit (Zimlich, 1979).

Others outside the department are also imitating the SDA approach. Most notably, the Education Department (ED) has created within the Office of the Assistant Secretary for Evaluation and Program Management a Service Delivery Assessment function modeled on the function in HHS. While the future of this unit is in doubt, since the Education Department may undergo major revisions, the first product of this ED unit was an influential study of bilingual education at the local level.

Finally, Congress has become aware of SDA and has used reports on more than one occasion. Twice, SDA findings have been cited on the floor of the House and Senate as evidence that services are needed at the local level. On another occasion, oversight hearings were held by a Senate subcommittee responsible for the services addressed by one SDA report. More recently, the General Accounting Office's new Institute for Program Evaluation has begun to examine the SDA function and its applicability to the GAO and other federal agencies.

Conclusion

On the basis of this description of the Service Delivery Assessment process, what generalizations can we draw regarding qualitative evaluations? One lesson must be that qualitative evaluations, when measured against the traditional criteria of methodological rigor, possess weaknesses that will invite criticism from quantitative evaluators. Since qualitative evaluators are a minority among federal evaluators (and probably among state and local evaluators as well), such criticism will have to be accepted or combated.

Sampling of both sites and respondents is one ground for criticism: The lack of random selection procedures can be argued to imply a lack of representativeness of findings. To the extent that random sampling is possible, this criticism is valid; it can be avoided by employing sophisticated sampling procedures. Such randomization can prevent SDA team members from being steered toward particular sites or respondents by their own biases or by others'. It is no less inexcusable for qualitative evaluators than for quantitative evaluators to forego careful selection of sites and respondents simply from lack of effort.

However, random sampling is not possible for many aspects of qualitative evaluation. The necessity of including or excluding certain sites or respondents with specific traits, the difficulty in obtaining information on the subtle local differences that affect service delivery, and the flexibility needed to pursue referrals all prohibit randomized procedures. Since the only alternative to nonrandom selection in these areas is to exclude this valuable information from the study, qualitative evaluators employ much purposive sampling.

Staffing for site visits is also a concern, since all qualitative information is first assessed by field staff before it is recorded for later analysis. Of course, any research process involves some intermediate steps between direct client responses and data analysis, but qualitative evaluations rely heavily on the judgments and talents of field staff. Many SDA team members, especially full-time SDA staff, are well trained and experienced in observations and discussions. These staff are the backbone of the SDA process and perform the bulk of field efforts, especially in tasks that are particularly difficult or sensitive.

However, others, albeit in decreasing proportion, take part in SDA field work and contribute information for analysis, and their contributions are less consistent. Indeed, their lack of familiarity with either the substance or the process of site visits is responsible for their diminished involvement in SDAs. To the extent possible, other qualitative efforts might consider limiting field staff to persons with known competence in the required duties. It is our experience that training, especially the short-term training required for a short-term project, is often not sufficient to ensure high-level performance from new personnel.

A related weakness, yet also a strength, of qualitative evaluation is the open-ended nature of the information-gathering process. Unlike predetermined evaluations that use standardized instruments or measures, qualitative evaluations are designed to pursue unexpected information as it appears. SDA uses several techniques to achieve this goal, including minimally structured discussion guides and repeated instructions to team members to remain flexible. The resulting information often supplies some of SDA's more interesting findings. However, this flexibility yields nonuniform information from team members, since not all field staff have pursued or probed the same issues with the same respondents. Nor have all field staff followed the same order or techniques for eliciting information. It can be hoped that as a result of the numerous team members involved in a project, the hundreds of discussions, the several methods of analysis, and the final distillation by the lead region, these differences in information-gathering techniques will be diluted. Yet the dilemma remains, and qualitative evaluators need better techniques for eliciting fairly uniform types of information in a decidedly nonuniform process.

Analysis of information from site visits also poses problems. Given the nonuniformity of information, how can findings be distilled? Three separate techniques used in SDAs have been described in this chapter, and it has been suggested that triangulation of methods helps to compensate for the idiosyncracies of any one approach. Yet there remain the problems of weighting information from different sources, conducting content analyses on records of varying depth, and blending information gleaned from discussions, observations, document analyses, and other methods. Currently, the analysis of qualitative evaluation is at least as much art as it is science, and methods remain undeveloped. It is perhaps this area that offers the most potential for major contributions in qualitative evaluation.

Yet, in spite of these areas of concern, SDA illustrates that qualitative evaluation can become an accepted contributor to the decision-making process. The reason for such acceptance is quite simple: SDAs are useful to top officials in planning, managing, and evaluating department programs. "To meet standards of utility, evaluation reports must be informative to practitioners and must make a desirable impact on their work" (Stufflebeam, 1974, p. 7). SDAs make this desirable impact because they meet Stufflebeam's six criteria for evaluation effectiveness: relevance, importance, scope, credibility, timeliness, and pervasiveness.

Service Delivery Assessments are useful because they are relevant to the needs of decision makers. Too often, evaluation projects are viewed by program managers as of more interest to researchers than to those who must wrestle with the problems of service delivery on a day-to-day basis (Pratt, 1980). Given this perception, it is not surprising that managers pay little attention to either the needs or the findings of many evaluators.

SDA adopts a different approach, preferring to consider itself a tool that aids top management to address issues of interest. Throughout the development of issues, conduct of site visits, drafting of reports and briefings, and presentation of findings, SDA staff and program staff work closely to ensure that program concerns are addressed. This does not imply that the objectivity of SDA staff is compromised, since it is possible to work closely yet to maintain an independence from program pressures.

SDAs are also important, since they respond to the Secretary's current needs and receive the attention of the highest officials of the department. Thus, they receive the full cooperation and resources that are needed to complete them. A common complaint about evaluation efforts is that the important issues are not examined. SDA, and other evaluations that aim to be useful, must make special efforts to avoid this mistake.

The scope of an SDA is important, since some important issues may be addressed while others may not. To be useful, an evaluation must address all issues of interest. SDA, through the extensive preassessment efforts as well as the regular review by program staff and experts, remains open to new issues as they arise. Often, the site visits suggest new issues to consider, and sometimes these new issues are unknown to program staff. A useful evaluation system is sufficiently flexible to incorporate new issues as they arise.

Like all evaluations, an SDA must be credible to be useful. While this credibility implies respect for the methods and procedures used in the study, it also requires a respect for the evaluator as an individual or group (Singer, 1979). SDA has the dual advantage of operating for the Secretary and of being managed by the Inspector General, neither of whom can afford to condone efforts that are less than fully objective. Even so, many suspicious program managers have changed their opinions of Service Delivery Assessments only through personal experience, and to that extent an impeccable track record is essential for any evaluator.

One of the most useful traits of an SDA is that it is timely. "If a decision must be made by a certain date and the information is late, the data will have little value. . . . However, most decision makers do not have the time or the resources for extended studies" (Staats, 1980, p. 20). Stufflebeam says that this "is perhaps the most critical of the utility criteria. This is because the best of information is useless if it is provided too late to serve its purpose" (1974, p. 9). Clearly, an evaluation must be completed in time to assist the decision makers. However, this timeliness implies an almost inevitable trade-off with methodological rigor. Each step of an evaluation requires time, and usually the more time, the better. Certainly, SDA staff would prefer to have more time for preassessment, design, training, site visits, and analysis. Yet, if the alternative to coping with time pressures is to miss the deadline for being useful, SDA clearly prefers to provide its best information on time. Unfortunately, at least from a policy perspective, not all evaluation efforts make this decision.

The final criterion for useful evaluation is that it be pervasive. This means that the findings are disseminated to all involved parties in an understandable form. The personal involvement of the Secretary and the Inspector General ensures that SDA findings reach the necessary individuals within HHS. This type of support should be the aim of all evaluations. Yet, the SDA staff themselves have a major responsibility to ensure that the findings are presented clearly and concisely (Nathan, 1979). The emphasis on short and readable documents and briefings helps SDA to disseminate its findings, and the personal briefing with the Secretary resolves any misunderstandings that may occur.

In summary, Service Delivery Assessment has become a useful

evaluation tool largely because it satisfies several important criteria for effectiveness. It allows the managers of diverse, complex service programs to remain informed about and responsive to the realities existing at the "client's end of the pipeline." Equally important, it provides this grassroots perspective quickly enough to affect upcoming decisions. As the field of program evaluation turns from exclusive reliance on experimental methods (Smith, 1978), Service Delivery Assessment provides one example of an innovative approach. It can be hoped that other examples will soon emerge and that the combined lessons of SDA and these other models will enable the entire field of evaluation to advance.

References

Brickell, H. M. *Needed: Instruments as Good as Our Eyes.* Kalamazoo: Evaluation Center, College of Education, Western Michigan University, 1976.

Califano, J. A., Jr. "Service Delivery Assessment." Memorandum to Heads of Principal Operating Components, Washington, D.C., March 6, 1978.

Cochran, N. "Cognitive Processes, Social Mores, and the Accumulation of Data: Program Evaluation and the Status Quo." *Evaluation Quarterly*, 1978, *2* (2), 343–358.

Cox, G. B. "Managerial Style: Implications for the Utilization of Program Evaluation Information." *Evaluation Quarterly*, 1977, *1* (3), 499–508.

Demaline, R. E., and Quinn, D. W. *Hints for Planning and Conducting a Survey and a Bibliography of Survey Methods.* Kalamazoo: Evaluation Center, College of Education, Western Michigan University, 1979.

Demkovich, L. E. "The Rewards and Frustrations of the Federal Bureaucracy: An Interview with Hale Champion." *National Journal*, June 16, 1979, pp. 998–1000.

Drucker, P. F. *Management: Tasks, Responsibilities, Practices.* New York: Harper & Row, 1973.

U.S. General Accounting Office. "Evaluation and Analysis to Support Decisionmaking." Washington, D.C.: U.S. General Accounting Office, 1976.

U.S. General Accounting Office. "Finding out How Programs Are Working: Suggestions for Congressional Oversight." Washington, D.C.: U.S. General Accounting Office, 1977.

Freeman, H. "Future Developments in Evaluation Research." In C. Abt (Ed.), *Problems in American Social Policy Research.* Cambridge, Mass.: Abt Books, 1980.

Guba, E. G. *Metaphor Adaptation Report: Investigative Journalism.* Paper and Report Series No. 4. Portland, Ore.: Research on Evaluation Program, Northwest Regional Educational Laboratory, 1978.

Harrington, P. J., and Sanders, J. R. *Guidelines for Goal-Free Evaluation.* Kalamazoo: Evaluation Center, College of Education, Western Michigan University, 1979.

Hendricks, M. "A New Approach to Program Evaluation at HEW." In C. Abt (Ed.), *Problems in American Social Policy Research.* Cambridge, Mass.: Abt Books, 1980.

Nathan, R. "Ten Rigorous Rules for Relevant Research." In C. Abt (Ed.), *Costs and Benefits of Applied Social Research.* Cambridge, Mass.: Council for Applied Social Research, 1979.

Patton, M. Q. *Utilization-Focused Evaluation.* Beverly Hills, Calif.: Sage, 1978.

Pratt, J. "State-Level Impacts of Social Policy Research." In C. Abt (Ed.), *Problems in American Social Policy Research.* Cambridge, Mass.: Abt Books, 1980.

24

Rossi, P. H. "Issues in the Evaluation of Human Services Delivery." *Evaluation Quarterly,* 1978, *2* (4), 573–599.

Rossi, R. J., and McLaughlin, D. H. "Establishing Evaluation Objectives." *Evaluation Quarterly,* 1979, *3* (3), 331–346.

Scheirer, M. A. "Program Participants' Positive Perceptions: Psychological Conflict of Interest in Social Program Evaluation." *Evaluation Quarterly,* 1978, *2* (1), 53–70.

Scriven, M. "Pros and Cons About Goal-Free Evalution." *Evaluation Comment,* 1972, *3* (4), 1–4.

Scriven, M. *Evaluation Bias and Its Control.* Kalamazoo: Evaluation Center, College of Education, Western Michigan University, 1975.

Singer, J. W. "When the Evaluators Are Evaluated, the GAO Often Gets Low Marks." *National Journal,* November 10, 1979, pp. 1889–1892.

Smith, N. L. *The Development of New Evaluation Methodologies.* Paper and Report Series No. 6. Portland, Ore.: Research on Evaluation Program, Northwest Regional Educational Laboratory, 1978.

Staats, E. B. "Why Isn't Policy Research Utilized More by Decision Makers?" In C. Abt (Ed.), *Problems in American Social Policy Research.* Cambridge, Mass.: Abt Books, 1980.

Stake, R. E. *Program Evaluation: Particularly Responsive Evaluation.* Kalamazoo: Evaluation Center, College of Education, Western Michigan University, 1975.

Stufflebeam, D. L. *Meta-Evaluation.* Kalamazoo: Evaluation Center, College of Education, Western Michigan University, 1974.

Zimlich, N. "HDS Delivery Level Assessments for FY 1980." Memorandum to Regional HDS Administrators, Seattle, Wash., August 23, 1979.

Michael Hendricks is assistant director for policy coordination, Office of Service Delivery Assessment, U.S. Department of Health and Human Services. His academic training includes postdoctoral study in methodology and evaluation research at Northwestern University.

*This chapter chronicles the history of a program designed
to develop methods for criminal justice evaluation.*

New Methods in
Criminal Justice Evaluation

George Silberman

This chapter focuses on a research-funding program in the U.S.
Department of Justice. In the three years during which I was associated
with that program, organizational names and affiliations underwent
considerable change, so I begin with a brief chronology of events.

I first came to Washington as a staff member in the Office of
Evaluation (OE) of the Law Enforcement Assistance Administration
(LEAA). LEAA was created in 1969 to combat the crime problem. The
agency had four line offices, one of which, the National Institute of
Law Enforcement and Criminal Justice (NILECJ), was the research
arm of the organization. The OE was one of three divisions within
NILECJ, and it was responsible for supporting evaluations of both
LEAA-funded programs and "major criminal justice initiatives" at the
state and local levels.

In the course of funding and overseeing evaluations, I soon
reached a conclusion that I found to be shared by other staff and
administrators: the quality of evaluations was not going to improve
until the methodological base upon which these studies rested was
strengthened. Based on this conclusion, it was argued that NILECJ
should start a program on the methodology of evaluations. This argu-

N. Smith (Ed.). *New Directions for Program Evaluation: Federal Efforts to Develop New Evaluation Methods,* no. 12.
San Francisco: Jossey-Bass, December 1981

ment was well received, and in September 1977, a new division was created in NILECJ, the Office of Research and Evaluation Methods (OREM). In October 1979, Congress removed NILECJ from LEAA, constituted it as a semiautonomous research organization within the Justice Department, and renamed it the National Institute of Justice (NIJ).

When OREM was created, its mandate in the area of evaluation methods was the general prescription to "advance the state of the art." Exactly how that was to be accomplished was left to the discretion of the staff. The first thing that had to be decided was the structure of what eventually became the Methodology Development Program (MDP). Three questions required answers: How should proposals for funding be solicited? Who should be informed of the program? and How should proposals be selected for grants?

During discussion of how to solicit proposals for funding, two distinct strategies were considered. One was for us to identify issues that we wished to see addressed; that is, the solicitation would list all the areas that we considered legitimate for funding—for example, how to quantify the severity of sanctions, how to measure implementation, how to refine time-series models, and so on. The other approach, which we selected, was for us to say that any attempt to make an advance in evaluation methodology would constitute an appropriate submission. Although this "open" approach limited the control that we could exercise over the direction of the MDP, it was chosen for two reasons. First, researchers could propose subjects in which they were truly interested; they did not have to alter their designs in order to meet rigidly established outlines for acceptability. Second, by allowing submitters this freedom, the topics that would be proposed were not restricted to the methodological problems of which NIJ staff were aware.

Our answer to the second question—who we should tell about the program—was as many people as we could. We assumed that research that addressed methodological problems often faced by criminal justice evaluators was taking place in many substantive areas outside of criminal justice. As a result, someone who had to measure satisfaction with police services might benefit from previous research that measured satisfaction with health services.

To answer the third question—how to pick the winners—we had two options. One was to rely heavily on internal staff in making selections, thereby assuring some match between the grants let and internal research priorities. This approach, however, ran counter to our decision to encourage researchers to define their own projects freely, and it was therefore rejected. Instead, we decided to rely totally on external peer review. The primary benefit of doing so was that it allowed the eventual consumers of methodological advances — the evaluators and the researchers — to select for funding projects that held the most promise for solving problems that they encountered in their daily work.

This discussion of program structure is not offered as evidence of professional modesty on the part of the OREM staff. It is included to impress upon the reader that the program reflected major developments in the field and not merely personal beliefs about what was significant.

Let us review some of the research supported under the MDP. In a previous article (Silberman, 1980), I discussed all ongoing projects. Since that time, however, the number of projects has increased to a point where exhaustive treatment is impractical. For that reason, I will describe some research supported by the program that illustrates its breadth. A complete list of funded research and detailed information on individual projects can be obtained by writing to the Program Manager, Methodology Development Program, OREM/NIJ/DOJ, 633 Indiana Avenue, N.W., Washington, D.C. 20541.

Variable Specification Studies

At the heart of every evaluation lies the basic question of what happens when a program or policy is introduced into a certain environment. The types of consequences that concern evaluators vary, resulting in either impact or process studies, and the study designs vary as a result. All evaluative efforts are similar, however, in that the critical independent variable is whether or not an intervention took place. It seems appropriate, therefore, to begin this discussion of research supported by the MDP with a project which argues that past evaluations were simplistic in their treatment of this variable.

The traditional approach to program evaluation involves a comparison between an environment that has a program and an environment where there is no program (either because it is a different environment or because the program has yet to be introduced). When all appropriate intervening factors are controlled for, the assumption is that program impact is equal to the differences observed between the two environments. Employing this design, the evaluator is restricted to two values for the program variable, *did exist* or *did not exist*. However, anyone who is familiar with program implementation realizes how imprecise these response categories are. Implementation can take place at different levels. Ongoing research at Florida State University, therefore, argues that a better measure of intervention would include information on two program dimensions, strength and integrity. Integrity refers to the extent to which the program in the field parallels the program on paper; it is measured by the magnitude of the difference between the planned and implemented interventions. Although the distinction between these two entities seems to be clear, many evaluators have failed to make it.

The other dimension, strength, is analagous to the concept of dosage. If one wished to determine whether aspirin cures headaches, the number of aspirin tablets administered to subjects would be included in the analysis. If this were not done, and if insufficient levels of the drug were administered, one could conclude — erroneously — that aspirin does not reduce pain. Transferring this lesson to program evaluation, the researchers argue that the strength of an intervention (for example, number of additional prosecutors, frequency of counseling sessions, changes in the level of police patrol) must be considered in any attempt to assess its consequences.

If we accept the contention that interventions should be treated as continuous, not as discrete, phenomena, the next concern becomes how we go about doing so. One major objective of the Florida State University project is to develop measures of strength and integrity for programs concerned with offender rehabilitation. Perhaps even more significantly, the research hopes to identify methods by which such measures can be derived from a wide variety of programs.

Refining the manner in which we measure frequently encountered variables is the concern of a number of other projects in the MDP. One effort focuses on crime rate, which is perhaps the most common dependent variable in criminal justice evaluations. That there are problems with this variable is clear from the literature, which is replete with criticisms of the major source of data on crime, the Uniform Crime Reports. Further, these criticisms have not gone unheeded, since they led to the multimillion-dollar surveys of victimization supported by the Bureau of Justice Statistics. These surveys are intended to produce better estimates of how much crime is occurring than estimates based only on incidents reported to the police. In future computations of crime rates, the victimization surveys are expected to increase the validity of the numerator, number of crimes. The concern of the MDP-funded project, however, is with the other figure in the computation, the population. Traditionally, this figure has represented the aggregate population for a given jurisdiction. The problem with this definition of population will become clear from the following example: Two suburban communities each have a population of 100,000. In each jurisdiction, 1,000 commercial robberies have taken place during the year. For this reason, the commercial robbery rate for both is assumed to be the same, one per hundred. If we learn, however, that one community has 500 commercial establishments, while the other has 1,000, a very different picture of crime emerges: Establishments in the former community are being victimized at twice the rate at which establishments in the latter community are being victimized. The point is that aggregate population is irrelevant in computing the rate for a crime that can only be committed against specific segments of the population. In such instances (auto theft, residential theft, statutory rape, and so on), the correct rate would be the number of incidents divided by the population at risk (number of automobiles, private residences, juveniles). It may also be appropriate to weight individual members of the population at risk so as to account for known differences in probability of victimization. For example, those concerned with auto theft may wish to consider the relative probability of theft of garaged cars and of cars left on the street. In the case of rape, it might be appropriate to focus on the number of single women—because they are the more frequently unescorted—between the ages of fifteen and twenty-five—because they are the most frequent victims of that crime. Research in this area is investigating the concept of population at risk, and it hopes to provide appropriate numerations for computing rates for each of the eight felony offenses. It is expected that these new rates will help evaluators to reach useful conclusions on the impact of crime reduction efforts.

A second variable often used to assess the impact of criminal justice programs, and one that has become increasingly popular in the last few years, is fear of crime. Attempts to measure fear present evaluators with considerably greater difficulties than attempts to measure the level of criminal activity. There is no central repository for data on fear, and any information must usually be obtained through a primary data-collection effort. In designing such an effort, the evaluator confronts a major methodological problem: How do you translate a policy-level concept, which is typically imprecise, to the operational level, where specificity in definition is essential? In order to answer this question, we must ask three more: First, how many dimensions are contained within the concept of fear? For example, does the respondent distinguish between fear of physical harm and fear of property loss? Second, what are the relevant dimensions? Are they, for example, fear of going out at night, fear of burglary while absent from the house, fear that relatives will be victimized, fear of being sexually abused? Third, what relationships, if any, exist between the several relevant dimensions of fear, and do these relationships differ among various populations? For example, are all individuals who are concerned about personal injury resulting from crime also fearful for their spouses, or is this pattern exhibited only by males?

These issues are being explored by a third MDP project. This research hopes to provide a measure, or a set of measures, that can be used to determine types and levels of fear of crime. Another product of this research that has significance for evaluators will be the description of methods employed by the researchers in developing the measure or measures. These methods could be useful in other areas where dimensionality is in question (for example, satisfaction with health services, sense of economic security).

Value Estimation Studies

The preceding discussion was concerned with the manner in which variables are defined, the assumption being that, once the variables are defined, data gathering can proceed. In criminal justice, however, and to some extent in other substantive areas, there are certain variables for which information cannot be obtained. In these instances, the evaluator must rely on procedures that estimate values. A second group of studies supported by the MDP attempts to develop, refine, or validate estimation procedures.

One project focuses on a measurement problem faced in all evaluations. As already noted, evaluations determine program impact through comparative analysis. Sometimes, this involves a single jurisdiction where the value for some variable (for example, crime rate) before an intervention is compared with the value after the intervention. In other instances, comparisions are made between the variable in jurisdictions where there is a program and jurisdictions where there is not. The most frequent design, referred to as the *interrupted time-series quasi-experiment*, makes both comparisons. In essence, however, the two comparison groups are essentially surrogate measures for the true dimension of interest: the value of the dependent variables had there been no intervention. One MDP project suggests that, although we obviously cannot observe the variable after the program has been implemented, as if there were no intervention, we may be able to estimate values for it.

This can be accomplished by using one of a class of statistical models originally developed as forecasting tools. These models, referred to as *Box-Jenkins, ARIMA,* or *stochastic models,* make the basic assumption that every value in a time series is a function of some previous value that has passed through a change "filter."

Further, by analyzing any series of sufficient length with a variety of statistical procedures, one can reach a determination about that filter. Once it is known, the task of projecting future values in the series becomes relatively simple. Figure 1 illustrates how such projections can be employed by the evaluator.

The solid line denotes observed crime rates over a four-year period, with the vertical broken line indicating the point in time of some intervention (for example, a gun-control law). If one analyzes only the observed series, one will probably conclude that the intervention had no impact, since crime rates immediately bounding the intervention point are approximately equal. However, if one builds a stochastic model based on the series prior to intervention (line segment 1) and uses that model to forecast expected values in the absence of intervention, the evaluation will reach dramatically different conclusions. The values forecast by the model (line segment 3) indicate that the crime rate should have gone up significantly at just about the time when the intervention took place. Since the crime rate remained relatively stable, one can conclude that its failure to rise resulted from the intervention. The impact of this intervention can, therefore, legitimately be assumed to be the magnitude of the difference between the observed and expected series (A).

A second MDP project concerned with estimation techniques focuses on methods for estimating the number of criminals. For a large

Figure 1. Differences Between Observed and Forecasted Values

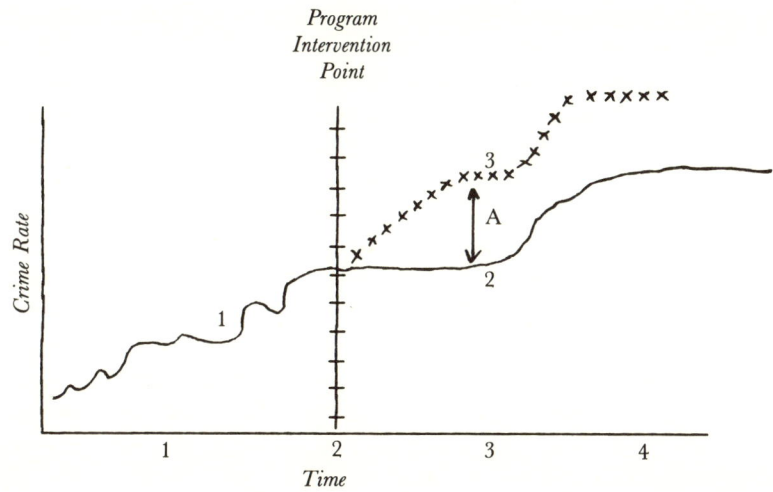

class of programs, principally those which fall into the category of reha-
bilitative efforts, this variable seems a more direct measure of impact
than the frequently encountered crime rate. However appropriate the
number of criminals seems to be as an outcome measure, one would be
hard pressed to find a single evaluation that used this variable. No
doubt this is a consequence of the difficulties inherent in enumerating a
population whose most consistent characteristic is the intent to remain
invisible.

The problem of determining the size of hidden populations is
not new. Zoologists charged with the task of determining the number of
zebras in a national park or even the number of fish in a lake have had
to deal with this issue. In response, they developed a number of statistical models all based on the assumption that the frequency with which
any single individual is encountered is a function of the total area and
the density of the population. Since the area is known, one can reliably
determine the density by counting the frequency of contacts. The MDP-
funded research is attempting to adapt these models for use in criminal
justice, with the principal concern being the biasing effects of the way
in which individuals are "encountered." Should the research prove successful, it will allow us to make accurate estimates of a number of hidden populations, including drug users, alcoholics, and violent offenders.

The techniques under investigation are necessarily observational. Clearly, one cannot go out and ask all the hawks in Colorado to
identify themselves. When estimating the number of offenders, however, the possibility exists that survey techniques could be used for enumeration. The obvious problem with this approach is that individuals
are unwilling to indict themselves. Another MDP project offers some
hope for eliminating this barrier by resorting to a technique developed
about fifteen years ago, randomized response. This procedure can be
illustrated by an example: A hundred individuals are assembled in a
room. They are asked to raise their hands if they have ever committed
a violent crime. Obviously, the hesitancy among the respondents
would compromise the accuracy of any data gathered in this fashion.
Randomized response would put the question somewhat differently:
Individuals are asked to answer one of two questions posed at the same
time, and the observer is never sure which question is being answered.
For example, the hundred individuals could be asked to flip a coin and
to raise their hands *either* if the coin came up heads *or* if they had ever
committed a violent crime. Since only the respondent knows whether
the coin comes up heads or tails, the observer can never be sure which
question is being answered. The observer does know, however, what
the expected distribution of heads and tails is, namely, fifty-fifty. And

with this knowledge, the observer can estimate the aggregate number of offenders among the hundred people in the room.

The MDP-sponsored research on randomized response is concerned with extending the technique so that it can provide interval-level data (for example, how many times have you?) and with determining the relative validity of randomized response as compared with traditional self-reporting procedures.

One other project in this general area of deriving estimates for behavior that is difficult to observe deserves mention. It is concerned with situations in which aggregate-level data are available to the evaluator but individual-level data are preferable. For example, take a situation in which the impact of a reduction in the speed limit from sixty-five to fifty-five miles per hour is at issue. In the first step, data are secured to indicate the number of individuals in each of three categories for both the pre- and postchange periods: those driving slower than fifty-five miles per hour, those driving between fifty-five and sixty-five miles per hour, and those driving faster than sixty-five miles per hour. If these data are displayed in contingency table form (Figure 2), it is clear that the marginal values are known, but the individual cell values are not.

One can use this information to reach some conclusions. For example, the number of individuals driving faster than sixty-five miles per hour has decreased, the total number of individuals who obey the law has decreased, and the majority of individuals drove between fifty-five and sixty-five during both periods. However, these data cannot answer a number of important questions, including questions about individuals who changed driving habits as a result of the law. Nevertheless, without this information, the evaluator cannot answer the critical policy-related question of why some individuals who drove legally prior to the change continued to do so after, but others did not.

**Figure 2. Contingency Table of Driving Patterns
Before and After Change in Speed Limit**

		Postchange		
		Slower than 55	Between 55–65	Faster Than 65
Prechange	Slower than 55				20%
	Between 55–65				60%
	Faster than 65				20%
		35%	55%	10%	

Inferring individual level from grouped data is the concern of ongoing research at the University of Oregon. The hope there is that an estimation procedure can be developed that will provide valid cell values for situations like the one just described.

Data Analysis Studies

The final class of studies to be discussed deal with the analysis of data. As with variable specification and value estimation, analysis should not be envisioned as a discrete stage of the evaluation process. In reality, almost every decision made by the evaluator either derives from or has impact on some other dimension of the study. The taxonomy presented here (that is, specification, estimation, and analysis) serves only to facilitate discussion; it is not meant to establish these categories as independent or unrelated. In evaluations, however, categorization or classification is often required for reasons that are substantive, not editorial. This section begins, therefore, with a review of two projects focused on analytic procedures designed for classification purposes.

The number of classification algorithms has grown steadily in the last few decades. Although many of these procedures are similar, no two are exactly alike, and evaluators must select a procedure with very little indication of which procedure best fits their needs. The primary objective of the first MDP project concerned with classification is to provide the evaluator with enough information to allow the optimal algorithm to be selected for a given application. This research, which recently concluded, argues that there are three decision points in the classification process. The first involves determination of the objective of the process. The evaluator may want to create classes that are predictive (for example, risk to the community, amenability to treatment), that can illuminate causal relationships, or that are merely descriptive. The second decision involves selection of a specific algorithm (for example, hierarchical clustering, multidimensional scaling, discriminant function analysis). Finally, the evaluator must establish the criteria by which the classification scheme itself will be evaluated (for example, intragroup homogeneity, coverage, intergroup distance).

The final product of this effort contains an overview of all classification procedures applicable to criminal justice evaluation and research. More significant perhaps, it includes a table that lists all the possible objectives of classification and indicates all the appropriate algorithms for each. The final piece of information on this table indicates the evaluative criteria that should be applied to the results of the analysis and evaluative criteria that should not. This information should assure greater consistency over the three decision points that have been mentioned.

One criterion that has been used in evaluating the adequacy of attempts at classification is coverage. Simply stated, coverage refers to the percentage of the target population that was actually placed in some class. According to a second MDP project, too much emphasis has been placed on this criterion in past classification efforts. The researcher argues that in most cases there is an inverse relationship between coverage and the validity, and consequent utility, of the constructed classes. That is to say, the more individuals one attempts to classify, the less accurate each of the classifications becomes. As an alternative to the classical approaches, therefore, it has been suggested that techniques be investigated to maximize validity, even if this occurs at the expense of coverage. Three such techniques—typal analysis, Lorr's technique, and inverse factor analysis—are the focus of this ongoing research. Its primary concern is which of the three techniques presents the most valid classes. The project, however, does not assume that these procedures and the more traditional coverage-maximizing approaches are mutually exclusive. In fact, it assumes that the most appropriate classifications would entail a two-stage process. The first stage uses one of the three validity-maximizing procedures. All individuals who remain unclassified are then placed in one of the constructed classes by using more traditional approaches.

Problems of classification have long been a special concern of psychology. Other disciplines, however, have also addressed classification issues, and, although the terminology differs, there are some striking similarities. This overlap is pronounced for the area generally referred to as sociometrics, in which the basic question is who belongs with whom. Here, too, two MDP projects deserve mention. One project is investigating the potential for criminal justice evaluation of procedures that can be grouped under the heading of network analysis.

In recent years, the tendency to construct programs that place the responsibility for the delivery of a given service not on one but on a variety of groups has been growing. Examples of this tendency can be seen in juvenile programs in which police, school administrators, and parent organizations work together to prevent delinquent behavior; rehabilitation programs for ex-offenders which require that parole officers, independent counselors, and families all interact in order to smooth the offender's re-entry into society; and victim assistance programs that involve prosecutors and psychiatric personnel in efforts to minimize the trauma experienced by victims of violent crime. In evaluating these programs, it is important to consider the nature of the interaction among the various groups. Yet evaluations rarely deal with interaction in other than broadly qualitative terms. The MDP project on network analysis hopes to change this state of affairs by developing techniques that can provide empirically based measures both of the quantity and of the quality of interactions among groups involved in complex service delivery systems. There are three primary issues of concern to this investigation: What type of data are necessary for measuring interaction? How are these data best to be collected? and What are the most appropriate techniques for analyzing these data?

The second project concerned with group construction is attempting to refine a set of procedures, known as *blockmodels* for use by criminal justice evaluators. The major advantages of blockmodels over other sociometric techniques is that they allow identification of floaters and bridges. Floaters are individuals or groups who change their affiliations over time. Bridges are individuals or groups who serve to link one or more of the identified blocks. The major potential of the blockmodel is to allow evaluators to deal with the question of interaction in a context that approximates reality more closely than other models in that it allows for changes in affiliation and it recognizes that the same individuals can belong to several groups.

Another MDP project is concerned with the statistical problems presented by the nonequivalency of groups. In both experimental and quasi-experimental designs, all comparisons made between experimental and control groups assume that the two groups are equivalent, yet we know that this is frequently not the case. In order to deal with the nonequivalent control group situation, statisticians have developed a variety of procedures designed to correct bias. The objective of the MDP project is to compare three procedures that have been used in this context — LISREL analysis, factor-loglinear regression, and analysis of covariance — in an effort to determine when each is best applied.

Other projects that have analytical questions as their primary focus include efforts to refine techniques for pattern recognition, extend Rasch models to allow for polychotomous data input, investigate the implications of data aggregation and disaggregation, develop procedures for dealing with dependent variables that have truncated distributions, adapt measures of statistical power for use in the design of evaluations, and explore alternative methods for estimating cost and production functions.

It should be noted here that the efforts just named, like other MDP projects that have not been mentioned, have been omitted from the discussion not because of personal preference but because of my inability to describe the work in two paragraphs or less. It is obvious that this criterion has no bearing on the significance of this research for the field of evaluation. With this qualification in mind, I offer some personal observations on the current state and the future of criminal justice evaluation methods.

Some Personal Observations

This chapter began with a chronicle of the events that led to creation of the MDP. As stated there, the rationale for this program was that evaluations could improve only if methodological advances were made. Any review of the programs must, therefore, answer two questions: Were methodological advances made? and Did the quality of evaluations improve?

It can be hoped that the projects just discussed make a convincing case for an affirmative answer to the first question. As a result both of the funded research and of corollary research, we can now define variables of interest with greater precision, measure phenomena that were otherwise impossible to quantify, and analyze data with greater confidence in both the reliability and the validity of the conclusions.

Despite these advances, however, I believe that the field of criminal justice has not witnessed significant improvements in the quality of its evaluations. (Ironically, one methodological advance still to be made is a universally accepted, operational definition of what a "quality" evaluation is.) This is not to say that some excellent evaluative studies have not been done in the area, nor do I mean to impugn the integrity or competence of analysts engaged in criminal justice evaluation. The point is that, given the methodological breakthroughs that have been made, we could have expected more improvement in the quality of evaluations in this area. That this expectation has not been realized is, I believe, a function of three factors yet to be discussed.

Administration of the MDP was a rather labor-intensive undertaking. That is, essentially one staff person was responsible for soliciting applications, reviewing proposals, selecting peer-review panels, preparing necessary documentation for awards to be made, and overseeing the research once it was funded. Given the magnitude of the program—12,000 direct mail solicitations, announcements in professional newsletters, as many as 150 proposals submitted for a single round, up to fifty reviewers per round, and more than thirty-five active grants to be monitored—there was not much time to consider issues related to dissemination of results. The assumption was that successful projects would publish in scholarly journals. However, the individuals whose efforts were supported under the program had very different backgrounds, and as a result their findings appeared in such diverse disciplinary publications as the *American Economic Review, Psychometrika, Evaluation Review,* and the *Journal of the American Statistical Association,* to name only a few. This absence of a central repository of information on the program, when combined with the problems traditionally associated with acceptance and use of new technologies (that is, the complexity of new methods, the inherent conscrvatism among potential user populations) suggests one reason why evaluations did not benefit from the methodological advances: evaluators simply did not know about the resulting advances.

A second reason why significant improvements in evaluations did not result from the MDP is illustrated by Figure 3 below.

The relationship posited between the two dimensions in Figure 3 relies heavily on Kuhn's (1970) work on the nature of scientific progress. This relationship can be depicted as a step-function, not as a simple linear progression. That is to say, methodological advances accumulate until a sufficient number exist for an advance in the quality

Figure 3. The Relationship Between Methodological Advances and Improvements in Evaluation Quality

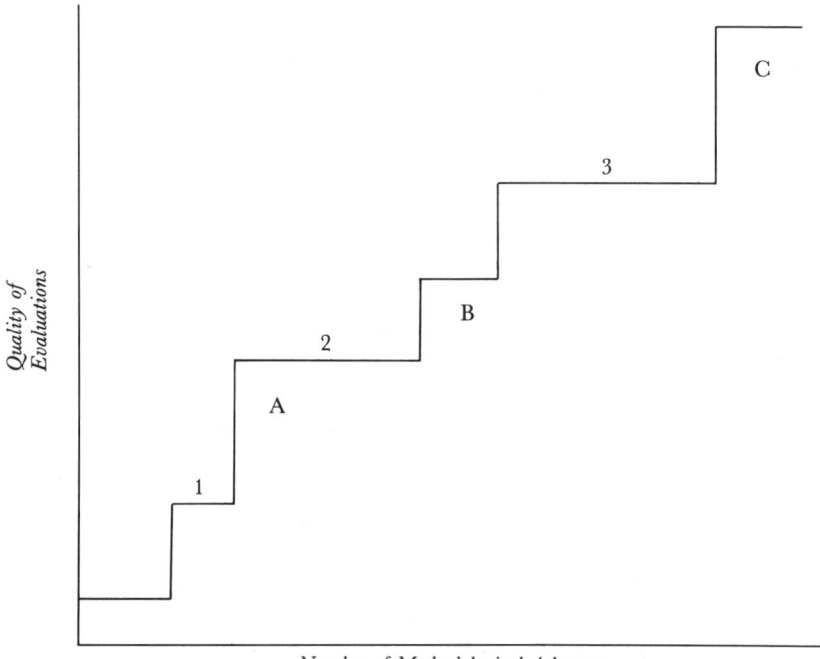

Number of Methodological Advances

of evaluations to be realized. This is quite different from the traditional assumption that every change in one dimension results in change along the other. Translating this relationship to the case of a single evaluation effort, the point is that, if it has five methodological problems, it may not do any good to solve only four of them. That is, it may be necessary to solve all five problems before the quality of the evaluation can improve. In addition, as Figure 3 shows, there is no necessary relationship between the number of advances in methodology and the magnitude of the improvement in quality. As a result, a single advance (line segment 1) may lead to a sizeable improvement (line segment A), while several advances (line segment 2) may improve evaluation quality only slightly (line segment B).

However, even if this is an accurate depiction of the way in which methodological advances contribute to the state of evaluation, the reader is right to question why so many advances (a total of thirty-eight projects were funded) have not been sufficient to lead to improvements in quality. The answer to this question — and my third reason for feeling that the quality of evaluation has remained essentially unchanged — results from the disproportionate development of evaluation methods and evaluative theory.

Inevitably, all investigations of methodological issues reduce to attempts to answer the question *how*. How one defines variables, how one collects data, and how data should be analyzed were the three general questions addressed by projects reviewed in this chapter. However, while answering the question how is an important component of all efforts to increase our knowledge, it is not sufficient. We must also know *when*. For example, when should environment be included as an intervening variable? When should fear of crime serve as the outcome measure? When are cross sectional designs inappropriate? Finally, we must also know *why*. For example, why should we include variable A in the analysis and exclude variable B? Why do we expect outcome A to result from a program and not outcome B? Why is counting the most appropriate kind of analysis in a particular evaluation? Without answers to these questions of when and why, the process of designing an evaluation becomes a series of educated guesses.

Obviously, the other side of the coin is that if we know all these answers, evaluation, as well as all research, would no longer be necessary. My contention, therefore, is not that all these answers must be known before questions are posed but that the current state of criminal justice evaluations is such that the tools available extend beyond our understanding of when to use them and that this understanding will come only with advances in theory.

40

References

Kuhn, T. S. *The Structure of Scientific Revolutions.* Chicago: University of Chicago Press, 1970.

Silberman, G. "Recent Advances in Evaluation Methods." In M. Klien and K. Teilman, (Eds.), *Handbook of Criminal Justice Evaluations.* Beverly Hills, Calif.: Sage, 1980.

Until recently, George Silberman managed the methodology development program at the National Institute of Justice. Currently he is in charge of the state-of-the-art effort at the Institute for Program Evaluation, a new organization within the U.S. General Accounting Office.

To enable decision makers to become more aware of the levels of confidence that can be placed in the results of particular computerized decision models, means of establishing levels of confidence for such models are discussed.

Toward Guidelines for Evaluating Large-Scale Computerized Models

Bruce W. Thompson

The Comptroller General was given very broad responsibility and authority for the evaluation and analysis of federal programs and activities under the Budget and Accounting Act of 1921 and the Accounting and Auditing Act of 1950. Section 204 of the Legislative Reorganization Act of 1970 supplemented the Comptroller General's authority and indicated current congressional interest in analyses of programs. The Congressional Budget Act of 1974 further strengthened the congressional emphasis on the evaluation of programs, the statement of legislative objectives and goals, and the improvement of evaluation methods. Among other things, the 1974 act requires the Comptroller General to develop and recommend to Congress methods for review and evaluation of government programs and activities carried on under existing law. The U.S. General Accounting Office (GAO) has used a variety of approaches in performing this task. For example, it has published guidelines for use in auditing efficiency, reviewing program results, and conducting impact evaluations. This chapter describes one evaluation methods development activity undertaken by the GAO—the task of determining how much confidence to place in the results provided by a computerized model (U.S. General Accounting Office, 1979). The

N. Smith (Ed.). *New Directions for Program Evaluation: Federal Efforts to Develop New Evaluation Methods,* no. 12.
San Francisco: Jossey-Bass, December 1981

41

approach taken by this effort provides guidelines for the gathering of evidence on which to base reasonable opinions, conclusions, judgments, and recommendations concerning the confidence that can be placed in a model's results. It should, therefore, be useful in planning a model-evaluation effort. It should also be useful to persons active in model development, since the evaluation aspects of model building need to be considered at the start of the effort and carried out during model development.

Why GAO Became Involved

This particular effort originated in 1974 in a letter from the Chairman of the Committee on Science and Technology, U.S. House of Representatives, to the GAO. In this letter, the Chairman noted that much of the information in the Federal Energy Administration's forthcoming Project Independence Blueprint "was obtained by the use of computer simulation models." The Chairman stated, "I should like to request GAO to undertake a thorough review and analysis of the methodology used in the computer programs, including the following aspects: (1) the major assumptions made in the model, (2) enumeration of any specific computational methods, (3) the source and reliability of the input data, (4) the sensitivity of output information to the input data, and (5) results of tests of the computer simulation models." Thus, GAO was thrust into the comprehensive evaluation of large-scale models by this congressional request to evaluate the Project Independence Evaluation System (PIES), the formal name of the model used to support development of the Blueprint.

The difficulty of this task soon became apparent. There were no generally accepted guidelines or standards to outline how one might proceed. In performing the analysis, GAO assembled and reviewed program material and the status of model evaluation, and numerous experts in the general field of modeling were interviewed. The GAO findings on PIES were documented in a report to Congress (U.S. General Accounting Office, 1976). This effort was followed by a GAO-initiated project in which the Transfer Income Model (TRIM), a large-scale model used in welfare policy analysis, was reviewed and evaluated. TRIM was selected because of its widespread use within government to analyze a broad range of welfare programs and the complex interrelationships of those welfare programs with other income security programs, federal tax policies, and employment and wage policies. For example, TRIM had been used to analyze AFDC, SSI, Food Stamp, and federal Individual Income Tax programs; modifications to those programs; variations of a housing allowance program; and negative income tax proposals, such as the Income Supplement Program and the Allowances for Basic Living Expenses Program. It was also used to support the work of President Carter's Welfare Reform Task Force. Agencies that had used TRIM or that were using it at the time of the review and evaluation included the Departments of Health, Education and Welfare, Housing and Urban Development, the Treasury, and Agriculture; the then Federal Energy Administration; the Congressional Budget Office; the Committee on Housing Administration; House Information Systems; and several State governments. This project, too, resulted in a report to the Congress (U.S. General Accounting Office, 1977).

The models that were the subject of these reports were but two of a large number of models used by the federal government to assist policy analysts and decision makers in shaping their policy recommendations and decisions. These models are similar in that they are large-scale computerized models designed or used to help in making decisions about public programs that involve large sums of federal money and affect the lives of millions of Americans. They are large-scale in that the system that they represent is large — in the number of individual parts, in the number of different kinds of parts, in the number of functions performed, in the number of inputs, and in absolute cost.

While modeling is an extremely useful analytical approach, it is important to avoid the temptation to view a model as a black box that automatically gives reliable, valid answers. For various reasons, decision makers sometimes use a model's results without being fully aware of the theories, assumptions, approximations, and judgments that went into development of the model. Also, they may be unclear about how these factors affect the validity and reliability of the model's predictions. For cases in which the model is at least partially implemented by means of a computer, the speed with which the computer performs immense numbers of calculations and produces large amounts of output very rapidly can give a deceptive air of reliability to the results. All too often, decision makers fail to ask how much confidence should be placed in the results provided by the model, and, when they do ask this question, all too often there is no sound basis for an answer.

Model evaluation should not be a purely retrospective task. If no foundations have been laid and no thought has been given to evaluation until the model is complete or nearly so, then the task of the auditor or evaluator is more difficult. The understanding of a model that is required to evaluate it can take months to achieve in the absence of appropriate documentation. Therefore, it is very important for the evaluative aspects of model building to be considered at the start and to be carried out during model development as well as after the model has become operational. Model builders should realize at the beginning that their products may be evaluated with a set of criteria like the one discussed here. If they do, they will know what their models may be measured against, and this will encourage them to view the evaluative criteria as a natural product of good model building. In other words, model evaluation must be an ongoing process.

The full-scale evaluation of a complex model can be an expensive, time-consuming effort requiring diverse talents and skills. Ideally, any model whose results will be used in the decision-making process should be subjected to such evaluation. In reality, this will not always be possible because of constraints on time or resources. In such cases, if use of the model plays a significant part in the decision-making process, *some* level of evaluation should still be considered. In some cases, time will permit no more than a quick but careful look by an expert in the field — what we refer to as a face validity check; in other cases, it may be possible to perform some, but not all, of the detailed analysis described in this chapter. The result of this evaluation should be provided to the decision maker, together with an assessment of the risks involved in using the model without more extensive evaluation.

The use of complex, large-scale models by many government agencies is increasing due to improved training for analysts and to the development and refinement of analytical decision-making methodologies. One cannot expect managers in senior positions to have a detailed understanding and appreciation of these methodologies. Thus, there is a need for procedures — or guidelines — that will enable independent investigators to assess the validity of a model's results so as better to guide the use and interpretation of that model by senior managers. Many models are so large and complex that evaluation by an individual working alone is precluded. Thus, to evaluate large-scale models in a reasonable amount of time, a multidisciplinary evaluation team should be formed. This team should consist of personnel knowledgeable in the functional areas being modeled, the environment of the decision maker or other user of the model, mathematical modeling, computer science, and statistics.

Evaluation of a model, as the term is used here, does not mean second-guessing the intent and results of the model's developers or sponsors. Rather, evaluation gives interested parties a set of criteria to accumulate evidence regarding the credibility and applicability of the model, whether or not they were involved in its origins, development, and use. One such set is proposed and discussed in the following pages (see Figure 1).

There are three primary reasons for advocating evaluation of complex models: First, for many models, the ultimate decision maker is far removed from the modeling process (this is especially true in governmental areas), and a basis for accepting or rejecting the model's results by such a decision maker needs to be established. Second, users of a complex model developed for other purposes must be able to learn how applicable the model is to the new problem area. Third, for complex models, even if there is extensive interchange between decision makers and model developers, it is difficult for decision makers to comprehend fully the results of carrying out the modeling steps (that is, the impact of a model's assumptions, data availability, and other elements in the modeling process) without some formal, independent evaluation based on established criteria.

It is very important to recognize that a model must not be judged only in the abstract against certain ideal goals. Careful consideration must also be given to its purposes, to the manner and the environment in which it is used, and to other feasible approaches that could be used to solve the problem. What may be a relatively satisfactory operating model for one objective may be very unsatisfactory for another.

The criteria proposed in this chapter are very general in nature; that is, they do not depend upon the subject matter of the underlying methodology. Therefore, two things need to be emphasized: First, these criteria reflect concerns that any decision maker or model evaluation team would wish to address before they relied upon the results

Figure 1. Criteria for Model Evaluation

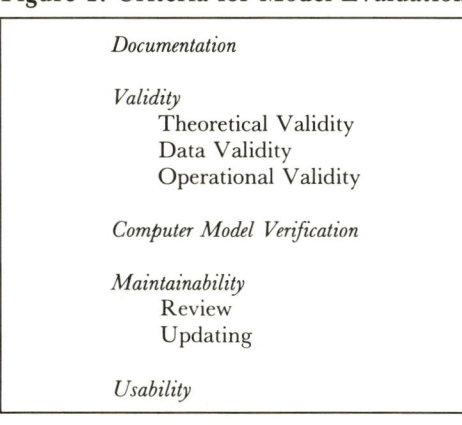

Documentation

Validity
    Theoretical Validity
    Data Validity
    Operational Validity

Computer Model Verification

Maintainability
    Review
    Updating

Usability

obtained from a given model. Second, the team will have to use a great deal of ingenuity, judgment, and experience when adapting these criteria to a specific model.

These criteria apply to any model evaluation effort. The extent to which they can be applied in any given case will depend not only on the judgment and experience of the evaluators but also on the needs of the model's users. Two important caveats are in order: First, this chapter is focused on large-scale computer models. While the author feels that the criteria described here should apply to most model evaluation efforts, he does not attempt to specify the entire class of models to which they apply. Second, since the author wishes to focus upon large-scale computer models used to help analyze major programs, the model evaluation process is viewed in this chapter as a very extensive undertaking. However, to employ the same level of effort for all model evaluations would be wasteful. Many times, a quick but careful reading of available documentation on a model by an expert in the area (that is, a face validity check) will enable a potential user to decide whether to use the model. An entire spectrum of possible levels of evaluation separates the face validity check and the type of detailed analysis described in this chapter.

Documentation

As the term is used here, *documentation* is written (or otherwise recorded) information about a model. This definition is purposely very general, and it highlights the fact that there are different purposes. It will be convenient here to distinguish between two levels of documentation: descriptive documentation and technical documentation. The former consists of general information about the model, such as its underlying theory, assumptions, limitations, constraints, and relationships to other models with which it is linked. The latter consists of information that is sufficiently detailed to allow technical evaluation of the model; such information includes details on the methodology used and the mechanization that permit others to duplicate and operate the model.

The developer needs to document what has been done, why, and how. This documentation should also include claims for the effectiveness of the model and evidence to substantiate those claims. Moreover, the record of the modeling process should be clear and intelligible to an informed, interested audience, and it should provide sufficient detail to permit independent evaluators to replicate its results. The clarity, completeness, and conciseness of model documentation is also critical to the process of model evaluation. Since the quality of the documentation cannot be assessed until the team has reviewed it in detail, the evaluation process begins and ends with documentation.

Validity

There is no reason to believe that a model is capable of approximating reality so well that its results can be accepted without reservation. One should not assume that the model faithfully represents the reality it was designed to reflect. The capability of the model to represent reality to the satisfaction of the decision maker or analyst who is using it is referred to as *model validity*, and the process of establishing the model's fidelity of representation is called *validation*. The definition and the determination of the degree of validity obtained is the major task of evaluation. It is important to realize that reality is in the mind of the perceiver, in this case the decision maker or the analyst. This makes an already difficult task even more difficult, and the process of validating a model requires interaction between the model's developers and its users.

Frequently, the outputs of a complex model are predictions. In such cases, the task of the evaluation team is to determine the accuracy of these predictions. Where possible, the team should compare the model's outputs against historical results or the results of field experimentation. When a model is properly developed and documented, such analyses have been performed by the model's developers. In such cases, the task of the evaluators is to assess the developers' predictions and supporting tests. However, the evaluation team may have to perform some tests of its own or at least to replicate some of the documented tests.

In most complex modeling situations, researchers have found that decision makers often are not involved in details either of design or of validation. The final model structure tends to be the product of analysts and computer programmers. For a complex model of an existing situation, historical data are often very hard to obtain.

In sum, then, no validation procedure is appropriate for all models; the tasks required for model validation must be adjusted to accommodate the model's structure, the documentation, and other information available to the evaluators. Validity is viewed as being comprised of three main subcategories—theoretical validity, operational validity, and computer model verification.

Theoretical Validity. Models are particularly useful tools, and they are frequently used by analysts and decision makers for systematic investigation of questions or problems encountered by governmental planners or decision makers. The questions or problems are investigated by using the model as a surrogate for the real-world situation. The nature of the conclusions obtained through use of the model and the confidence that can be placed in them depend in part on the results produced by mathematical analysis of the model itself. They also depend on the relationship between the problem and the model — the parts of the problem that the model represents and how well it represents them, the parts of the problem that the model distorts or fails to represent and how badly it does so.

Theoretical validation requires evaluators to review the theories that underlie the model and the major stated and tacit assumptions that are embodied in those theories or that have been made in order to develop or adapt a theory to the problem. The applicability and restrictiveness of these assumptions to the internal and external problem environments as viewed by decision makers must be examined. That is, do these assumptions affect the model in such a way as to produce results for a problem that is not the problem originally stated? Have the underlying theories been adequately tested? Is it reasonable to assume that the underlying theories are applicable to the problem at hand? Evaluators must determine how the divergences uncovered by this review limit the validity of the model.

Evaluators must also verify that the transition from the theoretical model of reality (or perceived reality) to the mathematical model has been made correctly. This requires them to identify and assess the reasonableness of the most important assumptions made by the modelers in formulating the mathematical model. This is not as easy as it seems, for assumptions come in many forms. Explicitly stated assumptions are easy to identify. The difficulty lies in isolating the unstated or implicit assumptions. The implicit assumptions may be present either in the underlying theory or in the methodology used to apply the theory to the problem. Sometimes, they are affected by the implicit or unintended biases of the model's developers and computer programmers.

Data Validity. Here the evaluation concern is two fold: the accuracy, completeness, impartiality, and appropriateness of the original data; and the manner in which the model transforms the original data. The distinction between these two aspects of data validity is important. It is not sufficient to determine that the original data are accurate, complete, impartial, and appropriate. For example, a microsimulation model could specify such sources of nonwage income as interest, rent, and dividends as data inputs. However, the only data source available might provide information only on total nonwage income. While the original data may very well be accurate, complete, impartial, and appropriate for use by the model, the evaluator should determine whether disaggregation of the original data has been accomplished correctly.

To validate the data, the evaluator will have to answer such questions as these: Do the data identify and measure the desired problem elements? Are the data sources clearly defined, and have the responsibilities for data collection been established? Are the procedures for the collection and updating of data workable? Are the data obtainable within reasonable cost, time, and operational assumptions? Do the data collection procedures make impartial recording of data possible?

Operational Validity. It is in the nature of models not to be able to reproduce exactly or to predict infallibly the real-world situation. Operational validity assesses the importance of these errors and divergences for the use of the model. Such assessment requires interaction between the evaluation team and the users. This is very important, as it is the team's main check on its understanding of the users' perception of reality.

Evaluators should be concerned with the divergence between the actual outcomes and the outcomes predicted by the model. For some models, statistical tests can be utilized; for example, by comparing historical time series. Evaluators should determine whether such tests can be applied and whether they have been applied properly by the developers. As intermediate computational results — parameters — are usually used in the model to further analysis, the team also needs to determine whether there are errors in computed parameters and whether procedures to minimize such errors have been utilized. The evaluators must attempt to uncover such divergences and errors, their magnitudes, and their impact. The outcome of this operational validity review should list computed parameters and decision variables and identify the extent to which errors and divergences in these computations can occur. To accomplish their task, evaluators will have to answer such questions as these: To what extent do the assumptions of the model and their divergences degrade the use of the results in the operational situation? Do the data requirements in terms of cost, time, accuracy, and operations preclude gathering of the necessary model inputs? Do the logic and numerical elements of the model as transformed into the computer program invalidate the computational process? Are the predictive divergences of the model of great enough magnitude to make the model results unacceptable? Have the results of any trial solutions been inconsistent with the expectations of decision makers? If so, how can use of the model be justified? What changes have been made, or what changes should be made?

Computer Model Verification

To verify a model, the evaluators must ensure that it has attributes imputed to it by the developer and that it behaves as intended. Basically, verification has been accomplished if it has been demonstrated that the computerized model runs as intended. That is, evaluators must also be concerned with the validity of the translation of the mathematical model statement and formulation into a numerical computer process. This is a complex, multifaceted problem and requires that evaluators identify explicitly and state in measurable terms the model's intended purposes. They must also determine whether there is sufficient evidence to establish that the mathematical and logical relationships are internally consistent; that the mathematical and numerical results are correct and accurate; that the logical flow of data and the intermediate results are correct; that the important variables and relationships have been included; that the computer program as written accurately describes the model as designed; that the program is properly mechanized and debugged on the computer; and that the program runs as expected.

Although these aspects are interrelated and not independent, it is important that they be verified separately, because any one of them might not hold in a given case. Thus, that the program has been written accurately and mechanized properly on the computer does not guarantee that it will also run correctly.

Clearly, evaluators will usually be constrained to base their evaluation on the available documentation. This puts a heavy burden on developers to prepare complete documentation that describes their verification process (for example, test problems and results of debugging procedures). However, whenever possible, evaluators must attempt to clarify any deficiencies that they detect by discussing them with developers. The evaluators should be able to replicate the tests conducted by the developer.

Maintainability

The next major evaluation criterion is model maintainability, which is concerned with how to make an acceptable model continue to be an acceptable representation of the real system during its life cycle. Maintainability has two aspects, review and updating.

Review. Review is a preplanned and regularly scheduled program for reviewing the accuracy of the model over its life cycle. Evaluators must be sure that a review procedure has been established and that it is functioning properly.

Some questions that evaluators should ask are these: Is there a formal procedure that requires the users, model developers, current model maintainers, and solution implementers to meet, discuss, and decide what to do about divergences between the model predictions and the actual outcomes or about proposed model and data changes? Is there a procedure to determine whether the model is still valid at a given point in time, whether it should no longer be used unless specified changes are made, or whether it should no longer be used under any conditions? Are change implementation procedures fail-safe (that is, the current operating system cannot be destroyed through mechanical or human error), do they encompass a proper testing methodology, and most important, do they produce the necessary documentation?

Updating. Evaluators need to be satisfied that a procedure has been established to collect and analyze information that will enable users to determine if and when the model parameters or model structure should be changed and that there is a process for making such changes.

Some of the questions relevant to updating are these: Are there procedures for detecting when input data have changed? If so, are the controls workable, and are the changed data collected in a timely fashion so as to ensure that the model's calculations are not degraded or incorrect? Does someone have responsibility for updating data sets, for analyzing their accuracy, and for determining the propriety of introducing updated data into the system? What procedures have been established to ensure that new data are entered without error? Has the computer program been written in a form that can be readily modified?

A related aspect that evaluators must assess is the adequacy of the training program associated with the model. Formalization of a training program depends on the model's application. However, training normally includes such items as formal lectures for computer systems personnel and other users and briefings to decision makers on the model and on how to interpret the model's output. It is important for revisions to the model to be made known to systems personnel and decision makers; for model results to be presented to users in familiar and acceptable format; and for users to understand how the model should be used. As changes in the model are made, there must be ways of reflecting such changes in the model documentation. Evaluators should determine whether an adequate process for updating and disseminating information about such changes has been established.

Usability

Factors that affect a model's usability include:

- *Availability of data.* Even if the data are known to exist, they may not be available for general use. For example, a particular model may require data that the Bureau of the Census has collected but not yet released; until such data are available, the model is not usable. How are privacy and freedom of information issues handled?
- *The understandability of the model's output.* Often, computer-produced output is not in a form that is understandable; that is, it may be only a string of numbers, with no explanatory text. But if the results of the model are incomprehensible to the user, for all practical purposes, the model is not usable.
- *The presentation format chosen.* How representative are baselines (for example, base year)? Are the sensitivity data selected to show only one type of finding? What is the distribution of model results?
- *The transferability of the model to another computer system.*
- *The accessability of the model.* For example, is it classified?
- *The size of the model.*
- *The length of a typical run.*
- *The costs in money and personnel to set up and run the model.* For example, how efficient is the computer model design as judged by the number of different runs needed to gain reliable insights?

The preceding list is neither exclusive nor exhaustive. Its aim is merely to suggest some factors that can affect the usability of a given model. The relative importance of these factors depends upon the problem at hand, and it is up to the evaluators to determine this.

Conclusion

The first major application of the approach described in preceding sections has been relatively well received by the pertinent stakeholders. This application, an evaluation of the use of the Transfer Income Model (TRIM), appeared as a report to Congress that contained several recommendations for improving the use of TRIM. As a result of these recommendations, an ongoing subcommittee on microsimulation of the Federal Committee on Statistical Methodology was organized by the Department of Commerce. This subcommittee, made up of persons involved in conducting microsimulations and in using data produced by microsimulations is studying aspects of microsimulation modeling that have a bearing on the estimation of errors. A series of commissioned seminars has been completed, and work is in progress on a working paper that summarizes findings to date. As mentioned earlier, the approach to model evaluation presented in this paper is taken from the document, "Guidelines for Model Evaluation." There is evidence that this report has assisted model evaluators, helped to educate evaluators, and made a contribution to the state of the art in model evaluation. It has been used in university classes on policy modeling as a teaching tool; excerpts were published in the March-April 1980 issue of *Operations Research*; an executive agency is providing the document to its own validation staff as well as to contractors; a senior research associate of the West German government is using it in a review of a large-scale model; and it has been used by GAO evaluators as a basis for evaluating several models.

However, a number of shortcomings still exist in this approach. For example, it fails to discuss available analytical alternatives to the model. This is a flaw because a model should be judged not in the absolute but in relation to the alternatives available. It is possible for a model to be judged poor but still to be the best tool available.

Another shortcoming is that the guidelines do not deal explicitly with the composite model (that is, one that a variety of methodologies have been employed to create), nor do they identify quantitative measures of "goodness of fit" for the various types of models. Thus, one major issue that requires further development is identification of procedures for satisfying the criteria set out in the approach. It is expected that subsequent experience will probably reveal changes in the relative importance of the criteria as well. In sum, these guidelines and the attendant criteria are themselves subject to evaluation and subsequent modification. This is as it should be, and the result of this evolutionary process should be an improvement in the technology of model evaluation and, ultimately, in the usefulness of complex models for policy analysis and decision making.

References

U.S. General Accounting Office. *An Evaluation of the Use of the Transfer Income Model — TRIM — To Analyze Welfare Programs* (PAD–78–14). Washington, D.C.: U.S. General Accounting Office, 1977.

U.S. General Accounting Office. *Guidelines for Model Evaluations* (PAD–79–17). Washington, D.C.: U.S. General Accounting Office, 1979.

U.S. General Accounting Office. *A Review of the 1974 Project Independence Evaluation System* (OPA–76–20). Washington, D.C.: U.S. General Accounting Office, 1976.

54

Bibliography

Apostel, L. "Formal Study of Models." In H. Fredenthal (Ed.), *The Concept and the Role of the Model in Mathematics and Natural and Social Sciences.* New York: Gordon and Breach, 1960.

Berman, M. B. *Notes on Validating/Verifying Computer Simulation Models.* Santa Monica, Calif.: Rand Corporation, 1972.

Brewer, G. *Politicians, Bureaucrats, and the Consultant: A Critique of Urban Problem Solving.* New York: Basic Books, 1972.

Chaiken, J., and others. *Criminal Justice Models: An Overview.* Santa Monica, Calif.: Rand Corporation, 1975.

Clark, J., and Cole, S. *Global Simulation Models: A Comparative Study.* New York: Wiley, 1972.

deNeufville, R., and Stafford, J. H. *Systems Analysis for Engineers and Managers.* New York: McGraw-Hill, 1971.

Deutsch, K. W., and others. *Problems of World Modeling: Political and Social Implications.* Cambridge, Mass.: Ballinger, 1977.

Eilson, S. "Mathematical Modeling for Management," *Interfaces,* 1974, *4* (2), 32–38.

Emshoff, J. R., and Sisson, R. L. *Design and Use of Computer Simulation Models.* New York: Macmillan, 1970.

Fishman, G. S., and Kiviat, P. J. *Digital Computer Simulation: Statistical Consideration.* Santa Monica, Calif.: Rand Corporation, 1967.

Fromm, G., Hamilton, W. L., and Hamilton, D. E. *Federally Supported Mathematical Models: Survey and Analysis.* Washington, D.C.: U.S. Government Printing Office, 1975.

Gass, S. I. "Evaluation of Complex Models." *Computers and Operations Research,* 1977, *4,* 27–35.

Gass, S. I. "A Procedure for the Evaluation of Complex Models." In *Procedings of the First International Conference on Mathematical Modeling.* Columbia: University of Missouri, 1977.

Gass, S. I., and Sisson, R. L. *A Guide to Models in Governmental Planning and Operations.* Potomac, Md.: Sauger Books, 1975.

Greenberger, M., Crenson, M. A., and Crissey, B. L. *Models in the Policy Process.* New York: Russell Sage Foundation, 1976.

Holcomb Research Institute. *Environmental Modeling and Decision Making.* New York: Praeger, 1976.

Honig, J., and others. *Review of Selected Army Models.* Washington, D.C.: Department of the Army, 1971.

Kleijnen, J. P. C. *Statistical Techniques in Simulation, Parts I and II.* New York: Marcel Dekker, 1974.

National Bureau of Standards. *Guidelines for Documentation of Computer Programs and Automated Data Systems.* Washington, D.C.: National Bureau of Standards, 1976.

Operations Research Society of America. "Guidelines for the Practice of Operations Research." *Operations Research,* 1971, *19* (5), 1123–1258.

Pugh, R. E. *Evaluation of Policy Simulation Models.* Washington, D.C.: Information Resources Press, 1977.

Quade, E. S. *Analysis for Public Decisions.* New York: Elsevier, 1975.

Sage, A. P. *Methodology for Large-Scale Systems.* New York: McGraw-Hill, 1977.

Schellenberger, R. E. "Criteria for Assessing Model Validity for Managerial Purposes," *Decision Sciences,* 1974, *5* (5), 644–653.

Shubik, M., and Brewer, G. D. *Models, Simulations, and Games: A Survey.* Santa Monica, Calif.: Rand Corporation, 1972.

Strauch, R. E. *A Critical Assessment of Quantitative Methodology as a Policy Analysis Tool.* Santa Monica, Calif.: Rand Corporation, 1974.

U.S. General Accounting Office. *Audit Guide for Assessing Reliability of Computer Output.* Washington, D.C.: U.S. General Accounting Office, 1978.

U.S. General Accounting Office. *Advantages and Limitations of Computer Simulation in Decision Making.* Washington, D.C.: U.S. General Accounting Office, 1973.

U.S. General Accounting Office. *Improvement Needed in Documenting Computer Systems.* Washington, D.C.: U.S. General Accounting Office, 1974.

U.S. General Accounting Office. *Ways to Improve Management of Federally Funded Computerized Models.* Washington, D.C.: U.S. General Accounting Office, 1976.

Urban, G. L. "Building Models for Decision Makers." *Interfaces*, 1974, *4* (3), 1–11.

Van Horn, R. "Validation of Simulation Results." *Management Sciences*, 1971, *17* (5), 247–257.

Weiss, C. H. *Evaluation Research.* Englewood Cliffs, N. J.: Prentice-Hall, 1972.

Zeigler, B. P. *Theory of Modeling and Simulation.* New York: Wiley, 1976.

Bruce W. Thompson is group director of the Data Analysis Group in the Institute for Program Evaluation at the U.S. General Accounting Office.

Mental health values are now underrepresented in evaluation methods for mental health programs, and emerging evaluation methods differ widely in their promise for addressing this situation.

Emerging Evaluation Methods in Mental Health Services

Charles Windle
Eugenie Walsh Flaherty

This chapter is a chi-square test, that is, it contrasts expected approaches to the evaluation of mental health services with observed approaches. We hope that it can reach significant conclusions. We mean to say more than that rhetoric differs from reality. Rhetoric should differ from reality, for it is a form of inspiration, not a form of description, and the importance of inspiration in society may increase as basic economic needs are filled and as our attention can rise to psychological and moral values.

The contrast that we wish to make concerns the types of goals, objectives, and methods that should be expected to characterize program evaluation if the values espoused by the mental health professions were used to shape program evaluation. Such mental health-oriented program evaluation would have special features that might make evaluations more useful in improving services. However, we feel that this potential of evaluation has not yet been realized.

The views expressed are those of the authors and do not necessarily represent those of the National Institutes of Mental Health.

N. Smith (Ed.). *New Directions for Program Evaluation: Federal Efforts to Develop New Evaluation Methods*, no. 12. San Francisco: Jossey-Bass, December 1981

Our analysis has four parts: First, we describe what should be expected for program evaluation dealing with mental health services if the values that the mental health discipline asserts to be important were taken seriously. Second, we discuss the types of evaluation of mental health services that appear to exist in 1980. Third, we describe some recent trends in the development of program evaluation methods for mental health services. Fourth, we suggest some approaches to bridge the gap between the types of program evaluation that are consonant with mental health values and current practice.

Mental Health Service Values

Before we attempt to identify the major values that underlie mental health services, we need to admit that our attempt will be exploratory. There is much ideological dispute within and among core mental health professions and among these professions, the general public, and representatives of other professions. To try to characterize the values that underlie a profession is to describe both the values that these professionals hold and the values that logic seems to require as a result of the content of the profession. Formal mental health service is provided mainly by four professions: psychiatry, psychology, social work, and nursing, with psychiatry in the dominant position. Other professionals have gained some recognition in the movement of mental health into the community in what has been called the third mental health revolution (Hollander, 1980). These various professions, of course, differ in ideology. Even more instability can be caused by changes in values over time. Mental health services have been subject to changing fashions (Bowen, 1979). Only to the extent that there are common values and that these values differ from those of other societal groups is it reasonable to try to characterize the values of the mental health services. We believe, however, that we can identify a number of such values. Since program evaluation is by definition a tool for improving a specific program, the values which guide that program should be an important part of the orientation of program evaluation. The values that shape mental health services should influence the types of program evaluation that mental health services use.

Humanitarian Service Ethic. The most fundamental value of mental health treatment ideology is humanitarian concern. The welfare of persons with actual or potential mental health problems is the explicit goal of service (Halmos, 1970). The cynicism that stems from sociological sophistication makes us recognize that these ethical values are more formal and rhetorical than accurate descriptions of dominant motivations (Becker, 1970; Goode, 1969). The self-interest of professionals can lead them to act in ways that violate this ethic (Rothman, 1980). However, the service ideal may have some guiding and constraining influence on the selection, recruitment, and orientation of persons who go into human service professions, and it may also influence the professional codes of ethics that operate, however weakly, in peer-group control. The orientation of mental health professionals toward considering as their client the person who manifests mental health problems, rather than that person's family or society at large, further facilitates the humanitarian orientation, although this approach can also result in blaming the victim (Ryan, 1971).

In program evaluation, the humanitarian service ethic could be expected to result in a preference for criteria dealing with clients' welfare rather than the cost savings and in a disposition to use evaluation results to improve and expand services rather than to increase efficiency or to cut waste.

Client outcome is found to be the preferred evaluation topic among clinicians (Flaherty and Olsen, 1978), although the feasibility and practical utility of this approach are doubtful (Windle, 1979). Conversely, the Community Mental Health Centers (CMHC) Program has been criticized for paying too little attention to fiscal planning or service costs (Macro Systems, Inc., 1973; U.S. General Accounting Office, 1974).

There is a clear tendency for evaluation to be used for program justification and expansion (Windle and Volkman, 1973), but this tendency serves the interests of professionals as much as the interests of clients, and it characterizes many programs regardless of their formal humanitarian service ethic (Carter, 1971). It should also be noted that the selective focus on problems and the selective use of results that are good advocacy can be bad science and violate principles of research necessary to obtain accurate information or to improve understanding (Bermant and Warwick, 1978).

Rationalism. The accepted ideology of the Western industrialized world holds that problems can best be overcome through reasoning. Mental health embraces this ideology in attributing importance to client insight during therapy and to academic preparation for practitioners. However, since the mental health field has its roots in theories about the operation of the unconscious, mental health should be less dominated by the ideology of rationalism than other fields. Nonetheless, program evaluation appears frequently to make naive rationalistic assumptions about the importance of formal program goals and the use of study results by rational decision makers. This naiveté seems greatest at the early stages of a program evaluation effort or an evaluator's career (Windle, 1979).

The general concept that special knowledge is necessary to solve problems could be applied in at least three ways.

First, the importance of special expertise could be extended to program evaluation, thus promoting the concept that highly professional specialists should operate technically sophisticated forms of program evaluation. This specialization could take the form of concentration on the experts' forte, exotic methodology, or it could lead evaluators to discount the views of program administrators. Instead of taking managers' goals as the criteria, evaluators would base their judgments of the institutions' pathology on their own expertise in public administration and sociology, and they would work to apply program change technology to reform programs (Davis and Salasin, 1975).

Second, rather than having evaluation serve as a form of motivation to produce more responsive or appropriate behavior, it could focus evaluation on a search for specific items of factual information that could translate into program-improving decisions.

Third, if it placed more importance on service professionals than on expertise in general, it would argue that evaluation should remain in the hands of the clinical specialists, and it would call for a peer-review type of evaluation. The relative status of clinicians and evaluators will help to determine which interpretation of rationalism prevails.

Individualism. As part of the ideology of individualism accepted by the Western world and in particular by the United States, the medical profession identifies defects within and focuses treatments not on the broad social environment but on individuals and their immediate environments (Rose, 1979). The medical model tends to cause program evaluation to look for the causes of problems in the abilities or decisions of individual program staff. Thus, it is compatible with the rationalistic view of programs and of the role of evaluation in aiding managers to make decisions. This view, which values the wishes of individuals over the wishes of society at large, also promotes self-improvement over accountability as the purpose of evaluation.

Mental Health as a Criterion. The subject area of mental health is psychological. Thus, one could expect that the primary interest of mental health professionals is in persons' feelings and cognitive states, and one could expect these psychological states to be given high priority among the criteria used to evaluate mental health service programs. Such criteria would include not simply changes in clients' psychiatric symptomatology but also in their satisfaction with services and in their other attitudes toward programs.

The essence of program evaluation is the values whose achievement is to be assessed. Valuing is a psychological process, and it is intimately involved in many mental health problems. Thus, mental health practitioners should be experts in identifying and assessing people's values. The program evaluation activities expected for mental health programs, then, should work to specify criterion value dimensions, and they should emphasize criteria that bear on individuals' subjective appraisals.

Community Mental Health Ideology. There exists in the health care field a community mental health ideology that seems to some extent to contradict some medical care values. Gottesfeld (1972) isolated six factors in community mental health ideology. The most variance was found on the issue of community context. This value argues that treatment should be provided in community rather than in institutional locations; community people as well as professionals should be involved in care giving; and caregivers should work in open, democratic ways rather than in hierarchical teams. The community context value implies a concern not only with strictly physical values but with social values as well, and it calls for the community to be involved in various aspects of the evaluation process — as providers of criterion values and as collaborators in the planning and conduct of evaluations.

The second dimension described by Gottesfeld conflicts even more with the more fundamental medical values. This issue, radicalism, emerges from "a dissatisfaction with the progress that has been made in community mental health and a belief that rapid, drastic changes are needed" (Gottesfeld, 1972, p. 33). This issue argues for political involvement, methods that reach larger masses of people and a change in administration that moves toward community control. Applied to program evaluation, this view would argue that evaluations should be performed not by staff of the institutions evaluated but by outsiders, and even by persons who do not represent the disciplines involved in service delivery.

The third factor identified by Gottesfeld is traditional psychotherapy, which emphasizes psychotherapy and long-term treatment on a base of psychoanalytic theory. This position is opposed by people who believe that such treatment is generally not effective or who feel that it is not feasible for large numbers of persons. If applied to program evaluation, this value would suggest that traditional research practices should be abandoned for the innovative methods that have immediate use for programs.

The last three factors that Gottesfeld identified are prevention, extension of the definition of mental health, and role diffusion. Both prevention and extension of the definition of mental health require social factors to be considered as relevant to mental health problems. This goes beyond the scope of the usual medical care orientation. For program evaluation, both imply a need to consider the nature of the programs being assessed and the variables that may be relevant to their outcome very broadly. If role diffusion was applied to program evaluation, the evaluator would become less an assessor than an implementer of the results of assessment. This could make the program evaluator an "action rescarchcr" and formative rather than summative funclions of evaluation would be emphasized.

In summary, many charateristics of mental health services could shape the approaches used for evaluation of these programs. However, the variety and the occasional inconsistency of these characteristics limit their usefulness as predictors.

There is also no good way to tell which characteristics will have the greatest influence, since program evaluation has been imposed on mental health services from the outside rather than rising out of the mental health movement itself. In fact, as we shall consider in the next section, this exogenous origin suggests that there may be little connection between the nature of service programs and the type of program evaluation to which they are subjected.

Types of Program Evaluation Used in Mental Health Services

Exogenous Origins. Probably the most important feature of program evaluation of mental health services as it now exists is its exogenous origins. While hospitals, clinics, and other organizations that provide mental health services sometimes want information about the program, having this information frequently takes lower priority for program staff than other activities, and the type of information most desired by organizations is often not evaluative, or at least it is not unbiased. The program evaluation activities of both the CMHC program and the National Institutes of Mental Health (NIMH) received a major impetus from congressional mandates. During the first decade of the CMHC program, program evaluation was optional for centers. Most centers did some program evaluation, but many did only a few different kinds, and about one fifth did none (Windle and Volkman, 1973). Several studies of the program criticized centers for doing little evaluation to guide their management (Chu and Trotter, 1974; Martens and Warren, 1971; U.S. General Accounting Office, 1974). In consequence, Congress added a program evaluation requirement to the 1975 Amendments to the CMHC Act. A definite increase in the amount of program evaluation in centers followed (Kirkhart, 1979; Majchrzak, 1980).

For NIMH, as for a number of other federal programs, a specific, continuing, planned program of evaluation was initiated only when Congress authorized a categorical one percent expenditure of program funds for evaluation. For the CMHC program, Congress specified several types of evaluation activities and several topics that evaluation should address. Although centers do not blindly conform to federal requirements, these specifications do help to shape centers' program evaluation activities.

For both NIMH and individual CMHCs, program evaluation has focused on service processes, such as accessibility, continuity, and financing, rather than on client or community outcomes; it has been done largely under the direction of managers or technique-oriented evaluators, not of clinicians or lay citizens; and it has tended to crystallize the results in reports that are not easy to disseminate, and for this and other reasons there has been little dissemination of results.

With the passage of P.L. 96–398, the Mental Health Systems Act of 1980, evaluation approaches for mental health services shifted toward externally imposed accountability systems that focus on prescribed service processes (Kepler-Seid, Windle, and Woy, 1980). This law specifies that federally funded service agencies should use standardized measures of performance to report their achievements.

Methods Advocated in Mental Health Evaluation Literature. One way of identifying the evaluation approaches peculiar to mental health services is to see what approaches are described in books addressed to the mental health services and to compare them with the approaches described in books on other service areas. For this review, the authors examined eight books whose titles concerned evaluation of mental health programs. Six were prepared by the National Institutes of Mental Health directly or under contracts (Davidoff, Gutentag, and Offutt, 1977; Hagedorn, Beck, Neubert, and Werlin, 1976; Hargreaves, Attkisson, and Sorensen, 1977; Landsberg and others, 1979; Peters, Lichtman, and Windle, 1979; Zusman and Wurster, 1975), and two were by other individuals (Coursey and others, 1977; Posavac, 1979).

These eight books generally portray evaluation of mental health programs as similar to evaluation of other human service programs. However, Posavac (1979) suggests that the area of mental health services is distinctive for its variability and for the unsupervised role of providers. These features seem relevant to two of the approaches that Posavac and other authors advance for mental health evaluation, individualized goal attainment and peer review. Davidoff, Guttentag, and Offutt (1977) claimed in 1977 that the evaluation of community mental health centers was in the vanguard of other services.

Most of these texts on mental health program evaluation adopt the systems management model of program implementation (Elmore, 1978), which assumes that programs are directed by rational managers who have the ability and interest to exercise control over the organization's efficiency and effectiveness in pursuing its goals. Thus, evaluation tends to be viewed as "part of the process of education and continuing education" (Mechanic, 1975, p. 23). Program values are usually implicit in the goals set by policymakers and administrators. Information is collected on both service process and outcome. Several of the NIMH-sponsored books are tied closely to the specific topics and approaches of the CMHC Amendments of 1975. This means that they emphasize service processes. The books focus on assessment techniques for a range of topics rather than on ways of using information. When they do discuss the use of results, the discussion is often quite general and implies that incremental improvements, not radical reform or curtailment of waste, is their main use. Assessment technology seems to provide the main basis for most of the context of these publications.

Trends in Developing Program Evaluation Methods for Mental Health Services

The National Institutes of Mental Health has recognized the appropriateness of federal support for developing program evaluation methods useful in evaluating mental health services. There are several mechanisms by which this role is carried out. The topic is included in services-related research funded extramurally through research grants. In addition, Congressional authority for NIMH to evaluate the service programs funded by NIMH has led to development of methods both for NIMH to use in its own evaluations and for individual service facilities to use for self-evaluation (Windle and Ochberg, 1975). While one can see why it would be necessary to develop methods for national-level evaluation before such evaluations were conducted, it is less clear why funds for national-level evaluations should be used to develop methods for local-level evaluations. A possible rationale is that NIMH might be able to aggregate local evaluations through analysis to produce national-level conclusions (Cook and Shadish, in press). This rationale is frequently used to justify government support of local data systems, since NIMH depends upon the reports of local agencies to build a national statistical picture. The argument is much less convincing for program evaluation, however. Program evaluation differs from other types of research for its focus on program-specific conditions, both in the problems and variables investigated and in the adaptation of conclusions and presentation to win the acceptance of local decision makers. Therefore, it is doubtful that the types of questions addressed in local evaluations would help to answer national-level questions. In fact, an attempt to shape local evaluations in order to make them additive, for example, by using similar definitions of variables and by publishing results, could destroy their appeal and usefulness for local managers. This rationale was not, in fact, advanced when national-level funds were allocated to develop local evaluations, and no efforts were made by NIMH to collect and aggregate local-level evaluations. The frequent use of national-level evaluation funds to develop procedures or manuals to help local-level evaluators seems to the authors to have occurred largely as an extension of NIMH's general orientation to assist local agencies, researchers, and universities. For example, when the one-percent evaluation funds first became available, NIMH had a number of project proposals under development to help local community mental health centers to do evaluations. When there was a desire to get studies under way promptly, proposals that were available from past NIMH activities were interpreted as within the new mission.

The second cause of this questionable use of funds was some disappointment within NIMH about how little use of evaluation study results was made at the national level (Stockdill and Sharfstein, 1976; Windle and Bates, 1974). Since there seemed to be good use of the products developed to help local facilities and since NIMH received credit for providing these products, it seemed more useful to produce the materials popular at local levels than the national-level reports.

The approaches to program evaluation supported by NIMH during the 1970s for use by local mental health facilities ranged widely in types of procedures and assumptions.

Structured Use of Clinical Judgment. Procedures for structuring peer review by professionals of the work by other professionals is one type of program evaluation that has been applied to health services in order to "ensure quality." As costs of health care increased and as a higher proportion of reimbursement came from third-party payers, government and insurance companies sought ways to contain program costs. A procedure that relied upon the judgments of other physicians was accepted as a compromise by physicians. NIMH supported research by Yale University to develop procedures applicable to mental health services for use by Community Mental Health Centers (Reidel, Tischler, and Myers, 1974). In 1978, an intensive survey of a small sample of centers found that, although most centers were still in the process of developing quality assurance procedures, center staff were optimistic about the potential of this procedure (Flaherty and Olsen,

1978). However, it remains to establish the extent to which, and the conditions under which, this approach will actually improve services.

Goal-Attainment Scaling. An approach to program evaluation designed to capture the idiopathic features of individual clients' problems and the individuated treatment appropriate to solve these problems is the Goal-Attainment Scaling (GAS) technique developed by Kiresuk and Sherman (1968). The National Institutes of Mental Health has supported considerable development work to refine and disseminate this program evaluation method. As a consequence, much technical assistance has been made available by the Program Evaluation Resource Center in Minneapolis to enable interested persons to try this approach in a wide range of circumstances. In addition to workshops, conferences, and consultations, a special journal devoted to techniques for evaluating goal attainment, the *Goal Attainment Review*, was published for several years (1974–1977). As might be expected, distinctive tailoring of the goal-attainment scales to fit individual problems is a primary weakness of the approach, since the scaling procedures that achieve comparability among programs or among individuals remain difficult to apply and validate (Calsyn and Davidson, 1978).

As often happens with program evaluation, the primary benefits of Goal-Attainment Scaling seem to be by-products. That is, GAS facilitates services by increasing their relevance through its focus on goals and involvement of clients. The popularity of this technique seems to have peaked with the fairly large dissemination effort of the Program Evaluation Resource Center in Minneapolis during the 1970s.

Citizen Evaluative Review. The Community Mental Health Centers Amendments of 1975 included a requirement that each community mental health center, "in consultation with the residents of its catchment area, review its program of services and the statistics and other information [required by the law in the center's evaluation] to assure that its services are responsive to the needs of the residents of the catchment area" (P.L. 94–63, p. 16). If carried out, this participative form of evaluation could take any one of a large number of forms, depending upon the technical detail involved and the roles of center staff and residents of the catchment area. An evaluation of the way in which the requirements of program evaluation in the CMHC Amendments of 1975 were actually being carried out in 1978 suggested that very few centers were in fact involving residents of the catchment area in the evaluation effort, other than members of their own governing and advisory boards (Flaherty and Olsen, 1978). However, a group of community mental health centers in Florida conducted a study with

NIMH support to develop, field test, and prepare materials to assist other centers in using this procedure in a productive fashion. A variety of types of citizen groups was organized to work with center staff in reviewing the centers' evaluations. It was found that even groups composed of former clients made recommendations that frequently were implemented by centers. Different types of groups, of course, gave different types of recommendations. Thus, the ex-patient groups seemed most alert to problems in the quality of care, while persons who represented other agencies focused more upon administrative and interagency issues (Zinober and others, 1980). A manual based on the work of the Florida consortium to help centers implement citizen evaluation review is in preparation (Zinober and Dinkel, 1981). More general publications to help lay citizens participate in evaluations of mental health service programs have also been developed with NIMH support (MacMurray and others, 1976; Peters, Lichtman, and Windle, 1979).

Program Performance Measurement. With the passage of the Mental Health Systems Act of 1980, the National Institutes of Mental Health began to prepare for another form of program evaluation. Experience with the intensive focus on a self-evaluation type of program evaluation, as mandated by the CMHC Amendments of 1975 for local Community Mental Health Centers, suggested that an accountability approach was likely to have greater value for services than a self-evaluation model, which often turned into advocacy for the agency that was doing the evaluation (Windle, 1979). The Mental Health Systems Act specified that grantees of funds for services should enter into a contract specifying the standards by which performance of funded activities would be monitored and evaluated, a schedule for this performance, the incentives for the grantee to meet such standards, and the role of the Secretary of the Department of Health and Human Services and of consumers and representatives of affected communities in this monitoring and evaluation. To assist in this process, the law specifies that "the Secretary shall prescribe standard measures of performance designed to test the quality and extent of performance by the recipients of grants and contracts under [this law] and the extent to which such performance has helped achieve the national or other objectives for which the grants . . . were made. . . ." (Sec. 316). This form of evaluation seems to place the burden on the oversight agencies in the federal government and the states to perform evaluations and to use their results to improve local centers. The activity of local centers seems to focus on choosing, generating, and reporting measures of their performance that the oversight agencies judge to be relevant. This requirement does not seem to compel the local agency to analyze evaluation results and reach conclusions, as research always does; instead, it can be satisfied by use of an information system after the program decides what statistics are most relevant.

This requirement for a performance measurement type of evaluation to be conducted primarily by the monitoring agencies and to include community residents is not unique. The Bureau of Community Health Services in the U.S. Public Health Service has had such a system for a number of years (Bureau of Community Health Services, 1978). Other agencies have attempted similar systems with varying degrees of success (Elmer, 1979; White, 1975; Zedlewski, 1979). This approach has been advocated by the U.S. General Accounting Office (1978), which even produced a guide for evaluating performance measurement systems (U.S. General Accounting Office, 1980).

In line with the general trends toward greater emphasis on accountability, the office of the Secretary of Health, Education, and Welfare (now Health and Human Services) instituted an Operations Management System based on performance measures for selected programs, including the Community Mental Health Centers program. The National Institutes of Mental Health selected thirteen measures that covered three types of goals of the Community Mental Health Centers program: accessibility, productivity/efficiency, and financial viability. Statistics by which these thirteen indicators could be measured are to be drawn from data supplied by federally funded centers to the National Institutes of Mental Health in an annual statistical report (Taube, 1980). The thirteen performance measures are described as additional tools to help centers, states, and regional offices evaluate progress toward goals, not as replacements of existing regional office and state monitoring activities.

The first set of data on the thirteen performance measures for centers under the Secretary's Operations Management System will be available in the summer of 1981. These could be the basis for some informal or formal evaluation of use either for local facilities (when feedback from NIMH is provided to them) or for federal and state monitoring to improve centers through technical assistance and other forms of oversight. The considerable potential of performance measurement for focusing the program on particular goals and for rendering agencies accountable has promise of increasing the effectiveness of services. It also carries some threat from possible misdirection of efforts toward criteria that can be measured easily and from development of adversarial relationships between agencies on the one hand and the general public and potential clients on the other. These threats are a good reason why there should be much careful study of how a performance measurement system should be used and of the particular indicators, standards, and collection and dissemination procedures that should be employed (Keppler-Seid, Windle, and Woy, 1980). The possibility of support for such research endeavors depends both upon the funds available at federal and state levels and upon the initiative of evaluators, managers, and interested citizens who propose technically sound and socially useful projects.

Bridging the Gap Between Popular Evaluation Methods and Mental Health Service Values

We believe that the four evaluation methods which we see emerging in mental health service evaluation differ in their congruence with the values that underlie mental health services. To be explicit about our views of the consistency of values and evaluation approaches, we rated each of the evaluation approaches on its degree of congruence with each of the mental health service values described earlier. The ratings of congruence are shown in Table 1. In general, we see citizen evaluative review and goal-attainment scaling as fairly consistent with these values and clinical peer judgments and program performance measurement as fairly inconsistent. These views are our own, however, and others may disagree. Others may also disagree about the values that we identified as values of mental health services. In fact, some staff working in community mental health centers may also not subscribe to these values (Wagenfeld, Robin, and Jones, 1974). As the CMHC program matures (or assumes a new form as suggested by the Mental Health Systems Act) and the social, economic, and political environment changes from nurturance to hostility, the values of community mental health advocates can be expected to change. However, we assume that these defections from community mental health values will be only temporary and that in the long run the types of program evaluations that are most appropriate for mental health services will reflect these values. If this is so, and if our views are correct that some of the current trends in evaluation conflict with these values, thought should be given as to how program evaluation can give greater recognition to mental health values.

Two approaches seem possible. One is to emphasize techniques that manifest mental health values and deemphasize techniques that do not. Thus, citizen-controlled evaluation and goal-attainment scaling might be encouraged, while program performance measurement might be discouraged. Other techniques do not seem popular now in mental health program evaluation, but they could be used more extensively.

Table 1. Congruence of Four Evaluation Methods with Mental Health Service Values

Mental Health Service Values	Emerging Evaluation Methods in Mental Health Service Programs			
	Clinical Judgment (Quality Assurance)	Goal-Attainment Scaling	Citizen Evaluative Review	Program Performance Measurement
Humanitarianism		+	+	−
Low rationalism	−	−	+	−
Individualism	+	+		−
Mental health as criterion	+			−
CMHC ideology				
1. Community context	−		+	−
2. Radicalism				
3. Nontraditional psychotherapy	−		+	
4. Prevention	−			−
5. Extended definition of mental health	−	+	+	
6. Role diffusion	−		+	

+ The authors judged this value to be given high weight in the evaluation method.
− The authors judged this value to be given low weight in the evaluation method.

For example, the multiattribute utility approach (Edwards, Guttentag, and Snapper, 1975) recognizes the values of stakeholders who are often ignored.

Consumer satisfaction assessments also have an advantage in their orientation toward the values of service recipients. However, as such assessments are usually employed, they lack differentiating ability, they produce unrealistically favorable portrayals of consumer attitudes, and they are used for program advocacy, not for client advocacy (Gutek, 1978). Modifications in the methods used to evaluate client satisfaction might solve some of these problems, especially if client control over the design and use of the instruments increased and the emphasis upon measuring, which appears to be the domain of experts, was replaced by an emphasis on "reform," a political process that requires action by community members in their citizen role (Windle and Paschall, in press).

House (1980) points out that some other, less common approaches to evaluation, such as case studies, quasi-legal trials by jury, and an art criticism approach, are relatively democratic or non-elitist, subjectivist in their methodology, and oriented more toward personal understanding than toward social efficiency as outcomes. These approaches seem more consistent with mental health values than the usual program goal-oriented and system analysis evaluation procedures.

The other approach to the conflict between mental health service values and program evaluation approaches is to modify the program evaluation approaches so they better reflect mental health values. The clinical judgment approach should be expanded to consider other issues than clinical criteria—humanitarian concerns, for example. Since decisions by clinicians always involve more than clinical considerations (for example, costs and the personal desires of staff), it would be appropriate for the many nonclinician stakeholders to participate in these aspects of the review of service utilization.

For performance measurement, a much wider array of improvements seems both necessary and possible. The general direction that these modifications should take was suggested by Kelly (1980), who noted that different approaches to measurement of public sector productivity derive from alternative ideological views of the role of politics in program implementation. An "institutional-universalist paradigm" assumes that external, rational criteria exist from which standards and norms can be extracted. This leads to a political economics perspective, which bases its indices on input-output ratios and cost-benefit analyses. A "participatory-selectivist paradigm rejects standardization in principle and stresses the internal subjective world of the client-consumer" (Kelly, 1980, p. 77). This sociological-psychological perspective leads to assessments of client satisfaction and analysis of coproduction. While the economic orientation leads to simpler measures focused on program output, the sociological-psychologocial orientation requires inquiry into "who received precisely what, when, where and in what amounts" (Kelly, 1980, p. 79). Kelly suggests that Heaton's Service Productivity Rating System (1977) may provide a starting point for synthesis of the two perspectives.

Conclusion

There are at least two positions that one can take toward the large discrepancy that we find between mental health values and the methods used to evaluate such programs. One interprets the discrepancy as another example of social program failure, consistent with the general disillusion concerning the effectiveness of social programs and with distrust of the altruism of service providers. The other regards program evaluation as a specialty in its own right, with its own values and techniques (Morell and Flaherty, 1978). If program evaluation is regarded as a separate profession, there can be little expectation that program evaluation practice will reflect the values of the particular fields to which it is applied. This perspective is consistent with the largely exogenous origins of program evaluation in mental health programs. Even this perspective, however, would acknowledge that discrepancies between the values of program evaluation and of the programs to which it is applied are relevant to the cooperation expected of a program and its evaluators and consequently to the effectiveness of program evaluation.

Our discussion has dealt with the many values of mental health services and the extent to which they appear in program evaluation. A contrasting approach is to start with the values of program evaluation and search for them in mental health programs. Probably the most serious problem that this approach would uncover is the absence of an experimental approach within most programs. It is difficult for many practitioners to accept the view that their particular program is only one approach to a goal and that it is in continuing need of critical review and improvement. Instead, practitioners tend to think that the existing program is the best solution to the goal, that the organization must be committed to it to make it work, and that it must be defended against all detractors and competitors (Campbell, 1969).

The resistance to an experimental orientation is not unique to mental health programs, but even here, one can argue that, insofar as mental health deals with psychological barriers to adaptation, mental health professionals should be aware of, and able to correct, such shortsighted and self-limiting tendencies as overcommitment to specific programs. In all, the introduction of program evaluation to mental health programs offers both disciplines an opportunity for basic reorientation that should enhance their functioning.

References

Becker, H. S. "The Nature of a Profession." In H. S. Becker (Ed.)., *Sociological Work.* Chicago: Aldine, 1970.

Bermant, G., and Warwick, D. P. "The Ethics of Social Intervention: Power, Freedom, and Accountability." In G. Bermant, H. C. Kelman, and D. P. Warwick (Eds.), *The Ethics of Social Intervention.* Washington: Hemisphere, 1978.

Bowen, A. "Some Mental Health Premises." *Milbank Memorial Fund Quarterly,* 1979, *57* (4), 533–551.

Bureau of Community Health Services. *Instruction Manual for the BCHS Common Reporting Requirements.* Rockville, Md.: U.S. Department of Health, Education, and Welfare, 1978.

Calsyn, R. J., and Davidson, W. S. "Do We Really Want a Program Evaluation Strategy Based Solely on Individualized Goals? A Critique of Goal-Attainment Scaling." *Community Mental Health Journal*, 1978, *14*, 300–308.

Campbell, D. T. "Reforms as Experiments." *American Psychologist,* 1969, *24*, 409–429.

Carter, R. K. "Clients' Resistance to Negative Findings and the Latent Conservative Function of Evaluation Studies." *American Sociologist*, 1971, *6*, 118–124.

Chu, F. B., and Trotter, S. *The Madness Establishment*. New York: Grossman, 1974.

Cook, T. D., and Shadish, W. R., Jr. "Metaevaluation: An Assessment of the Community Mental Health Center Congressionally Mandated Evaluation System." In W. R. Tash and G. Stahler (Eds.), *Innovations in Mental Health Evaluation*. New York: Academic Press, in press.

Coursey, R. D., Specter, G. A., Murrell, S. A., and Hunt, B. (Eds.). *Program Evaluation for Mental Health: Methods, Strategies, and Participants*. New York: Grune and Stratton, 1977.

Davidoff, I., Guttentag, M., and Offutt, J. *Evaluating Community Mental Health Services: Principles and Practice.* Washington, D.C.: U.S. Government Printing Office, 1977.

Davis, H. R., and Salasin, S. "The Utilization of Evaluation." In E. L. Struening and M. Guttentag (Eds.), *Handbook of Evaluation Research*. Vol. 1. Beverly Hills, Calif.: Sage, 1975.

Edwards, W., Guttentag, M., and Snapper, K. "A Decision-Theoretic Approach to Evaluation Research." In E. L. Struening and M. Guttentag (Eds.), *Handbook of Evaluation Research*. Vol. 1. Beverly Hills, Calif.: Sage, 1975.

Elmer, V. "The State of Performance Indicators in Housing." Paper presented at the Evaluation Research Society Conference, Minneapolis, October 1979.

Elmore, R. F. "Organizational Models of Social Program Implementation." *Public Policy*, 1978, *26*, 185–228.

Flaherty, E. W., and Olsen, K. *An Assessment of the Utility of Federally Required Program Evaluation in Community Mental Health Centers*. Vol. 1. Philadelphia: Philadelphia Health Management Corporation, 1978.

Goode, W. J. "The Theoretical Limits of Professionalization." In A. Etzioni (Ed.), *The Semiprofessions and Their Organization*. New York: Free Press, 1969.

Gottesfeld, H. *The Critical Issues of Community Mental Health*. New York: Human Sciences Press, 1972.

Gutek, B. A. "Strategies for Studying Client Satisfaction." *Journal of Social Issues*, 1978, *34*, 44–56.

Hagedorn, H. J., Beck, K. J., Neubert, S. F., and Werlin, S. H. *A Working Manual of Simple Program Evaluation Techniques for Community Mental Health Centers.* Washington, D.C.: U.S. Government Printing Office, 1976.

Halmos, P. *The Personal Service Society*. London: Constable, 1970.

Hargreaves, W. A., Attkisson, C. C., and Sorensen, J. E. (Eds.). *Resource Materials for Community Mental Health Program Evaluation*. (2nd ed.). Washington D. C.: U.S. Government Printing Office, 1977.

Heaton, H. *Productivity in Service Organizations*. New York: McGraw-Hill, 1977.

Hollander, R. "A New Service Ideology: The Third Mental Health Revolution." *Professional Psychology*, 1980, *11*, 561–566.

House, E. R. *Evaluating with Validity*. Beverly Hills, Calif.: Sage, 1980.

Kelly, R. M. "Ideology, Effectiveness, and Public Sector Productivity: With Illustrations from the Field of Higher Education." *Journal of Social Issues*, 1980, *36*, 76–95.

Keppler-Seid, H., Windle, C., and Woy, J. R. "Performance Measures for Mental Health Programs: Something Better, Something Worse, or More of the Same?" *Community Mental Health Journal*, 1980, *16*, 217–234.

Kiresuk, T., and Sherman, R. "Goal-Attainment Scaling: A General Method for Evaluating Community Mental Health Programs." *Community Mental Health Journal*, 1968, *4*, 443–453.

74

Kirkhart, K. E. *Program Evaluation in Community Mental Health Centers*. Unpublished doctoral dissertation, University of Michigan, 1979.

Landsberg, G., Neigher, W. D., Hammer, R. J., Windle, C., and Woy, J. R. (Eds.). *Evaluation in Practice: A Sourcebook of Program Evaluation Studies from Mental Health Care Systems in the United States*. Washington, D.C.: U.S. Government Printing Office, 1979.

MacMurray, V. D., Cunningham, P. H., Cater, P. B., Swenson, H., and Bellin, S. *Citizen Evaluation of Mental Health Services: An Action Approach to Accountability*. New York: Human Sciences Press, 1976.

Macro Systems, Inc. *Trends in Sources of Funds for Community Mental Health Centers*. Silver Spring, Md.: Macro Systems, Inc., 1973.

Majchrzak, A. *Organizational Parameters of the Evaluation Process: A Study of Community Mental Health Centers*. Unpublished doctoral dissertation, University of California, Los Angeles, 1980.

Martens, H. A. and Warren, C. R. *The Multiagency Community Mental Health Center: Administrative and Organizational Relationships (Vols. 1 and 2)*. Springfield, Va.: National Technical Information Service, 1971.

Mechanic, D. "Evaluation in Alcohol, Drug Abuse, and Mental Health Programs: Problems and Prospects." In J. Zusman and C. Wurster (Eds.), *Program Evaluation*. Lexington, Mass.: Lexington Books, 1975.

Morell, J. A., and Flaherty, E. W. "The Development of Evaluation as a Profession: Current Status and Some Predictions." *Evaluation and Program Planning*, 1978, 1, 11–18.

Peters, S., Lichtman, S. A., and Windle, C. *Citizen Roles in Community Mental Health Center Evaluation: A Guide for Citizens*. Washington, D.C.: U.S. Government Printing Office, 1979.

Posavac, E. J. (Ed.). *Impacts of Program Evaluation on Mental Health Care*. Boulder, Colo.: Westview Press, 1979.

Public Law 94–63, Sec. 206. (c)(1)(B).

Reidel, D. C., Tischler, G. L., and Myers, J. K. *Patient Care Evaluation in Mental Health Programs*. Cambridge, Mass.: Ballinger, 1974.

Rose, S. M. "Deciphering Deinstitutionalization: Complexities in Policy and Program Analysis," *Milbank Memorial Fund Quarterly*, 1979, 57, 429–460.

Rothman, D. J. *Conscience and Convenience: The Asylum and Its Alternatives in Progressive America*. Boston: Little, Brown, 1980.

Ryan, W. *Blaming the Victim*. New York: Pantheon, 1971.

Stockdill, J. W., and Sharfstein, S. S. "The Politics of Program Evaluation: The Mental Health Experience." *Hospital and Community Psychiatry*, 1976, 27 (9), 650–653.

Taube, C. A. "A Description of the Revised 1981 Management System for the Federally Funded Community Mental Health Centers." Rockville, Md.: National Institutes of Mental Health, 1980.

U.S. General Accounting Office. *Need for More Effective Management of Community Mental Health Centers Program*. Washington, D.C.: U.S. General Accounting Office, 1974.

U.S. General Accounting Office. *Federal Agencies Should Use Good Measures of Performance to Hold Managers Accountable*. Washington, D.C.: U.S. General Accounting Office, 1978.

U.S. General Accounting Office. *Evaluating a Performance Measurement System: A Guide for the Congress and Federal Agencies*. Washington, D.C.: U.S. General Accounting Office 1980.

Wagenfeld, M., Robin, S., and Jones, J. "Structural and Professional Correlates of Ideologies of Community Mental Health Workers." *Journal of Health and Social Behavior*, 1974, 15, 199–210.

White, B. F. "The Atlanta Project: How One Large School System Responded to Performance Information." *Policy Analysis*, 1975, 1, 659–691.

Windle, C. "Developmental Trends in Program Evaluation." *Evaluation and Program Planning*, 1979, *2*, 193–196.

Windle, C., and Bates, P. "Evaluating Program Evaluation: A Suggested Approach." In P. O. Davidson, J. W. Clark, and L. A. Hamerlynck (Eds.), *Evaluation of Behavioral Programs*. Champaign, Ill.: Research Press, 1974.

Windle, C., Majchrzak, A., and Flaherty, E. W. "Program Evaluation at the Interface of Program Echelons." In R. F. Rich (Ed.), *Translating Evaluation into Policy*. Beverly Hills, Calif.: Sage, 1979.

Windle, C., and Ochberg, F. M. "Enhancing Program Evaluation in the Community Mental Health Centers Program." *Evaluation*, 1975, *2* (2), 31–36.

Windle, C., and Paschall, N. C. "Client Participation in Community Mental Health Center Program Evaluation: Increasing Incidence, Inadequate Involvement." *Community Mental Health Journal*, in press.

Windle, C., and Volkman, E. M. "Evaluation in the Centers Program." *Evaluation*, 1973, *1* (2), 69–70.

Zedlewski, E. W. "Performance Measurement in Public Agencies: The Law Enforcement Evaluation." *Public Administration Review*, 1979, *39*, 488–493.

Zinober, J. W., and Dinkel, N. R. (Eds.). *A Trust of Evaluation: A Guide for Involving Citizens in Community Mental Health Program Evaluation*. Tampa, Fla.: Florida Consortium for Research and Evaluation, 1981.

Zinober, J. W., Dinkel, N. R., Landsberg, G., and Windle, C. "Another Role for Citizens: Three Variations of Citizen Evaluation Review." *Community Mental Health Journal*, 1980, *16*, 317–330.

Zusman, J., and Wurster, C. F. *Program Evaluation*. Lexington, Mass.: Lexington Books, 1975.

Charles Windle is a member of the Division of Biometry and Epidemiology in the National Institutes of Mental Health. Recently, he organized a section on accountability, program evaluation, and information use within a division of the American Psychological Association.

Eugenie Walsh Flaherty, an independent consultant, is founder and coeditor, with Jonathan Morell, of Evaluation and Program Planning. *Her current interests include policy analysis in the health field, evaluation of mental health programs, needs assessment for drug rehabilitation programs, and research in adolescent sexuality and contraception use.*

New evaluation methods are being developed by adapting techniques from geography, philosophy, journalism, economics, film criticism, photography, and other areas.

Creating Alternative Methods for Educational Evaluation

Nick L. Smith

Since the passage of the Elementary and Secondary Education Act (ESEA) in 1965, evaluators in education have been struggling to develop methods that satisfy both the canons of scientific research and the practical needs of the nation's educators. Although most attention has been placed on educational measurement and the use of systematic, widespread testing as a means of fulfilling evaluation purposes, many evaluators have become interested in approaches that draw on the traditions of other fields, such as anthropology, economics, law, journalism, and literature.

This chapter reports on a multiyear effort funded by the National Institute of Education to develop alternative evaluation methods for use in local school districts and state departments of education. This effort, which began in 1978, has undertaken to identify, translate, and test methods currently employed in other fields for use in education. The chapter discusses the need for new evaluation methods in educa-

The work reported in this chapter was supported in part by the National Institute of Education under Contract No. 400–80–0105 but does not necessarily reflect the views of the Institute or of the Northwest Regional Educational Laboratory.

N. Smith (Ed.). *New Directions for Program Evaluation: Federal Efforts to Develop New Evaluation Methods*, no. 12. San Francisco: Jossey-Bass, December 1981

77

tion, the context of evaluation practice in which new methods will function, and the kinds of new methods now being developed for use in education, and it illustrates some of the contributions that this work is making to evaluation methodology. Much of the work reported here is currently in progress, although some of it has been reported in the professional journals. Two recent books contain reports on this work, *Metaphors for Evaluation: Sources of New Methods* (Smith, 1981a) and *New Techniques for Evaluation* (Smith, 1981b).

Need for New Evaluation Methods

In the last few years, interest in the development of new evaluation methods for education has increased. This interest has been evident among theorists, practitioners, and educators alike. I have discussed this recent concern with new methods at greater length elsewhere (Smith, 1981c), so I will only highlight a few points here.

Although testing is the predominant operational definition of evaluation for evaluation practitioners in local school districts and state education departments, the professional literature does not reflect this picture. The traditional view is that the true experiment is the only legitimate form of educational evaluation. Proponents of experimental methods warn of the dangers of quasi-experiments and other methods (for example, Boruch and Rindsdopf, 1977; Campbell and Boruch, 1975; Cook, Cook, and Mark, 1977; Gilbert, Light, and Mosteller, 1975); others (for example, Cooley and Lohnes, 1976) have argued that evaluations of major educational systems must necessarily be multivariate, longitudinal, large-sample, and expensive. In recent years, this traditional view has been challenged by such writers as Parlett and Hamilton (1976) and Guba (1978), who argue that the traditional approach has many faults. Authors critical of the traditional approach have advocated use of naturalistic methods and qualitative data and approaches based on models other than those provided by scientific, experimental research. They have attacked the traditional approach on the grounds of feasibility, desirability, and even ethics. The proponents of the traditional approach have countered with evidence purporting to show that randomized controlled experiments are indeed feasible, that they need not result in unethical treatment of subjects, and that they do not necessarily preclude use of qualitative data or attention to local differences. The debate continues.

There is general agreement, however, among evaluation practitioners and theorists, both those committed to traditional approaches and those searching for new options, that the activity of evaluation has yet to fulfill it promise; that is, it has not yet lived up to its social role as a provider of relevant, useful, timely information on the value of educational and social programs. While both groups of theorists acknowledge the problem, both groups also debate the manner in which evaluation methods ought to be improved. Those who favor traditional approaches respond to the challenge with redoubled efforts to improve existing procedures, while the others believe that radical alternatives are required.

There is also evidence that evaluation practitioners are looking for new approaches to their work. Although the most pressing problems of evaluation within local school districts and state departments result from lack of resources and professional staff, some practitioners have argued for new methods (Law, 1980; Stenzel, 1980). Lyon (1979) reports that information about effective evaluation practices is one of the four items judged most likely to improve unit effectiveness for metropolitan school districts having enrollments of 45,000 students or more.

Similarly, in a study of evaluation units in twenty-five state departments of education (Caulley and Smith, 1978; 1980), twelve states reported that they had inadequate methods for some evaluations, while fifteen states indicated that decision makers needed information that they did not know how to supply. Eighteen of the twenty-five states, or 72 percent, indicated that they would like to try new evaluation methods.

Even educators have indicated support for alternative approaches to evaluation. Bernard McKenna (1980), in testimony on behalf of the National Education Association, has argued for new approaches to evaluation, and a recent needs assessment of Northwest educators (Northwest Regional Educational Laboratory, 1980) ranked program evaluation as the area needing greatest emphasis in the coming decade.

Evaluation theorists, practitioners, and educators agree on the need for improving evaluation and for considering alternative methods of gathering and presenting evaluative information.

Context of Evaluation Practice in Education

One of the reasons most often cited for the development of new methods in evaluation is that current procedures are not well matched to the context within which evaluation practice occurs in education. In fact, there has been relatively little study of evaluation practice itself. Only with the recent interest in improving the utility of evaluation have there been studies of the settings in which evaluations are conducted. If new methods are to improve practice, they must be compatible with these settings. We need to know what routine evaluation practice is really like.

Evaluation in Local School Districts. Although there were research units in local school districts prior to 1965, the passage of the Elementary and Secondary Education Act in that year placed new demands for evaluation on local districts. The pressure for evaluation came largely from critics of public education; public educators showed less enthusiasm. The subsequent fifteen years, however, have seen a dramatic increase in evaluation capability at the local education agency (LEA) level.

There are approximately 15,000 public school districts in the United States, most of them small, with fewer than 5,000 students. There are approximately 750 districts with 10,000 students or more; 43 percent of these larger districts have centralized units for program evaluation (Lyon and others, 1978). Thus, there are at least 323 LEA evaluation units in the U.S. today.

Lyon and her colleagues (1978) surveyed evaluation units in school districts having enrollments of 10,000 or more. They report that 89 percent of the metropolitan districts, 59 percent of the large districts, and 33 percent of the medium districts have an evaluation unit. Further, 85 percent of these evaluation offices were established after 1965. Thirty-seven percent of these units report directly to the superintendent, while 44 percent report through one intermediary, and 20 percent report through two or more intermediaries. Only 39 percent of the units are located in instructional offices; the rest are located in administrative or support offices. The average evaluation unit spends more time working on school administrative concerns than on instructional concerns.

Lyon and others (1978) report that, while these units are primarily responsible for formal assessment within the district, they are not exclusively responsible for that activity. Only 26 percent of the units report doing all the district evaluation of state, federal, and local programs. Further, most of these units accomplish their work with the use of in-house personnel. Almost half of the units spend no money on consultants. These units have staffs ranging from zero to ninety full-time professional members, but 58 percent of the units have two professional staff or fewer.

Ninety-seven percent of these units report that their budgets are one percent of the total district budget or less, with about half of the units reporting that their budgets are adequate. Local funds, rather than federal or state funds, are the primary source of support for local evaluation. In fact, the modal office is entirely locally funded. The profile of funding sources for the average office is 65 percent local, 18 percent federal, 15 percent state, and 1 percent other.

These offices evaluate elementary, intermediate, and secondary education. About 75 percent of the units view assessment of student achievement as the dominant focus of their data-collection efforts. Seventy-five percent also agree that testing is their major method of data collection. Lyon and others (1978) note that individual offices show considerable variation in the nature of their local functions and activities. The offices express little agreement on what constitutes basic evaluation practice or on the priority of various evaluation activities. However, they tend to spend more time on summative than on formative evaluation and to pay little attention to process evaluation or program costs. The developmental work of these units emphasizes evaluation instruments and tests over instructional programs or products. Seventy-one percent of the units administer district-wide, norm-referenced testing programs, and 48 percent administer district-wide, criterion-referenced testing programs.

While several evaluators who practice in local school districts have described what it is like to work in such settings (for example, Holley, 1978; Holley and Lee, 1977; Polemeni, undated; Stephens and Barber, 1978; Webster and Stufflebeam, 1978), their reports tend to remain in the fugitive literature. However, these writings do serve to highlight some of the problems faced by evaluators in local school districts, such as serving the information needs of competing audiences, implementing experimental designs in a context of changing conditions, inadequate resources, resistance from school personnel to data-collection requirements, and difficulty in communicating evaluation results, especially politically sensitive results.

Evaluation Practice in State Education Agencies. Evaluation practice in state education agencies (SEAs) has been studied even less. Caulley and Smith (1978; 1980) surveyed twenty-five state departments of education, twenty-one of which had centralized program evaluation units. They found as much diversity across the state agencies as Lyon and others (1978) had found across local school district units. State units reported staffs ranging between one and seventy-two full-time personnel, with the modal unit having between one and eight full-time staff. These units devoted from 0 to 100 percent of their time to program evaluation, with the average state devoting approximately half of its time to program evaluation. These units conducted or monitored between 1 and 300 evaluations a year and contracted out between 1 and 250 evaluations a year. However, most units conducted or monitored between fifteen and twenty-five evaluations a year and contracted very few to third-party evaluators.

The types of methods used by state department evaluators reflect methods used in local school districts. Most state education agencies emphasize objective assessment, with pre- and posttesting in experimental designs, and testing is their primary mode of data collection. A few states employ auditing and accrediting approaches, using some interviewing and classroom observation. All states use written reports as their primary reporting technique, with only five states using either oral presentations or press releases to report their evaluation studies. As for local units, the most pressing problems for state evaluation units are shortage of staff and lack of financial resources.

Law (1980) has described the setting within which state agency evaluators work in these terms: "[State evaluation units] are embedded in a state agency and, hence, are bureaucratic by definition; they are in a political environment; they report to a variety of audiences; they operate under severe constraints of time and human and financial resources; they tend to be in a reactive mode. The units tend not to be innovative in their approach to evaluation, since they operate under legislative and regulatory mandates. Departure from conventional custom and procedure is perilous, and, thus, the mode of operation tends to remain as it was a decade ago" (Law, 1980, p.3).

A series of papers written by SEA evaluation managers sheds further light on the setting within which SEA evaluation takes place. In a review of this work (Smith, in press), I have summarized the SEA evaluation context as follows: "It is clear . . . that influences from the federal, state, and local level all work to constrain the nature of evaluation practice within state departments of education. Such influences regulate the organization and staffing of such units as well as determine what is evaluated, what methods are used, and who communicates with whom. These papers portray SEA evaluation units as engaging in many activities; evaluation being operationally defined to include monitoring, impact assessment, information preparation, research synthesis, planning, and policy preparation, with the majority of attention and effort devoted to testing activities. Little attention seems to be paid to causal studies or to the assessment of worth. Further, there is little explicit attention to analysis of values or of value claims, although a great deal of attention is paid to political analysis. These units are characterized by a lack of autonomy and independence. An SEA evaluation unit is one piece of a large organizational enterprise and, as such, staff members cannot play the role of 'third-party contractors' that is often played by their university counterparts. Within these units, political and legal considerations are frequently more important than technical considerations, with most evaluation attention focused on management assistance of policy analysis to the general exclusion of the improvement of instruction" (Smith, in press).

These descriptions of LEA and SEA evaluation practice indeed present a picture sharply different from much of the early literature on evaluation method. The view of evaluation as merely a technical specialty most akin to academic field research certainly does not appear to be compatible with the reality of practitioners.

Development of New Evaluation Methods

Having discussed the need for new evaluation methods and outlined the nature of evaluation practice in education, I will consider some new approaches now being developed, and in the final section, I will discuss some of the results of this work.

The Variety of Work on New Methods. Currently, much effort is being devoted to the development of new evaluation methods for use in educational settings. Most of this work is being conducted privately by researchers who have little direct financial support. Most educational evaluators are aware of the work by Guba (1978), House (1980), Stake (1975), Eisner (1979), Parlett and Hamilton (1976), and others. There is work in progress, however, which has not yet been generally discussed in the evaluation literature; this work is focused on new evaluator roles (for example, the "public" evaluator, the "lay" evaluator, the "team" evaluator) and on application of new techniques and perspectives in evaluation (for example, signal detection theory, case studies, fiction, critical social inquiry, and metaanalysis; see Smith, 1980b for a list and more detailed description of such work). This is just a sample of the new approaches currently being pursued by individual researchers and evaluators.

Various federal agencies are also funding programmatic work to develop new evaluation methods, as discussed in the other chapters of this sourcebook and elsewhere (Smith, 1980a). In education, the National Institute of Education (NIE) is funding several major attempts to improve evaluation methodology at state and local levels. In FY 1980, $1,317,100 was spent on such research, including a study of the "stakeholder" evaluation utilization strategy, a study of exemplary uses of local testing and evaluation information, studies of local evaluation design and use, studies of quantitative evaluation methods, and studies of evaluation utilization (Charles Stalford, NIE, personal communication). It is to one of these NIE-funded projects that we now turn.

The Work of the Research on Evaluation Program. Among
its other activities, the Research on Evaluation Program at Northwest Regional Educational Laboratory conducts research supported by
the NIE to develop new evaluation methods. Since its beginning in
1978, the methods project of this program has produced more than
sixty technical reports and involved more than ninety specialists in
development and testing of new evaluation methods. These specialists
have included philosophers, journalists, lawyers, geographers, sociologists, psychologists, educators, political scientists, economists, artists,
as well as scores of evaluation practitioners. The purpose of this project
is to improve the practice of evaluation in local school districts and state
education departments by researching and developing new evaluation approaches and techniques, by testing and revising these methods
in collaboration with evaluation practitioners, and by preparing systems and materials to support consultation, training and implementation of the new methods.

In developing new approaches to evaluation, this project has
followed the strategy of identifying existing procedures in other fields
and of adapting these procedures for use in educational evaluation. For
example, the project has worked to adapt the cost-effectiveness analysis
developed in economics for use in school finance problems and in
instructional program cost studies; trend surface analysis developed in
geology for use in studies of the regional distribution of educational
needs and services; display techniques developed in art for use in evaluation communication; and optimization techniques developed in
operations research for use in evaluation of facilities and educational
transportation problems. This project focuses primarily on educational
program evaluation and only to a lesser extent on product, system, and
personnel evaluation. We are concerned primarily with the larger evaluation units in the country, which have sufficient internal support and
expertise to adopt and implement alternative evaluation strategies. We
are concerned with evaluation, broadly construed, and its interface
with other educational functions, such as policy, finance, planning,
research, and management. Because other programs of new method
development have focused attention on local educational agency evaluation (for example, the work now being conducted by the Center for
the Study of Evaluation at the University of California, Los Angeles),
we tend to focus on evaluation within state departments of education,
although some of our work is being conducted at the local level.

The work of the project involves four activities. First, the project initiates the conceptual development of alternative approaches by
specialists familiar with other disciplines and with educational evalua-

tion. This conceptual work is subsequently reviewed both by content specialists and by evaluation practitioners. Second, the project supports field trials of these new methods by practitioners in natural settings. To the extent possible, practitioners incorporate the approaches into their ongoing work. Third, the project develops training and support materials to be used in implementation, local adaptation, and refinement of the approaches. Fourth, in order to develop new methodological approaches that are conceptually sound and of practical utility, much needs to be known about the nature of evaluation practice. Consequently, the project also carries on a parallel line of research on the nature of evaluation practice as it naturally occurs.

A sample of project reports will give the reader an idea of the range of the work now being pursued. Most of these reports will appear soon in scholarly journals or in the books mentioned earlier.

- Metaphor Adaptation Report: Investigative Journalism
- Techniques for the Geographic Analysis of Evaluation Data
- Poetry Criticism as a Perspective for Education Evaluation
- Philosophy as a Metaphor for Evaluation
- Law as a Metaphor for Evaluation
- Educational Evaluation: Adaptations from Geography
- Painting as an Evaluation Metaphor
- Architecture as a Metaphor for Evaluation
- Phenomenology, Multiple Realities, and Educational Evaluation
- Committee Hearings as an Evaluation Format
- Evaluation Case Histories as a Parallel to Legal Case Histories
- Metaevaluation: Alternative Perspectives
- Product Evaluation
- Educational Evaluation Through Operations Research
- Photography as an Evaluation Technique
- Casebook on Cost Analysis in Educational Evaluation
- Educational Evaluation and the Creation of Stories
- The Use of Exploratory Data Analysis in Educational Evaluation
- The Evaluation Document: Philosophic Structure
- Some Contributions of General Systems Theory, Cybernetics Theory, and Management Control Theory to Evaluation Theory and Practice
- Conceiving and Representing: Their Implications for Educational Evaluation

In this project, we have adopted the position that, in order to improve evaluation practice, information on methodological alternatives should be based, first, on experience, not on value preferences of individual evaluators; second, on public trials of the methods, not on private studies, where little is known about the actual conduct of the evaluation; and, third, on a variety of settings, so the robustness and general applicability of methods can be assessed. Isolated uses of a new method can be suggestive, but they do not provide the breadth of experience needed adequately to assess the utility of a given evaluation approach. One of the purposes of this project is, therefore, to provide information on alternative evaluation methods of this type. There are, of course, a variety of ways in which such information is gathered in the field of evaluation (Smith, 1979).

There are differences in the nature of the methodological development work when it is conducted not as the private research of an individual investigator but as part of a funded, programmatic research effort. Much of the private research already mentioned is individual activity pursued by researchers because of their own interests, under an indefinite time line and usually with limited resources. As a funded programmatic effort, our project's activities tend to be somewhat more formal and systematic; they group activities that are heavily client-centered, clearly time-bound, and supported by ample resources.

We attempt to maintain a heavy practitioner flavor in our effort, from initial conceptual development through field testing. Our work is aimed not only at devising new methods and testing their utility but also at fostering the adaptation of suitable approaches in SEA and LEA settings. The literature on educational innovation (for example, Berman and McLoughlin, 1975; Cheever, Neill, and Quinn, 1976; Fullan and Pomfret, 1975) suggests that, in order to maximize the adaptation of these new methods, the method development and test work should be conducted in conjunction with practitioners where there is a locally felt need, an inside advocate, a problem orientation, attention to adaptation to the local setting, and early phase-out of external support. We attempt, therefore, to maintain close contact not only with specialists in such fields as journalism, sociology, and art but with a large number of evaluation practitioners in state departments and local districts. The need to understand the context of evaluation practice as seen by the daily practitioner has led us to parallel research on the nature of evaluation practice. There is not space here to elaborate on our research efforts in this area, so it must suffice to say that we are using such procedures as surveys, participant observation, case studies, and self-report studies by evaluation practitioners in order to identify and document the nature of evaluation practice.

Contributions to Improved Evaluation

What advances are being made in evaluation as a result of the work on new methods being conducted by the Research on Evaluation Program? One definite outcome is an expanded view of evaluation method. The project is uncovering a wide range of new tools for use in evaluation, and it is increasing the scope of problems that can be addressed in evaluation studies. New conceptual distinctions of relevance in evaluation are also being discovered.

The sample of these new contributions to evaluation theory and practice reported here can only suggest some of the many avenues opening for the elaboration and improvement of evaluation in education.

New Techniques and Operational Procedures

This section samples the techniques and procedures identified in other fields that have been considered for application to educational evaluation. This list should serve to give the reader an idea of the range and nature of alternatives now possible in evaluation.

Social Area Analysis and Trend Surface Analysis. Epidemiologists and geologists use similar procedures (social area analysis and trend surface analysis, respectively) to map spatial relations among phenomena of interest. For example, by mapping the incidence of a certain disease on a map of a metropolitan area, an epidemiologist can study the relationships between that disease and such factors as transportation patterns, location of medical facilities, and characteristics of the citizen population. Upon reflection, it is clear that many problems in the evaluation of educational programs are basically geographic in nature. For example, how do we know that remedial resources are located in areas of greatest need? What is the relationship between local school district compliance with state regulations and the district's proximity to the state office? What is the relationship between the location of the teacher's residence and his or her commitment to the community life of the local school? How can school boundaries be set to minimize student transportation time? These educational questions could be addressed in evaluations through the use of classic procedures employed by epidemiologists, geologists, and geographers.

Concept Analysis. Philosophers spend much of their time analyzing concepts. Through the use of clear cases, contrary cases, and borderline cases, they can clarify the meaning of an important concept in order to state clearly what counts as an example of that concept. Many evaluations could benefit from the use of such techniques to clarify the basic foci of their efforts. In evaluating a special education program, for example, evaluators need to be clear on many questions before they can conduct the evaluation. They need to be able to say what they mean by "remedial" reading, what they can take to be a clear case of a "disadvantaged" individual, what they mean when they describe an individual as "gifted," and what they mean by "effective" instruction. Greater conceptual clarity through the use of procedures commonly employed by philosophers could greatly sharpen the precision of evaluation thought.

Legal Histories. Lawyers sometimes produce legal histories of important state and federal legislation. Through the study of legislative drafts, transcribed testimony, proposals, bills, committee hearings, and reports, the purpose and meaning of the legislation can be clarified. Legislative histories are used to limit the scope of application of a law or to impose limitations on the meanings of particular words thought to be ambiguous. These histories also enable lawyers to make interpretations in light of the social conditions extant at the time when the legislation was produced. Much evaluation in education is, in fact, mandated through legislation, and evaluators' use of legislative histories might clarify the nature of the educational program being evaluated and illuminate the intent of the legislators who required it to be evaluated. Through the creation and study of legislative histories, evaluators would be better able to deduce appropriate evaluative criteria that were responsive to the intent of the legislators.

Document Tracking. Journalists use various procedures to take advantage of documented evidence in building a story. For example, journalists who know how things normally work can deduce what types of physical records or documents have to be produced in order to accomplish a given financial or legal transaction. Having a suspicion about what has occurred, the journalist can then search for evidence of its occurrence in the appropriate documentation. Similarly, evaluators can use existing educational records systems to investigate such issues as the handling of truancy or vandalism problems within the school, to evaluate the adequacy of counseling services, or to track the flow of educational personnel within a large school system. Journalists rely extensively on existing documentation and interview data to construct a story, and these two sources of evidence are often overlooked by educational evaluators.

Procedures Rehearsal. Some artists engage in extensive procedural rehearsal before painting. This is particularly true in watercolor painting, where a mistake cannot be easily rectified. Before beginning to paint, watercolorists will often mentally walk through each step, identifying what brush to use, how much to wet the paper, which pigments to apply in what order, and so on, rehearsing each procedure until they have all procedures clearly in mind. Some evaluations would profit if evaluators mentally rehearsed each step, looking for barriers, anticipating problems, considering contingencies, and so on. Mental rehearsals of evaluation activities (rather like conceptual pilot tests) can sharpen attention not only to methodological detail but also to possible contingencies in the evaluation setting.

Structural Analysis. Some critics of poetry, film, and literature use techniques of structural analysis that enable them better to understand how the piece achieves its artistic end. They study how the form and content of the piece relate to its function and impact. Using such procedures as tagmemics to analyze the themes of a story, a critic can show how its structure enables it to achieve its desired impact. Meta-evaluation can apply the procedures of structural analysis to analyze the nature of evaluative reports. These procedures can be used to study the way in which the selection of a topic, the organization of the material, and the use of discursive language, numerical data, and visual aids contribute to the effective transmission of evaluative information.

Modeling. Operational research methods, such as decision theory, cueing theory, and simulations, are used to model industrial phenomena in order to increase the chances of producing the desired conditions and outputs. These procedures can be used in education to address such problems as allocating instructional resources, addressing the adequacy of student scheduling procedure, and evaluating the impact of competing teacher assignment strategies.

New Concepts and Distinctions for Evaluation

A number of concepts or distinctions used in other disciplines might prove of use in educational evaluation. Here is a sample:

Minimum/Maximum Projections. In planning investigative studies, journalists often make minimum/maximum projections, in which they indicate to their editors what, at a minimum, they will be able to deliver and what, if all goes well, the maximum outcome of their efforts will be. Since investigative journalism is a risky and expensive business, such projections allow editors more easily to weigh the payoffs against the costs of investigative studies. If similar distinctions were used in evaluation, evaluators could think in terms not of a single study but of a sequence of activities leading to a final evaluative "story." Giv-

90

ing minimum/maximum projections would allow the evaluator greater operational flexibility, while it would increase the evaluation funder's control over the level of investment.

Fit. In evaluating structures, architects make judgments about architectural fit. By considering the purpose of the structure, the materials employed, the nature of the setting, and the constraints upon materials design and location, architects assess how well the structure meets the requirements of the situation. Similarly, in doing metaevaluation, evaluators might consider not only the methodological adequacy of the evaluation study but its fit to the context. That is, how well do the design, results, presentation, and basic construction of the evaluation fit the socioeducational context, resources, and situational constraints within which the study was conducted? With this model, metaevaluators could make an overall assessment of the adequacy of the evaluation to its purpose, time, and setting—a broader form of review than the conventional methodological critique.

Levels of Evidence. In law, different levels of evidence are required, depending upon the nature of the case. For example, preponderant evidence may be sufficient in an administrative hearing, but conclusive evidence is required in a criminal trial. In evaluation, however, most discussions of method seem to imply that conclusive evidence is always required in all settings. Evaluators may wish to consider the conditions under which less than conclusive evidence would be a sufficient basis for the decisions or actions of educational decision makers.

Fairness. While scientists are persistently concerned with objectivity in their work, journalists are more concerned with fairness. Journalists who do not believe that objectivity is possible in their work take steps to ensure that all sides of an issue are fairly presented and that each position is adequately heard. Perhaps evaluators should be concerned more with the fairness of their procedures rather than with the objectivity of their procedures, particularly in evaluations of broad and complex social and educational programs that reflect multiple viewpoints.

Satisficing. Geographers have noted that certain decisions are based not upon optimizing conditions but on obtaining satisfactory resolution of competing conditions. Thus, they suggest that individuals' behavior is better described as "satisficing" than as "optimizing." Individuals engage in nonoptimal behavior because of differences in goals, differences in their level of knowledge, and differences in their aversion to personal risk and uncertainty. Educational evaluations are often based on the assumption that optimizing all beneficial conditions is the ideal solution. Perhaps evaluators ought to recognize that individuals do not always seek optimal conditions but sometimes settle for satisfactory conditions. Such a view has implications for the evaluative criteria used in evaluation studies.

Compelling the Eye. Artists are concerned about keeping the viewer's attention inside the boundaries of a painting. If, for example, the perspective of a wharf leads the viewer's eye out of the painting, the painter may construct a heavy pier at one side to stop the visual flow and insert a few seagulls overhead to redirect the viewer's eye back to the point of prime interest. Similarly, evaluation reports might seek to compel the reader's mind to focus on one primary message. All secondary messages, data, and examples would reinforce and lead the reader back to the primary topic of the report. This heuristic suggests that nothing which does not relate directly to the prime topic would be included in the report, a condition not prevalent in most of today's evaluation reports, which accumulate marginally relevant statistical data.

These are just a few of the many new procedures and conceptual distinctions that are emerging from our work on new evaluation methods. This work promises to greatly expand our conception of evaluation.

Future Prospects

What can contribution of this effort to the improvement of evaluation theory and practice be expected to be? In considering this question, let us think about the ways in which methodological innovations take place. Many factors influence whether a methodological innovation is accepted and implemented well enough to change the nature of practice. Holton (1973) reminds us of ways in which strong personalities in a field can alter methodological habit. Kuhn (1970) has, of course, told us a great deal about the social nature of methodological innovation. Evaluation practitioners are already very familiar with the ways in which political and legal factors influence the methods used; consider, for example, how state legislatures mandate the use of criterion-referenced rather than norm-referenced tests in state assessment efforts and the ways in which the Office of Education has prescribed statistical models to be used in evaluation of Title I programs. It is clear, therefore, that whether a particular innovation influences practice depends to a great extent on factors other than the conceptual and empirical evidence concerning its quality. Basically, whether the work produced by this project will have significant effect on evaluation theory and practice is an empirical question.

As discussed earlier, there is considerable interest and support at this time for the development and use of alternative approaches in evaluation. The work of this project is broadening the range of alternatives available, and it is collecting some of the conceptual and empirical evidence needed to make reasoned selections of methods. A small part of the work of the project is devoted to the study of methodological development itself. It is our intention to use our experience to provide support to evaluators in LEAs and SEAs that will enable them to develop and refine their own methods. Perhaps the greatest benefit that can come from this work is not the replacement of one traditional method by another but a change in the basic point of view concerning evaluation methods. I hope that a wide range of methods continues to be developed and that refinement in evaluation practice is continuing. As practitioners become increasingly familiar with these approaches, they should be in a better position to reject standard techniques that are irrelevant to their purposes and select the best method for the situation from among the alternative approaches. It is likely that the work of this project will have some influence on the nature of evaluation theory. Indeed, one must reconsider what is even meant by the term *evaluation* when so many methods are available for performing it. Recognition of the several varieties of important social service possible under the general heading of evaluation should lead to greater tolerance for intellectual variety in educational evaluation.

References

Berman, P., and McLoughlin, M. W. *Federal Programs Supporting Educational Change.* Vol. IV: *The Findings in Review.* Santa Monica, Calif.: Rand Corporation, 1975.

Boruch, R. F., and Rinkskopf, D. "On Randomized Experiments, Approximations to Experiments, and Data Analysis." In L. Rutman (Ed.), *Evaluation of Research Methods: A Basic Guide.* Beverly Hills, Calif.: Sage, 1977.

Campbell, D. T., and Boruch, R. F. "Making the Case for Randomized Assignment to Treatments by Considering the Alternatives: Six Ways in Which Quasi-Experimental Evaluations in Compensatory Education Tend to Underestimate Effects." In C. A. Bennet and A. A. Lumisdaine (Eds.), *Evaluation and Experiment: Some Critical Issues in Assessing Social Programs.* New York: Academic Press, 1975.

Caulley, D. N., and Smith, N. L. "Field Assessment Survey." Research on Evaluation Program Paper and Report Series, No. 10. Portland, Ore.: Northwest Regional Educational Laboratory, 1978.

Caulley, D. N., and Smith, N. L. "Program Evaluation in State Departments of Education." *Evaluation News,* Winter, 1980, pp. 37–38.

Cheever, J., Neill, S. B., and Quinn, J. *Transferring Success.* San Francisco: Far West Laboratory for Educational Research and Development, 1976.

Cook, T. D., Cook, F. L., and Mark, M. M. "Randomized and Quasi-Experimental Designs in Evaluation Research: An Introduction." In L. Rutman (Ed.), *Evaluation Research Methods: A Basic Guide.* Beverly Hills, Calif.: Sage, 1977.

Cooley, W. W., and Lohnes, P. R. *Evaluation Research in Education.* New York: Irvington, 1976.

Eisner, E. W. *The Educational Imagination: On the Design and Evaluation of School Programs.* New York: Macmillan, 1979.

Fullan, M., and Pomfret, A. *Review of Research on Curriculum Implementation.* Ontario, Canada: Ontario Institute for Studies in Education, 1975.

Gilbert, J. P., Light, R. J., and Mosteller, F. "Assessing Social Innovations: An Empirical Base for Policy." In C. A. Bennet and A. A. Lumsdaine (Eds.), *Evaluation and Experiment: Some Critical Issues in Assessing Social Programs.* New York: Academic Press, 1975.

Guba, E. G. *Toward a Methodology of Naturalistic Inquiry in Educational Evaluation.* Monograph Series in Evaluation, No. 8. Los Angeles: Center for the Study of Evaluation, University of California, 1978.

Holley, F. M. "Changing Primary Evaluation Clients." Paper presented at the annual meeting of the American Educational Research Association, Toronto, Canada, March 1978.

Holley, F. M., and Lee, A. "The Real World of Public School Evaluation." Paper presented at the annual meeting of the American Educational Research Association, New York, April 1977.

Holton, G. *Thematic Origins of Scientific Thought: Kepler to Einstein.* Cambridge, Mass.: Harvard University Press, 1973.

House, E. R. *Evaluating with Validity.* Beverly Hills, Calif.: Sage, 1980.

Kuhn, T. S. *The Structure of Scientific Revolutions.* Chicago: University of Chicago Press, 1970.

Law, A. "The Need for New Approaches in State Level Evaluations." Paper prepared for the Northwest Regional Educational Laboratory, Portland, Ore., 1980.

Lyon, C., Doscher, L., McGranahan, P., and Williams, R. *Evaluation and School Districts.* Los Angeles, Calif.: Center for the Study of Evaluation, University of California, 1978.

Lyon, C. "New Perspectives on School District Research and Evaluation." In *What Do We Know About Teaching and Learning in Urban Schools?* Vol. 9. St. Louis: CEMREL, Inc., 1979.

McKenna, B. "Critical Needs for Research and Development in Evaluation: Holism Versus Partialism." Public testimony given at the annual meeting of the American Educational Research Association, Boston, April 1980.

Northwest Regional Educational Laboratory. *Regional Needs Survey Results.* Portland, Ore.: Northwest Regional Educational Laboratory, 1980.

Parlett, M., and Hamilton, D. "Evaluation as Illumination: A New Approach to the Study of Innovative Programs." In G. V. Glass (Ed.), *Evaluation Studies Review Annual.* Vol. 1. Beverly Hills, Calif.: Sage, 1976.

Polemeni, A. *The Politics of Evaluation.* New York: Office of Educational Evaluation, Board of Education of the City of New York, undated.

Smith, N. L. "Requirements for a Discipline of Evaluation." *Studies in Educational Evaluation,* 1979, *5,* 5-12.

Smith, N. L. "Federal Research on Evaluation Methods in Health, Criminal Justice, and the Military." *Educational Evaluation and Policy Analysis,* 1980a, *2* (4), 53-59.

Smith, N. L. "The Programmatic Development of New Methods in Educational Evaluation." Research on Evaluation Program Paper and Report Series, No. 45. Portland, Ore.: Northwest Regional Educational Laboratory, 1980b.

Smith, N. L. (Ed.). *Metaphors for Evaluation: Sources of New Methods.* Beverly Hills, Calif.: Sage, 1981a.

Smith, N. L. (Ed.). *New Techniques for Evaluation.* Beverly Hills, Calif.: Sage, 1981b.

Smith, N. L. "Developing Evaluation Methods." In N. L. Smith (Ed.), *Metaphors for Evaluation: Sources of New Methods.* Beverly Hills, Calif.: Sage, 1981c.

Smith, N. L. "The Context of Evaluation Practice in State Departments of Education." *Educational Evaluation and Policy Analysis,* in press.

Stake, R. E. *Evaluating the Arts in Education.* Columbus, Ohio: Merrill, 1975.

Stenzel, N. "Critical Needs for Research and Development in Evaluation: Mutated or Radical Evolution?" Public testimony given at the annual meeting of the American Educational Research Association, Boston, April 1980.

Stephens, C. E., and Barber, L. "Serving Some Clients of Research and Evaluation Inhibits Serving Others." Paper presented at the annual meeting of the American Educational Research Association, Toronto, Canada, March 1978.

Webster, W. J., and Stufflebeam, D. L. "The State of Theory and Practice in Educational Evaluation in Large Urban School Districts." Paper presented at the annual meeting of the American Educational Research Association, Toronto, Canada, March 1978.

Nick L. Smith, director of the Research on Evaluation Program at the Northwest Regional Educational Laboratory in Portland, Oregon, served as president of the Evaluation Network in 1980. He is the editor of two new books on evaluation methods, Metaphors for Evaluation: Sources of New Methods *and* New Techniques for Evaluation.

Index

Strength, concept of, 28
Structural analysis, technique of, 89
Stufflebeam, D. L., 21, 24, 81, 94
Swenson, N., 74

T

Taube, C. A., 68, 74
Tebbutt, J., 5n
Thompson, B. W., 2, 41–55
Tischler, G. L., 65, 74
Transfer Income Model (TRIM), 42–43, 52
Trend surface analysis, technique of, 87
Trotter, S., 62, 73

U

U.S. Department of Education, service delivery assessment by, 18–19
U.S. Department of Health and Human Services (HHS), Office of Service Delivery Assessment (SDA) of: acceptance of, 21–23; analysis of, 1, 2, 5–24; background of, 5–7; credibility of, 22; data analysis by, 14–16, 20–21; design by, 10–11; dissemination of, 22; impact of, 17–19; issues of, 19–21; preassessment in, 8–10; reporting findings of, 16–17; requirements for, 6–7; sampling procedures of, 11, 13–14, 19; scope of, 21–22; site visits by 13–14, 20; staff for, 12–13, 20; timeliness of, 22; topic assignments in, 7–8; triangulation by, 15–16, 20
U.S. Department of Health, Education, and Welfare, 6–7; Operations Management System of, 68
U.S. Department of Justice (DOJ), 25–40
U.S. General Accounting Office (GAO), 9, 10, 24, 53, 55, 59, 62, 68, 74; evaluation by, 1, 2, 41–53; Institute for Program Evaluation of, 19

U.S. Public Health Service, 68
Updating, for model maintainability, 51
Urban, G. L., 55
Usability, as evaluation criterion, 51–52

V

Validity: of data, 48–49; as evaluation criterion, 47–49; operational, 49; theoretical, 47–48
Value: and change filter, 30–31; estimation of, 30–34; and hidden populations, 31–33
Van Horn, R., 55
Variables, specification of, 27–30
Verification, as evaluation criterion, 49–50
Volkman, E. M., 59, 62, 75

W

Wagenfeld, M., 69, 74
Warren, C. R., 62, 74
Warwick, D. P., 59, 72
Webster, W. J., 81, 94
Weiss, C. H., 55
Werlin, S. H., 63, 73
White, B. F., 68, 74
Williams, R., 93
Windle, C., 2, 5n, 57–75
Woy, J. R., 63, 69, 73, 74
Wurster, C. F., 63, 75

Y

Yale University, clinical judgment research by, 65

Z

Zedlewski, E. W., 68, 75
Zeigler, B. P., 55
Zimlich, N., 18, 24
Zinober, J. W., 67, 75
Zusman, J., 63, 75

Statement of Ownership , Management, and Circulation
(Required by 39 U.S.C. 3685)

1. Title of Publication: New Directions for Program Evaluation. A. Publication number: 449-050. 2. Date of filing: 9/28/79. 3. Frequency of issue: quarterly. A. Number of issues published annually: four. B. Annual subscription price: $30 institutions; $18 individuals. 4. Location of known office of publication: 433 California Street, San Francisco (San Francisco County), California 94104. 5. Location of the headquarters or general business offices of the publishers: 433 California Street, San Francisco (San Francisco County), California 94104. 6. Names and addresses of publisher, editor, and managing editor: publisher—Jossey-Bass Inc., Publishers, 433 California Street, San Francisco, California 94104; editor—Scarvia B. Anderson, ETS, 250 Piedmont Avenue NE, Atlanta, Georgia 30308; managing editor—William Henry, 433 California Street, San Francisco, California 94104. 7. Owner: Jossey-Bass Inc., Publishers, 433 California Street, San Francisco, California 94104. 8. Known bondholders, mortgages, and other security holders owning or holding 1 percent or more of total amount of bonds, mortgages, or other securities: same as No. 7. 10. Extent and nature of circulation: (Note: first number indicates average number of copies of each issue during the preceding 12 months; the second number indicates the actual number of copies published nearest to filing date.) A. Total number of copies printed (net press run): 2982, 3493. B. Paid circulation, 1) Sales through dealers and carriers, street vendors, and counter sales: 85, 40. 2) Mail subscriptions: 1226, 1490. C. Total paid circulation: 1311, 1530. D. Free distribution by mail, carrier, or other means (samples, complimentary, and other free copies): 125, 125. E. Total distribution (sum of C and D): 1436, 1655. F. Copies not distributed, 1) Office use, left over, unaccounted, spoiled after printing: 1546, 1839. 2) Returns from news agents: 0, 0. G. Total (sum of E, F1, and 2—should equal net press run shown in A): 2982, 3494. I certify that the statements made by me above are correct and complete.

JOHN R. WARD
Vice-President

NEW DIRECTIONS
FOR PROGRAM
EVALUATION

Number 8 • 1980

NEW DIRECTIONS FOR PROGRAM EVALUATION

A Quarterly Sourcebook
Scarvia B. Anderson, Editor-in-Chief

Number 8, 1980

Training Program
Evaluators

Lee Sechrest
Guest Editor

Jossey-Bass Inc., Publishers
San Francisco • Washington • London

TRAINING PROGRAM EVALUATORS
New Directions for Program Evaluation
Number 8, 1980
 Lee Sechrest, Guest Editor

New Directions for Program Evaluation (publication number
449-050) is published quarterly by Jossey-Bass Inc., Publishers.
Subscriptions are available at the regular rate for institutions,
libraries, and agencies of $30 for one year. Individuals may
subscribe at the special professional rate of $18 for one year.

Correspondence:
Subscriptions, single-issue orders, change of address notices,
undelivered copies, and other correspondence should be sent to
New Directions Subscriptions, Jossey-Bass Inc., Publishers,
433 California Street, San Francisco, California 94104.
Editorial correspondence should be sent to the Editor-in-Chief,
Scarvia B. Anderson, Educational Testing Service, 3445 Peachtree
Road N.E., Suite 1040, Atlanta, Georgia 30326.

Library of Congress Catalogue Card Number LC 78-73932

International Standard Serial Number ISSN 0164-7989

International Standard Book Number ISBN 87589-855-6

Cover design by Willi Baum

Manufactured in the United States of America

Contents

Editor's Notes

The publication in 1968 of Donald T. Campbell's paper "Reforms as Experiments" would probably be accepted by most persons as a reasonable watershed for the origins of the current interest and movement in evaluation research. Since that time the field, if indeed it is one, has grown rapidly. There are at present two societies, several journals, and many books devoted to evaluation research. Meetings are proliferating so that there are special conferences, sections within conventions, and local arrangements beyond counting—all having to do in some way with program evaluation. All these phenomena are occurring within or affecting not only several traditional academic disciplines such as psychology, sociology, and political science, but also many subject matter fields such as education, health care, and criminal justice. They are also occurring within all levels of government, in private industry, foundations, educational institutions, and so on.

Psychology has certainly been the central discipline within the evaluation research movement, but quite a few other disciplines have also been involved from the early stages. More recently, however, professionals are appearing who are not so easily identified as belonging to any particular academic discipline, nor, in some cases, even to any distinct subject matter area. These persons are variously termed evaluators, program evaluators, and evaluation researchers, but it is their Shane-like character of tough, no-nonsense "guns for hire" that is notable. Is this the direction for the future? Are we to have specialists in evaluation who lack any other identity or will we, and should we, continue to have workers for whom evaluation research is only one of their tools, only a part of their identity?

Training for evaluation research is of even more recent origin than the field itself and is understandably inchoate. Whatever we do, it will grow and evolve, but it may be that its growth can be directed and forced if we exert our efforts. If we are wise, we can send growth in directions that will be in the best interests of society. The chapters in this volume concern the training of evaluation researchers; hence they address issues fundamental to the growth of evaluation research as a field or as an activity. The perspectives represented are diverse. Contributors include persons whose professional identities much antedate the field and a recent graduate of a training program; those whose major identity is that of evaluation researcher and those for whom evaluation research is only a part of professional identity; those who train and those who ultimately use the services that evaluation researchers supply.

The diversity of views guarantees that the writers will not agree completely; yet neither is there the type or level of disagreement that would justify despair at ever concurring on the critical features of evaluation research training programs. My personal hope is that these chapters will forward the discussion even if they do not produce resolutions.

Lee Sechrest
Guest Editor

Lee Sechrest is professor of psychology at
Florida State University.

Should evaluation research move toward the status of an independent field or discipline or should it be nurtured as a subspecialty within academic and problem areas? Since the field is new, it may be too early to settle on any single model for training.

Evaluation Researchers: Disciplinary Training and Identity

Lee Sechrest

Apparently evaluation research is a growth industry. As is usually true of such industries, the growth is only partially constrained, it proceeds in directions determined more by historical accident than by intent, and it is more than a bit unpredictable. Scientists, academicians, and professionals are usually not happy with such a state of affairs, having, in general, a substantial preference for more rational, incremental, and planned development. Consequently, not long after it became evident that evaluation research might eventually constitute a field or area of activity and that at least some students should be trained for that activity, evaluation researchers already in the field began to be concerned about what was appropriate training and what the field might eventually become. Obviously, the early workers were groping in the dark. This writer, one of those early in the field, is reminded of a probably apocryphal story about a psychoanalyst who claimed to have had 1,000 hours of training analysis from an analyst who had had 300 hours of analysis from one who had none at all. Those of us who were first in the field had no training in evaluation research and nothing to guide us but our general methodological training and our intuition. That worked for a while, but now pressing questions are beginning to be asked: Is there a common core of evaluation research knowledge? What is the appropriate professional identity for evaluation researchers? What is the training required to achieve that identity? Where will that training be best obtained?

Is Evaluation Research a Profession?

As others have noted (Anderson and Ball, 1978) there are divergent views about the status and appropriate training of evaluation researchers. Some say that evaluation research is a job, and, therefore, that training should be "on the job"; others say that evaluation research is a profession, and, therefore, that training should be formal, following the professional model. Nearly everyone now would probably agree that evaluation research is some of both; the differences in opinion arise over the proportions. Anderson and Ball (1978) surveyed sixty-four evaluation research "experts"—that is, senior persons in the field, almost none of whom had been formally trained in evaluation research—and received forty-four replies (a response rate of 69 percent, better than most surveys). In general, the respondents seemed to lean toward a professional model for training. However, when ideas about specific evaluation research capacities were examined, the view was somewhat more refined. Some requirements for evaluation research involve fairly well-defined, technical skills—for example, research design and statistical analysis—and there was a fair amount of consensus that these skills are best acquired through formal training. Other evaluation research requirements center more on issues of outlook and style, and there was similar consensus that these characteristics may be more dependably acquired in an actual work setting.

It was perhaps somewhat premature that Anderson and Ball titled their book *The Profession and Practice of Program Evaluation*, since it is still not clear that program evaluation is a profession. Recently, however, Morell and Flaherty (1978) looked at evaluation research from the standpoint of the sociology of occupations, and they noted that evaluation research was developing characteristics typical of a profession: A goodly number of training programs are specifically designated evaluation research training programs. The number of conferences on training in the field is growing. There is an Evaluation Research Society (ERS), which holds an annual meeting. Nor is this a narrowly based special interest group; there are other, somewhat competing and related organizations, such as the Evaluation Network and the Association for Applied Behavioral Science. An interest in establishing some sort of minimal standards for the practice of evaluation research, that is, for certification of evaluation researchers has emerged. There is growing concern for ethics, manifested, for example, by the chapter that Anderson and Ball devote to that issue, and the ERS committe on ethics. And, finally, that there is growing concern for professional standards with respect to quality of performance is manifested by, among other things, the draft *Standards for evaluations of educational programs, projects, and materials* developed by the Joint Committee on Standards for Educational Evaluation (1978). It seems clear that evaluation research has developed at least some of the characteristics of a profession, but it may still be too soon to tell what it will eventually be like. There is a saying that "if it walks like a duck and it talks like a duck, it probably is a duck." However, this is not to say that it is easy to tell from looking at a baby duck just what it will grow up to be.

Evaluation Research as a Professional Specialty

It is not necessarily the case that evaluation research *must* become a separate profession simply because it looks a little bit like one at the beginning. As an alternative, evaluation research might develop as a professional specialty cutting across but mostly lying within other identifiable disciplines. Thus, there would be psychologist evaluation researchers, economist evaluation researchers, and medical evaluation researchers, to name only these. What would link these diverse groups together would be a common interest in and recognition of the necessity for high quality evaluations of social interventions, knowledge of basic evaluation research methods, commitment to objectivity, and the like. Perhaps good models for such a profession do not as yet exist, but the idea is not without precedent. For example, use of the term *mental health workers* is not uncommon as a generic designator, though this ignores the fact that several different disciplines—professions, if you must—are subsumed under that title. Similarly, one encounters references to *health care professionals*, which implies a shared interest that cuts across disciplinary lines. On the face of it, there is no obvious reason why the term *evaluation researchers* could not be used to designate a group of professionals in different disciplines who share a core of common interests. What discipline or professional area does *not* need evaluators?

In this writer's view, the present heterodoxy in evaluation research training is most reassuring. We are much too young a profession—or specialty, if you will—to settle on a single model or even a few models. We can do for a while with some chaos while we test a variety of approaches and ideas. It would be a mistake to foreclose on a single track program for training evaluation researchers. We do not know, for example, which mix of problem area content and methodology is best, nor whether the mix is the same for all areas; how much of what kind of quantitative training should be given (see Fienberg, in this volume); or what emphasis should be placed on the political aspects of evaluation. Consequently, each training effort is, in some sense, a quasi-experiment for testing ideas about training.

Most other professions did develop in the seemingly haphazard way advocated here. There was never anything like a standard medical training curriculum in this country until the famous Flexner report of 1910, which recommended that a scientifically based curriculum be provided in universities. Until very recently, training in law was provided by a wide diversity of proprietary, part-time, correspondence, and even nonschool programs, which had very little standardization. Evaluation research should be able to tolerate some ambiguity until recommendations can be based on something other than intuition. To quote one of the more rigorous and demanding evaluators of recent history, "Let a hundred flowers bloom!"

One potentially invaluable source of information—feedback from graduates of our training programs as they go out into the field (see Brown, in this volume)—should soon be available. We might benefit from an extension of the Anderson and Ball study (1978) to recently trained evaluators actively plying their trade. Feedback would be helpful if it were systematic.

Despite the advantages of diversity, some realities seem likely to force those training evaluation researchers to develop a fairly standard model. One obstacle seems to this writer almost certain to force evaluation research training into the mold of a specialty within disciplines. That is, there is simply too much for one person to learn for the nondiscipline-based evaluation research professional model to be feasible. Already the methodology of evaluation research is extremely diverse and wide-ranging, it is often highly technical, and it is growing by leaps and bounds. The survey by Anderson and Ball (1978), which recorded what present experts thought evaluation researchers ought to know, is highly instructive in this regard. Thirty (that is, two thirds) of the 44 respondents listed the following as essential content areas and skills: descriptive statistics, inferential statistics, statistical analysis, quasi-experimental design, experimental design, data preparation and reduction, correlation and regression methods, survey methods, major literature and reference sources useful for evaluators, method of controlling quality of data collection and analysis, sampling application of interviews, questionnaires, ratings, alternative models for program evaluation, psychometrics, professional and ethical sensitivity, and expository skills. Almost every other content area or skill imaginable was regarded as desirable, if not essential (Anderson and Ball, 1978, pp. 172–173).

Why should so many skills be required? The answer undoubtedly lies in the fact that the demands of evaluation research are so diverse and unpredictable. The requirements may change drastically from one evaluation project to the next; for example, the same evaluator may be asked on one job to understand a fairly small-scale randomized experiment with a clear-cut behavioral outcome measure and on the next to confront a large-scale quasi-experiment, which, if the evaluator is lucky, involves a pre- and post- community survey, necessitating analysis by structural equations to be related in the end to a cost-benefit analysis. Without some disciplinary boundaries and in the face of demands for virtual omniscience, the ultimate responses of most evaluators would be variable, unpredictable, and almost certainly inadequate.

Disciplinary boundaries are likely to place at least some limits on the extent of expected knowledge, since various academic and professional disciplines have both content and method specialties. In the interests of preserving reason, it is probably best for those specialties to be maintained for the most part. Thus, psychologists have specialized in research design, statistical analysis of experimental data, measurement, and behavioral measures. Sociologists have specialized in survey methods, pioneered the techniques of path analysis, and developed highly sophisticated sampling procedures for community studies. Economists, physicians, and political scientists have all developed their own areas of expertise. I do not advocate that disciplinary boundaries should be preserved in any absolute way, only that they should be normative; that is, that disciplinary boundaries should provide general expectations about what persons within each discipline should know.

Another reason for favoring training within disciplines is that theory is often the weakest feature in an evaluation enterprise. Time after time, those whose job it is to evaluate a project find that there is little if any explicit theoretical rationale for the intervention, for the design that is to be employed, for the measures that are to be obtained, or for the temporal arrangements of interventions and measures. To cite just one example, in evaluations of police interventions it is not uncommon to find that crime rates are used to assess outcomes, although there is no imaginable way in which the intervention under study could deter the crime, as in studies of the effects of police patrols on crimes occurring indoors. Methodology alone may possess too few tools for conceptual analysis to be maximally effective in planning and structuring evaluations. Persons trained within a discipline can bring their own theoretical constructs to bear on problems. Those theoretical constructs may not be the right ones, but at the very least, if their purpose can gain attention, they are likely to force some theoretical and conceptual issues to be clarified.

By bringing another conceptual slant to bear on the problem and its proposed solution, the person grounded in a discipline may also help those involved in a program to foresee the potential negative effects of the intervention. Although it is only a hypothesis, this writer suggests that, while the potential positive effects of an intervention are likely to be seen by those who devise a program, the potential negative effects are more likely to be seen by those who approach the problem from a different conceptual perspective. Consider, for instance, the advocacy of intestinal bypass surgery as a way of controlling obesity. Those who viewed the problem from a perspective other than that of obesity control per se would seem to be more likely to anticipate the possible effects of such surgery in other areas of life, such as interpersonal functioning. Neill and others (1978) reported on a number of cases of intestinal bypass surgery. In every case, weight loss occurred, but in every case, the weight loss produced serious marital problems. Perhaps a psychologist or a sociologist with an interest in family problems could have foreseen this side effect of the surgical procedures, certainly, they would have a better chance of foreseeing it than a methodologically astute but atheoretical research methodologist.

The Fish Scale Model of Omniscience

It is the contention of this writer that most evaluations of programs of any size and complexity will require the talents and viewpoints of a multidisciplinary team. Neither the broadgauged individual evaluator nor the single discipline team is likely to be adequate to the task of evaluating more than the simplest of interventions. The critical task, then, becomes one of needs assessment: what skills and viewpoints are likely to be needed in order to accomplish a complete and interpretable evaluation? Obviously, after these needs are assessed an appropriate and effective team must be assembled. The evaluators who compose this team must have been socialized to their task in such a way that they understand and can communicate with one another; each must be sympathetic to the others' roles and they all must be prepared to share responsibility.

The concept of the "Renaissance man" is familiar enough although it is seldom exemplified. Clearly, the idea of a person who knows almost everything was considerably more meaningful, if not literally tenable, when there was much less to know. Even in a field as circumscribed as program evaluation, the notion that one could actually know everything that there is to know seems incredible. Therefore, if we are to envision the kind of knowledge and wisdom that is required for adequate planning and implementation of evaluation research, we will need a different model. It has already been suggested that a team provides a reasonable model.

Some time back, Donald T. Campbell (1969) noted the improbability of achieving what he termed the "Leonardesque aspiration" of broad competence in science. Campbell suggested that the route to "omniscience" was likely to be through shared, rather than individual, wisdom, and he suggested fish scales as an appropriate metaphor for shared wisdom. Though no one fish scale covers very much, by their overlapping the fish scales cover the entire fish. Campbell contrasted the overlapping of fish scales with the ordinary state of affairs in disciplinarized science, where there are clusters of persons who share a common core of knowledge and gaps—often large ones—between those cores. Campbell went on to propose that we should attempt to produce fish scales in our training programs and foster that type of overlapping knowledge in our own professional and academic activities. Thus, the basic core of psychology would be that which enables psychologists to have a sense of shared identity and to converse at a basic level; beyond that core, each psychologist should be trained to relate to some other field or specialty or problem area.

Projected onto evaluation research, the fish scale model suggests that each person should have both some sense of disciplinary identity and, in addition, a competence enabling that person to work with members of some other field. What is envisioned by this model is a large set of workers who, by reason of their overlapping competencies, can evaluate the entire universe of social interventions. The finding by Pelz and Andrews (1976) is relevant here; according to these researchers, organizations that were most effective in solving problems were characterized by a good bit of "dithering," which occurs when members of an organization agree on goals but disagree on the means of accomplishing them.

The fish scale model may appear risky, for it clearly anticipates that even for those in the same discipline the amount of overlapping knowledge will be limited. Campbell was very serious in posing the fish scale model. He believed that one should avoid reading the same journals, attending the same meetings, and involving oneself in the same projects as colleagues in one's own discipline. He believed that the sum of knowledge would be increased if colleagues shared with each other the knowledge that they acquired in their separate intellectual pursuits. He also believed that the definition of disciplinary lines is arbitrary and that individual scholars might, in effect, create their own unique "discipline" at the boundary between two classically defined disciplines. Thus, for example, it might be possible to create the specialty of "econopsychologist" or "psychoeconomist" by acquiring the knowledge and methodological skills necessary to operate in the area between those two disciplines. George Katona, to name one person, did something of that sort. Such a person could very well not know some of the economics that most economists knew—for example, econometrics—and some of the psychology that most psychologists knew—for example, psychophysiology. Similarly, such a person could very well not know all the methods customarily employed in both fields, but this person would know the methods required to function in the interstice.

Thus, a fish scale evaluator would be a person sufficiently well-grounded in one traditional discipline and its methods to be able to relate to other colleagues in that discipline and to deal with its major problems and at the same time sufficiently at home in another field to be aware of its problems and to be able to communicate with those functioning in that field; this person would thus be prepared to bring the concepts and methods of the academic discipline to bear on the applied field. For example, a psychologist working in police research would bring to that problem area various measurement skills and perspectives, concepts relevant to officer performance, and skills in research design and statistical analysis. A sociologist involved in the same research would contribute concepts useful in understanding the interface between the police and the community they serve, such methodological skills as survey research, and such statistical skills as path analysis or multiple contingency table analysis.

To train fish scale evaluators, those firmly grounded in and committed to traditional academic disciplines will probably have to relax their rules a bit, become a bit more tolerant of those who do not possess all of the traditional knowledge, and become comfortable with students whose commitment to that discipline is only partial. This may be asking a lot. Those responsible for such training will have to encourage students to develop subspecialties within other disciplines or fields; this may require them to sacrifice some control over students.

Learning to Learn

Though this writer subscribes in general to the fish scale model for training, there is one limitation on most training models that is severe. We usually do not have the foggiest idea what a student will be doing in the long run. This limitation is particularly troublesome if the number of jobs open to trainees is so limited that a student has to be ready to take whatever is available, and it is even more so when the field itself is in a state of flux. Both these conditions seem currently to prevail in the field of evaluation. We may painstakingly train a student to work in criminal justice evaluations—providing that student with a background in a discipline such as sociology, training in relevant statistical and design techniques, and experience in criminal justice research—only for the student to discover that there are no criminal justice jobs available when he or she graduates or that there are no jobs available in a part of the country that is geographically desirable.

Some time ago, the concept of learning to learn was introduced in psychology; this concept held that under the proper conditions, organisms, including humans, could be trained to become increasingly adept at solving new problems. We need to develop that capacity in our evaluation research trainees. Ideally, an evaluation researcher should get better and better at adapting to new problem areas, so that instead of becoming a narrow specialist in one particular field, the experienced evaluator would display increasing efficiency in dealing with problem areas never before encountered.

The goal of an all purpose evaluator may seem to resemble the ideal of the Renaissance man that we have already rejected. However, it is not that the evaluator should know everything but that what is known should become increasingly applicable to whatever problems are faced. Surely the problems encountered in different fields cannot be so diverse that concepts and methods are not transferable. It has been the writer's experience that the basic problems are very much alike, whether one is engaged in health research, for example, or in police research. These problems include difficulties in defining and measuring variables, in providing for control over delivery of treatment and in assessing the manner in which treatment is delivered, in developing appropriate comparison groups, and in selecting statistical analyses which are optimal for the data set in light of the particular questions posed. What seems to differ is the terms in which these problems are talked about, and, perhaps, their order of priority. But once one has learned to ask whether a particular intervention will be accepted by the physicians who must implement it, it becomes natural to ask whether an intervention will be accepted and implemented by the police officers who are to be involved. Somehow, we need to train students not to regard themselves as fully "educated" or "trained" by the time they receive their degrees, but as embarked on a process of education that does not end until they stop functioning altogether. One way to achieve this end may be to get students involved early on in a variety of projects, or at least in more than one.

One of the potential advantages of the fish scale model is that it may make it slightly easier to get students—and even their teachers—to accept the limits of their competence. Since the fish scale model relieves them of the obligation to know everything in their own primary field, it may be easier for them to admit even broader limitations on competence. Under the fish scale model, the well-trained person will either rely on others for missing expertise or undertake a self-training effort to acquire some specific competence. The humbling knowledge that one does not know everything, particularly if accompanied by the firm confidence that one at least knows something, may make it easier for the fish scale evaluator to work cooperatively, perhaps as a member of an evaluation team.

The Consulting Role

In the writer's experience, one of the commonest functions for an evaluation research specialist is that of consultant, which is also, however, one of the functions probably least anticipated in the training of students. The consulting role is a rather special one, since it is very apt to be limited with respect to time, involvement, and responsibility; yet it can be absolutely critical to the success of a project. The one aspect of the consulting role that is not much limited is the range of the problems and content areas that are brought to the attention of the consultant. Especially when functioning more or less as a pure methodologist, the evaluation consultant may be involved in almost any content area imaginable. This writer, for example, has consulted on projects involving police operations, health education, early childhood education, nutrition, bilingual education, leadership effectiveness training, psychotherapy outcome research, teenage contraception clinics, remedial reading, juvenile delinquency, mental health services, management of diabetic conditions, and emergency medical services. This list is only partial, but it well illustrates the diversity of problems that an evaluation research specialist may confront.

There are a number of characteristics which seem necessary if one is to function effectively as a consultant, especially across diverse problem areas. It is not clear that all the characteristics required can easily be acquired in training; some of them may be a matter of personal style. This is not the place to develop an exhaustive list of characteristics desirable in a consultant, but three may be mentioned as potential goals of training: flexibility, tolerance, and ability to learn.

It should be fairly obvious that a substantial degree of intellectual flexibility is required if one is going to consult as a methodological generalist. One must be able to shift modes of discourse, relate to a wide variety of persons with diverse interests, and move readily from one problem to another. It may be difficult to train persons in the flexibility that effective consulting requires but if training is to be accomplished, it seems likely that it should begin early and that students should be urged to involve themselves in a wide variety of problems.

Sophisticated—that is, truly useful—evaluation research consultants regularly find themselves dealing with methodologically unschooled professionals and administrators working in problem areas whose methodologies scarcely deserve even the label. Some evaluation researchers seem to find it difficult to unbend sufficiently to understand the problems and outlook of client groups and to begin from where they are. It is terribly tempting to recommend a sophisticated randomized experiment with impeccable measures, and then to sigh with disgust in the face of protests that the plan is utterly unfeasible. Effective consultants must have considerable tolerance for the muck and mire of the real world and the beleaguered folks who work in it. Again, it is not clear that tolerance can easily be taught; however, if it is to be taught, the process must begin early. One can only recommend, then, that students should be involved from the beginning with the kinds of problems and people that they will eventually have to deal with.

Finally, an effective consultant has the capacity to listen carefully and thoughtfully to clients, other professionals, other consultants, and a great many other persons from whom something may be learned. As observed by this writer, the ineffective consultants seem to have a fairly standard set of recommendations, which they make on a moment's notice to anyone with a problem. Effective consultants are those who are willing to listen to others until they are confident they have a genuine understanding of the problem and the role that each participant is to play in solving it.

They are able to listen to the views of others even if those views differ diametrically from their own, because in a successful evaluation almost all views may eventually need to be accommodated. Once more, it seems that to the extent that training can be successful, an early exposure to diverse experience and views provides the best beginning.

Specialized Knowledge Within Problem Areas

It should not be inferred from the preceding discussion that the writer believes that almost any evaluator can move into any problem area and begin to function effectively after acquiring little more than a few new vocabulary terms. Different problem areas have important knowledge requirements, which are not always easily acquired. For example, different problem areas are associated with quite different types of data, and different types of data have problems of their own. Most data on crimes, for example, are likely to be quite unstable, because standards for reporting crimes are so variable and because reporting is so easily influenced by transient local policies. Officially recorded causes of death often bear little relationship to the actual reasons for death. Data on health problems may not be available at appropriate and useful levels of aggregation, and so on. Because diverse problem areas require specialized knowledge, it is usually important that evaluations be team efforts.

How effectively an evaluator can function without an existing familiarity with a problem area will obviously depend upon the complexity of the problem for which help is sought, what specifically is required of the evaluator, and the extent and intensity of involvement which will be possible. Not all problem areas are so highly technical or unduly complicated that a well-informed outsider cannot fit right in with no problems. Involvement in a program designed to increase car pooling for workers at a large industry should not require a great deal of initial preparation, since no very specialized knowledge is involved. However, it might take a great deal of time to become able to participate usefully in an evaluation of intervention to improve quality of life for patients in end-stage renal disease. In some instances, the advice or other help required from a given evaluation researcher may be so limited or specific that no great knowledge of the field is required—for example, advice on designing the sample for a survey. Even if a field is complex and specialized, an otherwise well-prepared evaluator should be able to become an effective team member if the time frame for the project permits a gradual integration of staff. There are probably few problem areas that are so complex that an intelligent, well-trained evaluation researcher could not learn enough in a few weeks' time to comprehend the problems and contribute to their solution. In this writer's experience, if evaluation researchers have the traits of flexibility, tolerance, and willingness to listen, and if those traits are accompanied by lively inelligence and sufficient energy, there is little justification for excluding that person from an evaluation team for want of prior experience in the problem area.

Quantitative and Qualitative Knowing

As will be evident from the chapters by Boruch and Reis, Wortman, Cordray, and Reis and Fienberg in this volume, evaluation is likely to be a highly quantitative enterprise. Of necessity, many of the decisions that have to be made about programs and other social interventions will be quantitative in nature. Moreover, the variety of quantitative data and processes that may be encountered in perusing the evaluation literature is truly formidable: survey data, experimental data, archival data, observational data; correlational analysis, categorical data analysis, multivariate analysis; and so on. All these data are collected and analyzed in particular ways so as to permit us to know, or to think that we know, something. Usually, that knowing ends up being expressed in some simplified binary form, such as larger or smaller, more or less. (Sometimes it ends up being expressed in the even simpler, if less satisfying, form of "we can't tell.") Accordingly, quantitative knowing is of great importance, and training for evaluation research must include preparation for producing such quantitative knowledge.

However, as Campbell (1974) has made so clear, another kind of knowledge also has great importance for the evaluation researcher—namely, qualitative knowledge. The value of qualitative knowledge is more apparent in process evaluation than in outcome evaluation, but without knowledge of process, outcome often has little meaning. Issues of process in intervention studies can generally be distilled into the separate but related questions of the inherent capacity of the intervention to produce change and the degree to which the planned intervention was actually implemented. These issues have been referred to as strength of treatment and integrity of treatment (Sechrest and Redner, 1979). Qualitative knowledge most often bears on questions of strength of treatment or integrity of treatment. Thus, for example, if one knows that an intervention was carried out by relatively untrained persons it may be unjustified to suppose that the intervention should have worked, because the treatment may not have been strong enough to produce the intended effect. And if one knows that attendance at treatment sessions was often poor, one may doubt whether the integrity of the treatment was maintained and, again, whether it should be expected to have had any effect. Similarly, if one knows that participants in a program, whether they are the providers or the recipients of services, had negative or otherwise pessimistic attitudes toward the program, one has important information with which to adjust one's interpretations of outcome findings.

In order to make accurate, fully informative evaluations of program effectiveness, then, it is necessary to have complete information, much of it qualitative, on the nature and conditions under which the intervention was implemented. Those who are training evaluators seem to be failing, since the kind of information that is needed is very rarely included in evaluation reports. Reviewing studies of rehabilitation of criminal offenders, Sechrest and Redner (1979) noted that treatments were so cursorily described that it was difficult to know what they consist of, let alone what would have to be done to replicate them. Little attention is paid to issues of program integrity, and it is rare to find that the attitudes of program participants were assessed. Similar concerns about reports of group treatments of juvenile offenders have been voiced by Julian and Kilmann (1979), but the problems extend well beyond the area of offender rehabilitation, for in a series of reviews Kilmann and his colleagues have noted deficiencies in reports on the effectiveness of student counseling groups (Henry and Kilmann, 1979), treatments for sexual deviations (Kilmann, Gearing, and others, in press), treatments for sexual dysfunctions (Kilmann and Auerbach, 1979), and the use of nonprofessional therapists in treatment of mental and behavioral disorders (Kilmann, Scovern, and others, in press). Without question, deficiencies in the reporting of qualitative data about social interventions are widespread.

Even when sufficient qualitative data to make judgments about program strength and integrity are provided, the picture is not encouraging. Quay's analysis (1977) of a widely cited study of the effectiveness of group counseling for prison inmates (Kassebaum, Ward, and Wilner, 1971) showed clearly that the treatment as planned was woefully weak, and that as delivered it may have been virtually nonexistent. Wortman and St. Pierre (1977) analyzed the well-known Alum Rock School Voucher program, and their account shows that as finally achieved the intervention was of a very limited nature, scarcely resembling the school voucher program as conceived. Evidently, training programs for evaluation researchers should pay systematic attention to the need for qualitative data on programs and to ways in which such data may be produced.

Again, it may take further development of the concept of the evaluation team to meet this need. As Campbell (1974) suggests, not everyone may be equally comfortable with qualitative data or equally adept at producing it. There is probably much to be said for encouraging evaluation researchers, like other professionals, to concentrate on the things that they do best. This may well mean that more use should be made in evaluation research efforts of members whose discipline has made them well-versed in the traditions of qualitative research; for example, anthropologists and sociologists are accustomed to the role of participant observer. Those of a more quantitative bent must be trained to recognize the contributions of the qualitative researchers and to work closely with them. At the very least, all evaluation researchers must be trained to recognize the necessity for documenting the processes of program design and delivery. Again, the best recommendation would be that preparation for that recognition should begin early and involve practical interdisciplinary experience.

Utilization-Based Evaluation Research

Patton (1978) has called attention to the desirability of building the utilization of evaluation directly into the very evaluation research scheme. Although it is no simple task to say just what utilization means—for example, if the effects of a program are judged to be too limited to justify the political risks of implementing the program, are the outcome findings "unutilized"?—it is obvious that the intent of program evaluation is some impact on decision making and policy. It then follows that training in evaluation research should include training in research that has some potential for utilization. Unfortunately, the fact of the matter is that we know very little about the kind of research that has potential for utilization, let alone how to train others to do it. There are at least two interesting facets to the problem, however, and both merit attention as research problems in their own right.

The first facet of the utilization problem involves the question whether there are more and less persuasive ways of answering a research problem within the same constraints of cost and scientific integrity. To put it another way, the issue is whether there are trade-offs in the ways of doing research that result in research with the same net scientific integrity but with differential credibility as a basis for policy recommendations. For example, consider the following possible research strategy alternatives:

- A single-site, carefully managed project versus a multiple-site, more loosely managed project;
- A large experimental effect on a few program recipients versus a small experimental effect on many program recipients;
- A single relevant outcome measure on many respondents versus several relevant outcome measures on a few respondents;
- A small, tightly controlled experiment versus a larger, less well-controlled experiment.

In fact, we do not know which of the strategies may be the best generally, let alone in any one specific case. However, it may be possible to do research on the question. Sechrest and others (in press) attempted to study the value of such various strategies in persuading hospital administrators to work for implementation of new programs, but the results were largely inconclusive, because the hospital administrators were so unsophisticated about research that they could not respond effectively to the task given to them and because most of them had already made up their minds about the research questions and seemed impervious to the evidence with which they were presented.

The second facet of the problem of increasing the potential for utilization of research involves the most effective ways of presenting research findings. On the one hand, articles written for one's scientific colleagues are likely to be unintelligible to a lay audience. On the other hand, articles written for lay audiences may be decried by other scientists as misleading and oversimplified. The problem is how to present findings in such a way that both scientific and lay audiences will reach the same conclusions about the findings and their interpretation. Imagine, for example, the task of presenting the findings from a three-way ANOVA table with some significant main effects and interactions so that a lay audience would draw the same conclusions as a statistician. It is clear that this task is a difficult one.

To this writer's knowledge neither of these issues is much addressed by evaluation research training. There is little on these issues in the evaluation literature. Yet each issue is certainly researchable and each is in need of research. As yet we do not have a great deal to offer in the way of definitive training on these issues: the best that we could do, in all probability, would be to awaken students to the potential importance of these issues and to urge that both be carefully considered in the planning and conduct of evaluations. At the very least, potential utilizers of the evaluation should be consulted during the planning of the research; after the research is completed, understanding of the findings could be investigated.

Training the Research Utilizer

In the early 1970s, this writer participated with colleagues at Northwestern University in the development of a summer training program in evaluation research methodology, to be directed at persons already in the field and doing evaluations (Sechrest, 1973). This program was funded by NIMH. The original proposal had involved a dual program in which each evaluator's "boss," presumed to be a decision maker, was to receive a short but intensive training designed to produce understanding of the nature of scientific program evaluation, of the findings that such evaluations could produce, and of their implications in relation to program design, development, and implementation. This part of the proposed training program was not funded. It might have been a good idea.

As a result of this writer's experience with hospital administrators and hospital medical directors, he concluded that hospital administrators had to receive some training in how to understand research and research outcomes if they were to become effective utilizers of research findings. Along with Ayres D'Costa, the writer prepared a document, under the auspices of the Association of University Programs in Health Administration, that was meant to be incorporated into training programs for health administrators. Unfortunately, AUPHA was never able to publish the social science materials of which the evaluation research document was a part, so another opportunity to educate decision makers was lost. A third effort at educating potential utilizers occurred when the writer organized a conference on research on emergency medical services; that conference did produce a document addressed to decision makers (Sechrest, 1978).

The writer continues to believe that much is to be gained by involving potential evaluation research utilizers in training programs. They would not be expected to delve into all the intricacies of research methodology and management. However, they would profit from training designed to show them why and how a scientific evaluation needs to be done, how research findings emerge, and how they are interpreted. To the extent possible, training programs should allow research trainees to work directly with administrators for whom the work would be likely to have practical meaning. Not only would research trainees develop a better understanding of how to do research with potentially maximized impact but they would also have an opportunity to provide indirect training to the administrators. The payoff could be substantial.

Evaluation Research Training: Some Recommendations

Until a persuasive alternative plan is developed and tested, evaluation research training should remain based in the various disciplines for which evaluation services are most needed (for example, education and health) and from which the most substantial methodological contributions are likely to come (for example, psychology, sociology, and statistics).

From the very beginning, evaluation research trainees should be provided with diverse experiences with respect to problem areas and with a conceptual framework permitting them to construe the similarities and differences between those areas.

Students wishing to acquire special expertise as evaluation researchers should acquire a core of knowledge, particularly related to basic theoretical and methodological concepts within their discipline, but they should also be encouraged to acquire related knowledge in other disciplines or problem areas, even at the sacrifice of breadth of knowledge in their own disciplines.

Formal academic training must be relied upon to produce the desirable breadth of outlook and to foster interdisciplinary and interproblem involvement. The self-interests of eventual employers are likely to make on-the-job training more narrowing.

Evaluation research training cannot be accomplished in vacuo, and it will be necessary for those who do the training to be directly involved in doing evaluation research themselves. Only in that way will they have the interests and contacts required to ensure the appropriate experiences for their students.

Until we are all certain that we know what we are doing, we should not promote a single model for evaluation training. Let us, collectively, experiment with a variety of models and learn from our shared experiences.

However, to the extent that what is proposed in this paper may be taken as a model for evaluation research training, it should be disregarded altogether by those who think they have a better way of doing the job.

References

Anderson, S. B., and Ball, S. *The Profession and Practice of Program Evaluation.* San Francisco: Jossey-Bass, 1978.

Campbell, D. T. "Ethnocentrism of Disciplines and the Fish Scale Model of Omniscience." In M. Sherif and C. W. Sherif (Eds.), *Interdisciplinary Relationships in the Social Sciences.* Chicago: Aldine, 1969.

Campbell, D. T. "Qualitative Knowing in Action Research." Kurt Lewin Memorial Address, Society for the Psychological Study of Social Issues, meeting with American Psychological Association Annual Convention, New Orleans, September, 1974.

Henry, S. E., and Kilmann, P. R. "Studies of Counseling Groups in Senior High School Settings: An Evaluation of Outcome." *Journal of School Psychology,* 1979, *17,* 27-46.

Joint Committee on Standards for Educational Evaluation. *Standards for Evaluations of Educational Programs, Projects, and Materials.* Draft report. American Educational Research Association, 1978.

Julian, A., and Kilmann, P. R. "Group Treatment of Juvenile Delinquents: A Review of the Outcome Literature." *International Journal of Group Psychotherapy,* 1979, *29,* 3-37.

Kassebaum, G., Ward, D. A., and Wilner, D. M. *Prison Treatment and Parole Survival.* New York: Wiley, 1971.

Kilmann, P. R., and Auerbach, R. R. "Treatments of Premature Ejaculation and Psychogenic Impotence: A Critical Review of the Literature." *Archives of Sex Behavior,* 1979, *8,* 81-100.

Kilmann, P. R., Gearing, M., and others. *The Treatment of Sex Deviations: A Review of the Literature.* In press.

Kilmann, P. R., Scovern, A., and others. "The Effect of Nonprofessional Therapists: A Review of the Outcome Research." *Journal of Community Psychology,* in press.

Morell, J. A., and Flaherty, E. W. "The Development of Evaluation as a Profession: Current Status and Predictions." *Journal of Evaluation and Program Planning,* 1978, *1,* 11-17.

Neill, J. R., and others. "Marital Changes After Intestinal Bypass Surgery." *Journal of the American Medical Association,* 1978, *240,* 447-450.

Patton, M. Q. *Utilization-Focused Evaluation.* Beverly Hills, Calif.: Sage, 1978.

Pelz, D. C., and Andrews, F. M. *Scientists in Organizations.* (Rev. ed.) Ann Arbor, Mich.: Institute for Social Research, 1976.

Quay, H. C. "The Three Faces of Evaluation: What Can Be Expected to Work." *Criminal Justice and Behavior,* 1977, *4,* 341-354.

Sechrest, L. "Training in Evaluation Research: Development of a Program." Paper presented at American Psychological Association Annual Convention, 1973.

Sechrest, L. (Ed.). *Emergency Medical Services: Research Methodology.* NCHSR Research Proceedings Series, DHEW Publication No. (PHS) 78-3195. Washington, D.C.: Department of Health, Education and Welfare, 1978.

Sechrest, L., and others. "Use of Research in Policy Decisions." *Medical Care,* in press.

Sechrest, L., and Redner, R. "Strength and Integrity of Treatments in Evaluation Reports." In L. Sechrest, S. G. West, and others (Eds.), *Evaluation Studies Review Annual.* Vol. 4. Beverly Hills, Calif.: Sage, 1979.

Wortman, P., and St. Pierre, R. G. "The Educational Voucher Demonstration: A Secondary Analysis." *Education and Urban Society,* 1977, *9,* 492–571.

Lee Sechrest is professor of psychology at Florida State University.

*Given the broad scope of research methodology, what
should a realistic training program require?*

Training for Evaluation
Research: Some Issues

Paul M. Wortman
David S. Cordray
Janet Reis

Training programs in the social sciences have proliferated during the last
two decades. In psychology, for example, departments have expanded from
general experimental (that is, learning and perception) to include programs in social, developmental, and quantitative methods. A notable feature of this evolution in the social sciences is the growing interest in
applied work, specifically in program evaluation. In fact, the shift in
attitudes toward program evaluation has been so dramatic as to warrant a
relabeling of the specialty: no longer is it a "miscellaneous" career opportunity but an official alternative to an academic career (Woods, 1976). The
reasons for the coming of age of evaluation research and its accompanying
training programs stem from a number of sources.

  This brief historical introduction will outline some important
factors behind the promotion of evaluation activities. It will not attempt to

Development of this paper has been supported by NIMH Methodology and
Evaluation Research Training Grant No. 1-T32-MH 15113-01.

unravel the complex causal network underpinning the growth of the field, nor is its exposition of influential factors complete. The intent is to place evaluation research and methodology programs within a historical context as a basis for comments on existing programs and suggestions for future developments. While evaluation is a multidisciplinary activity, its roots lie largely in psychology. Thus the perspective will be largely a psychological one.

The origins of program evaluation can perhaps be traced to one of the oldest motives known to humankind, the desire to build a better society for the benefit and enjoyment of its citizens. In psychology, the origins date back to Lewin's writing on "action research" (1946) involving research for social change. Interest in program evaluation was accelerated during the 1960s by the national experience with planned social change. The nation's grappling with the problems identified by the Great Society and its legislative successors has revealed in expensive detail just how large and complex those social problems are (Aaron, 1978). Despite large expenditures of money, high hopes, and good will, our society remains racially segregated, environmentally polluted, and beset with the economically contradictory events of high unemployment and high inflation. The apparent ineffectiveness of social programs combined with shrinking government purchasing and spending power has led to demands for conscientious monitoring of program efficacy. The popular call for auditing of proposed societal solutions has been reflected in and augmented by work of proponents of an "experimenting society" (Campbell, 1969, 1971) that consciously evaluates major ameliorative social programs.

Psychologists have been at the forefront of this activity. Motivated both by an interest in moving away from their "vigorously irrelevant past" (Caplan and Nelson, 1973) and by the development of appropriate methodologies (Campbell and Stanley, 1966), one group advocated involvement with work having social utility. Criticisms within the profession prompting change toward greater utility have been directed at the perceived imbalance between the scientific acceptability and the social utility of different investigatory methods. The priorities associated with these two factors are now often reversed for the two most common modes of investigation, controlled laboratory studies and field research. Many young professionals now prefer methodologically messy but more immediately relevant applied work.

Another factor in the rise of evaluation research, derived in part from those noted above, is changes in the job market for Ph.D.s. Since this discussion focuses on training programs aimed at preparing students to enter the job market, the condition of that market for psychologists merits mention. The issue of job openings in psychology translates immediately for most professionals into opportunities within the academic sector which raises some interesting questions about graduate school socialization. The possibilities that young people have today of obtaining positions in institutions of higher learning are remote. Economic analyses of the demand-supply dynamics of the academic labor market show that doctorate production is expected to peak between 1981 and 1985, at the very time when academic employment is projected to be at its lowest level in several decades. As a result, a new Ph.D. has an estimated 20 percent probability of securing an academic position during the 1980s. This figure represents a 15 percent drop from the late 1970s. Demographic trends have converged to produce a large number of doctoral candidates but a smaller undergraduate cohort group, high material expectations, enrollment-driven academic budgets, and graduate student-driven academic departments. This situation appears to preclude an amicable or easy passage through the Ph.D. surplus period (Cartter, 1976). Senior faculty are likely to continue to draw young people into the academic arena because of the need for students to fill their classrooms and research assistants to staff their laboratories.

Growing interest in applied social science research as an alternative to academic careers is reflected not only in the establishment of new training programs but also in the proliferation of new journals and the establishment of new professional organizations. New journals include this *New Directions* quarterly, *Evaluation Quarterly* (Sage), *Evaluation and Program Planning* (Pergamon), and *Evaluation* (Minneapolis Medical Research Foundation). Three new professional groups have also emerged (Evaluation Network, Evaluation Research Society, and Council on Applied Social Research) to meet the needs of the discipline (Riecken and Boruch, 1978). Given this shift into applied areas such as program evaluation, it is important to consider those components of graduate training that are necessary to produce competent evaluators.

Graduate Training in Evaluation Research

Sechrest (1976) makes a persuasive case that owing to a scientifically based research tradition, psychology is particularly well suited for training program evaluation personnel. The emphasis placed on experimental research methodology, quantitative analysis, and operationalization of behavior via multiple measures/methods is cited as cogent to the evaluation enterprise. Nevertheless, Robert Sommer (1977), a psychologist at the University of California, Davis, has remarked of recent graduates of his program who entered the evaluation marketplace that "almost without exception these students have complained that they received little in their graduate training to prepare them for this sort of activity [evaluation]" (p. 1).

It is not that the training received in graduate departments is of little value to those who assume evaluation research positions, but that training needs to be tailored to the needs of the evaluation discipline. Thus, we sympathize both with Sechrest's position and the students referred to by

Sommer. While the scientific—that is to say, the experimental— perspec tive instilled in graduate programs provides a useful framework from which to judge the quality of empirically derived knowledge, utilization of these principles in evaluation requires attention to the feasibility, appropriateness, and comprehensiveness of these methods. The following discussion will address the questions of what type and what form of graduate training should be provided to prepare an individual to become an evaluation researcher.

Thinking about what types and forms of training would prepare an individual to cope with the technical and practical requirements of evaluation, brings to mind a number of questions about *what* evaluation research is and *how* it should be conducted. At present, there is not a consensus among experts in the field on the answers to these questions (Cronbach, 1977). We endorse Campbell's (1969) emphasis on rigorous assessment of the impact of social innovations. Graduate training should focus on the acquisition of rigorous methodological skills and emphasize continual assessment of the validity of causal inference derived from the application of specific design strategies. This experimental orientation provides the basic foundation upon which evaluation research training can be built. Counterbalancing this obvious need to emphasize training aimed at high-quality (that is, valid) evaluation research is open acknowledgement by leaders in the field of the constraints imposed by political considerations operating in the evaluation setting. Weiss (1972, p. vii) aptly describes evaluation research as the application of "methods and tools of social research" to an "action context that is intrinsically inhospitable to them." Thus, training in evaluation research should emphasize ways of maximizing the quality of the research effort within the confines of the situation within which it is carried out.

Content of an Evaluation Training Program

Graduate training typically involves the completion of a specified sequence of research courses and the acquisition of research experience. In this regard, training programs in evaluation do not differ from more traditional programs. Where they do differ is with respect to the content of the courses and the settings within which the research experience is obtained.

Research design, quantitative methods, and measurement techniques form the core content of an evaluation research training program. These are not unfamiliar topics, particularly for graduate programs in psychology. An admittedly unsystematic examination of course offerings in graduate catalogues of numerous institutions reveals that one course in research design, one three-course sequence in statistics, and one course in issues in measurement are almost universally required of candidates in such programs. Of course, the adequacy of these courses for training evaluation personnel depends heavily on their content. In the following sections we will describe the course work which seems necessary for training evaluation researchers.

Research Design. Unlike laboratory-based psychological research, where the predominant research design strategy entails some variation of the experimental paradigm (characterized by the random assignment of experimental units to treatment conditions and control over the implementation of treatment), practicing evaluation researchers must have an arsenal of alternative design strategies in their methodological repertoire. While Boruch and his colleagues (Boruch, 1974, 1975; Boruch, McSweeny, and Soderstrom, 1978) have successfully answered critics who claimed that the experiment is infeasible, unethical, limited in scope, and not useful for decision making, there remain numerous research settings where alternative research strategies must be used. For example, quasi-experimental designs (Campbell and Stanley, 1966; Cook and Campbell, 1976, 1979) are said to be "sufficiently probing" to be useful when experimental procedures are not feasible. Indeed, considerable progress has been made in recent years towards the refinement of these strategies. For example, Reichardt (1979) provides a comprehensive discussion of the analysis of nonequivalent control group designs, and McLeary and McCain (1979) provide an equally comprehensive discussion of the analysis of interrupted time-series designs. Both of these general alternatives to the experimental model seem likely to be profitably utilized in the evaluation context. Campbell (1974) strongly recommends the inclusion of qualitative methodologies in evaluation research, not as alternatives to more quantitatively oriented research but as complementary techniques. From a design perspective, the evaluation researcher must take an eclectic perspective, and the training must reflect this orientation.

However, researchers must not only be familiar with these alternative strategies but they must also have a firm understanding of their strengths and weaknesses. Thus, training should not only provide exposure to these alternatives but it should also impart a critical attitude to their application and provide trainees with standards for assessing the quality of the knowledge they derive from use of these methods. Cook and Campbell (1976, 1979) thoroughly explain the rationale behind the application of quasi-experimental strategies in applied settings. The creative use of multiple design strategies within a single study (for example, the patched-up design outlined in Campbell and Stanley, 1966) should also be emphasized. Appreciation of the logic of the research process (that is, systematic assessment of rival explanations) rather than the blind application of techniques quickly demonstrates the relevance of seemingly rigorous designs for practical application in the evaluation research context.

Program Evaluation As a Substantive Area. The sociopolitical context within which evaluation research is conducted also requires formal consideration. This is an area in which traditional research training programs are likely to be deficient. As such, a course which systematically examines the context and the constraints that frequently are imposed by that context is likely to be quite beneficial. The importance of such considerations is aptly described by Muirhead and Wortman (1974), who recount how a well-conceived evaluation design was spoiled by the treatment administrators' motivations for conducting an outside evaluation, severe time constraints, difficulties in obtaining approval for access to comparison groups, and budgetary constraints. This is not an unusual situation. Indeed, Riecken, Boruch, and others (1974) have devoted considerable attention to technical issues, such as management of the research team, execution of the design, and confidentiality, which are pervasive in the evaluation of social interventions. While it is not always clear how one could avoid these difficult issues, they occur with notable frequency in the field, and unless the evaluator is prepared to contend with such facts of life, the quality of the evaluation effort is likely to suffer, and the experience is bound to be disheartening to the evaluator who is not street-wise.

Beyond the implementation of the research methodology, the researcher must acquire familiarity with certain less traditional forms of research. Within a comprehensive evaluation strategy, issues associated with program process monitoring, assessment of program implementation, and specification and operationalization of program goals and objectives need to be considered. Further, such procedures as goal-attainment scaling, cost-benefit analysis, and social-impact assessment may be required or requested by some members of the program constituency. Clearly, adequate preparation for assuming the role of evaluator requires familiarity with issues that are distinctively associated with program evaluation and not likely to appear in traditional discussions of social science research methods.

Quantitative Analysis. As already indicated, a cursory examination of graduate-level course offerings in selected colleges and universities reveals that almost all require a three-course sequence in advanced statistical analysis. Typically, this sequence begins with an examination of the theory and practice of statistical inference, proceeds to an enumeration of the multiple models of analysis of variance and regression/correlation, and concludes with an introduction to multivariate analysis strategies. While much of this material is appropriate and necessary, a practicing evaluator is likely to require additional concentration on the application and interpretation of these procedures. Inasmuch as factorial designs are less prevalent in evaluation research, concentration on an applied, generalizable multiple regression/correlation model seems best suited to the evaluation setting (Cohen and Cohen, 1975). Generalizations to assessment of change (with and without fallible covariates), path analytic strategies, and linear and nonlinear analyses of growth can be derived from this basic material.

In addition to an understanding of the technical details associated with these procedures, effective communication of the meaning of the results obtained from them is an essential component of the evaluation researchers' role (Ricks, 1976). These skills need to be developed as part of the training program.

Measurement Issues. To complement the formal consideration of research design and statistical analysis, there is a need for considered attention to measurement issues. In addition to traditional notions of reliability and validity of response variables, sensitivity of these variables with respect to the treatment and assessment of the treatment, at the macro level of implementation and at the individual level of reception (Boruch and Gomez, 1977), represents a major issue confronting evaluation researchers. Further, following the arguments by Webb, Campbell, and others (1966) favoring multiple operationalism and the use of existing unobtrusive data sources, attention to the identification, assessment, and exploitation of existing data sources could be incorporated into an applied measurement course.

Field Practicum: Methodology and Evaluation Research. The preceding discussion has emphasized the acquisition of an understanding of the nature of the evaluation setting and the technical, methodologically oriented content of courses. However, approaching evaluation research training exclusively from a textbook methodological orientation runs the risk of producing individuals who could be described as methodologically muscle-bound; these individuals would suddenly realize that the training they had received was too academic to be meaningfully and readily applied in their new work setting. While examination of case study materials (Muirhead and Wortman, 1974) can sensitize students to the feasibility and appropriateness of their tools, there is no substitute for the experience gained from hands-on application of research skills in a field setting. This type of experience is a necessary component of the evaluation training program. Within the field practicum, students, under the supervision of an experienced evaluator, should be given an opportunity to become involved with all phases of the evaluation process: planning, negotiation of the strategy, execution of the strategy, and reporting of evaluation findings to the sponsoring agency. Since seeing an evaluation study through to its completion is a time-consuming affair, it is likely that at least one full academic year of part-time commitment will be necessary. Munz (1977) reports success with a "vertical team" approach to providing field experience in evaluation research. With this approach, senior-level students, under the supervision of faculty members, work closely with new students to provide a useful resource within the department and to guarantee continuity of research activities. Other approaches to supervised field training include placing students in government agencies, private foundations and research institutes, or service organizations, an approach similar to the clinical internship provided in clinical psychology programs.

If the field practicum is a required aspect of the graduate training program, the methodologically sophisticated individual will be less likely to experience a sharp discontinuity upon leaving the academic environment to assume the role of evaluation researcher. The experience obtained by students within the field setting serves two additional purposes. First, it provides a means for students to assess those areas where they might want to pursue additional training prior to completion of their academic training. Second, the training program itself can benefit from these experiences if they are used as the basis for decisions regarding expansion and/or alteration of program content.

Training Models

Although the preceding discussion has assumed a traditional predoctoral training model, there is another, pragmatic and problem-oriented approach to the training model. Typically, this involves focused short-term training at the postdoctoral level for practitioners working in applied settings, such as mental health centers, schools, and government agencies, who are directly responsible for social programs and their evaluation. These people need to be taught specific methodological techniques in experimental design, measurement, and statistics that can be applied directly to the program being evaluated. Thus, this is an applied "how-to-do-it" problem-solving approach. This practitioner model is often realized in small workshops of a few days duration held at regional or national conventions. Topics are narrowly focused and covered in some depth. Less often, the scope and duration of the topics are expanded into material sufficient for summer institutes or workshops (Wortman, 1977; Wright, 1977).

Practitioner Model. The focus of the practitioner model is skill training. It is assumed that the participants have a need to know the material as well as having a problem and/or setting in which to apply it. Thus a field research practicum is not appropriate to this type of training. Instead, the emphasis is on a variety of techniques usually based on an analytic method. Table 1 describes the curriculum of a summer institute held at Northwestern University between 1973 and 1977. This summer program in evaluation research consisted of an initial eight-week session at Northwestern and a subsequent year of supervised research at the trainee's work site. An optional second summer at Northwestern was available to those who had made substantial progress in their evaluation projects—progress meriting further staff consultation. The materials appended describe the didactic of the first-year curriculum. This course, which included a computer laboratory in applied statistics, comprised the bulk of the in-

Table 1. Illustrative Syllabus for an Evaluation Research Survey Course

Session	Topic	Reading	Laboratory Topic	Reading
1	Introduction and Overview	Riecken, Boruch, and others (1974, pp. 1–39) Wortman (1975)	Introduction to computing; SPSS	Nie, Hull, and others (1975, pp. 1–34)
2	Validity	Cook and Campbell (1979, pp. 37–94)		
3	Randomization	Campbell and Stanley (1966, pp. 13–34) Boruch (1975a)		
4	Quasi-Experiments (a) Nonequivalent Control Group Designs		Statistical analysis of non-equivalent control group	Cook and Campbell (1976)
5	(b) Time Series	Campbell and Boruch (1975) Cook and Campbell (1976)		
6	(c) Regression-Discontinuity	Riecken, Boruch, and others (1974)		
7	(d) Correlational designs		Time series analysis	Glass, Willson, and Gottman (1975)
8	Combining True and Quasi-experiments	Boruch (1975b)		
9	Measurement	Webb, Campbell, and others (1966, pp. 1–34) Riecken, Boruch, and others (1974, p. 117–151) Boruch and Gomez (1977)		
10	Elements of Testing	Nunnally and Wilson (1975, pp. 227–288)	Cluster analysis approaches to scale construction	Everitt (1976, pp. 1–41)
11	Introduction to Linear Models	Mendenhall (1968, pp. 48–84)		

Table 1 (continued)

Session	Topic	Reading	Laboratory Topic	Reading
12	Competing Methods of Analysis	Campbell and Boruch (1975) Reichardt (1979	Structural equation models	Hilton (1976, Chapter 10)
13	Metaevaluation	Cook and Gruder (1978)		
14	Evaluation as Research	Riecken, Boruch, and others (1974, pp. 153–201)		
15	Politics of Evaluation	Williams and Evans (1969) Riecken, Boruch, and others (1974, p. 203–243)	Multivariate analysis	Harris (1975, pp. 1–30)
16	Formalizing Hypotheses for Evaluation Projects	Gilbert, Light, and Mosteller (1975, pp. 151–159) Cook and Campbell (1976, pp. 223–246)		
17	Confidentiality	Campbell, Boruch, and others (1977) Riecken, Boruch, and others (1974, pp. 245–295)		
18	Cost Analysis	Dorfman (1965, pp. 117–171) Gilbert, Light, and Mosteller (1975, p. 159–168)	Factor analysis	Jöreskog (1969)
19	Goal Attainment Scaling	Kiresuk (1975) Kiresuk and Sherman (1968)		
20	Public Interest in Evaluation	Krause and Howard (1974) Riecken, Boruch, and others (1974, pp. 245–255, 271–277)		
21	Policy Making	Gilbert, Light, and Mosteller (1975, p. 63–80, 111–135, 168–197) Weiss (1973)		
22	Summary: Evaluation Perspective			

struction. In addition, a seminar course focused on the particular problems of the trainees and the staff in conducting field work and other advanced topics in evaluation research.

The material covered in the summer program represents a brief overview for the larger predoctoral program described above and, in fact, for the doctoral program that emerged at Northwestern in 1975. Thus, students were familiarized with basic concepts in quasi-experimental design, measurement, and a variety of statistical approaches useful in program evaluation. The purpose was more informational than instructional; that is, mastery was not the primary objective, although many fellows did pursue and master techniques that were relevant to their needs. Similarly, the program abstracted analytic procedures often studied in more intensive workshops associated with longer programs. However, no familiarity or sophistication was assumed (it was in most of the workshops). In short-term learning situations, the emphasis is most often on detailed mastery of specific techniques, such as maximum-likelihood factor analysis, and the computer programs used to perform them. The trainee is expected to know something about the technique and to have some experience with it.

In retrospect, the best training approaches appear to be either the short, focused workshop experience or the longer research-oriented pre- and postdoctoral training programs now developing. The former is useful for updating and extending skills, on the model of health care professionals who are required to show evidence of continuing education for recertification. The latter model, more traditional in the social sciences, is better suited for acquiring new training.

Research Model. In addition to the usual predoctoral students, postdoctoral fellows can play an important role in evaluation research programs. Not only do they fit in with the realities of current NIMH funding, which is increasingly emphasizing such support, but also with the realities of evaluation research. The conduct of evaluation research is a labor-intensive activity. A "vertical team" composed of a faculty member, a postdoctoral fellow, one or two graduate students, and perhaps even an undergraduate research assistant, provides the manpower necessary for applying the evaluation research principles taught in the classroom to actual program evaluations. Often, these experiences are located within the university. For example, at Northwestern we have been involved in evaluating the effectiveness of the Law School's juvenile assistance clinics, a new integrated science curriculum, and a randomized clinical trial of oxygen therapy for patients with chronic lung disease.

While these and other field work practitioners make possible pragmatic experiences in the conduct of program evaluations, including design and measurement, they do not stress data analysis. In order to satisfy the need for training in data analysis, data sets have been acquired for secondary analysis (see the chapter by Boruch and Reis in this volume). Secondary analysis involves the systematic scrutiny of the elements of a social reform from an experimental or quasi-experimental perspective (Campbell, 1969). The aim of such analysis is to assess the credibility of the findings and to reinterpret them in the least ambiguous manner. This is a useful pedagogical technique, which allows students to develop and apply new, competing methods of analysis that either remove or minimize the bias implicit in conventional approaches. Typically, standard analytic methods, such as analysis of covariance, are applied inappropriately to unusual situations, such as those lacking random assignment to the program, and hence they yield biased estimates of program impact. In addition, the political and fiscal import of a program often demands that analysts with different perspectives examine the data for the sake of more valid conclusions. The sheer size and complexity of some programs suggest that multiple analyses are justified to obtain maximum information for the research and development dollar. Thus, for the past four years, the Northwestern group has conducted a project on secondary analysis (Boruch and Wortman, 1978), which involves doctoral and postdoctoral trainees in the reanalysis of educational data sets (Wortman, Reichardt, and St. Pierre, 1978).

Variations in Evaluation Training: Illustrative Examples

Perloff and Schulberg (1977) cite two papers that claimed to have uncovered between eighty and one hundred formal programs that offered training in evaluation research. The actual number of programs, their disciplinary ties, and the extensiveness of their curriculum is unknown at this time. The Evaluation Research Society (Ross Conner, personal communication) is currently conducting a survey in an attempt to answer these questions. One thing that is clear is that academic programs vary widely in the emphasis, extensiveness, and type of training provided. In general, evaluation programs are either social research oriented or quantitatively based. The former are distinguished by an emphasis on field methodology, whereas the latter have traditionally contributed to the development and refinement of statistical procedures (for example, Stanford's education department). Given recent concerns regarding licensing, standards for evaluation, and the quality of evaluation research, it might be profitable to examine different types of training programs. We would like to introduce a second set of distinctions in addition to the dichotomy described above. That is, some programs make evaluation research a specialization, while social problem oriented programs make evaluation a subspecialty and traditional programs have incorporated evaluation research into their course curriculum. The purpose of these distinctions is to provide a framework for brief descriptions of five graduate programs.

Northwestern University, Department of Psychology, Division of Methodology and Evaluation Research. The general purpose of this program of studies is to provide both pre- and postdoctoral students with an opportunity to acquire substantial skills in experimental and quasi-experimental design, data analysis, methods of measurement, and the field research techniques essential for planning and evaluating social programs. The program emphasizes the methods and conduct of evaluation research. Students take two courses in measurement, two courses in the linear models approach to data analysis in addition to the usual three-course statistics sequence, and a year-long field research practicum. The students are exposed to the design and related courses during their first year. It is not until their second year that they engage in field work.

Given the wide variety of evaluation activities, students are required to complete a six-course minor during their first two years. This not only eliminates the risk of developing methodologically muscle-bound evaluators but also provides them with the substantive competence (Wortman and Muirhead, 1977) necessary for proper evaluation. In order to design and conduct useful evaluations, it is important that evaluation professionals be experts in the particular application area as well. The traditional image of the evaluator as an ex post facto data analyst and salvager of weak designs has been shown to be inappropriate and unworkable. At Northwestern, students are trained to be active participants in prospective program evaluations.

Unlike the program at Northwestern with its major emphasis on training in methodological strategies and in a minor substantive area, the social problem oriented programs reverse this orientation. Each of these programs has as its academic focus a commitment to the examination of substantive issues related to social problems and offers courses relating to evaluation as a minor area of specialization.

University of California-Irvine, Program in Social Ecology. This program represents an interdisciplinary "effort to apply scientific methods to the analysis of a wide range of problems arising out of the complex interaction among persons and their physical and social environment" (University of California-Irvine Bulletin, 1977–1978, p. 221). Graduate training is organized into three broad interest areas: the role of the environment in producing normal and atypical behavior, the role of social control, and the role of the criminal justice system in ameliorating or exacerbating social problems.

Of particular interest to the issue of training for evaluation research is the course work in evaluation research offered through the Irvine program. All candidates for the Ph.D. degree are required to complete a four-quarter sequence in research methodology consisting of one course in research methods, a two-course sequence in advanced statistics, and a course in program evaluation. A course ("Issues in Social Intervention") focusing on assessment and design of interventions is also required. A variety of supplementary courses relevant to evaluation training (for example, an advanced course in evaluation research and courses in ethics and professional issues) and a mechanism for award of academic credits for participation in a field setting are also provided by the program.

Claremont Graduate School, Psychology Department. This program has two major areas of specialization, social/environmental psychology and cognitive psychology, with preparation in three major "career streams." In order of departmental priority, these career streams provide training for field research in the assessment and amelioration of social problems, for science-based professional practice, and for conventional academic careers.

As partial fulfillment of the course work leading to the Ph.D., students are required to complete a sequence of research courses consisting of an introduction to research (with a required research assistantship), a sequence of three advanced statistics courses, and at least one additional course in methodology. The Claremont program has a distinctive approach to specialized research courses in that numerous single-topic half-semester modules are offered. Examples of these modules include computer applications, correlational techniques, applied multiple correlation/regression, statistics for quasi-experiments, psychometric methods, observational analysis, evaluation research (applied and theory), and multivariate analysis. This flexible training format allows the student to become familiar with numerous issues associated with the conduct of applied research. The department's commitment to the value of field experience is reflected in its provision to accept four to twelve units of field placement credit per semester, with a maximum of twenty-four units applicable towards the degree. Further, the recent formation of the Claremont Graduate School Center for Applied Social Research provides an institutional base for providing supervised field research experience.

Two older programs, which represent the best of traditional programs, have an eye open to alternative careers for their students: the graduate program in Measurement Evaluation and Statistical Analysis (MESA) in the Department of Education at the University of Chicago and the graduate program in educational psychology at the State University of New York at Buffalo. These departments are unique in being staffed by well-known faculty remarkable both for their impressive academic credentials and their interest in evaluation. The faculty members' receptiveness toward evaluation projects may stem from their affiliation with education, a field that engaged in evaluations long before evaluation became popular among more straight-laced psychologists.

University of Chicago, MESA program. The philosophical and technical focuses of the MESA program are designed to complement each other. Education is seen as a process of change; students are equipped with quantitative methods of research to study this change. In addition to the acquisition of an understanding of test construction and evaluation, experimental design, and statistics, students are expected to nurture an interest in a substantive area of education of their own choice. The areas are so broadly defined as to cover the full gamut of social science interests. Perhaps in deference to its prestigious academic roots, the official description of career opportunities for MESA graduates is dominated by academic appointments. As mentioned earlier, developments in the job market may serve to increase faculty interest in alternative careers for their students and an increased highlighting of experiences in evaluation. The program's public relations brochure does not indicate its degree of commitment to specialized training in evaluation.

State University of New York, Buffalo, Department of Educational Psychology. This program ranks in the same league of excellence as the MESA program and echoes many of the same themes. Traditional methodological and statistical course work is stressed, as well as interdisciplinary training in the other social science departments. The graduate bulletin does not reflect the prevalent attitude toward evaluation, which is positive. A fair amount of support and interest is offered by the faculty to students interested in developing an expertise in program evaluation.

The training provided by these five programs varies in its extensiveness. The breadth of knowledge of evaluation principles decreases as one moves from specialty programs to traditional programs, although none of the programs described here could be considered deficient in that respect. For purposes of setting standards of evaluation training, it might be useful to recognize that different training programs have different goals; institutions should be encouraged not to oversell programs in their evaluation training if that is not their major mission. Evaluation research is a complex undertaking and superficial training is likely to seriously hamper its future.

Future Directions for Evaluation Research

To provide a summary of the training activities that have evolved over the past decade, we have attempted to specify the origins of contemporary interest in evaluation research, described the type of substantive training necessary for conducting evaluation research, described current modes of training, and provided illustrations of programs that currently provide graduate training in evaluation research. As the field continues to grow and new issues arise, the structure and format of training is likely to require further modifications.

As a research-based, knowledge-generating enterprise, the utility of evaluation research will ultimately depend upon the quality of the information generated by individual evaluation efforts. In this regard, recent discussion has concerned the need to develop standards of conduct for evaluators and standards for assessing the adequacy of training programs. The latter concern has been given legitimacy by the NIMH mandate for the inclusion of an evaluation component in NIMH-sponsored training programs. Further, recent discussions of institutional provisions for ensuring quality control in evaluation have included proposals for eventual certification of individuals as competent evaluation professionals (Anderson, 1978). Given the newness of evaluation research and the interdisciplinary background of its participants, credentialing issues would be extremely difficult to resolve. Therefore, as a quality-control mechanism, licensing and/or professional certification probably fall in the category of long-range strategies for ensuring quality.

Other, short-range solutions to quality control need to be considered. For example, in-house evaluation conducted by the training program staff (Wright, 1977) should be promoted. Feedback from program participants on the usefulness and adequacy of various program components (for example, course work, workshops, field practicum) serves the purpose of ensuring that relevant information is being transmitted. Further, supervised research experience, with feedback to the trainee, can ensure that evaluation principles are properly applied. Both of these forms of internal evaluation mechanism are cited as examples of the responsibility that training programs should assume to ensure that their graduates are competent to perform evaluation research.

Another, more formal mechanism for assessing, and ultimately ensuring, the quality of information generated by evaluation researchers is the use of secondary analysis. Secondary analysis is currently being conducted by government agencies (for example, the General Accounting Office) and by independent evaluation researchers. Reassessment of results through secondary analysis can affirm or refute the primary evaluators' conclusions and serves as a screening device that insulates the potential users from the primary evaluator. While the results of a secondary analysis do not necessarily provide a "seal of approval," such analysis can ensure that contemporary methodological standards, necessary to support a recommendation/conclusion, have been employed.

Given the expense and time required for adequate secondary analysis, competently trained persons who have responsibility for initial data collection and research design will be required if evaluation research is to have its intended impact on the decision-making process. The next few years will undoubtedly see an intensification of interest in the development of standards and guidelines for evaluation research. In addition, decisions regarding organizational jurisdiction over assessment, certification, and recertification of evaluation professionals will have to be considered. As these issues are resolved, they are likely to have considerable impact on the type and form of graduate training that is offered. We have attempted to provide an overview of evaluation training that we believe is both sensitive to practical and technical evaluation issues and of a nature to promote quality evaluation research.

References

Aaron, H. J. *Politics and the Professors: The Great Society in Perspective.* Washington, D.C.: The Brookings Institution, 1978.

Anderson, S. B. "Standards Committee Seeks to Establish Evaluation Guidelines." *Evaluation Research Society Newsletter,* 1978, *2* (2), 4.

Boruch, R. F. "Bibliography: Illustrative Randomized Field Experiments for Program Planning and Evaluation." *Evaluation,* 1974, *2* (1), 83–87.

Boruch, R. F. "Coupling Randomized Experiments and Approximations to Experiments in Social Program Evaluation." *Sociological Methods and Research,* 1975, *4,* 31–53.

Boruch, R. F. "On Common Contentions About Randomized Experiments for Planning and Evaluating Social Programs." In R. F. Boruch and H. W. Riecken (Eds.), *Experimental Testing of Public Policy: The Proceedings of the 1974 Social Science Research Council Conference on Social Experiments.* Boulder, Colo.: Westview Press, 1975a.

Boruch, R. F. "On Common Contentions About Randomized Field Experiments." In R. F. Boruch and H. W. Riecken (Eds.), *Experimental Testing of Public Policy: The Proceedings of the 1974 Social Science Research Council Conference on Social Experiments.* Boulder, Colo.: Westview Press, 1975b.

Boruch, R. F., and Gomez, H. "Sensitivity, Bias, and Theory in Impact Evaluations." *Professional Psychology,* 1977, *8,* 411–434.

Boruch, R. F., McSweeny, A. J., and Soderstrom, E. J. "Randomized Field Experiments for Program Planning, Development, and Evaluation: An Illustrative Bibliography." *Evaluation Quarterly,* 1978, *4* (2), 655–695.

Boruch, R. F., and Wortman, P. M. "An Illustrative Project on Secondary Analysis." In Robert Boruch (Ed.), *New Directions for Program Evaluation: Secondary Analysis,* no 4. San Francisco: Jossey-Bass, 1978.

Campbell, D. T. "Reforms as Experiments." *American Psychologist,* 1969, *24,* 409–429.

Campbell, D. T. "Methods for the Experimenting Society." Paper presented at meeting of American Psychological Association, Washington, D.C., September 1971.

Campbell, D. T. "Qualitative Knowing in Action Research." Kurt Lewin Award Address, Society for the Psychological Study of Social Issues, meeting with the American Psychological Association, New Orleans, September 1974.

Campbell, D. T., and Stanley, J. C. *Experimental and Quasi-Experimental Designs for Research.* Chicago: Rand McNally, 1966.

Caplan, N., and Nelson, S. D. "On Being Useful: The Nature and Consequences of Psychological Research on Social Problems." *American Psychologist,* 1973, *28,* 199–211.

Cartter, A. M. *Ph.D.s and the Academic Labor Market.* New York: McGraw-Hill, 1976.

Cohen, J., and Cohen, P. *Applied Multiple Regressional Correlation Analysis for Behavioral Science.* Hillsdale, N.J.: Lawrence-Erlbaum, 1975.

Cook, T. D., and Campbell, D. T. "The Design and Conduct of Quasi-Experiments and True Experiments in Field Settings." In M. D. Dunnette (Ed.). *Handbook of Industrial and Organizational Research.* Chicago: Rand McNally, 1976.

Cook, T. D., and Campbell, D. T. *The Design and Analysis of Quasi-Experiments for Field Settings*. Chicago: Rand McNally, 1979.

Cronbach, L. J. "Remarks to the New Society." *Evaluation Research Society Newsletter*. 1977, *1* (1), 1–3.

Dorfman, Robert (Ed.). *Measuring Benefits of Government Investments*. Washington: Brookings Institution, 1965.

Everitt, B. *Cluster Analysis*. New York: Wiley, 1976.

Gilbert, J. P., Light, R. J., and Mosteller, R. "Assessing Social Innovations: An Empirical Base for Policy." In C. A. Bennett and A. A. Lumsdaine (Eds.), *Evaluation and Experiment*. New York: Academic Press, 1975.

Glass, G. V., Willson, V. L., and Gottman, J. M. *Design and Analysis of Time-Series Experiments*. Boulder, Colo.: Colorado Associated University Press, 1975.

Harris, R. J. *A Primer of Multivariate Statistics*. New York: Academic Press, 1975.

Hilton, G. T. *Intermediate Politometrics*. New York: Columbia University Press, 1976.

Jöreskog, K. G. "A General Approach to Confirmatory Maximum Likelihood Factor Analysis." *Psychometrika*, 1969, *34*, 183–202.

Kiresuk, T. J., and Sherman, R. E. "Goal Attainment Scaling: A General Method for Evaluating Comprehensive Community Mental Health Programs." *Community Mental Health Journal*, 1967, *4*, 433–435.

Kiresuk, T. J. "Goal Attainment Scaling at a Community Mental Health Center." In W. A. Hargreaves, and others (Eds.), *Resource Materials for Evaluating Community Mental Health Centers*. Part IV. *Evaluating the Effectiveness of Services* Rockville, Md.: National Institute of Mental Health, 1975.

Krause, M. S., and Howard, K. I. *Program Evaluation in the Public Interest: A New Research Methodology*. Evaluation Research Paper No. 4, Evanston, Ill.: Northwestern University, 1974.

Lewin, K. "Action Research and Minority Problems." *Journal of Social Issues*, 1946, *2*, 34–46.

McCleary, R., and McCain, L. J. "The Statistical Analysis of the Simple Interrupted Time-series Quasi-experiment." In T. D. Cook and D. T. Campbell (Eds.). *The Design and Analysis of Quasi-experiments for Field Settings*. Chicago: Rand McNally, 1979.

Mendenhall, W. *Introduction to Linear Models and the Design and Analysis of Experiments*. Belmont, Calif.: Wadsworth, 1968.

Muirhead, S., and Wortman, P. M. *The Death of a Design: A Case Study from the Experimenting Society*. Evaluation Research Series Paper No. 2. Evanston, Ill.: Division of Methodology and Evaluation Research, Northwestern University, 1974.

Munz, D. C. "Evaluative-applied Psychology: A New Career Alternative." Paper presented at annual convention of American Psychological Association, San Francisco, 1977.

Nunnally, J. C., and Wilson, W. H. "Method and Theory for Developing Measures in Evaluation Research." In M. Guttentag & E. Struening (Eds.), *Handbook of Evaluation Research*. Vol. 1. Beverly Hills, Calif.: Sage, 1975.

Perloff, R., and Schulberg, H. C. "Evaluation Training Models and the Search for a Theory." Paper presented at annual convention of American Psychological Association, San Francisco, 1977.

Reichardt, C. S. "The Statistical Analysis of Data from Nonequivalent Group Designs." In T. D. Cook and D. T. Campbell (Eds.). *The Design and Analysis of Quasi-experiments for Field Settings*. Chicago: Rand McNally, 1979 (in press).

Riecken, H. W., and Boruch, R. F. "Social Experiments." *Annual Review of Sociology*, 1978, *4*, 511–532.

Riecken, H.W., Boruch, R. F., and others. *Social Experimentation: A Method for Planning and Evaluating Social Intervention.* New York: Academic Press, 1874.

Ricks, F. A. "Training Program Evaluators." *Professional Psychology.* 1976, 7, 339–343.

Sechrest, L. "The Psychologist as Program Evaluator." In P. J. Woods (Ed.), *Career Opportunities for Psychologists: Expanding and Emerging Areas.* Washington, D.C.: American Psychological Association, 1976.

Sommer, R. "No, Not Research, I Said Evaluation!" *American Psychological Association Monitor,* 1977, *8*, 1, 11.

Webb, E. J., Campbell, D. T., and others. *Unobtrusive Measures: Nonreactive Research in Social Sciences.* Chicago: Rand McNally, 1966.

Weiss, C. W. *Evaluation Research.* Englewood Cliffs, N.J.: Prentice-Hall, 1972.

Weiss, C. H. "Where Politics and Evaluation Research Meet." *Evaluation,* 1973, *1*, 37–45.

Williams, W., and Evans, J. W. "The Politics of Evaluation: The Case of Head Start." *Annals of the American Academy of Political and Social Sciences,* 1969, *385*, 118–132.

Woods, P. J. (Ed.). *Career Opportunities for Psychologists: Expanding and Emerging Areas.* Washington, D.C.: American Psychological Association, 1976.

Wortman, P. M. "Evaluation Research: A Psychological Perspective." *American Psychologist,* 1975, *30*, 562–575.

Wortman, P. M. "Evaluation Research: New Training Programs for New Careers." *Professional Psychology,* 1977, *8*, 361–367.

Wortman, P. M., and Muirhead, R. S. "Toward the Proper Conduct of Social Program Evaluation." *Evaluation,* 1977, *4*, 189–192.

Wortman, P. M., Reichardt, C. S., and St. Pierre, R. G. "The First Year of the Educational Voucher Demonstration: A Secondary Analysis of Student Achievement Test Scores." *Evaluation Quarterly,* 1978, *2*, 193–214.

Wright, S. R. "The First Two Years of the Summer Institute in Evaluation Research." *Evaluation Quarterly,* 1977, *1* (1), 183–187.

*Paul M. Wortman is a program director in the
Center for Research in the Utilization of
Scientific Knowledge, Institute of Social Research,
University of Michigan.*

*David S. Cordray is an assistant professor in the
Division of Methodology and Evaluation,
Department of Psychology, Northwestern University.*

*Janet Reis is a research associate in the
Center for Health Services Research and
Policy, Northwestern University.*

Administering research and overseeing evaluation researchers make evident the critical role that attitudes and outlook play in comparison to sheer technical skill.

Training Evaluators of Social Experiments and Social Programs

Joseph H. Lewis

The question is often asked, "Are good evaluators born or made?" Even those who believe strongly that the important characteristics of good evaluators are born to them usually agree that there is also an element of making as well, since evaluators need some degree of quantitative skill, which can only be acquired. The question then becomes, "Given that some training is required, what should it be and how should it be done?" This article sets out some views on this second question.

First, it must be said that there is insufficient experience and practically no relevant data upon which to base a demonstrably right answer. Obviously, then, an answer must be an expression of opinion. It follows that the reader has a right to know enough about the writer's background to be able to discount the prejudice which no doubt colors his views.

In the very early 1940s, before the United States was officially at war with the Axis powers in World War II, civilian scientists working with the U.S. Navy to help it respond to the technological challenges presented by Nazi magnetic and acoustic mines and by Nazi U-boats were impressed by the initial applications of what was just beginning to be called operational research. By 1942, three different operational research groups had been formed in Naval Headquarters in Washington, and the writer, an electrical engineer with an advanced degree in economics and business administration (minor in psychology) who had been engaged in designing and building experimental floating power plants for deperming naval vessels and merchant ships, was asked to become a charter member of one of them.

This group was headed by a physicist. Other charter members were a mathematician, from academe, and a geophysicist, from a major oil company. As the U.S. mobilized its resources for war, more civilians from a variety of backgrounds joined the group, which merged with another. Obviously, none of its members had been trained in operational research, and no one had time to ask whether it was a science, an art, or a craft or, indeed, whether it was an "it" or a "they." Only later, in the middle 1950s, did such questions figure in the agenda for national and international meetings of practitioners. (By that time, the U.S. contingent had decided, after much earnest argument among themselves and with their British counterparts, to call it operations research; while the British had respectfully but firmly concluded that it should remain operational research.) What we early operations researchers had in common was a bent for problem solving, a willingness to question accepted wisdom, a thirst for empirical data about the operations of systems under field conditions, not just their physical or technical characteristics, and a desire to see any useful knowledge that we should develop or acquire applied in the field.

The operations we studied were largely tactical in nature, although in the aggregate they contributed to strategic campaigns. We often participated in these operations as observers, so that we could understand the meaning of the data we collected across time, circumstance, or geography. The operations were conducted or directed by trained professionals. The professionals held strong views about what worked and why. Their views were based largely upon personal experience. Professional sailors and flyers were tempted to view analysis of war operations by civilians as laughable if not also dangerous. Acceptance of the utility of operations research, operations analysis, or operations evaluation—as it was variously called by U.S. practitioners—was generally slow in coming and by no means universal.

What scientific empirical study of field operations in war meant, fairly often, was results improved by factors ranging between two and one hundred. That it was done by men of such diverse backgrounds and experience meant that the techniques we used were borrowed from the variety of disciplines represented by those conducting the studies. By today's standards, most of the techniques used were not sophisticated, although there were some exceptional developments like search theory. However, their application to operation research *was* sophisticated for that day.

The easiest sorts of operations to understand and improve were those in which the limits were set by physics, such as turning rates of aircraft or warships, sinking rates of depth bombs, visibilities to the eye or to sonar and radar sensing devices. Most difficult to deal with analytically were those in which the limits were set by human capacities. Operations research, which came to be known as OR, was able to make little if any contribution to army ground operations during World War II.

After the war, as OR was widely adopted throughout the defense establishment and made major inroads in industry, its practitioners became professionally self-conscious. As the demand for practitioners increased, questions naturally arose about how to increase the supply. Should the increased demand continue to be met by attracting people of suitable bent from established disciplines? Which disciplines? Should students be taught OR before they adopted one of the established disciplines? Should they be taught OR instead of an established discipline? Should students be undergraduates? Graduates? Should the ultimate aim be for all OR practitioners to be trained at the doctoral level (a much less common level of training in the early 1950s than it became during the Viet Nam war)? What should OR students be taught? Since OR approaches and techniques were almost entirely borrowed or adapted from older disciplines and since the processes of borrowing and adapting were still going on, how could a "whole" curriculum be identified? The essence of OR had been its focus upon empirical knowledge of operations and operators acting in the field; how could this be taught in the classroom? These were some of the questions raised.

Out of the controversies of those days came doctoral programs in OR at a number of colleges and universities around the country, led off, if memory serves, by the Massachusetts Institute of Technology. (The nature of the process by which academe responds to market opportunities as they arise in the external professional world is touched on by Lewis, 1971.)

The first products of academic training in OR were viewed skeptically by many old-timers. In spite of the use of case studies and some limited field practice in local industries, they felt that many trainees were wet behind the ears. Even where limited field practice had taken place, the way for it had been smoothed by a benevolent—or anxious—professor, and if the going got rough, its continuance could be similarly sheltered. Some old-timers worried that a sense might emerge that methodology was everything, whereas they believed that what mattered the most was understanding how to find the fundamental characteristics of the operation to be studied, how to ask the right questions about it, and, above all, how to persuade those who conduct the operation and who must therefore risk the consequences of the study to accept its findings. Anyone who could do these things, they said, could find the people who possessed, or knew where to borrow, the appropriate methodologies. The newly trained OR practitioners sometimes felt that such views had a largely defensive purpose for those who had succeeded in the "old days" but who might not now be able to qualify as entrants in their own profession. This was doubtless sometimes true.

I believe that the same self-consciousness, the same quest for identity, the same need and opportunity to expand in numbers that once prevailed in operations research is shared today by evaluators of social programs and social experiments. OR was supplemented and then superseded in many defense applications by systems evaluation, systems analysis, and policy analysis, first in defense and then in domestic matters—first, urban; then, environmental; now, energy. The same issues have been addressed again and again, and the outcome has nearly always been the same: some doctoral level programs have been established; some newly trained practitioners have emerged; academic careers in teaching, research, and publishing have been created and sustained; but a substantial share of practitioners has always come from older disciplines. Some practitioners developed by each of these sources have succeeded. Some have not.

The meaning of success is neither singular nor universal. For some, it means managing teams of analysts, researchers, and evaluators. For others, it is successful publication in selected journals. For some, it is solving a methodological problem. For others, it means answering the main question. For still others, the key lies in sensing and solving the politics of research so that an experiment can be initiated and then sustained long enough to know what happened. For many, it is a mixture of these things and still others, like helping young entrants to grow and flower.

It is my impression that the question of evaluating social experiments is the most complex and difficult enterprise so far attempted by researchers and analysts who want to know what happens, ultimately in generalizable terms, as the result of operations conducted by real agencies in the real world. The potential for conflict between those operationally involved and the evaluators of social experiments is higher than it is in social program evaluation, because in experimentation the constraints on the directors and conductors of the operation under study are both more numerous and more explicit and therefore more subject to enforcement or to warfare between parties if they are not enforced. Social experiments represent the ultimate in operations limited not by physics but by human capacities and characteristics.

In experimentation involving such social service delivery agencies as the police, for example, what takes place is a temporary but still very real shift of power from administrators and practitioners to evaluators. If what is to be tested is the use of women on patrol, administrators must agree in advance to assign patrol officers to duties, shifts, areas, burdens, and hazards without regard to sex. They must agree to induce or to compel compliance with those assignments among dispatchers, sergeants, and partners for the duration of the test. Even in today's changing world of gender-related values, the natural tendency of most policemen is to protect women partners, to fear for their own safety, to worry about consequent loss of effectiveness in tight situations, to resent this intrusion into a previously all-male domain, and this natural tendency is constrained by the requirements of the experiment—that is, of the evaluators. Field and higher ranking supervisors are limited in their ability to distribute their resources as they deem best suits the needs of the moment. Managers pay an internal political price when they make their subordinates and police officers endure unnatural constraints and do unpopular things. They may also have to pay that price in terms of their own career.

Further, if some traditional element of police practice like routine preventive patrol is to be tested by experimentation, it must be withheld in some areas to make the experiment valid. Although there may be no empirical evidence that such a practice produces the results traditionally claimed for it, or even that it matters one way or the other, police and the public have assumed that it does for several generations. Police agency philosophy, organizational structure, equipment, budgets, and operations have been based on such assumptions. Police managers and police officers alike held sincere and very strong views about the dangers of such experimentation prior to its having been done safely first in Kansas City, and subsequently elsewhere (Kelling and others, 1974, 1975; Schnelle and others, 1975.) Some felt so strongly that they violated not only the rules of the Kansas City experiment but also the explicit orders of a popular and powerful chief. When this was detected by the evaluators and by department monitors of the experiment, the experiment was stopped and corrective actions were taken. Some of these actions altered the career prospects of some officers. When the experiment was restarted, it ran under control for the full planned period. In this case, the chief had the capacity and the willingness to pay the internal political price necessary to safeguard the experiment. This is by no means always the case.

Moreover, when practices established with the public over a long period of time or new practices not familiar to the public are to be tested, the managers and conductors of the operations under study run an additional risk which the evaluators do not share. In the case cited above, because of his unusual public popularity, independence from local control, and long and effective tenure, Chief Kelley's decision to test routine preventive patrol was accepted with equanimity by the people of Kansas City. Nothing went wrong during the experiment to endanger the public. It was, of course, agreed in advance that, if dangerous crime increased in the areas from which routine preventive patrol had been removed, the chief would stop the experiment. Chief Kelley knew that there was always a risk that citizens would fear what he proposed to do and that this fear could jeopardize his popular political support, and hence his budgetary support as well. He knew that if something did go seriously wrong and he stopped the experiment, it might still be too late to ensure his survival in office. Other chiefs with less tenure, less popular support, and less independence from local control must rightly fear the potential external political consequences of manipulating service practices to conduct tests for the purposes of evaluation. A publication about such an evaluation may better prepare evaluators for the next experiment, but it cannot restore a fallen chief to his job. In a world in which police chiefs in major cities hold their jobs for an average of less than three years, survival is a motivation not to be treated lightly.

These internal and external political facts of life are not, of course, limited to police services. Every manager of a public service delivery operation faces them and must deal with them as best he can. It is not surprising, then, that these managers generally regard research and, above all, evaluation as something that is done *to* them; the pay-offs are far from clear or certain, while the risks are immediate, obvious, and serious, both professional and personal. Inducing acceptance and effectively promoting maintenance of experimental conditions in the face of these natural perceptions by those who must adopt and maintain unnatural postures and conditions for rigidly specified periods of time if evaluation is to have a chance requires far more of evaluators than, say, skills in the use of multiple regression techniques. For an excellent elaboration of these aspects of conducting social experimental research, see Kelling (in press). For an account of Police Foundation learning from experience in experiments involving police services, see Lewis (1970).

Only somewhat less daunting is the task of social program evaluation in the absence of experimentation. While other forms of evaluation are generally less rigorous than experimentation and do not place the same constraints on managers and operators, the element of personal and professional threat may still arise and the delivery of social services shares with social experimentation the complexities that stem from situations in which human capacities define the limits. Both evaluation of social experiments and social program evaluation have benefited from and built upon their predecessors: physical experimentation and mathematics constitute the ultimate foundation, while OR, systems analysis, and policy analysis form the immediate background in one line of ancestry and psychology, sociology, political science, and economics form the immediate background in the other. Both evaluation of social experiments and evaluation of social programs are still developing. While both have grown remarkably during the seventies, the application of their findings is only beginning, while their acceptance and use by legislators and administrators is still embryonic. Nevertheless, they are already providing teaching and research careers in universities. New professional societies of researchers and practitioners have recently been founded to codify what evaluations are and to give them an identity. Publishers are finding the subject area a fruitful one—the fourth annual review publication is being edited—and the arguments about whether the field is or may become a discipline in its own right are going forward. So, once again, the present situation resembles that of the early-to-middle fifties.

Another notable common thread that characterizes these two somewhat related approaches to understanding the workings and outcomes of the operations of organizations is that both operations and social program research are conducted, by and large, by teams of researchers, analysts, and evaluators. Individuals have been noteworthy in the invention, adaptation, or perfection of particular techniques; as developers, managers and facilitators of team performance; and as potent teachers, critics, synthesizers, reanalysts, and editors, but the work in the field has generally been done by teams. Sometimes they were the vaunted multidisciplinary teams. The first multidisciplinary teams were largely accidental; later, they were much sought after, despite the difficulties encountered in forming them consciously, because they promised wider technique-borrowing capacity and offered enriched perspectives to all those who participated. Sometimes the teams were composed of or at least dominated by a single discipline. In the early days of OR, this might be physics or mathematics or some branch of engineering. Later, in systems analysis, economists tended to dominate. By the time practitioners of policy sciences had acquired sufficient professional self-consciousness to name themselves and to set up doctoral training programs, the many strains of activity from which the policy sciences had developed were reflected by the fact that advanced training programs were begun almost simultaneously in graduate schools of economics, political science or government, business, and urban affairs (itself an amalgam of many disciplines). At the present time, evaluation methodology, program evaluation, experimentation, and so on are being taught largely in schools of psychology. Nearly all of the so-called softer sciences are now more quantitative in outlook and approach than they were before. Nearly all these training programs turn out researchers who, to the extent that they expect to achieve their potential in empirical field research, expect to do so as members of teams. There seems little likelihood that the necessity for the team approach to evaluation of social programs and experiments will diminish. An instructive account of how one well-known evaluation team in the field of police experimentation was developed is contained in Kelling (1977).

Finally, one other observable characteristic of evaluation should be mentioned: it is itself without substance. What gives it substance is what is being evaluated. This has consequences for how evaluation should be taught as well as for how it must be learned.

The future is by no means always a simple extrapolation from the past, but when it is not, man has so far generally been poor at predicting it.

If the particular past experiences that this writer has sketched are prologue, then we have some idea what to expect.

First, when a substantive area of organizational operations is first addressed by scientific inquiry, those who perform the inquiry must, perforce, be drawn from established disciplines.

Second, the major empirical work will be done by teams of analysts, researchers, and evaluators from one or more of those disciplines. Initially, these investigators are attracted by the nature of the problem itself and their sense of its importance.

Third, as soon as enough teams are working in a growing new field of operational inquiry, professional self-consciousness will set in, professional societies will be formed to name the new discipline, to give it identity and dignity, and to raise its standards. Doctoral programs, first in schools of the disciplines that dominate the earliest and strongest teams, later in others, will attempt direct training in the new discipline. In the nature of things, it is only with great difficulty that such courses can teach any more than a smattering of the substance about which evaluations have been or may some day be done; these courses will, perforce, concentrate on techniques and methodologies related to data collection, processing, and analysis.

Fourth, when the newly named discipline is more mature—as is the case of social program research—its practitioners will be drawn both from established disciplines and from the new graduate programs. In the first few years of this period, the older and generally the senior members of evaluation teams will come from established disciplines. The younger and junior members will represent both the established disciplines and new programs, with presumably an increase from year to year in the numbers of those with direct graduate training in the new discipline—say, evaluation. It is reasonable to suppose that eventually an equilibrium between practitioners from each source, representing some balance of supply and demand, will emerge. There is presently no way to know what that equilibrium will be. In the case of such older relatives of program evaluation as OR, it is evident that substantial numbers still continue to come from older disciplines which have a substantive base—that is, they are about something substantial in addition to the methodologies for studying it, rather than about methodology alone.

As individual evaluation practitioners mature, they generally expect to rise in their profession. Given the wide range of views of success, as noted earlier, rising in their profession will not always mean the same thing to different practitioners. Some will want to become methodological stars. Others will want ultimately to acquire increased management responsibilities.

These, in principle, represent quite different balances of skills and viewpoints. But the Peter Principle prevails in evaluation, too, and the people who rise to increased management responsibilities more often show evidence of skills at applying methodology than of notable management capabilities. This is quite natural. In the nature of things, the junior people in teams begin with the most routine aspects of either data acquisition and processing or of analysis. It is hard to imagine how else it could be. So it is inevitable that their first responsibility for management or for political relationships with the conductors and directors of the operation under study will very likely be based upon demonstrated excellence in an unrelated skill and only indirectly, if at all, on evidence of the skill implied by the new duties and opportunities associated with their rising.

With few exceptions, excellent individual scientists prove to be terrible managers of research teams and inept political facilitators of what evaluation teams must do. The exceptions become so by becoming more interested in—and discovering talents and tolerance for—managing, training, and facilitating than in the continued practice of their own science. They can and ought to be synthesizers, an essential role for a manager of evaluations.

At any given time, an evaluation team will ordinarily consist of a number of junior members, who acquire and clean data and perform analyses of it under the direction of senior researchers, while the whole enterprise is managed and politically facilitated in its work by a director of some sort. If entrants to teams are at the master's or doctoral level, methodological aptitude or even brilliance may be demonstrated early. One year may see palpable movement, so the task specialization talked about here is not necessarily very rigid. It is also true that the relationship between operators and evaluators—the politics of evaluation—can sometimes be grossly affected by junior data collectors if management is not careful about training and controlling such matters or if management is unlucky. But the divisions of labor suggested here will hold most of the time.

What difference, then, does it make how evaluators get their training? What is the difference between practitioners trained in evaluation as such, and those trained in disciplines which have a substance as well as methods of studying it? Given the general division of labor within teams, it probably does not matter very much at the outset if one can safely assume that the range of methodologies taught in evaluation courses includes adequate training in those relevant to the evaluation at hand and that individuals attracted to the study from established disciplines also know how to use the relevant methods. (Key decisions—decisions about what methods *are* relevant—will commonly be made at the first level of evaluation supervision or at even higher levels.) By and large, its seems reasonably likely that both requirements will be met most of the time. For those who see their goal as one of excellence in methods, or as involving research in methods, it seems that one would be as likely to succeed as the other.

48

Given that knowledge of the substance and politics of what is being evaluated plays such a prominent role at higher levels of evaluation management responsibility, it is this writer's prejudice that, if there were to be some long-run difference in the fortunes of the two kinds of trainees, it would emerge there. It may be somewhat easier to link substance and its study for people trained in disciplines which have a substance than it is for those whose training concentrates on the methodologies of study.

One way or another, we learn everything we know. Can "it" be taught and learned absent from life, in abstraction, in academe? Obviously, my prejudice is that most of what is important in facilitating and directing teams must be learned on the job, over time. It may be just a little easier if early training has been substantively oriented. But I hasten to add that, at that level, personal differences may overwhelm any differences produced by training. Only time will tell.

References

Kelling, G. L. "Development of Staff for Evaluation." In *Emergency Medical Services: Research Methodology.* HEW Publication No. (PHS) 78-3195. Washington, D.C.: U.S. Government Printing Office, 1977.

Kelling, G. L. "Politics as Social Science Methodology." In M. J. Saks (Ed.). *Advances in Applied Social Psychology*, in press.

Kelling, G. L., and others. *Kansas City Preventive Patrol Experiment: A Summary Report.* Kansas City, Mo.: Police Foundation, 1974.

Kelling, G. L., and others. *Kansas City Preventive Patrol Experiment: A Technical Report.* Kansas City, Mo.: Police Foundation, 1975.

Lewis, J. H. "Policy and Sciences and the Market." *Policy Sciences,* 1971, *2* (3), 287–300.

Lewis, J. H. "Evaluation of Experiments in Policing: What Are We Learning." *Evaluation Quarterly,* 1978, *2* (2), 315–330.

Schnelle, J. F., and others. "Social Evaluation Research: The Evaluation of Two Policy Patrolling Strategies." *Journal of Applied Behavior Analysis, 4* (Winter), 353–365.

Joseph H. Lewis was director of evaluation for the Police Foundation from 1971 to 1979. He is now semiretired and living in Sorrento, Maine.

*Inextricably entwined with research methods are the
quantitative skills required to develop, manage, and
analyze the complex data sets that almost always
characterize evaluation projects. But is there any
common core of quantitative skills that all evaluation
researchers should possess? And should quantitative
skills be taught within the context of an evaluation
research program?*

Quantitative Training
for Evaluation Research

Stephen E. Fienberg

The term *evaluation research* has perhaps as many definitions or descriptions as there are individuals who claim to practice it. While the focus of this chapter is on quantitative training for evaluation researchers, there is an inherent difficulty in separating out or distinguishing quantitative methods from more general methodological issues involved in their use. Thus, definitions of both methodology and evaluation research are required. Throughout this chapter, evaluation research is taken to be use of the scientific method, through the design, collection, and analysis of data, to assess the extent to which programs or activities achieve specified objectives.

This definition directly identifies all the aspects involved in training evaluation researchers: scientific method (in the context of one or more of the social sciences); methodology (the design, collection, and analysis of data); social programs (their design and structure as they relate both to theoretical constructs and goals and to the practical aspects of implementing programs); and specifying program objectives. Although these components can in principle be separated, they are inevitably intertwined when one evaluates any particular social program, whether it be police patrols, a community mental health program, a manpower training program, an electricity rate experiment, or a work-release prison program. Such programs can be broad, encompassing a multitude of experiments and sub-programs, or they can be highly specific.

There is a sense in which my definition of methodology is both intentionally broad and narrowly focused, depending on one's vocational or professional training or perspective. By defining methodology as the design, collection, and analysis of data, I have purposely made it synonymous with one of the standard definitions of statistics. In this sense, then, methodology is equivalent to quantitative methodology or statistical methods, and many would interpret this as a narrow definition. Yet I view statistical training in the broadest of senses, one which includes the interface of statistics with substantive areas and the "art" of questionnaire design, since statistical methods cannot be divorced in their application from subject-matter content if they are to remain useful. Statisticians are viewed by many social scientists as mathematicians, and the problems on which they work as abstract. Yet the major advances in statistical methodology have come in connection with real-world problems. As the most innovative and creative statistician of the past century, Sir R. A. Fisher (1925, p. v), says: "For several years prior to the preparation of this book, the author had been working in somewhat intimate cooperation with a number of biological research departments at Rothamsted; the book was very decidedly the product of this circumstance. Daily contact with statistical problems as they presented themselves to laboratory workers stimulated the purely mathematical researches upon which the new methods were based."

The constant interaction between statistical methods and the problems to which they are to be applied is a theme that bears repeating. In principle, there is little difference between evaluating the effects of a certain fertilizer on the growth of a variety of wheat, the outcome of a psychotherapeutic intervention or some other limited, specific treatment applied to individuals, and the outcome of a food program aimed at improving nutrition. Indeed, similar experimental designs might well be appropriate for all three tasks. Yet only a thoughtless researcher would automatically treat the three problems as the same, ignoring the differences that exist, for example, in the physical situations involved and in the impact that these would have on experimental control and the measurement of outcomes.

The questions to be explored in this chapter can now be defined as follows: What is the minimum set of quantitative skills that should be possessed by all evaluation researchers? Need these skills be taught as part of a formal training program? What is the role of on-the-job training as it relates to methodology? How can we facilitate continuing education for evaluation researchers so as to better equip them to deal with complex situations?

In attempting to answer these questions, and especially the first, I was reminded of a classic paper by Bode, Mosteller, and others (1949). These authors were concerned primarily with the natural and physical sciences, whereas in the present discussion we are concerned with the social and policy sciences. Moreover, they focused on undergraduate training, whereas our focus is on graduate or professional training. Yet their basic statement on the unity of science is worth repeating here, with slight changes in wording: All science began as part of "natural philosophy and radiated outwards"; even in this modern era it should be possible to recapture this universalistic spirit. Scientific method is common to all sciences. Almost every science is more easily taught and developed by using some of the equipment of the others. As the doctrine of planning experiments and observations and of interpreting data, statistics has a common relation to all sciences (p. 553).

I view the evaluation researcher as a social-scientific generalist, for whom these basic ideas are directly applicable. The third proposition in this basic statement deserves some elaboration because of its importance to evaluation researchers. By narrowly focusing on a small set of quantitative techniques or paradigms in widespread use in their own discipline, researchers often make only incremental contributions. Yet others working on exactly the same problems, who borrow from techniques used by scientists in other fields, can make major breakthroughs. Similar statements can be made about the teaching of the social sciences, although the consequences may not seem as dramatic. Through the use of statistical ideas that are common to several fields together with detailed examples of applications from each, a teacher of social-scientific generalists can present a broad scientific outlook that will aid them in the understanding of new problems. This is related to the concept of *learning to learn* discussed by Sechrest in this volume.

Essential Quantitative Skills

What are the basic quantitative methodological skills that all evaluation researchers should possess? How should these skills be acquired? The premise of these questions is that all evaluation researchers must possess some such skills. In a survey of evaluation experts, Anderson (1978) found that six topics were rated as essential or desirable by virtually all respondents: descriptive statistics, statistical analysis and inference, quasi-experimental design, experimental design, correlation and regression methods, and sample survey methods. Although I might not have chosen to organize the entire set of skills represented by these particular topics, most experts would recognize these items as necessary components of a basic course or sequence of courses in statistical methods or techniques.

I believe that all evaluation researchers should have methodological training in statistical methods equivalent to a full-year or a three-quarter sequence at the minimum. While some have acquired such training in the past by self-guided study or through on-the-job training, the level of competence required for these skills strongly argues for formal statistical training. For this reason, I advocate that a methodology sequence be a basic requirement in any Ph.D. program in evaluation.

My own preference is for a statistics sequence organized to elucidate methods for conducting statistical studies, methods of gathering data, and data analysis and inference making. The actual topics covered in such a sequence is not as crucial as its orientation toward the use of the methods being taught, especially in drawing inferences about causation. Such an orientation will inevitably lead to a study of the role of well-designed statistical experiments, complete with randomization, as the method of choice in evaluation research. To paraphrase the well-known statistician George Box (1966), to find out what happens to a system when you interfere with it, you must actually interfere with it and observe what happens, not just passively observe it. To rule out alternative explanations, such experimentation is best done in carefully controlled situations. This is as true in the setting of social experimentation and social programs as it is in agricultural, biological, or industrial settings.

The full-year sequence that I have suggested is predicated on the view that there is a core of statistical principles and techniques that needs to be mastered before one can proceed to the more sophisticated tools of time series analysis, MANOVA, structural equations, and so on. The full-year sequence would concentrate on this core, although it might also include a brief overview of other techniques. I do not believe that this sequence would achieve depth at the cost of narrowness; the issue is one of basic education necessary to avoid superficiality. All too many graduate students in evaluation research have their heads filled with such buzzwords as "intervention analysis," "seasonally adjusted time series," "structural coefficients and causal models," and the like, when they still have not mastered ideas about simple comparisons of groups. Such students cannot specialize in the application of ARIMA time series models without an understanding of where these models fit in the broader methodological perspective.

Should the minimal formal methodological training stop with the sequence in statistical methods? I think not, for without a detailed demonstration of the use of these methods in actual program evaluations, most students or trainees would have little idea of the difficulties associated with the transfer of statistical concepts from the textbook to the real world. Thus, I would propose a second sequence of methodology courses as part of the core Ph.D. evaluation program. This sequence would focus on case studies and address such issues as developing an evaluation model; learning what to measure and how; measurement reliability, including validity assessment; data processing and data quality control; and handling missing observations and missing variables. If specific advanced statistical techniques were viewed as being especially desirable for evaluation work, they could be incorporated into this sequence. I am not sure which subset of techniques I would single out myself.

An instructor of statistical and related quantitative methods typically attempts to illustrate elementary methods or principles of experimentation using relatively simple examples, which have been tidied up to reinforce a single concept or idea. As a consequence, the examples that students must deal with in introductory methodology courses are often misleading in their simplicity. Thus, this second sequence of courses, which involves a form of secondary analysis of selected case studies, is critical to an understanding of the problems that real-world evaluation studies must ultimately confront (See the chapter by Boruch and Reis in this volume).

The actual case studies used in this second sequence could vary according to the nature of the training program or they could represent a diverse collection, such as a negative income tax experiment, a study of community-based corrections programs, or an attempt to assess the potential impact of health insurance legislation. Two excellent surveys of recent social experiments by Gilbert, Light, and Mosteller (1974) and by Ferber and Hirsch (1978) provide a long list of appropriate examples.

Key ingredients in any review of the case studies are exploration of alternate evaluation designs and methods of data analysis and review of the use of study findings in actual policy-making situations (Fairley and Mosteller, 1977). In addition, there should be some attention to ethical and legal constraints on experimentation and data collection. Meier (1972) gives an excellent discussion of these issues in the context of the 1954 Salk polio vaccine trials.

Statistical methods beyond those in the standard statistics sequence need to be introduced in a sequence for evaluation researchers (for example, time series analysis and change-point methods), as should ideas on such statistically related topics as unobtrusive measures and test and scale reliability.

Among the benefits that could accrue from this second methodology sequence is a recognition among trainees that the statistical approach is flexible and that there is a need to go beyond the elementary statistical methods. Learning that it is often desirable to seek methodological assistance in designing a study to evaluate a social program can be a crucial lesson. Moreover, through a detailed examination of case studies, evaluation research trainees may begin to learn how to deal with questions involving the allocation of resources for policy research in the redesign of experiments (Rivlin, 1974).

Sechrest's chapter in this volume discusses Donald Campbell's fish scale model of omniscience, in which the route to omniscience lies through shared, rather than individual, wisdom. The preceding comments are reasonably consistent with the fish scale model, but they also imply that the fish scales—in this case the trainees in an evaluation research program—all must have some overlap, this overlap representing the core knowledge about basic statistical concepts and techniques that all must possess. The nonoverlapping aspects of the fish scales would then come from advanced statistical skills of a somewhat specialized nature, as well as from training in substantive areas or disciplines.

Related Quantitative Skills

Many evaluation researchers make extensive use of quantitative skills that are complementary to or even markedly different from those just described. This is as it should be, and graduate programs in evaluation research should, as some already do, emphasize training in such additional skills as financial record auditing, cost-benefit analysis, demographic methods, econometric methods, operations research, psychometric methods, and statistical decision theory.

Such training should not be viewed as a substitute for the training to be provided by the methodological course outlined in the previous section. Indeed, courses on many of these topics would build directly on material covered in the basic methodology courses. As with the courses on statistical methodology, additional training in these related quantitative skills should be coupled with case studies that provide a detailed illustration of their applications.

It is not necessary for every evaluator to be expert in all these areas or even in one. What is important is that an evaluator should be able to recognize the need for a nonstandard or specialized set of quantitative techniques in an actual evaluation problem and to seek assistance from an expert who can provide the requisite advice.

A fascinating proposal included in the curriculum for the scientific generalist (Bode, Mosteller, and others, 1949), was for a course in "judging, guessing, and the scientific method." The purpose of the course was to encourage individuals to bring their education and intelligence to bear on estimation and prediction problems for which they have inadequate information. This seems just as appropriate for the modern evaluation researcher as it was for the scientific generalist of thirty years ago. Such a course would draw on statistical skills acquired earlier by the students and would most effectively be taught through the use of real examples. Mosteller (1977) provides a compendium of techniques for order of magnitude estimation of unknown numbers together with examples.

Fairley (1977) describes in detail the problems that arise when evaluating the probability of a catastrophic accident from the marine transport of liquefied natural gas (LNG). His problem involves "guestimates" made by the Federal Power Commission of seven separate probabilities that, multiplied together, yield an overall estimate of one chance in 4,664,179 per trip for a major LNG spill, and he points out the possible errors and uncertainties in the components. These typically involve the underestimation of potential risks by factors as high as five (that is, the probabilities may be five times higher than stated). Fairley also provides tentative guidelines for the evaluation of catastrophic accident probabilities in new problems. This material could be used to great effect in the proposed course. Case studies of such events and problems as the incident at Three Mile Island, military intelligence estimates, and the number of illegal immigrants and their impact on the U.S. economy could also be used in this course.

On-the-Job Training

More than one writer has questioned whether evaluation should be viewed as a profession or discipline and not simply as a job. As Anderson and Ball (1978, p. 168) note, "the latter perception seems to be against formal training and with advocacy of 'internship' or 'in-service' experiences." While I have come down foursquare in support of formal methodological training, it remains clear to me that such training will be of little value if it is not followed up or accompanied by some form of on-the-job experience.

Internships already play a major role in public policy programs at several universities, and I suspect that they will play an important role in evaluation research training programs of the future. The experience one gains from an internship, however, is quite different from formal training in the fundamentals of statistics. One can learn to use a particular method of analysis in a particular context (for example, multivariate analysis of variance with adjustments for covariates in the study of educational programs in a school district), but typically, when deadlines for reports are approaching, there is little time for the careful study of alternative methods and the grounds for choosing among them.

Continuing Education in Methodology

Even with strong formal training in methodology, a person actively engaged in program evaluation can rapidly become out of date. Ten years ago, few evaluation researchers would have received formal training in such methodological techniques as Box-Jenkins time series analysis, intervention analysis for quasi-experimental situations, loglinear models for contingency tables, or Tukey exploratory data analysis. Today these techniques seem to be in vogue. How then can we expect evaluators to keep abreast of new developments in methodology?

Four possibilities come to mind. All four pertain to continuing education in the broad sense and have implications beyond methodological training for evaluation research.

The first possibility is the development of a series of tutorial sessions on methodology, to be scheduled as part of professional meetings of evaluators. Sometimes called workshops, tutorial sessions on various topics have proved quite popular at meetings of such diverse organizations as, on the one hand, the American Society of Quality Control and the Institute of Management Sciences/Operation Research Society of America and, on the other, the American Psychological Association and the American Sociological Association (where they are called didactic seminars). Tutorial sessions typically last between two and three hours and serve as a brief refresher or as an introduction to a limited set of materials. If a participant is actually to utilize the ideas or methods presented, an additional investment of time is required.

Second, many professional societies offer continuing education in methodology for their members in the form of short courses. The American Statistical Association, for example, holds one or more two-day courses in conjunction with its annual meetings. Topics covered in recent years include exploratory data analysis, discrete multivariate analysis, data analysis of multivariate observations, with an emphasis on graphical techniques, and techniques for ranking and selection. Other professional associations have similar activities, although short courses so provided are not really oriented towards evaluators. In addition, several profit-making corporations and university faculties offer short courses, lasting between two and five days, on similar topics in statistics at frequent intervals, many of them in the summer. If this particular form of continuing education is to be of value to evaluation researchers, it will need to be adapted or at least augmented, since many existing short courses are oriented toward other applications. Moreover, the use of such forms of continuing education itself needs careful evaluation. The inadequacies of the brief but intensive review that is possible in a short course leads to the third possibility.

With the projected decline in college and university enrollment, many administrators are looking toward the development of programs for mature students. One aspect of such planning could well involve month-long intensive refresher courses for evaluators. These courses could review fundamental methodological ideas and introduce some innovative ones. They would be especially effective if they were linked to material taught in an evaluation research Ph.D. program and offered on a recurring basis. The one-month duration is a compromise between the all too brief short course and the typical quarter- or semester-length program. It would give the students time to absorb the methodological material presented and to explore its application in evaluation problems in which they were personally interested.

As the fourth possibility, I note that continuing education need not be confined to tutorial sessions or courses. As more in-depth and detailed evaluation studies are published, the printed word may well suffice to guide continuing methodological training. Printed materials could be organized for self-guided study and supplemented by videotape and even interactive tutorial packages structured for use with minicomputers.

The concept of continuing education has merit for almost all fields, but it may play a special role in the quantitative training of evaluation researchers, keeping them abreast of innovations in statistical methodology and reminding them of the basic concepts upon which all sound evaluation must ultimately rest.

References

Anderson, S. B., and Ball, S. *The Profession and Practice of Program Evaluation.* San Francisco: Jossey-Bass, 1978.

Bode, H., Mosteller, F., and others. "The Education of a Scientific Generalist." *Science,* 1949, *109,* 553–558.

Box, G. E. P. "Uses and Abuses of Regression." *Technometrics,* 1966, *8,* 625–629.

Fairley, W. "Evaluating the 'Small' Probability of a Catastrophic Accident from the Marine Transportation of Liquified Natural Gas." In W. Fairley and F. Mosteller (Eds.), *Statistics and Public Policy.* Reading, Mass.: Addison-Wesley, 1977.

Fairley, W., and Mosteller, F. (Eds.). *Statistics and Public Policy.* Reading, Mass.: Addison-Wesley, 1977.

Ferber, R., and Hirsch, W. Z. "Social Experimentation and Economic Policy: A Survey." *Journal of Economic Literature,* 1978, *16,* 1379–1414.

Fisher, R. A. *Statistical Methods for Research Workers.* Edinburgh: Oliver and Boyd, 1925.

Gilbert, J. P., Light, R. J., and Mosteller, F. "Assessing Social Innovations: An Empirical Base for Policy." In C. A. Bennett and A. A. Lumsdaine (Eds.), *Evaluation and Experimentation: Some Critical Issues in Assessing Social Programs.* New York: Academic Press, 1975.

Meier, P. "The Biggest Public Health Experiment Ever: The 1954 Field Trial of the Salk Poliomyelitis Vaccine." In J. Tanur, and others (Eds.), *Statistics: A Guide to the Unknown.* San Francisco: Holden-Day, 1972.

Mosteller, F. "Assessing Unknown Numbers: Order of Magnitude Estimation." In W. B. Fairley and F. Mosteller (Eds.), *Statistics and Public Policy.* Reading, Mass.: Addison-Wesley, 1977.

Rivlin, A. M. "Allocating Resources for Policy Research: How Can Experiments Be More Useful?" *American Economic Review,* 1974, *64,* 346–354.

Stephen E. Fienberg is professor of applied statistics at the University of Minnesota and will soon be at Carnegie-Mellon University.

*With evaluation tasks growing in size and
complexity, initial analyses of data are unlikely to be
complete, satisfactory, or persuasive...The usual
approaches to analysis of complex data sets from
evaluation projects can be enhanced by having the
data undergo secondary analysis.*

The Student, Evaluative Data, and Secondary Analysis

Robert F. Boruch
Janet Reis

In James Watson's account of his discovery of DNA structure (1968, p. 148), he observes that "As long as Francis [Crick] and I remained closed out from the experimental data, the best course was to maintain an open mind. So I returned to my thoughts about sex." This chapter adds a few options to those apparently available to Watson.

In particular, we examine the liberty engendered by secondary analysis of someone else's data and the way in which that liberty can be exploited by the student. The presumption is that the opportunity to reexamine the experience of an earlier research effort and to enlarge on it is fundamental to intellective enterprise. We focus on data generated by evaluation of social programs, rather than on data from social surveys. Secondary analysis is defined here as using data from evaluations in ways other than those planned or executed in the original research. This definition is broad

The research on which this chapter is based has been supported by the National Institute of Education and the National Science Foundation. Donald Fiske was kind enough to provide some comments on an earlier draft. It is also a pleasure to acknowledge the contribution of Louis Fogg, a student at the University of Chicago, whose questions helped to sustain our interest in the topic.

enough to encompass the various types of secondary analysis catalogued with awesome thoroughness by Cook and Gruder (1978/1979).

The Virtues of Secondary Analysis

Secondary analysis expands academic freedom of inquiry. In effect, it increases the number of laboratories available for research and facilitates the university's traditional role of generating ideas and critical assessments. Moreover, the expansion involves no inordinate increase in cost either to university or to student. The activity does not require a large budget, since the costs of designing the original evaluation and collecting the data have been met by others. The costs of data accession can occasionally be borne out of pocket, even out of the student's pocket, and analysis costs can often be met through small foundation grants or through regular university support.

Time is precious to the student if one of the objectives is to learn something and, incidentally, to graduate to a slightly higher income category. Secondary analysis does provide temporal benefits. The time that might otherwise be spent in a program evaluation on managerial and logistical field problems can be formidable; secondary analysis preserves this time for imaginative and conscientious analysis. The energy that might otherwise be expended on projects which cannot be evaluated or which can only barely be evaluated is directed toward understanding of a different and, in some cases, we argue, a sturdier sort.

The functions of secondary analysis are diverse for the student as well as for the mentor. Many have stressed methodological innovation. This effort may range from direct application of new technology, and the consequent learning about that technology, to imaginative creation of new methods for estimating program effects and to testing these new methods on data that are already well understood. The function may be theoretical and tied closely to contemporary social problems. In this respect, secondary analysis of evaluative data is nothing more than a slight but significant extension of the tradition of fitting competing models in the sciences to data, of refining the models, and of discarding less useful ones. Some students have dedicated their secondary analyses to developing policy, since generating independent judgments about the quality of earlier analyses and the ambiguity of their implications is no less important for the student than it is for the government adviser or analyst. The student may be more naive and less potent in this arena, but neither deficiency justifies not making the attempt. In any case, the student is also less likely to be fettered, or at least to be fettered differently, by the local customs which are generated in an evaluation, customs that obscure weaknesses or color reporting for the original analyst.

Secondary analysis can assist in the orderly construction of what Hemingway used to refer to as a crap detector: the student can develop that special skill which speeds identification of the obscure and dubious, the illusory and the deceptive. Relying partly on secondary analysis for this is less risky than relying solely on academic courses to teach the skill or on journals to provide examples. To be sure, the skepticism so developed may be inflationary—it is usually easier to criticize than to invent solutions or good explanations. But if the latter are also regarded as part of the task of secondary analysis, then the process can have the salutory effect of impeding the productions of scholarly complainers.

Secondary analysis can help the student learn how to structure the inquiry, because there are no standard rules for it, because we cannot always teach it well, and because we have the responsibility to provide the opportunity. Having the chance to generate questions that need answering, in an orderly way, and to make some conscientious decisions about what is answerable and what is not seems better than not having it.

Secondary analysis can help the student to learn catholicity in research, which cannot always be done in formal training. That catholicity extends to questions, for a fair number can usually be asked of the data regardless of their original purpose. It most certainly applies to the answer. It's doubtful that any major program evaluation can be content with a single answer in the primary analysis. The secondary analysis can be no less intolerant. That catholicity is pertinent to language, too, and at several levels. The student must plow through the government's "forward plans" and the accompanying plethora of acronyms, through the academic social scientists' "conceptual frameworks" and the equally generous provision of neologisms, and through the public's sometimes startling interpretations of each. There is also the opportunity to confront one's own ignorance when establishing the meaning of an "unbiased" sample, of a "randomized" experiment, and of other concepts which seem simple as taught but which have unnervingly subtle implications.

The student's excessive trust in the separate academic disciplines is likely to be shaken by applied research, including secondary analysis, and that is all to the good. No applied social research is undertaken without managerial, institutional, or ethical constraints, and the students will have to be acquainted with these to understand the origins, character, and quality of evaluative data. It has always been difficult to give students the opportunity to learn how to avoid or attenuate the influence of reductionism in normal education. The more holistic view is somewhat likelier to emerge in secondary analysis than in formal courses or, for that matter, in the formal data collection efforts typical of dissertation research.

Organizational Options and Implications

Introducing secondary analysis to college education is not an especially new enterprise. But well-articulated strategies for initiating and sustaining the effort have not been examined in the research or university management literature. There are some very clear options, however, a few of which will be described here.

The interested faculty member has always had a fundamental role, of course. Steve Zysanski's research (1962), which was encouraged by Professor Leroy Wolins, involved secondary analysis of small data sets underlying published articles on psychological experiments. The cost of such activity is low, since most data sets are small, and access to data is improving, thanks to new editorial policies; the *Journal of Personality and Social Psychology*, for example, requires that the data used as a basis for a published article be available for competing analyses. For larger, more complex projects, student teams and some moderate financial support may be warranted. In reanalyzing the Sesame Street evaluations, for instance, Thomas Cook assembled a small team of graduate students, obtained modest foundation support for their endeavor, and managed to produce a tidy, jointly authored volume reporting the work (Cook and others, 1975). The use of a formal academic seminar as a vehicle for analyzing a complex data set is nicely illustrated by Moynihan and Mosteller (1972). That effort, which involved graduate students and university faculty, provided both with an opportunity to focus on important pieces of a complicated and a massive data set and to make judgments about the problems that could be attacked. For such policy-relevant projects as this, the strategy has the distinct advantage of quality control.

Institutional data banks, especially those with a unified theme, provide regular opportunities. At Michigan State University, for example, Sidney Katz and Joe Papsidero organized a large group of data sets on long-term health care for the sake of policy-related secondary analysis. The arrangement there is such that the experienced policy analyst develops a policy paper and that secondary analysis by advanced graduate students provides evidence both to support and to oppose the statesman's thesis before the paper is published. The institutional data bank that serves a larger variety of student and faculty needs is exemplified by Wisconsin's Institute for Research on Poverty, Michigan's Institute for Social Research, and the National Opinion Research Center at Chicago, (Hyman, 1972). Such data banks provide access to a variety of data sets from a great many surveys and from a few social program evaluations. The policy governing access to these omnibus systems is well developed, and some systems issue newsletters on acquisitions and analyses; for example, Wisconsin's *Focus*, Michigan's *ISR Newsletter*, and the Research Triangle Institute's *Hypotenuse*.

The creation of courses with a bearing on secondary analysis is a slippery matter. To be sure, seminars that focus on data generated by a particular evaluation and that facilitate production of high calibre research have been useful for Harvard, among others, but it is not yet clear that more regular efforts of this or some other sort can be sustained. David, Robbin, and others (1978) undertook to assay regular didactic approaches in their pilot test of microdata collection methods during Wisconsin's intersession. They capitalized on the gripes and suggestions of students to produce what may be the first regular course for users, managers, and generators of machine-readable data files in the social sciences. The course the course developed by these writers reasonably covers accession, standards, policy, processing, and analysis. Rather more attention has been devoted to periodic workshops in this area than to seminars or regular coursework. So, for example, Herbert Walberg at the University of Illinois has been instrumental in devising a workshop for professional researchers (rather than predoctoral students) with interests in science education; the vehicle for instruction is the data generated by the National Assessment of Educational Progress surveys conducted during the past ten years. At the National Opinion Research Center, Rachel Rosenfeld and Christopher Winship are the principals in workshops on longitudinal analysis, again for professionals; these workshops use NORC's longitudinal surveys of high school students and the National Longitudinal Surveys of High School Experience. Michigan, the Research Triangle Institute, and other archives have mounted similar efforts. The indirect influence on students of any of these academic options (workshops and so on), and their costs, usefulness, and conduct are not yet regarded as matters for serious research.

Several institutional arrangements do not appear to have been attempted as yet. For example, there are no cooperative arrangements among universities to focus student attention on single national evaluation projects in the interest of independent estimation of project effects; for example, along the lines of interlaboratory testing programs. However, cooperative institutional efforts have been made to ensure that public data do become available for scholarly research. The Association for Public Data Users, for example, is an institutional group primarily dedicated to making government-generated data more accessible and useful to the research public.

Disciplines. The interest in secondary analysis is ordinarily registered by social scientists, including educational researchers, economists, sociologists, and psychologists, yet the activity invariably engenders questions for other disciplines as well. For instance, little coherent theory and virtually no empirical research has been produced in this particular field by the library sciences. File architecture and standards are determined more often by existing methods than by adaptation and invention of new methods. As a consequence, standards for cataloging, inventory, utilization, and documentation are underdeveloped. At least one new organization, the International Association of Social Science Information Technology, has been created to help resolve such problems.

The few monographs available to journalists on the interpretation of data, much less on the interpretation of evaluative data, suggest that schools of journalism might exploit secondary analysis to permit students to learn what Meyer (1973) suggested that they should learn and what Kruskal (1978a) suggests that they have not learned. For example, most journalists fail to recognize that statistical methods are a subtle foreign language, though indeed they should. As a consequence, we find Sale (1974) investing "regression analysis" with alarming power—the near perfect, and therefore invidious, ability to predict who will engage in campus protest and who will not—and we find Edwin Newman (1974) grumbling about regression analysis, exogenous variables, and an assortment of other entities that offend his lexical sensibilities. Engaging in the process with live data might help these errant critics. Departments of communication are relevant, too, if we may judge by television documentaries on problems that rely heavily on secondary analysis; for example, the excellent productions by Britain's NOVA on the discovery of the structure of DNA and on research into the probable causes of spina bifida.

Despite Karl Popper's remarkable contributions, it is very difficult to find philosophy of science courses that include assessment of data by students to help them learn more about the notion of evidence, its corroboration, and its verification. Nevertheless, data generated by experiments in weather modification, health care, agriculture, and education all involve the problems he explores and afford the student an opportunity to rediscover his principles. Good law schools have become less parochial than their curriculum suggests. Here, too, there are some opportunities. Field tests of telephone conferencing and other new procedures in administrative law, of sanctions and rehabilitation methods in criminal justice, and of safety rules in regulatory law have generated large data sets which could be exploited to help the student learn how to design one's own evaluation and how to interpret evaluations designed by others. For a profession which exhibits alarming innocence about numbers, this could not be all bad.

Reexamination of quantitative data by the conscientious historian has been stimulated by a variety of works, including Phillip Curtin's (1969) careful investigations on the slave trade. It is not difficult to find exciting historical descriptions of productive secondary analysis, such as Alexander Graham Bell's use of census data to explore heredity and deafness (Bruce, 1975) and vigorous efforts to detect corruption of public statistics prior to the Civil War (Davis, 1972; Regan, 1973). The spirit which drives this scholarship is remarkably consistent with efforts to reexamine contemporary data.

Finally, methodology courses may, of course, exploit the process of secondary analysis. Textbook examples are often tidy and therefore misleading. They are often more trivial than need be. Real data have at least been declared important by a group of experts rather than the author of a textbook. Engaging in secondary analysis becomes a vehicle for adding literary flesh to the statistical bone of such courses, in that badly made decisions can be distinguished from decisions that were informed but wrong, and the implications of those decisions are evident in the data.

Human Resources and Manpower Planning. Postdoctoral programs which rely heavily on secondary analysis are pertinent to redressing the imbalances in manpower distribution. In particular, development of such new areas as program evaluation typically involves a high demand for people with specific skills and a low supply of such individuals. Generating that supply expeditiously and without increasing the already large number of Ph.D.s is sometimes possible through such postdoctoral programs. Because these programs normally involve less than two years' time and since most stipends are puny, the use of existing data as a vehicle for retraining is almost essential. At least two federal agencies have provided support for postdoctoral internships with a strong emphasis on secondary analysis of evaluative data. For related reasons, the National Institute of Education funded Northwestern's Project on Secondary Analysis (Boruch and Wortman, 1978). The National Science Foundation's support of the Inter-university Consortium at Michigan and of other archives has been durable and generally dedicated to better secondary analysis of survey data.

Policy: Statistical Research and Manpower. Some vigorous efforts to make federal statistical policy more coherent have been undertaken by the President's Reorganization Project, by the Office of Statistical Policy and Standards at the Commerce Department, by the National Academy of Sciences Committee on Federal Statistics, and by the U.S. General Accounting Office. Each has partial responsibility for policy on data access, for generating improvements in access policy, and for policy related to quality of data which might be useful to researchers.

Most of these agencies stress survey data rather than data generated by evaluations of public programs. None of them attend explicitly to students' use of statistical data generated in program evaluations, yet the market for such data among students is remarkable, and this is recognized in some federal agencies (Datta, 1976). Further, the number and character of secondary analyses undertaken by students appear to be raw material for a legitimate science indicator and for monitoring the utility of data archives, of the program evaluations that provided the data for the archives, and of the scientific investment of resources in particular fields. Mapping this terrain is possible if universities, dissertations, or microuses of major evaluation data sets are sampled. That research should help in turn to judge the utility of the indicator, to assay the resources necessary to increase the production of high-quality evaluations, and to provide more effective justification for small graduate-level grant programs in the social and physical sciences.

Student Options

Choices for the student who has an interest in secondary analysis are constrained by institutional capabilities as they are in any research effort. To the extent that there are faculty members whose interests coincide and institutional mechanisms for supporting the research, secondary analysis will be relatively easy. Even without such faculty members, however, there is a fair amount of opportunity to exercise independent judgment and to make a telling assault on our collective ignorance.

Presumptions. The presumption that collecting new data produces more significant contributions to the sciences than secondary analysis must, of course, influence the student's choice to do one or the other. In the absence of additional information, the presumption has all the merit of the epigrams found in fortune cookies. To be sure, there often is considerably more flexibility in formulating a question and generating evidentiary answers in primary research. There is also a greater demand on the secondary analyst to produce something remarkable from resources that have already been examined by smart people. For these reasons alone, the mediocre student might prefer to abstain from the activity, except where the data are fresh. Judging from the contributions of such senior scholars as James Coleman, Donald Campbell, and Gene Glass, who are older than the average graduate student but at least as vigorous, it is not only laudable but necessary to work both sides of the street. Judging from the failures of the economists, to rely solely on existing data may suffice to answer some interesting questions but it is clearly not useful for answering others.

Inquiry and Acquisition. Scouting out interesting and possibly useful information beyond that available within the institution is not difficult. Catalogues of evaluation studies for which original data are, in principle, available have been generated by the U.S. General Accounting Office (1976). A real-time system that enumerates and abstracts evaluations is advertised as operational for the U.S. Department of Health, Education and Welfare (Aaron, 1978), and other information systems with partially overlapping purposes, such as the Smithsonian Institution's Scientific Information Service, can also be helpful. The *Bulletin of the Data Clearing House in the Social Sciences*, published in Canada, attempts to provide timely reports on the production of new data sets all over the world, including those generated from special purpose research projects and from creation of integrated thematic research files. Data from some older evaluation studies are being stored by the National Archives (Dollar and Armbacher, 1979); the creation there of an easy-to-access archive of such studies is promising. Even the best of these resources is imperfect, though, so new data sets must often be learned about and obtained directly from the study's sponsor or contractor.

The rules of access to data vary from one government agency to another, despite the uniformity of access implied by the Freedom of Information Act. The Law Enforcement Assistance Administration, for example, has created formal internal regulations that require any data generated in research that it sponsors to be made available to the community of researchers when the final report is published. Though there is no explicit policy at the U.S. Office of Education and the National Institute of Education, some staff within these agencies have been vigorous in encouraging secondary analysis of evaluations supported by those agencies (Hedrick, Boruch, and Ross, 1979). Judging from its early support of public use manpower surveys and its more recent support of large-scale program evaluations of income subsidy programs for parolees, the U.S. Department of Labor has espoused similar candor in making evaluative data available for secondary analysis. We are aware of only one private foundation, the Police Foundation, which has an explicit policy on access to evaluative data from the programs it supports. The practice has been to encourage secondary analysis of data from such projects as the Kansas City Policy Patrol Experiments, policewoman impact studies, response time studies, and a variety of other innovative research projects (Lewis, 1978). The information policies of local public agencies and private organizations are not as well documented and less uniform than the policies of federal agencies; this makes inquisitorial persistence and polite personal requests essential.

Decisions. Deciding whether a data set is worth reanalyzing is no mean task. Some sets are worthless except as illustrations of bad practice. Even here, though, it is not unreasonable to avail oneself of the opportunity presented by such cases for conscientious critique. Regardless of the original data, flaws are at least as numerous in evaluation reports as they are in journal articles and government reports, and some flaws are interesting enough to sustain sophisticated examination. Gentle models of the practice include Kruskal's (1978b) remarks on the National Science Foundation's Science Indicators monograph. Less gentle but equally conscientious exemplars include the criticism by Bowers and his student Pierce (1975) of Erlich's provocative work on the deterrence effects of capital punishment. It is also possible to catalogue stereotypical errors in reporting; for example, Huff's *How to Lie with Statistics* (1954) and Campbell's (1974) *Flaws and Fallacies in Statistical Thinking*. The style exhibited by these writers is especially attractive in evaluative research settings where the analyst must speak to an audience that includes nonspecialists.

Where the data warrant better than bad faith, it is more difficult to decide whether they are sufficient for important analyses. In principle, the problem here is no different from that involved in deciding whether a given research topic is worth one's attention. The extent to which that decision-making skill can be taught is limited, but because it must be learned, it is reasonable to expect the student to engage the problem. The problem presented by evaluative research is particularly intriguing because some judgments have already been made, presumably by wiser heads. Public standards are reflected in the existence of the data, technical standards are reflected in their quality, and theoretical or political standards are reflected in their nature. However, just as the concerns of the day converge to produce a particular research enterprise and the resulting data set, so will advances in our understanding produce new concerns and new ways of exploiting the information so produced.

Illustrations. Extolling the virtues of secondary analysis is gratuitous in the absence of illustration and therefore examples are presented here. Underlying each is the notion that small but distinct increases in what we know characterizes most research and that, in secondary analysis as well, dramatic findings are exceptional.

Watson's search for the structure of DNA is as remarkable an example as any. He was migratory in his search for pertinent data and persistent in his search for models to fit to those data. The problems he encountered in accessing the data (notably in obtaining Rosy's photographs of crystalline structures) were not atypical for the student without prestige. Identifying the intellective target and encountering a colleague with a mutual interest and agreeable spirit were crucial. Their joint decision to "imitate Linus Pauling and beat him at his own game" seems not to have done them much harm.

Testing elements of existing theory and building small theory through secondary analysis are not uncommon at the predoctoral level. So, for example, estimating the intellective ability of children is fundamental to a great deal of theoretical research in child development and to field tests of theory-based ameliorative programs, and the theory of estimation can sometimes be assayed nicely through secondary analysis. Gomez (1977, 1978), for instance, exploited data stemming from experimental tests of enrichment programs for Colombian children to explore new theory (Rasch models) for measuring abilities. As a student, his contributions lay in providing evidence that the new theory yields results which do not differ notably from those yielded by older theories for estimating ability, that the ability estimates produced under the new theory appear to have interval properties (very nice for the analyst), and that the abilities of individual children can be well described using a fairly simple mathematical model. The product is an increment, small but nonetheless notable, in our knowledge of how children register their abilities. In the long run, Gomez expects this work to help in establishing the effects of expensive programs designed to resolve problems of cultural, nutritional, and economic deprivation. More generally, Rezmovic and Rezmovic (1980; forthcoming) test theories used to measure psychological traits by translating literal conceptions into mathematical form and testing the fit of the model to live data. In the process, they, like Watson, Gomez, and others, contribute arguments that both confirm and contradict theory constructed by scholars on whose shoulders they stand. The product of their effort is not unambiguous, but it is thoughtful, conscientious, and, in certain respects, clever.

Education research also contains examples of the use of secondary analyses of data to study evolving social issues. One instance of refocused research attention prompted by wider social movements is the burgeoning interest in sex differences as a factor in educational achievement. Cross-cultural surveys in educational research have detailed the differences existing between male and female students in attitudes and academic performance (Finn, Katlowski, and Reis, 1978), yet for many years gender was ignored as a variable in explanations of students' performance. Educational experts had declared that race and socioeconomic status were the crucial determinants. Reevaluation of data, such as that contained in the International Evaluation of Achievement Data, has begun to redress the neglect of gender, to supply information that has a bearing on constructive policy change, and to refine theory.

It is not difficult to find illustrations which in principle are relevant to public policy as well as to theory. However, the fact that many secondary analyses are completed after a particular government decision is made makes them generally rather than specifically useful; they are probably most useful when the policy issue inevitably reappears. For example, there is Magidson's (1978) work on competing analyses of evaluative data on Head Start programs, executed while he was a graduate student of management. His analyses could be wrong, since the design of the original evaluation and the resulting data do not permit unequivocal conclusions, but it is unlikely that they are. Indeed, his analyses make fewer unrealistic assumptions about the data than the original attempt. In any case, his analyses provoke reaction from established scholars, as they should, and so enhance both his citation count and the clarity of the issues for the inquisitive scientist. As every good scholar knows, enhancing citation counts is a wonderful thing for the young scientist if the reactions are intelligent, although it is not such a bad thing if they are not. As a student at Iowa State University, Rindskopf (1976) used a similar approach to establish the effects of Title I-supported programs on reading achievement among economically deprived children. He is indebted to Gene Glass for both data and original analyses, and his analysis suggests that if one recognizes the fallibility of those data explicitly, then the conclusions reached can differ remarkably from those based on conventional textbook analyses, which assume that the imperfections are irrelevant.

Often, it is easier, and perhaps wiser, to perform secondary analyses that illuminate one's own earlier work. That is the approach taken by Minor (1977) in his analysis of evaluations of the television-based health education program, "Feeling Good." Minor and Bradburn (1978) found a few interesting effects of the program. Recognizing that viewing habits quite naturally varied and that earlier analyses had failed to take this into account, Minor used multiple indicators of viewing in his dissertation so as to determine the robustness of earlier conclusions. The same style is implicit in Gomez's illustration; he was also a principal on the research which generated data for his secondary analysis.

The student need not be content with the data at hand, especially if simple augmentation is possible. Conner (1977), for instance, decided that the published documents were insufficient to establish that randomized field experiments had been executed as claimed and to identify plausible reasons for failure or success in each instance. His case studies use both published and unpublished statistics as evidence in deciding whether results are consistent with public statements, and he supplements the statistical analysis with information collected through direct interviews. Rindskopf (1976) augmented existing survey data with information concerning reliability of tests, so as to build less implausible models of the effects of compensatory education programs than had been available. Rather more vigorous augmentation, using existing data archives, was undertaken by Fagerlind (1975) in dissertation research to ensure that estimates of the economic effects of schooling were more accurate than earlier ones obtained by Paul Samuelson and by Christopher Jencks.

If the student's effort has merit, it deserves to be advertised. The vehicle for this, temperately referred to as "publishing" by some scholars, is less perfect than we would like it to be. However, the opportunity to publish and thereby to invite criticism is critical in evaluative research. There is a large array of new journals with a declared interest in evaluation, and they publish the remarkable products of student endeavor as well as the work of established scholars; occasionally they publish the work of backward students as well. New journals include *Evaluation Quarterly* (Sage), *Program Planning and Evaluation* (Pergamon), and *Evaluation Magazine*. Such older journals as *American Sociological Review* and *American Educational Research Journal* reach audiences with more orthodox tastes in research, but these journals are not less pertinent and regularly publish reanalyses.

References

Aaron, H. "Statement." In *Hearings on Costs, Management, and Utilization of Human Resources Program Evaluation, 1977.* Committee on Human Resources, U.S. Senate. Washington, D.C.: U.S. Government Printing Office, 1978.

Boruch, R. F., and Wortman, P. M. "An Illustrative Project on Secondary Analysis." In R. F. Boruch (Ed.), *New Directions for Program Evaluation: Secondary Analysis*, no. 4. San Francisco: Jossey-Bass, 1978.

Bowers, W. J., and Pierce, G. L. "The Illusion of Deterrence in Isaac Erlich's Research on Capital Punishment." *Yale Law Journal*, 1975, *85*, 186–209.

Bruce, R. V. "Alexander Graham Bell and the Conquest of Solitude." In *Hearings on H.R. 10686, A Bill to Amend Title 13 of the United States Code.* Subcommittee on Census and Population, Committee on Post Office and Civil Service, U.S. House of Representatives. Washington, D.C.: U.S. Government Printing Office, 1975.

Campbell, S. K. *Flaws and Fallacies in Statistical Thinking.* Englewood Cliffs, N.J.: Prentice-Hall, 1974.

Conner, R. F. "Selecting a Control Group: An Analysis of the Randomization Process in Twelve Social Reform Programs." *Evaluation Quarterly,* 1977, *1,* 195–244.

Cook, T. D., and Gruder, C. "Metaevaluation Research." *Evaluation Quarterly,* 1978, *2,* 5–51.

Cook, T. D., and others. *Sesame Street Revisited.* New York: Russell Sage Foundation, 1975.

Curtin, P. D. *The Atlantic Slave Trade.* Madison: University of Wisconsin Press, 1969.

Datta, L. E. "The Impact of the Westinghouse/Ohio Evaluation on the Development of Project Head Start: An Examination of the Immediate and Long-Term Effects and How They Came About." In C. C. Abt (Ed.), *The Evaluation of Social Programs.* Beverly Hills, Calif.: Sage, 1977.

David, M., Robbin, A., and others. *Instructional Materials for Microdata Collection Methods in Economics.* Madison: Economics and Library Science Data and Computation Center, University of Wisconsin, 1978.

Davis, R. C. "Social Research in America Before the Civil War." *Journal of the History of the Behavioral Sciences,* 1972, *8,* 69–85.

Director, S. "Evaluating the Impact of Manpower Training Programs." Unpublished doctoral dissertation, Northwestern University, 1974.

Dollar, C. M., and Armbacher, B. I. "The National Archives and Secondary Analsis." In R. F. Boruch (Ed.), *New Directions for Program Evaluation: Secondary Analysis,* no. 4. San Francisco: Jossey-Bass, 1978.

Fagerlind, I. *Formal Education and Adult Earnings: A Longitudinal Study on the Economic Benefits of Education.* Stockholm: Almqvist and Wiksell, 1975.

Finn, J., Katlowski, R., and Reis, J. *Sex Differences in Educational Attainment.* Buffalo: Psychology Department, State University of New York, 1978.

Gomez, H. "Evaluating Longitudinal Data with the Use of the Rasch Model." Unpublished doctoral dissertation, Northwestern University, 1978.

Hedrick, T. E., Boruch, R. F., and Ross, J. "On Ensuring the Availability of Evaluative Data for Secondary Analysis." *Policy Sciences,* 1978, *9,* 259–280.

Huff, D. *How to Lie with Statistics.* New York: Norton, 1954.

Hyman, H. H. *Secondary Analysis of Sample Surveys: Principles, Procedures, and Potentialities.* New York: Wiley, 1972.

Kruskal, W. "Formulas, Numbers, Words: Statistics in Prose." *American Scholar,* 1978a, *47,* 223–229.

Kruskal, W. "Taking Data Seriously." In Y. Elkana and others (Eds.), *Toward a Metric of Science.* New York: Wiley, 1978b.

Lewis, J. "Some Views on Secondary Analysis." In R. F. Boruch, P. M. Wortman, and D. S. Cordray (Eds.), *Secondary Analysis.* San Francisco: Jossey-Bass, forthcoming.

Magidson, J. "Toward a Causal Model Approach for Adjusting for Preexisting Differences in the Nonequivalent Control Group Situation: A General Alternative to ANOVA." *Evaluation Quarterly,* 1977, *1,* 399–420.

Meyer, P. *Precision Journalism: A Reporter's Introduction to Social Science Methods.* Bloomington: Indiana University Press, 1973.

Minor, M. J. "Estimating Treatment Effects in Social Experimentation." Unpublished doctoral dissertation, Department of Behavioral Sciences, University of Chicago, 1977.

Minor, M. J., and Bradburn, N. M. *The Effects of "Feeling Good."* Chicago: National Opinion Research Center, 1976.

Moynihan, D. P., and Mosteller, F. (Eds.). *On Equality of Educational Opportunity.* New York: Vintage Books, 1972.

Newman, E. *Strictly Speaking: Will American Be the Death of English?* New York: Warner Books, 1974.

Regan, O. G. "Statistical Reforms Accelerated by Sixth Census Errors." *Journal of the American Statistical Association,* 1973, *68,* 540–546.

Rezmovic, E. L., and Rezmovic, V. "Empirical Validation of Psychological Constructs: A Secondary Analysis." *Psychological Bulletin,* 1980, *87,* 66–71.

Rezmovic, E. L., and Rezmovic, V. "A Confirmatory Factor Analysis Approach to Construct Validation." *Educational and Psychological Measurement,* forthcoming.

Rindskopf, D. "A Comparison of Regression-Correlation Methods for Evaluating Nonexperimental Research." Unpublished doctoral dissertation, Psychology Department, Iowa State University, 1976.

Sale, K. *SDS.* New York: Vintage Books, 1974.

U.S. General Accounting Office. *Federal Program Evaluations: A Directory for the Congress.* Congressional Sourcebook Series. Washington, D.C.: U.S. Government Printing Office, 1976.

Watson, J. D. *The Double Helix.* New York: Signet, 1968.

Wortman, P. M., Reichardt, C. S., and St. Pierre, R. G. "The First Year of the Education Voucher Demonstration: A Secondary Analysis of Student Achievement Scores." *Evaluation Quarterly,* 1978, *2,* 193–214.

Zyzanski, S. "Analysis of Variance Applied to Factors Which Do Not Have Comparable Scales." Unpublished doctoral dissertation, Iowa State University, 1962.

Robert F. Boruch is director of the division of methodology and evaluation in the department of psychology at Northwestern University.

Janet Reis is a research associate in the Center for Health Services Research and Policy at Northwestern University.

*Training programs should produce professionals
who can fulfill the expectations of federal consumers
of evaluation research services.*

Qualifications of Evaluators:
A Federal Perspective

William Lohr

Evaluation research has had to assume an ever more important role in the last decade, a role which has major implications for the federal government as evaluation of its many programs has been mandated by congressional action. These developments have many ramifications for those in federal agencies who must manage programs and for those who must make decisions based on evaluations. It is clear that evaluations must be based on the best and most sophisticated research methods and that familiarity with these methods implies the formation of a group of knowledgeable persons by means of formal training. While that training may vary in intensity and degree, it must include some basic issues and topic areas if a comprehensive understanding is to be developed. It is the purpose of this chapter to describe these issues and areas.

In any training effort, there are two major areas of inquiry which must be dealt with. The first is what evaluation research is and how it is carried out; the second involves the meaning and uses of evaluation and its applications to the decision-making process. Both these major areas must be treated in detail; all the major aspects of evaluation research must be

The views expressed in this article are those of the author and do not reflect government policy.

comprehensively examined, while each component must receive as intensive a view as time permits.

The trainees should be recruited from positions within agencies in which there is responsibility for program evaluations at a significant level. Thus, two kinds of people should be involved: those who are required to make decisions on program impact and program continuation or their direct advisors on such issues; and those whose positions indicate probable capability to design, conduct, and manage evaluation research projects. The requirements for the latter group should necessarily be more stringent and technically appropriate.

As evaluations increase in importance, comprehensive evaluation training of federal officials includes evaluation research to a greater extent, so that these individuals can acquire the ability to recognize, understand, and implement a program of rigorous and serious evaluation research projects. In this new and burgeoning field, it is essential that the levels of ability be markedly increased in order to improve the quality of the evaluation research. Although it may not be possible to train everyone associated with evaluations to a level of capability that would allow them to conduct this kind of research themselves, an overall familiarity with the various aspects of evaluation research should make them sensitive to the requirements and able to manage research of this type.

Initially, it is necessary to understand what in advancing evaluation research is essential from the federal perspective for training personnel both for the management and conduct of evaluations. A training program must include the basic notion of the "evaluability" of a specific program; the definition of the "treatment"; the identification of the independent and dependent variables; the development of measurement strategies, and sampling techniques and the conception of random selection; an understanding of the problems associated with confounding factors and potential "plausible rival hypotheses"; an appreciation, at least in basic fashion, of the range of analytic techniques available for understanding the data; a perception of the problems of data acquisition, quality, and relevance; and an understanding of the overall inferential power inherent in the research design. Moreover, it is equally essential that the evaluation trainee come to understand the need for timeliness in evaluation, the political climate in which these studies are carried out, the potential "threatening" nature of evaluations from the program managers' perspective, and finally the need to attend to costs and to the rapid dissemination of results in comprehensible form to those in a position to make decisions about a program's continuation.

As evaluation research has developed, so have the theoretical underpinnings and technical sophistication. The number of well qualified and highly skilled individuals trained by institutions offering outstanding programs in evaluation research is increasing. Nevertheless, opportunities exist for a wide variety of training programs in which federal employees might gain valuable basic and advanced skills in evaluation research techniques. To use these programs as intensively as they need to be used, administrative arrangements must be flexible and the programs themselves imaginative. What is being suggested here is that there should be a basic minimum core curriculum that would include the following dimensions, each area within which is subject to an ever-increasing depth of comprehension and inquiry.

Theoretical Dimensions

To begin with, it is indispensable that a clear and thorough understanding of what evaluation research consists of with regard to federal programs be conveyed by this curriculum. Although the word *evaluation* has many meanings, it is understood here to mean the use of research techniques to assess the impact and effectiveness of social programs in modifying the social well-being of people. In this context, a research design is tailored to measure the specific effects (whether intended or unintended) of a given program. The purposes and goals of the program in question are determined by an inquiry into the legislative and executive intentions that led to enactment of the program. Evaluation training must include the process of determining these intentions by reviewing the relevant history, legislation, and implementation. Examples of outstanding evaluations should be used to underscore this feature of evaluations. It must be remembered and emphasized that programs often have effects unanticipated by their original purposes and that these subsidiary effects may well be revealed by research into the nature and impact of program effectiveness.

Once the goals and intentions have been understood, training should focus on the definition and specification of the "treatment," simple or complex, intended by program implementation. However simple and straightforward a given "treatment" may seem on the surface, its nature is likely to be complex and difficult to define in simple terms. In a training course, specific examples can serve to underline the complexities of such definitional problems. Examples should include both those cases where evaluation requirements were well understood and those cases in which the outcome was flawed because the nature of the "treatment" was insufficiently grasped. Because the program in all its ramifications is the independent variable that generates hypotheses about anticipated effects, an understanding of its nature is crucial to successful evaluation.

Once the treatment has been identified, the training should use a set of hypothesized outcomes to focus on the anticipated effects or dependent variables. By this means, the scope of program effectiveness can be assessed, if not in magnitude, at least in its direction. An associated question is the measures appropriate to determine the magnitude of effects along these hypothesized dimensions. Attention should be given to the validity, reliability, and relevance of the measures chosen. Care must be exercised to choose measures that are minimally reactive, for it is possible to choose a measurement strategy that produces effects in and of itself. Moreover, the detection of intervening factors and of factors which confound interpretation must also be emphasized. It would be well to consider how to control for a wide variety of effects so that interpretability is maximized in the evaluation research situation.

The question of research design is central to effective and successful evaluations. Training courses may well employ a wide variety of excellent texts on this matter, each of which offers a spectrum of possible choices of experimental and quasi-experimental designs. It should be noted that research designs are not applied in "cookbook" fashion; they require the maximum use of ingenuity and imagination, particularly in the kind of complex situations encountered in so many federal programs. Here, the use of examples is a necessity. Strong, successful evaluation designs are an inexhaustible mine of inventive approaches to complex and difficult research questions. It is by understanding examples of inventive designs that the "art" of evaluation designs may become clear.

Another key issue in training is the use of sampling and its applications in evaluation studies. A basic grasp of this dimension of research is essential. The same is true of random assignment of experimentals and controls whenever this may be possible. The use of control groups and comparison groups and the possibilities and limitations of matching should be explored. In all these explorations, the question of representativeness of the samples used must also be dealt with.

Questions of data collection form an integral part of any training program. Data must, of course, reflect valid measurement dimensions and be reliable and of uniformly high quality. Associated with this are the sensitive issues of ethics and privacy, consideration of which should receive high priority. Moreover, any data collection strategy should be mindful of the issue of cost of collection, for it is in this area that due proportion must be observed.

Finally, training must include at least the basics of available statistical and analytical techniques that can be used in determining the magnitude of the impact, along various dimensions, of the program in question. Although such questions are often complex and highly technical, it is imperative that trainees reach at least a general understanding of these features of research, for it is on these techniques that the significance and inferential power of conclusions are based. Moreover, it is important to consider how findings judged significant by statistical and analytic techniques can be translated into terms understandable to those who must decide the merits of a program and reach some conclusions about its continuance.

Practical Dimensions

Whatever the technical excellence and inferential power of an evaluation research study, there are other important and practical considerations. However ingenious the design, however elaborate its measures and methods, however representative the sample, and however powerful the treatments in impacting the social welfare, the findings must be timely, believable, understandable, cost-beneficial, and cost-effective for those who are in a position to make decisions affecting the program. Any training course in evaluation research must consider these questions along with those of a more theoretical nature. It is here that the relevance of scientific inquiry must pass an important and crucial test.

Any evaluation worthy of the name must be timely. There is a proper time to begin an evaluation and a proper time to reach informative conclusions. This is not an insignificant problem, for an evaluation begun too soon cannot detect the maximum impact; while an evaluation that is begun too late may miss the point at which a decision must be made. The duration of an evaluation must not be too short to uncover effects and not too long to be of no use.

Evaluators must face the fact that their role may render them so threatening to the managers that their evaluations are in jeopardy of contamination and a resistance that destroys their integrity. They must also realize that some programs are not evaluable, due to mismanagement by program directors or to the diffuseness of program goals. Every aspect of such "threats" to valid evaluation must be considered in the training course.

More difficult to understand but still a genuine factor is the question of belief. Users of research must "believe" that scientific inquiry as embodied in evaluation research is worthy of credence. The value of research is widely accepted and believed for the physical sciences; for those realms of science removed from the so-called hard sciences, the same confidence is absent, and belief structures are subject to a serious lack of credibility, agreement or disagreement stemming not from evidence but from preconceived notions that can make evaluation a mere exercise in scientific irrelevance.

Even with the increased acceptance of evaluation research as a viable means of arriving at realistic conclusions about program effectiveness, there is still the serious question of translating these findings into terms that are understandable to those who must make decisions about the impact of a given program. This aspect of evaluation research deserves special emphasis. Even if a program's impact is statistically significant, what does this mean in practical terms to one who must make a decision? Is it significant to this person? To the people it serves? Is it worthy of the concomitant expenditures, given the necessary fiscal restraint inherent in the growing realization that resources are not unlimited?

Moreover, the findings of evaluation research must be written in readable English, unobscured by jargon and sophistries. Trainees should understand that clarity and directness, economy of expression and readability are essential to the dissemination and communication of useful and important conclusions in a manner that serves the overall best interests of legislators, administrators, and users of programmatic interventions.

The scope and dimensions of training programs in evaluation research must be comprehensive and thorough, attuned to the best in the theory and practice of scientific endeavor. Surely the capability to develop and organize such a program exists. For now, it is a question both of fostering such a training effort on the part of those with the requisite skills and abilities to offer such programs and of encouraging those in federal programs to support and promote such training on an ever wider scale. Only then may evaluation research assume its rightful place in the social consciousness of the nation.

William Lohr is associate chief of the Health Services Research and Evaluation Cluster, Division of Extramural Research at the National Center for Health Services Research.

*A recent graduate of an evaluation
research training program illuminates the
shortcomings of such programs.*

Effective Training of Program Evaluators: A Mixture of Art and Science

Elizabeth D. Brown

At one time, it was relatively easy to delineate an adequate training program for evaluators. Students were advised to gain a solid grasp of experimental design and methodology—advice often qualified by the caveat that there would not be many times when a rigorous experimental approach could be applied. Students were also directed to learn instrument construction, and some knowledge of statistics was advocated. Armed with information about these various areas, evaluators were considered sufficiently trained to get out there and decide if programs were working.

The question of what constitutes an adequate training model is far more complex today. Not only have program evaluators expanded their horizons to include an increasingly wide number of topics but the very activities understood by evaluation have also multiplied. No longer is the evaluator merely thought of as someone who comes in at the end of the program to find out if its goals have been met. Now administrators call upon evaluators to find out what types of programs or program changes are needed, to monitor the development of programs in order to maximize their potential effectiveness, to weigh the costs and benefits of programs, to determine if programs are meeting their stated goals, and to assess whether programs have been installed to the degree that they were supposed to be. As the number of issues and activities in which evaluators are involved has increased, so have the tools of the trade. Today's evaluators can seldom get by solely on the basis of methodological and statistical skills. This is not to say that methodological and statistical know-how is no longer the sine qua non for evaluation training. In fact, survey data reported by Anderson and Ball (1978) show that experts in evaluation training still place knowledge of statistics and research design with the skills most important for evaluators to acquire. However, so many additional proficiencies are demanded of today's evaluators that knowlege merely of experimental design and statistical applications is no longer adequate.

Indeed, the range of activities belonging to program evaluation is so wide that it is unlikely that most evaluators can master it in its entirety. Therefore, choices must be made about the topics and methods that are most relevant to specific kinds of evaluation. Individual trainees will then be able to tailor their training programs to reflect these choices.

At first sight, it appears that the way to begin the process is to determine the particular skills that are needed to perform adequately in a given area. This solution was tentatively proposed by Anderson and Ball, who then in effect withdrew it when they noted that evaluators are usually expected to perform like applied researchers and that therefore they need "a broad range of experience and a kit with many tools" (p. 183). I have no argument with that point. However, it seems possible for would-be evaluators to appraise the likelihood of their ending up in a particular role or setting at an early point in training; the results of such appraisal would point to plausible directions for the remainder of the training program. For example, most evaluation trainees can probably state a preference either for evaluating from within a given institution or program or for evaluating from an extrainstitutional position. In the former instance, the evaluator would be part of an ongoing staff and would most often conduct formative evaluations, ongoing evaluations of program effectiveness, needs assessments, and determinations of the types of client who are most and least helped by programs. In contrast, extrainstitutional evaluators would probably use their skills most often in summative evaluations and needs assessments and only seldom in activities typical of ongoing program evaluations. As this chapter will argue, once trainees are aware of their preferences in setting and role, the number of skills that they must acquire can be pared and the direction that training must take will become more apparent.

Evaluation: An Art or a Science?

Schulberg and Baker (1979) suggest that advances during the last decade have changed the nature of program evaluation. A decade ago, it was an art, but today it is an endeavor characterized by both scientific and artistic qualities. Although the authors attribute the continued presence of artistic aspects in evaluation to conceptual and methodological problems, I believe that good program evaluation requires the combination of art and science. Without activities classifiable as artistic skills, the necessary underpinnings for sound program evaluation would not exist. As a case in point, one of the first tasks facing all evaluators is to help administrators to delineate the vital components of programs and the most effective means by which outcomes may be measured (Weiss, 1972). Another important skill is knowing how to present evaluation data in such a way that results stand a chance of being utilized (Weiss, 1971). Still another basic skill that evaluators must acquire is knowing how to gain influence and build rapport so as to minimize possible resistance by staff and administrators to evaluation efforts (Tharp and Gallimore, 1979).

Undoubtedly, the need for these various artistic skills depends on whether the evaluator is working in an extrainstitutional setting or evaluating from the inside. However, even extrainstitutional evaluators need some exposure to the artistic side of evaluation, for they will at times be asked for help in clarifying program content and goals and in selecting outcome criteria. In addition, the limited amount of contact that outside evaluators have with program staff may impose a burden that can be lightened by artistic skills: staff who are distrustful of external evaluators and who feel no personal commitment to them may be uncooperative during the data collection process and even sabotage that effort.

Artistic skills are essential ingredients in training programs for in-house evaluators. Inside evaluators are called upon almost daily to use such skills to avoid alienating program staff: not only must in-house evaluators gain the continual cooperation of program personnel because of the ongoing nature of data collection but in-house evaluators are often charged with the responsibility for ensuring that time schedules and standards are met. Thus, these evaluators face the constant risk of estranging themselves from the nonevaluation program staff.

The other side of the art-or-science coin is also differentially important. Evaluation results have more credibility when evaluators are not officially connected with a project (Weiss, 1972), and thus extrainstitutional evaluators are more often called in to test program outcomes. Determining the overall effectiveness of programs, many of which comprise multiple and diversified components and include large numbers of personnel, requires all the expertise in research design, methodology, and statistical application that can be mustered. Therefore, evaluators working from an extrainstitutional position must be well trained in the scientific aspects of program evaluation.

However, even though in-house personnel conduct fewer outcome evaluations, these evaluators still need to know research design, particularly for the dvelopment or formative evaluation stages of programs. For example, a decision may be needed about which of two components makes a stronger contribution to the overall program. An inside evaluator who is knowledgeable about experimental design will be better able to address the problem and to determine which of the two components should be left in the program.

In summary, training for evaluators who plan to assume an extra-institutional role should be characterized by science but include some exposure to artistic skills, while training for in-house evaluators should emphasize artistic components but not neglect building in a solid scientific base.

Evaluation: Separate from or Part of Theory?

The question of whether evaluators need to be trained in the theory of a basic discipline as well as in evaluation is quite significant. In essence, what is being asked is if evaluators of educational projects, for example, need basic training in education as well as training in evaluation. For the sake of cost savings, it would be desirable if basic subject-matter training were not necessary for skilled evaluators. After all, training programs that encompass only the soft skills (or the art) of evaluation as well as those skills more often associated with its hard (or scientific) side already have enough to cover without trying to educate evaluators in the theoretical issues and substantive matters of a basic discipline.

However, for many evaluators, supplemental training in a basic discipline will greatly enhance their ability to function in the evaluator's role. As might be expected, the amount of basic training needed will vary as a function of two things: the amount of training necessary to make someone knowledgeable about the area and the evaluator's position inside or outside the program. In regard to the former, it may be observed that completion of an undergraduate program in education, for example, is usually sufficient to gain employment as a teacher. For this reason, no additional training in a basic area may be needed for graduates training as educational evaluators. In some other areas, such as mental health programs, the situation is different. An undergraduate degree in psychology will not equip a would-be evaluator to know what outcome measures are appropriate or to set reasonably good criteria against which outcomes can be measured. Therefore, the graduate training of evaluators who plan to work in specialized settings may need to include training in a basic discipline as well as in evaluation. The implication is, of course, that such training will take more time and be more costly.

Whether the evaluator is to work inside or outside of the program is also important in determining whether additional basic training is necessary. Because of a relatively recent change in the way their positions are viewed, in-house evaluators are more inclined to need additional basic training; with increasing frequency, in-house evaluators are thought of as professionals informed both about program development and about program evaluation. As a result of this new view, intraprogram evaluators are being called upon to evaluate an expanding number of program components and to design and introduce changes if evaluation data indicate that programs are not proceeding as expected. The reader is referred to Tharp and Gallimore (1979), who describe how closely meshed development and evaluation skills can be during the early life of a program.

External evaluators also can make use of a theoretical and substantive understanding of a given area, whether in designing an intervention strategy, selecting appropriate outcome measures, or choosing the time when those measures should be administered. For instance, if nonscreened rehabilitated alcoholics were placed in a supportive posttreatment work setting designed to reduce recidivism, outcome data would probably suggest that the intervention was ineffective. The evaluators would need to know a priori that such treatment works best on clients who have no family support system and that minimal effect should be anticipated for those clients who come from intact families (Moos, 1979). If only the rehabilitated clients without families were exposed to the treatment, the outcome data would probably proclaim the intervention a success. Needless to say, the considerable cost savings that would accrue from not offering treatment to clients who would not benefit from it is another argument in favor of training evaluators in the substantive issues of a basic discipline.

Almost certainly, many evaluators will be called upon at some time during their professional life to assess a program that lies outside of their field of expertise. Unless good counsel about the area's substantive issues is available from other members of the evaluation staff (Anderson and Ball, 1978), evaluators who must cross into foreign evaluative territory are advised to tread carefully and to take the time for self-education about the substantive and methodological issues of the area with which the program is connected.

Not only do evaluators need to know the substance and theory of a basic area but they are also in a unique position to feed information back into the basic area. One way to do this might be by dismantling programs (Gottman and Markman, 1978) and analyzing for the contributions of each program component to the overall effect. Another contribution to basic theory could be made by analyzing for the characteristics of the clients who succeed and fail in a given program. In these ways, evaluation could feed into the theory of a basic area.

Training: Within an Area or Across Areas?

The issue of the discipline in which evaluation training can proceed most fruitfully, or of whether indeed there is just one discipline, is worthy of exploration. In the survey reported by Anderson and Ball (1978), 46 percent of the respondents came from education departments, 25 percent represented psychology departments, and those numbered in the remaining 29 percent represented another seven different disciplines. Further evidence that most evaluation training is currently taking place within education departments is illustrated by Phi Delta Kappa's (an education society) listing 77 training programs in evaluation, a figure far surpassing the 30 programs listed by the National Institute of Mental Health (Anderson and Ball, 1978, p. 167).

Although most current training occurs within just two disciplines, there is little to suggest that the best experience can be obtained either from an education or from a psychology training program. Indeed, it may be that the most fertile training can be gained by going across disciplines, sampling whatever is of value, and then going on to learn something new or something presented from a different perspective. A similar approach was advocated by Worthen and Sanders (1973), who noted that training with experts from different disciplines may help evaluators to broaden the perspectives from which evaluation problems are viewed. In this way, new approaches to evaluation may be devised.

Consideration should be given to training models that centered students within a given discipline to acquire basic substantive and theoretical training and to gain an understanding of the research methodology traditionally used to study that discipline; then the students would go on to other disciplines to supplement this basic training. Obvious choices for supplementary training would be statistics, which could be provided by statistics departments; survey techniques, which could be provided by sociology departments; and cost analysis, which could be provided by economics departments. Other choices, not as readily apparent but equally valuable, include training by marketing departments, to gain a perspective on consumer issues; by anthropology departments, to find out how to do ethnographical recordings, which are so valuable during formative evaluation (Campbell, 1974); and by psychology departments to learn how to deal with personnel problems and attitude change.

Program Evaluation Versus Research

A key training issue that seldom receives attention hinges on the degree of integration between program evaluation and research. While some writers (Sommer, 1977; Sparer and Johnson, 1978; Worthen and Sanders, 1973) have discussed the similarities and differences between evaluation and research and others (Anderson and Ball, 1978) have talked about the close relationship between evaluation and research, little has been done on integrating these two investigative areas. Evaluation, which is still in its early childhood, has many questions, issues, and methods that need to be subjected to scientific inquiry via the research process.

For example, there appears to be too little inspection of the methods employed during program evaluation. Such issues as the best combination of techniques to be used in process evaluations, the most effective ways of allaying staff anxiety and distrust, and the means by which evaluation results may best be utilized all need to be studied more objectively. What happens all too often at present is that the advice of accomplished evaluators is blindly accepted; they have found that things proceed most easily and effectively if a given path is followed. Even if research only proves that the conclusions of some veteran program evaluators are valid, it would still be comforting to know that principles taken for granted are really worthwhile.

Another area in which research is needed is the area of values issues. What happens to program delivery, outcome, and utilization of evaluation results if the values of administrators, staff, and evaluators differ? What is the best way to work around these differences so that the delivery of services and the evaluation process can proceed smoothly? Again, objective study may provide some straightforward answers.

Still another value-laden issue worthy of exploration is associated with some of the criteria used to determine program worth. Legislatures and funding agencies are as often interested in cost and analysis as in program outcomes. Nevertheless, there is a flaw if programs start to tie their successes and failures in with clients' earning potential. For example, if a mental health delivery system reports that a certain number of clients returned to paying positions as a result of services received, the income available to the community as a result of the clients' increased buying power and the savings accrued by the community as a result of the clients' leaving the welfare rolls are likely constituents of equations expressing the program's cost benefits. However, such indices are fraught with bias, because women, minorities, the aged, and the undereducated usually earn less money than others. How can a program which serves many low wage earners be compared with a program whose clients are "worth more" because they can earn more? Evaluators must be prepared to study how such analysis affects the selection of persons for inclusion in programs and what the ramifications of cost analysis are for future funding.

Given the issues just enumerated, as well as others that lie beyond the scope of this chapter, we should consider preparing some students for a new role—that of evaluation researcher. Although there may be a limited number of trainees who opt to do research on evaluation-related issues and methods, ample opportunity should be provided for potential evaluation researchers to become thoroughly versed in evaluation methods and topics, traditional research approaches, and the philosophy of science. With this background, evaluation researchers should be able to generate questions and provide answers that are essential in building a substantive base for program evaluation.

Summary

There is no answer to the question what constitutes an adequate evaluation training program, because evaluation itself includes an extremely diverse set of activities, classifiable as either science or art. So many activities may be subsumed under either of these two categories that evaluation trainees will have to choose the direction their training is to follow. This paper suggests that one basis on which such a choice can be made is for trainees to decide whether they would prefer to be associated with an ongoing program or to come in as an outside evaluator.

Training for extrainstitutional evaluators should strongly emphasize scientific training, but it should also include the artistic components of evaluation and provide some familiarity with the theoretical and substantive issues of a basic discipline. In contrast, intrainstitutional evaluators need intensive training in the artistic components of evaluation and a solid theoretical orientation to a basic discipline; however, they should also receive some exposure to research design and methodology.

The training model suggested in this chapter would place students in a basic discipline for preliminary training. Supplemental training in unrelated disciplines would follow, so that trainees could learn to approach evaluation and its issues more broadly and from different perspectives.

The other major training need centers on the training of evaluation researchers. With the questions and answers that properly trained evaluation researchers would provide, evaluation could proceed with more certainty that its principles and methods are valid.

References

Anderson, S. B., and Ball, S. *The Profession and Practice of Program Evaluation.* San Francisco: Jossey-Bass, 1978.

Campbell, D. T. "Qualitative Knowing in Action Research." Kurt Lewin Memorial Address, Society for the Psychological Study of Social Issues, meeting with the American Psychological Association, New Orleans, September 1974.

Gottman, J., and Markman, H. J. "Experimental Designs in Psychotherapy Research." In S. L. Garfield and A. E. Bergin (Eds.), *Handbook of Psychotherapy and Behavior Change: An Empirical Analysis.* New York: Wiley, 1978.

Moos, R. H. "A Conceptual Framework for Treatment Evaluation." In D. Hamburg, J. Barchas, and P. Berger (Eds.), *Psychiatry and Behavioral Sciences.* New York: Oxford University Press, 1979.

Schulberg, H. C., and Baker, F. "Evaluating Health Programs: Art and/or Science?" In H. C. Schulberg and F. Baker (Eds.), *Program Evaluation in the Health Fields*. Vol. 2. New York: Human Sciences Press, 1979.

Sommer, R. "No, Not Research. I Said Evaluation!" *APA Monitor*, 1977, *8*, 1-11.

Sparer, G., and Johnson, J. A. "Evaluation of OEO Neighborhood Health Centers." In H. C. Schulberg and F. Baker (Eds.), *Program Evaluation in the Health Fields*. Vol. 2. New York: Human Sciences Press, 1979.

Tharp, R. G., and Gallimore, R. "The Ecology of Program Research and Development: A Model of Evaluation Succession." In L. Sechrest, S. G. West, and others (Eds.), *Handbook of Evaluation Research*. Vol. 4. Beverly Hills, Calif.: Sage, 1979.

Weiss, C. H. "Utilization of Evaluation: Toward Comparative Study." In F. G. Caro (Ed.), *Readings in Evaluation Research*. New York: Russell Sage Foundation, 1971.

Weiss, C. H. *Evaluation Research: Methods of Assessing Program Effectiveness*. Englewood Cliffs, N.J.: Prentice-Hall, 1972.

Worthen, B. R., and Sanders, J. R. *Educational Evaluation: Theory and Practice*. Worthington, Ohio: Charles A. Jones, 1973.

Elizabeth D. Brown is assistant professor of psychology at the University of Maryland.

Key concepts of the volume are summarized in the editor's concluding chapter.

Conclusions

Lee Sechrest

Although the preceding chapters approach the problem of evaluation research training from quite different perspectives, they appear to converge on a number of conclusions and to permit one or two more to be inferred.

First, the problems of evaluation research and the field itself are so diverse that no one model of training will suffice. Although in theory the diversity of products that is required could be produced within programs, it is more likely that it will grow out of programs that themselves reflect the diversity of the field. It is probably not reasonable to champion any one set of expectations about what should be included in an evaluation research training program, though it seems safe to say that sound training in research methodology and quantitative analysis are irreducible elements.

The surest way to foster the diversity that now exists and that seems to be needed is to encourage the development of evaluation research as a subspecialty within academic disciplines and subject-matter and problem-oriented fields. The various subspecialists thus produced will differ naturally in orientation, in content knowledge, and in many details of methodological and quantitative training. As long as the latter do not preclude rigorous training, the resulting diversity is much to be desired. The discipline of psychology has been in the forefront of the field, and although this may possibly continue to be the case, it should not impede the development of coordinate programs in other areas. It probably would be desirable within many universities to develop some common course offerings, particularly in research methodology and quantitative analysis, to attract students from many departments. As indicated in the preceding papers, there are good reasons other than diversity for recommending that training in evaluation research be carried out within academic disciplines or content areas.

It is difficult to be very specific about the minimum set of skills that the newly trained evaluation researcher should have. In many ways, attitudes or outlook may be as important as specific skills. Certainly the evaluation researcher must have an ability to work closely with others in a sensitive way. The field is no place for loners nor for those inclined to be oblivious of the attitudes, feelings, and problems of others. Attitudes and outlook are difficult to impart by direct instruction, but must be carefully nurtured in students who were selected because they seemed hospitable to the learning.

Evaluation research is so new a field that it does not have much lore. Eventually it may narrow, but at present its expanse is broad. Clearly, much in it is going to change, and the changes may be rapid and unpredictable. This suggests that evaluation research programs should prepare students for lifelong careers of learning and change. There is no dogma, nothing to be learned that can be guaranteed to endure. No evaluation research training program should permit its faculty or students to think that training will ever "finish." Even the Ph.D. degree should be regarded as little more than marking where the student is in a continuing course of learning and training that eventually must be self-guided. How to achieve that state of independence cannot be specified but the ability and willingness of students to act as independent scholars should be encouraged at every turn.

Finally, in evaluation research, as in nearly every other enterprise, there is no substitute for doing. Evaluation research training divorced from evaluation research is not, or should not be, imaginable. The preceding chapters make clear that there is much about evaluation research that seems not to be teachable, and that this can only be absorbed from direct involvement. Evaluation research is not a set of isolatable skills. It is a vital, living enterprise that can be fully appreciated only when one is engaged in it.

Lee Sechrest is professor of psychology at Florida State University.

Index

characteristics of evaluation researchers, 39; composition of evaluator teams, 47; doctoral programs in
operational research, 41–42; evaluation of police practices, 42–44;
evaluation of social experiments,
42; evaluation research on organizations, 45; operational research, 40–
41; substance of evaluation research,
46; World War II, 39–41

P

Patton, M. Q., 17
Pelz, D. C., 17
Perloff, R., 36
Pierce, G. L., 70

Q

Qualifications of evaluators, 73–78;
areas of inquiry, 73–74; basic statistical training, 76; believability of
evaluations, 77; data collection, 76;
essential results, 77; focus on anticipated effects, 75; jargon, 78; practical dimension, 77–78; program
effectiveness, 77; program goals, 75;
recruitment of trainees, 74; requirements of federal government, 74;
research design, 76; role of evaluator in federal government, 73; sampling techniques, 76; theoretical
dimensions, 75–76; threats of evaluations, 77; timeliness of evaluation, 77; training program opportunities, 74–75
Quantitative training for evaluation
researchers, 49–57; application of
statistical methods, 50; continuing
education in methodology, 55–57;
definition of scientific method, 49–
50; difficulties in distinguishing
quantitative methods, 49; doctoral
program, 52–53; essential quantitative skills, 51–54; evaluation researcher as social science generalist,
51; fish scale model, 53–54; minimum set of quantitative skills, 50;
on-the-job training, 55; related
quantitative skills, 54–55; suggested
sequence of statistics courses, 52
Quay, H. C., 17

R

Redner, R., 18
Regan, O. G., 72
Reichardt, C. S., 35, 72
Reis, J., 19, 37, 59, 71, 72
Rezmovic, E. L., 72
Rezmovic, V., 72
Ricks, F. A., 36, 37
Riecken, H. W., 35, 36, 37
Rindskopf, D., 72
Rivlin, A. M., 57
Robbin, A., 71
Ross, J., 71

S

Saks, M. J., 48
Sale, K., 72
Sanders, J. R., 87
Schnelle, J. F., 48
Schulberg, H. C., 87
Scovern, A., 17
Sechrest, L., vii, viii, 1, 17, 18, 36, 37,
87, 89, 90
Secondary analysis in evaluation research, 59–72; courses based on
secondary analysis, 62–63; decisions
in evaluation techniques, 67; disciplines required, 63; educational
research, 69; human resources and
manpower planning, 65; inquiry
and acquisition, 66–67; institutional data banks, 62; methodology
courses, 64; organizational options
and implications, 61–65; phyloso-
phy of science and evidence, 64;
policies in statistical research and
manpower, 65; presumptions, 66;
reusing data, 69; role of faculty, 62;
statistics and the English language,
64; student options, 66–70; using
secondary data, 59; virtues of secondary analysis, 60–61
Sherif, C. W., 17
Sherif, M., 17
Shulberg, H. C., 36
Soderstrom, E. J., 35
Sommer, R., 36, 37, 87
Sparer, G., 87
Stanley, J. C., 35
St. Pierre, R. G., 18, 37, 72
Struening, E., 36

New Directions Quarterly Sourcebooks

New Directions for Program Evaluation is one of several distinct series of quarterly sourcebooks published by Jossey-Bass. The sourcebooks in each series are designed to serve both as *convenient compendiums* of the latest knowledge and practical experience on their topics and as *long-life reference tools*.

One-year, four-sourcebook subscriptions for each series cost $18 for individuals (when paid by personal check) and $30 for institutions, libraries, and agencies. Single copies of earlier sourcebooks are available at $6.95 each *prepaid* (or $7.95 each when *billed*).

A complete listing is given below of current and past sourcebooks in the *New Directions for Program Evaluation* series. The titles and editors-in-chief of the other series are also listed. To subscribe, or to receive further information, write: New Directions Subscriptions, Jossey-Bass Inc., Publishers, 433 California Street, San Francisco, California 94104.

New Directions for Program Evaluation
Scarvia B. Anderson, Editor-in-Chief
1978:   1. *Exploring Purposes and Dimensions,* Scarvia B. Anderson, Claire D. Coles
        2. *Evaluating Federally Sponsored Programs,* Charlotte C. Rentz, R. Robert Rentz
        3. *Monitoring Ongoing Programs,* Donald L. Grant
        4. *Secondary Analysis,* Robert F. Boruch
1980:   5. *Utilization of Evaluative Information,* Larry A. Braskamp, Robert D. Brown
        6. *Measuring the Hard-to-Measure,* Edward H. Loveland
        7. *Values, Ethics, and Standards in Evaluation,* Robert Perloff, Evelyn Perloff

New Directions for Child Development
William Damon, Editor-in-Chief

New Directions for College Learning Assistance
Kurt V. Lauridsen, Editor-in-Chief

New Directions for Community Colleges
Arthur M. Cohen, Editor-in-Chief
Florence B. Brawer, Associate Editor

Statement of Ownership , Management, and Circulation
(Required by 39 U.S.C. 3685)

1. Title of Publication: New Directions for Program Evaluation. A. Publication number: 449-050. 2. Date of filing: 9/28/79. 3. Frequency of issue: quarterly. A. Number of issues published annually: four. B. Annual subscription price: $30 institutions; $18 individuals. 4. Location of known office of publication: 433 California Street, San Francisco (San Francisco County), California 94104. 5. Location of the headquarters or general business offices of the publishers: 433 California Street, San Francisco (San Francisco County), California 94104. 6. Names and addresses of publisher, editor, and managing editor: publisher—Jossey-Bass Inc., Publishers, 433 California Street, San Francisco, California 94104; editor—Scarvia B. Anderson, ETS, 250 Piedmont Avenue NE, Atlanta, Georgia 30308; managing editor—William Henry, 433 California Street, San Francisco, California 94104. 7.Owner: Jossey-Bass Inc., Publishers, 43 California Street, San Francisco, California 94104. 8. Known bondholders, mortgages, and other security holders owning or holding 1 percent or more of total amount of bonds, mortgages, or other securities: same as No. 7. 10. Extent and nature of circulation: (Note: first number indicates average number of copies of each issue during the preceeding 12 months; the second number indicates the actual number of copies published nearest to filing date.) A. Total number of copies printed (net press run): 2540, 2537. B. Paid circulation, 1) Sales through dealers and carriers, street vendors, and counter sales: 80, 40. 2) Mail subscriptions: 949, 949. C. Total paid circulation: 1029, 989. D. Free distribution by mail, carrier, or other means (samples, complimentary, and other free copies): 125, 125. E. Total distribution (sum or C and D): 1154, 1114. F. Copies not distributed, 1) Office use, left over, unaccounted, spoiled after printing: 1386, 1423. 2) Returns from news agents: 0, 0. G. Total (sum of E, F1, and 2—should equal net press run shown in A): 2540, 2537. I certify that the statements made by me above are correct and complete.

JOHN R. WARD
Vice-President